We hope you enjoy this book. Please return or renew it by the due date.

You can renew it at www.norfolk.gov.uk/libraries or by using our free library app.

Otherwise you can phone 0344 800 8020 - please have your library card and PIN ready.

You can sign up for email reminders too.

D1352398

NORFOLK ITEM

30129 081 860 091

NORFOLK COUNTY COUNCIL
LIBRARY AND INFORMATION SERVICE

DEAD
LANDS
LLOYD OTIS

U RBANE
Publications

First published in Great Britain in 2017 by Urbane Publications Ltd
Suite 3, Brown Europe House, 33/34 Gleaming Wood Drive, Chatham,
Kent ME5 8RZ

A CIP catalogue record for this book is available from the British Library.

ISBN 978-1-911583-25-7
MOBI 978-1-911583-27-1
EPUB 978-1-911583-26-4

Design and Typeset by The Invisible Man
Cover by OR8 Design

Printed and bound by CPI Group (UK) Ltd, Croydon, CR0 4YY

urbanepublications.com

ONE

London, August 1977
The Messenger

The cellar door closed and served as a stark reminder of the punishment he received for stealing. He was eight years old and comforts were at a bare minimum in a place where the light had long ago been banished. No food, just a bottle of water and a bucket to piss in. Aged twelve, the cellar's discomfort became his friend, one he could stand beside or hide behind whenever he

chose to. Over the next few years, the visits to the darkest place lasted for no more than an hour each day, but the beatings were something he swore he would never forget.

Aged sixteen, he took his revenge.

The moment he snatched a life, he felt free. It meant nothing, to watch the light fade from his tormentor's eyes, to witness the cranium's patchwork of congealed blood. Or to touch the sweat dampened leathered skin of the newly deceased.

He buried his tormentor under the glare of the moon and went to sleep that night, with the dirt from the makeshift grave still caked underneath his fingernails. He chose not to wash it away, or to cleanse himself, because its meaning empowered him. It became a turning point in his life, forcing him to realise his purpose which, for better or for worse, had led him to here.

He had invited himself to tour the house while he waited for her, looking at the photographs, trinkets, and other things that marked a glittering career. From the observations, he built a picture to prepare himself because he liked to relate and understand. He wanted to let his victims know that pain was not always the enemy; it protected the weak just as it hindered the strong.

*

The key turned in the lock and the door slammed. She had arrived. The person he had come to see opened the door and met his smile. His very best smile. She screamed but he was quick.

*

He couldn't peel his eyes away from her and the more his grip tightened the more her skin reddened. They both knew she would soon be another statistic and after they found her, the do-gooders would invade her privacy, follow strict procedures and scrutinise her belongings. They'd take notes, interrogate friends and lovers, and set up an investigation into her death.

It was the sort of bleak future that scared her. No future. A sudden end. He loosened his grip to watch her crawl away and inch closer towards the door, while the tedious rub of the carpet brushed against her bruised skin. It hurt and created a searing sting, but the majesty in her struggle heightened his curiosity as she neared the door, outstretching her fingers as if touching an angel of God.

Then he dragged her back.

Darkness followed.

Her desire to live didn't last as long as he had wished and after he removed his hands from around her crushed trachea, he collected his sports bag from the hallway. He unzipped it then unravelled the cellophane. A cheap gimmick, a prop, like his Halloween mask, and he took from it what he needed to wrap her body tight. He couldn't bear to see her face. It didn't look as pretty now as when he first saw her and on the flat of her stomach, he pulled her along to where he wanted, sometimes dragging her by the ankles.

At the end, he couldn't help but to admire his work and he took a moment to reflect. He was not an educated man, never had the patience for the learning, but that spurred him on. Intelligence could manifest itself in other ways and he exited her home as if it was his very own, knowing that the cloak of anonymity would be his most powerful ally in the days to come.

TWO

Arlo Breck stifled a yawn and watched the small crowd as they stood upon worn pavements littered with fallen leaves. Amongst the few were stoned students dressed in flower-power T-shirts and bell bottoms. The ends of their hair danced on their shoulders, and the voyeuristic ones had their faces painted with the pretence of innocence. Breck ignored the sharp chill

in the air alongside the tight pinch in his throat to duck underneath the police tape. It cordoned off the crime scene and he almost slipped when dog poop caught the underside of his imported Florsheim leather loafers. He managed to scrape it off on the edge of a kerb and, up ahead, spotted a junior officer. Breck grabbed his attention with a flippant wave. The officer logged his name and then he went through the makeshift tent that led into the house – right side first. It was something he always did when visiting a crime scene at the start of a new case. His very own zwangsstörung moment, and from a distance Patricia Kearns watched, wondering why she always had to be paired with the weird ones.

Blind to anyone else, Breck moved past the patterned wallpaper and an array of Victorian paintings. He headed straight towards an area protected by a group of uniformed officers. Some wore familiar faces while others didn't but Breck acknowledged them all with a courteous nod. Then he switched his attention towards the body.

He crouched down for a closer inspection of the victim, a single woman with a prominent career. She had been propped against the wall in a sitting position and wrapped tight in cellophane. What shocked him most were her eyes. They were still open. Breck held a hand to his mouth, disappointed that his years of experience failed to soften the blow of her lost wondering stare. He shot a glance over at the dangling phone receiver and tried to piece together a possible scenario. While he did so, Kearns padded in.

She paused to admire a bona fide signature from Paul Newman. It hung on the wall next to a shelved bottle of Cinzano. Breck didn't care for her star struck moment. He welcomed the company.

'Are we sure this one is ours?' he asked.

'Yes. It's been classed as a sensitive case due to her occupation. She's a finance director of a large city firm with a portfolio of big influential clients.'

'Have we got a name for the deceased?'

Kearns pulled out her notepad. 'Janet Victoria Maskell.'

'OK, let me have the evidence bags. I think I've found something.'

Breck had spotted a palm-sized plastic object on the floor next to the skirting board. Alongside a magazine with scribbled words on its cover. He lifted each item then dropped them into the separate bags that Kearns produced. She didn't even ask him for the details. He'd tell her soon enough.

'How long do you think it will be before the report is in from the Coroner's Office? A week or so?' he asked.

'Maybe. It's hard to say. Bart will perform the examination without delay but after that, well you know what it can be like. Or should I say what Frank can be like?'

'Yes, he may do it in a couple of days if he doesn't get distracted but I heard he's celibate nowadays. Anyway, we need to move fast on this. Let's say two hours tops. Use our special powers of authority to push it through. I'm sure he'll understand.'

Breck rose to his feet and zeroed in on a faint wiper-blade of red on the wall, that was almost obscured by the body. He also noticed the cellophane had accentuated a circle of bruising that covered Janet's face. She had taken a lot of punishment, and Breck had a multitude of questions worming around inside his head which he couldn't answer. Feeling frustrated, he left and dragged Kearns with him.

Breck handed the evidence bags to the junior officer to label up with his mind still stuck on what he had just seen.

'What else do we know about the victim?'

'She never married, hasn't got any children and from a business perspective, she may have collated a few enemies over the years too.'

'I'm happy for you to dig a little deeper into all of that and run a check on her landline for me.' Breck rubbed the bristles on his chin, thinking about the items he found.

'What do you want me to do next then?'

'Well, the first forty-eight hours in any investigation are crucial so it's a good time to get a house-to-house under way. Put some pressure on a few neighbours. See if they saw anything.'

'Consider it done.'

Detective Inspector Arlo Breck and Detective Sergeant Patricia Kearns, walked towards the Austin Allegro, a car that looked decent under the murky grey skies but somehow lost its appeal when the sun shone across its exterior. Kearns split away to organise the house-to-house, while Breck leaned against the car, wanting to inhale the air far away from the corrosive stench of the house. He saw nothing wrong with that and amongst the dispersing crowd he thought he recognised one or two. The daughter of a local vicar and a woman that had lost her son in The Troubles, but he couldn't be sure.

He slipped his hands into the pocket of his duffle coat and found an old packet of Benson & Hedges. He had kicked the habit a while ago so tossed the packet away without a second thought. A moment later Kearns returned, patting her strawberry blonde perm into place.

'I'm dying for a fag,' she said.

Breck responded with a smirk. 'Sorry, haven't got any. I stopped smoking ages ago.'

'The house-to-house inquiries will be under way in a second.'

'Good. Let's hope we get a firm lead from them – and make sure you're on top of it.'

Breck moved away from the car and slipped under the police cordon to venture over to where the crowd had been. Kearns watched him swing his gaze from left to right before settling on a view in front of the victim's home. Although it was odd it became compulsive viewing. All that was missing was the popcorn. Then Breck crossed the road to return to the Allegro but didn't expect to see Kearns still standing there.

'I need you to be hands on with this Pat and manage those house-to-house enquiries,' he told her. 'Don't let others do it.'

Kearns didn't take offence. 'You don't trust them?'

'Yes, I do, but I trust you more.'

The vote of confidence please Kearns and she padded away, failing to see their old friend Frank Cullen who had just arrived. At fifty-plus with a raspy tone to his highland vocals, Frank was a good height and well-spoken, with a distinguished air about him. Born in Edinburgh, he ventured to London in his early twenties only to fall in love with an older woman. The relationship fizzled out after a month but he decided to stay. Breck caught up with him and extended a hand.

'You're here early.'

Frank shook it. 'I came as soon as I heard, wanted to see what I'd be dealing with,' he said in reference to the victim. 'Anything I should know?'

'It looks like she suffered but I'm no medical examiner.'

'Thanks for the warning but I'd say you know what you're talking about.'

Breck followed Frank back up to the crime scene. Their conversation skidded between the weather, Frank's cats, Italian art, and that day's national news. But when they walked through the tent and into the house to view the body, normal service resumed.

Frank, a semi-religious man, crossed himself before he entered the room and took a good look at Janet. He mumbled something too and in the end Breck and Frank stood side-by-side staring.

'What do you reckon Frank?'

'The beating could have killed her but I see marks around her neck. Have you called Bart?'

'He's on his way. For some strange reason, you always arrive before him.'

'You know me. I often like to turn up at crime scenes to see what is coming my way. I can't break the habit.'

'Will there be any benefit to Bart rushing here right now?'

'For certain, but there'll be no benefit for her. She's dead.' Frank was being himself and meant it when he said it. 'Bart will confirm the time of death and all that so don't worry.' Frank took a step forward. 'Quite the artist our killer is.'

'Yes, quite the artist.'

'Why the cellophane?'

'Hard to answer that. Looks like he's a bit kinky but I'm keeping an open mind. It could be a woman we're after.' Breck used a free hand to sling a few strands of curled dark hair back into place. 'I'll catch you later,' he said before leaving the house for a second time.

Breck returned to the Allegro, sat inside and waited for Kearns. He combed through what he had seen, unsure if he should be surprised because it hadn't taken long for the first anomaly of the case to surface.

Kearns eventually opened the door and joined him inside. 'We've done the house-to-house and picked up a bit of background information but not so much about today. However, there was one possible avenue to pursue in the name of Wynda Brodie.'

'What did she say?'

'Nothing, she's not in at the moment. One of the lads recognised the door number and told me she's always ringing the station to complain about kids, and people she thinks looks suspicious. If anyone has seen anything it'll be her.'

'OK, we'll speak to her when we can.'

Breck wound down the window, raised the phlegm from his throat and spat it out. Under normal circumstances one lead was better than none but he had something else.

'We need to use all our resources to locate a person by the name of Alexander Troy.' He forced his eyes to narrow, binding his dense eyebrows together.

'Who is that?'

'It's the name on the credit card I found and the name scribbled on the magazine that's now in the evidence bag. I reckon he's our prime suspect and considering the mess he has made of Janet Maskell, it's best we stick URGENT on everything.'

THREE

The area of Cransham remained controlled by the mood swings of crime. Slotted next to Lewisham and stretching all the way to New Cross, the litter-stained streets were divided by racial tension and mistrust, under a socio-economic climate that offered little beauty, just a picture of deprivation and hopelessness.

It helped it to fast become a destination that even the dead would refuse to inhabit - if they had a choice.

Breck and Kearns worked within the Sensitive Crimes Unit (SCU), a silent arm of the Yard. They were housed in the offices of the local station and had greater powers than most to investigate crimes that were deemed sensitive. Crimes that affected the country's power brokers. With Janet Maskell being the account handler for a glut of the capital's big businesses, she fell within their remit.

Now back in the office, Breck stared at his desk in dismay. It was a mess.

A newspaper took up a quarter of the desk space with the job section on display – with a mark against roles he fancied. The only way anyone left the SCU was through retirement, or in a body bag. Those were the unofficial rules and Breck detested his own carelessness. He turned the paper over to see the sensationalist headline, 'War on Our Streets.' The report focused on an impending far-right march, fearing it would splinter the whole community and set race relations back years. Everyone in Cransham and its surrounding areas were nervous about it, even the Mayor's office pleaded with the Commissioner to stop it. Effective police work wasn't a job for those out for an easy ride, or susceptible to bouts of depression.

A scrunched-up ball of paper zipped past Breck's head. His eyes scanned the department. No one claimed responsibility.

'Not me,' one officer said.

'Me neither,' said another.

'Idiots,' he muttered under his breath then he folded the newspaper in half and put it inside his drawer.

Kearns had a glint in her emerald eyes while she held a mug of tea with both hands and stared at a box of index cards displayed on her desk. Breck hoped with what she had found, they would be able to build a visceral picture of the victim's life. He grabbed a seat nearby and brought himself closer.

'Well done with getting this info,' he said, combing through the box of cards as Kearns watched him read them. He relaxed back in the seat when he had finished.

'So Janet Maskell liked routine and would leave for work at six-thirty every morning, with the journey time being around one hour, or an hour ten if she stopped off to buy a coffee. For a period, she indulged in a few one-night stands when several men visited her home but the last serious relationship she had was in 1974, which ended eleven months before a holiday romance in Switzerland.' Breck straightened up in the chair as if it would help him to continue. 'The data we have suggests she's been single for the best part of a year which I'm not convinced of. What else is there?'

'She liked to keep fit, jogged most mornings and employed a gardener.'

'Do we know where this gardener is?' Breck picked up a pen and twirled it between his index finger and thumb.

'Away somewhere judging by a diary entry she made. One of her neighbours said she refused to use a housekeeper because she preferred to clean the interior of the house herself.'

'That sounds strange. If she wanted no one cleaning the house why would she want to employ a gardener?'

Kearns pushed her empty mug to one side. 'It's a good point but who are we to judge? People do what they want to do when the mood takes them.'

'I suppose. Anyway, where are we with finding Troy?'

'I'm still working on it but as you can tell it's taking time. Haven't you heard? Not everyone wants to talk to us nowadays.'

Breck grinned at Kearns' moment of sarcasm then they were interrupted.

'Patricia, in here now!' The officers turned in their seats to see their Detective Superintendent, Anil Bashir, standing outside his office looking like a bull about to charge. Kearns sprung out of her seat and went to see him, failing to notice a curious Breck following behind. After she entered Bashir's office, he peered through the glass panel. It allowed him to look straight inside and although he couldn't quite see Bashir, he had a clear view of Kearns. She seemed fine at first then turned ghost white.

Breck broke away for fear of being caught spying, a reprimand was the last thing he needed. He returned to his desk to wait until his partner resurfaced. Maybe it was nothing but when she returned, she was pale and shaken.

'Why did Bashir call you into his office?'

'It was just about my performance. He told me I needed to improve.' Kearns' response was a lie, one she had no choice but to give.

'Was that all? He seemed steamed up when he called you.'

'He was. I think he's just got a lot on. I'll get onto locating Alexander Troy again.'

Kearns had reached the door by the time Breck told her, 'All right see you in a bit,' and he already guessed she had not divulged everything from her conversation with Bashir. It bugged him but in the end he chose to let it slide. Although with hindsight he should have pressed for the truth. Considering what was to come, it would turn out to be one of his biggest ever mistakes.

*

Kearns left the Evidence Room still in a daze after her unexpected conversation, but there was no way she could escape from what Bashir said. The past she escaped from had come back to haunt her.

Kearns returned to her floor and if someone had asked her who she had met along the way, she'd be unable to tell them. She glided across to the other side of the floor and slammed a hand down in front of Beatrice Pierce. It startled the young detective constable and served as evidence that the women tolerated each other but didn't blend well enough to be the best of friends.

'Have you been briefed about the Maskell case?' Kearns waited for an answer that was slow in coming.

'Yes.'

'Good, that saves me going through it now. Take this.' She handed over a plastic wallet containing the credit card that Breck found. 'I need you to ring the card provider and find out where we can locate

Mr Troy.'

Beatrice looked at the Access credit card then sucked in both cheeks, uncomfortable with the request, but aware that she had no choice but to comply.

'I've got a lot of other things to do. What's the priority level?'

Kearns baulked. 'It's high priority and needs to be done now!'

'Not if I'm collating stats for the Superintendent.'

Kearns' blood boiled, but she didn't want a slanging match in front of everyone.

'A word of advice, love,' she said. 'It's hard enough being a woman in this place so give that some thought before you get cheeky with me. You'll need all the friends you can get as time goes by. Remember that.'

Beatrice turned away from Kearns' glare, sensing that an overlong lecture might be on the cards. She may have been the younger and more junior officer, but she wasn't afraid to stand her ground and carried her pretty swathe of dark hair well. It helped her sweet smile. Yet another thing to annoy Kearns with. A few tense moments passed before she accepted the instruction but by then Kearns had moved onto other matters occupying her mind. She made her way to the ladies' toilets, ran inside one of the cubicles and locked it shut, and in a matter of seconds Patricia Kearns vomited.

*

Breck became desperate for a development in the case to cheer him up and wished Kearns would bring good news soon. They had been successful in trying to locate family members of the deceased but had nothing much else to go on. That quickly changed when Beatrice arrived with an update.

'You OK?' he asked her.

'Yes, but we need to have a chat sometime soon. Let me know when you can fit me into your busy schedule.' Breck didn't fail to notice the sarcasm in her voice but she knew he wouldn't make an issue of it. 'From the details on the Access credit card, I've been able to locate the suspect.' Breck brightened up. 'Alexander Troy's a thirty-two-year-old valuation specialist with no previous, employed at one of the big investment firms in the city.'

'Which one?'

Beatrice placed both hands onto her hips. 'You'll love this, Van Bruen plc.'

'So now we know how he knew Janet Maskell.'

'Yes, they worked at the same firm. She was a finance director there.'

'Do we have his address?'

'The card is registered to an address right here in Cransham. However, I believe as we speak, he's at his place of work in Fenchurch Street in the city.'

The news pleased Breck. They could grab Troy and get a quick result. 'Have you seen Pat anywhere?'

'No, not after she was rude. I think she's jealous of me; you're the only one that gives her any attention.'

Breck didn't want to get involved and gave his sleepy eyes a rub while Beatrice mistook his tiredness for weakness. Even a reluctance to be in charge.

'I will make time for us to have a chat,' he promised, 'but right now I need to grab a few uniforms and visit our suspect.' Breck released a half-smile and left his seat, unaware that the investigation would prove to be far more important to Kearns than anyone would ever know.

FOUR

Alexander Troy didn't have a great start to the day. His pop-up toaster failed to work so breakfast didn't happen the way he would have hoped, and he couldn't find his favourite tie. To make things worse, he ended up having a fierce argument with a total stranger over a seat on the train. Despite this, there were other

important things to concentrate on, matters personal to him. Some of these, if unsuccessful, would put him at great risk. But in getting it right as he had done so far, he was on his way to achieving his goal regardless of who it hurt.

While he was getting himself together, Cransham's SCU were about to apprehend him for the murder of Janet Maskell. If he knew, then the calmness he displayed would have been replaced by sheer panic. He worked for Van Bruen, heavyweights in the finance sector, and it would destroy everything he had already put in place.

Troy was stationed on a top floor that segregated its ambitious employees into banks of two, to reduce the risk of distraction through idle gossip. Desks were weighed down with a multitude of files and footsteps were silenced by the frayed auburn carpet. The telephones were in constant use. A determined Troy was intent on retaining his status, for his ego and to preserve his secrets. A glance at his watch reminded him his girlfriend had already boarded her flight and he wished he could have been there to see her off. But right now, his career was in trouble and he needed to rescue it.

Troy ran a manicured hand across the trousers of his navy-blue suit to straighten it out. A creased suit was at the top of everyone's hate list and today he needed to be liked. He popped his keys into his briefcase which he carried around to make himself look important, even though there was nothing more than an orange and a newspaper inside. He slid it under his desk then went to see his boss Lizzie Daniels. She either played Schubert or Brahms at a low volume, which served as a protective shield against the lower classes. When Troy entered her office, Schubert's Symphony No. 8 filled the room.

He had attempted to win new business by setting up a contract without approval. It went against the rules and had now led to a make or break meeting. Getting fired wasn't an option. Not when he was so close.

Lizzie sat behind a rosewood desk imported from Spain, like Queen Nefertiti, with phone in hand, speaking to a stakeholder that boasted of having high profile friends in Parliament. Her heavy mascara, locked curls and painted rouge lips, transformed her into a thinking man's fantasy, and when she ended the call, she closed her eyes as if she was in the process of deep meditation. A technique she perfected while growing up in Chicago and it had already made hard boiled men crap their pants. Her clear varnished nails glistened under the faint light and Troy wondered what the hell was going on when her eyelids flapped open and she delivered a penetrating stare.

He stood there for a few seconds perplexed, wondering in what way it was that he could have wronged her since the last time they had spoken. Then it hit him.

She had become disappointed with his actions and the poor decisions he made. He now sat in the last chance saloon.

'You're one of my best workers Alexander so I'd hate to lose you over something like this but rules are rules.' She only elongated his name when she was pissed off at him.

'Once again, I want to say how sorry I am.'

'Yes, I'm sure you are but it doesn't change much does it?'

Troy couldn't argue with that. Lizzie gathered her things in preparation for their meeting with the CEO Wade Van Bruen, and together they left the office to make their way to Meeting Room Number One.

*

The Allegro screeched to a halt outside the Van Bruen building. Another police car arrived a minute or two behind. It caused a few people nearby to break off from what they were doing, and witness Breck exit then marvel at the building for a few seconds. He stretched his neck up to the skyline but failed to see the top, yet his adrenaline wouldn't allow him to pause for too long. It coursed through his veins now and with two uniformed officers by his side, he made his way through the swing doors towards the reception area.

The same auburn carpet that lined Troy's floor also took centre stage in reception, though less worn, and there were two women stationed behind the desk at opposite ends of the age spectrum.

The windows allowed visitors to look at what appeared to be a manufactured garden, and a rectangular wooden table, decorated with the latest business magazines for visitors to read, had chairs positioned either side. Breck pulled out his ID.

'Hello, I'm Detective Inspector Breck. I need to speak to Alexander Troy as a matter of urgency.'

'You want to speak to Mr Troy?' The more mature one attempted to find his extension on the switchboard.

'Yes, that's right; Mr Alexander Troy.'

She appeared to be flustered so Breck waited for her to compose herself. Then the younger woman behind the desk – with a face covered in stage make-up – pointed over his shoulder. Breck saw a man and woman exit a lift and a wry smile spread across his face at the bit of luck. He dashed over.

'Hello, Mr Troy?' There was a slight nod of confirmation. 'I'm Detective Inspector Breck.'

Troy glanced at Lizzie without any words before turning his attention back to Breck.

'What can I help you with officer?'

'I'd like you to accompany me to the station and answer a few questions please.'

'What is this about?'

'It relates to an incident that took place this afternoon.'

'This afternoon?' Troy was worried and ushered Breck out of Lizzie's earshot. 'What incident?'

'We'd like to know your whereabouts for the last few hours and what you've been doing?'

Troy's heart drummed hard against his chest. His thoughts spiralled. Was his girlfriend all right? What was this detective referring to? Had his earlier actions returned to haunt him?

'You see Mr Troy, we believe you were at the scene of a crime.'

'A crime? There's been a mistake I'm sure. I had lunch on Charing Cross Road then came into the office late afternoon after a prior agreement with my bosses.'

Breck wanted to know how Troy's credit card ended up at the

murder scene but before he could ask, Lizzie gatecrashed the conversation.

'What's going on here, Detective Breck. I'm the General Managing Director and Alexander's boss.'

'There's been a serious incident. We believe your employee can help us.'

It was rare to see women working in the city at director level, so the revelation surprised Breck but also pleased him. Meanwhile Troy became more uncomfortable. He inched his body away until Breck gripped his forearm.

'I will need to speak to you down at the station; a crime has been committed and we believe that you can help us with our enquiries.'

Troy panicked. 'Lizzie call our legal team please.'

'I wouldn't bother,' Breck advised. 'This is routine and Alexander could be out in no time.'

Lizzie appeared to be reluctant to argue with Breck and for the few moments they all stood still, time seemed to slow down. The break enabled Troy to consider his options and after another glance towards his boss, he calmed down.

'Am I being arrested, officer?'

Breck had a bush fire burning in his eyes. 'Yes, I'm taking you into police custody so that you can help us sort this out. We want to establish the facts.'

'The facts of what?'

Breck showed no compassion and sought to enervate Troy's resolve. He instructed the two uniformed officers, who stood by the entrance of the building, to come over and accompany the valuation specialist outside. They would wait in the car until he had finished speaking to Lizzie, wearing the same stony look which he greeted Troy with. He had no plans to remove it as the officers led Troy away and throughout, Lizzie stood rooted to the spot.

Breck softened his steely expression for her because he knew that the ripples of murder often claimed many unsuspecting victims. The people that believed in the accused. The ones that were misled.

Janet Maskell's next of kin had been notified of her death so

Breck could now let her employers know. Yet, for him it wouldn't be easy. This part of the job never was. It wasn't his first murder case, but he still hadn't become used to stamping out all signs of emotion when breaking bad news. He urged Lizzie to sit down on one of the visitor seats in the waiting area. Both receptionists were still watching.

'What is Alexander accused of doing?' she asked.

'We think he's connected to a very serious matter involving a Van Bruen employee.' Breck lowered his voice. 'I'm afraid that Janet Maskell, your finance director, has died.'

Lizzie's hands covered her mouth to stop her scream. The news wrenched her gut and she gave herself a few moments to let it all sink in.

'She's dead?' Breck delivered a sharp nod. 'How did she die?'

'I'm not at liberty to divulge that at the moment but I can confirm that Mr Troy is a suspect.'

Lizzie's head dropped. She could bark orders at careless staff, coerce stakeholders into doing whatever she wanted, but for once she was confused and powerless to do anything. She wiped a tear from her eye and faced Breck, forcing her mindset back into business mode.

'This is a tremendous shock as you can imagine. I can't believe it. I spoke to her just after 1:00 p.m. regarding the meeting because we were supposed to go through a few things beforehand.'

'How did she sound?'

'Janet was fine, totally fine. She said she'd be on her way in but when she didn't turn up I called again after 2:00 p.m. but received no answer. I think you'd better come with me and speak to my CEO. This is terrible news. He'll want to hear it from you rather than me.'

Breck understood the request while Lizzie rose to her feet and glared at the two receptionists. They were quick to look away and begin the process of pretending to be busy once again. When a tearful Lizzie walked through a set of double doors in silence, Breck followed right behind.

Lizzie took him into Meeting Room One. Wade Van Bruen was a name he had come across before within the business sections of various broadsheets. He recalled only a comment or two from reading those sections because he never paid too much attention to them. No need to. Breck thought of those times, knowing that taking more of an interest would've helped him to build a picture of Van Bruen, instead of going in blind as he was doing right now.

Van Bruen sat with his back to the door but as soon as they entered, he swivelled the chair around.

'Wade, sorry I'm late but this is DI Breck, and he has some rather sad news for us.' Van Bruen stood up, a towering six-foot-four, and shook Breck's hand.

'Mr Van Bruen.'

'DI Breck have a seat.'

'It's OK. I prefer to stand. However, you may want to sit.' Van Bruen glanced at Lizzie, looking for guidance, but her eyes were glazed with nothing forthcoming. He sensed the magnitude of what he was about to be told so returned to his seat. 'Your finance director Janet Maskell has died. Her body was found this morning.'

Tears now began to stream down Lizzie's face while the shock hammered Wade.

'How did it happen?'

'We are treating it as suspicious and are trying to ascertain further details. However, we have taken one of your employees, Alexander Troy, into custody to help us with our enquiries.'

'Troy? This can't be happening.'

'I'm sorry to be the bearer of bad news.'

Wade turned to Lizzie, his voice more urgent this time as the shock still rocked him. 'Is this true?'

'Yes,' she said before dabbing her eyes with a Kleenex tissue.

Wade took in a huge gulp of air, wondering how to best deal with the situation – keep a lid on it for as long as possible, or make an official internal statement?

'You say that you've taken Alexander Troy into custody?'

'Yes, that's right, we want to know his whereabouts.'

'What have you got on him?'

Breck was a little uncomfortable with the question. 'Let's just say that we have reason to believe he can help us with the investigation.'

Wade remained deep in thought and at first Breck believed it was down to the shock. But when he saw the odd exchange of stares between him and Lizzie, he guessed that there was something else.

'Does someone mind telling what's going on?'

'Troy had been due to have an important meeting today with Lizzie, Janet and me, to discuss his conduct over the acquisition of a new client.'

'How important?'

'Important enough for him to fear for his job.'

'Who found out about what he had been up to?'

Lizzie was ready once again to join the conversation. 'Isn't it obvious, Detective?' she asked but Breck's shake of the head was an admission it wasn't. 'Janet found out about Alexander breaking the rules and brought it to our attention. She was the one that wanted him sacked.'

FIVE

The police car pulled into the station's yard, an area where cracks spiralled across the brick wall, and the chipped paint on the window frames created abstract patterns. Breck was in a bullish mood as he escorted Troy inside the station like a hunter with his trophy. The normal uniforms knew Breck. Even though the SCU's could operate on a need-to-know basis if they

wanted, Breck preferred to be recognised and that's all that mattered.

They frogmarched Troy into the custody area. A black teenager sat handcuffed with blood wedded to his afro, and he battled a runny nose, complaining that no one would give him a tissue. It was a place devoid of colour and warmth with a dusty smell lingering in the air. Any hint of comfort remained absent as one would expect. Troy knew about places like this all too well, and while he stood in front of the Desk Sergeant, he missed Breck display compassion. The DI pulled a handkerchief from his pocket and wiped the teen's nose.

Troy was instructed to fill out a form and he couldn't stop his hands from shaking when he did. His head continued to spin as he handed over his watch, along with loose change. He realised then it was really happening and became stuck between playing along or figuring the best way to get the hell out. He mulled this over while he confirmed his name and address before having his rights explained. His fingerprints and a mugshot were taken, face on, then side on. When he finished, Breck escorted him down to a prison cell.

Troy never expected to be arrested today, and he sat dazed on a single bed with a mattress carved from granite. He had friends and needed those friends to help him now. Too many people would be burned if he remained locked up and he needed his name cleared. Troy searched for ways to end the nightmare while staring at the bluish-grey walls of his cell, still unable to take it all in.

Breck stood by and watched him for a few moments before closing the cell door, thinking that Troy was stupid for leaving his credit card lying on victim's floor. A stupid and careless action that would cost him his freedom, with greed in some ways perhaps buried at the heart of it. There could be nothing else.

Breck wondered where Kearns had got to and searched for her, but before he reached half-way upstairs, he bumped into Kearns walking down. He was a little annoyed and found it difficult to hide it.

'Ah there you are, where have you been? I had to move quickly and nab Troy at his place of work, so didn't have the time to find you.'

'Sorry, I wasn't well. Threw up in the toilet.'

'You OK?' In a flash his annoyance turned to sympathy. He put a comforting hand upon her shoulder. 'Are you feeling better?'

'I survived a divorce and a daughter that won't speak to me so this is kid's play. Go on then, tell me. What did I miss?'

'Our Alexander Troy is in a cell and now that you're here, we can have a chat with him. See where we stand.'

'What was his reaction to being taken in?'

'Denial of course and a bit of, *how dare I connect him to this crime*, when I pulled him in.'

'Guilty?'

'Hard to say but Janet Maskell wanted him sacked for breaking company rules. Possible motive right there.'

'All right, let me grab the supporting evidence and a glass of water then I'll meet you in the interview room.'

Breck watched with some concern as Kearns doubled back upstairs. She said she was fine but he wasn't convinced, while accepting that they could both do with a break. He wanted to get things moving so went on ahead, knowing that some cases could take a while to crack. However, this one looked like it'd be wrapped up pretty soon. All Breck had to do was question the prime suspect and confirm the motive then it'd be onto the next one.

After a rustle of movement and the sound of keys outside his cell, Alexander Troy glanced up to see the ominous figure of Breck at the doorway, alongside the uniformed officer he had grabbed along the way. Troy put Breck's height at around 5'11 and his defined shape suggested that he looked after his body. If he made a run for it Breck would catch him.

'Time to go. This way please,' Breck said.

Troy refused to budge. 'I want my phone call. I'm entitled to it.'

'You are and you'll get it in due course. This way please!'

A disgruntled Troy relented and followed Breck and the other officer down the corridor, and all the way into the interview room.

He sat down clasping both hands together and waited, telling himself that they had nothing on him, convincing himself that it was all a mistake. One he could clear up in an instant. Moments later

Kearns entered the room. She sat next to her colleague with a closed file and began the proceedings.

'Do you require legal representation?' Troy opened his mouth to answer the question but Kearns cut in. 'Though if you do, it would make your stay last that bit longer. We'd have to make phone calls on your behalf, rearrange this interview, and the paperwork takes a long time to process nowadays. You see we're short-staffed here.'

Troy recalled his 'telephone' request with Breck and guessed that although these two knew the rules they'd bend them to suit. Kearns' false sincerity was the oldest trick in the book.

'Look, I want to sort this out and get back to the office to save my job. Me being here as a suspect is embarrassing for my company.'

'I agree so let's clear this up, then you'll be able to go,' Breck replied. 'To reiterate, I'm Detective Inspector Arlo Breck. Joining me is Detective Sergeant Patricia Kearns and you have decided to conduct the interview without legal counsel.' Breck opened the file that Kearns had placed on the table which contained the information they had so far collated on Troy. He used a finger to adjust the rim of his black polo-neck, while Troy, an educated man, expected a difficult time.

The speed at which Breck began to tap his fingers on the desk made Troy feel uneasy. His eyes played ping pong, darting between the two officers, waiting for someone to jump from the shadows and tell him the interview was a joke, a prank of the sickest nature. No one appeared. Troy knew that these people were trained and could chew him up and spit him out. Remaining calm should be paramount. As he opened his mouth to speak he noticed that Kearns had her pen ready to write down his statement, but it wouldn't deter him from telling them what he had to.

'I'd like to start by asking where you were between noon and 2:00 p.m. today?'

'I was having lunch on Charing Cross Road between 1:00 p.m. and 2:00 p.m. Then I started work in the afternoon.'

'Where did you have your lunch?'

'In The Cambas. It's a pub.'

Breck cleared his throat. 'Were you on your own when you were having lunch?'

'Yes I was.'

'Are you seeing anyone, Mr Troy?'

'The questioning should be about my whereabouts today not about my personal life.'

Breck ignored Troy and continued to steer the interview. 'Are you sure you weren't with,' Breck paused for a moment to look at a name written in the file, 'Ceinwen. Is she your girlfriend?'

Troy wondered how they knew about her and what they knew, while Breck and Kearns waited for him to respond. Then Troy relaxed a little, figuring that they had a name, perhaps from Lizzie but nothing else.

'From what I know you've pronounced the name wrong. It's not 'sign-win' it's 'kine-win' and no, 'I've never heard of her. Whoever she is, I don't know her.'

Breck didn't appreciate the pompous attitude. Neither did Kearns. 'Let's narrow this down,' Breck said. 'Where were you from noon to 1:00 p.m. today?

'Doing stuff?'

'What stuff?'

'Bits and pieces, I can't remember the detail.'

'So you have no alibi for that exact time?'

'I guess I don't. I visited no one in particular.'

Kearns jumped in. 'Why travel to Charing Cross Road just to have lunch when there are decent cafes and pubs around Cransham?'

'I had time to kill and wanted a change of scenery.' Troy smirked which was not the best thing to do under the circumstances. Kearns brought the questioning back a step. 'What was your reason for starting work in the afternoon?'

Troy considered his words. 'I had things at home I wanted to sort out.'

'Like what?' He stared at Kearns, not knowing what to add. 'What sort of things?'

Troy folded his arms. 'If you must know my boiler stopped working, so I tried to get it to work again. Wasn't successful though.'

He then averted his gaze away as if the whole process of questioning was a waste of his precious time. An act that riled both officers and Breck re-entered the questioning, determined to up the ante.

'Do you know Ms Janet Maskell?'

'Yes, I do. She's the finance director at my company.'

'What is your relationship with her?'

Troy broke out into a mock laugh. 'It's professional, nothing more. What are you insinuating?'

'Mr Troy, Janet Maskell is dead. We found her in her home this afternoon.'

Troy stared at Breck with a blank expression. 'Dead? I don't understand, how did she die?'

'We were hoping you'd tell us. She was the one that found out about your dodgy dealings at Van Bruen.' A reply failed to materialise from Troy. Kearns opened the file and took out a set of Polaroid photographs. She laid them on the table to ensure he could see the morbid images one-by-one, and the sight of a deceased Janet Maskell made him heave. It twisted his stomach in knots and he took a while to compose himself. 'The suspect is now being shown exhibit ONT11.' Kearns pulled out a clear plastic wallet from the file. It contained a glossy women's magazine. Troy's face turned to stone and his hands tightened around the arms of the chair when he saw his name written on it. 'She wrote down your name, why?'

'I can't provide an answer to the question but there must be a million people out there with my name.'

'I'd agree with that but not all of them have this card. The suspect is now being shown exhibit ONT12.'

Kearns pulled an Access credit card from the file. It was held within another clear plastic wallet and she made sure Troy saw his full name.

Breck pointed to it. 'That too was found in the victim's home. Is it yours?'

'Yes, it seems to be.'

'How do you explain that then?'

'Explain what?'

'Look, we can do this all day long if you want to but the truth is this, a woman that you know is now dead. You have a motive and your alibi is non-existent.'

Breck glared at him, convinced Troy was hiding something but he couldn't identify what.

Kearns pitched in. 'Where's the murder weapon; the heavy-duty tool or whatever you used to kill her with?'

'I don't know what you're talking about. I mean it. Despite the evidence you have which doesn't amount to much, I did nothing. I don't understand why Janet wrote my name down, or how my credit card ended up in her home. Something isn't right.'

'You're correct there, something isn't right. We've checked the wallet you handed over when you were brought in and there isn't a credit card inside. That's because it's right here. Exhibit ONT12. Let me ask you again. What was your relationship with Janet Maskell?'

A knock at the door then interrupted proceedings which annoyed Breck and he was surprised to see Bashir enter the interview room. Kearns left her seat and spoke with him but didn't seem to like what she heard. Breck couldn't decipher what was going on from where he sat. After Bashir had left, she called him over.

'What's going on Pat?'

'It doesn't look like this is going to be a straightforward case to wrap up.'

'What do you mean by that?'

'Come with me. You're not going to like it.'

Troy watched them exit the room to be replaced by a junior SCU member. He guarded the door, looked young and fresh, and Troy knew the waistline would be the first thing to go out the window for these guys if they didn't keep an eye on it. He figured he had nothing to lose so tried to strike up a conversation.

'Hey, do you know what's going on around here? One minute I'm being questioned, the next I'm being put on hold and people are walking out.' The officer ignored the question which pissed Troy off a little. 'There's just the two of us here so you can tell me. I won't say a thing.' Troy had no real conviction in his request; he just hoped something would come of it.

The officer opened his mouth to speak which gave Troy hope but that soon diminished. 'Shut it. I don't speak to scum.'

'You prick,' Troy retorted.

A moment later Breck and Kearns returned wearing rotten expressions. The junior officer left but stuck his middle finger up at Troy before he did. Kearns reached the table first, vexed, and Breck approached afterwards, running a hand through his hair. He was on edge.

'We have a problem and I want you to be truthful with me,' he warned Troy.

'Anything to help you DI Breck, that's why I'm here, isn't it?'

Breck's glare chilled every part of Troy's body as the words slipped out. 'What is your real name?'

Troy glanced at Kearns to see whether or not it was a trick but she didn't smile. He switched back to Breck. He didn't smile either.

'My name is Alexander Troy!'

'This is not the time to play games. What is your *real* name?' Breck's voice stabbed long and hard, and the detective inspector drenched the sentence in suspicion, leaving the words to hover. Troy couldn't understand what had prompted it. Why would they doubt who he was? After several long moments Breck broke the silence. 'A victim of a recent attack, claims the perpetrator was a man fitting your physical description. In the altercation that occurred, the victim had his wallet stolen.'

'What's that got to do with who I am?'

Breck threw his head towards the ceiling in frustration then snapped it back down.

'He can provide proof of a valid bank account, passport, even a National Insurance number in the name of Alexander Troy! Do you understand? I must warn you that as well as murder, impersonation fraud is an offence.' Troy ran over the events of the day so far and recalled the argument with a man about a seat on a train. That was it. Nothing else.

'Yes, I had a few choice words with a stranger but nothing like you're suggesting.'

'That's not the way we heard it.' A defiant Troy had to accept the mess he was in.

'You'd better get real comfortable. It looks like you'll be here a while.'

The SCU officers were products of their time, stuck in a gritty place where anything was possible, where good morphed into bad and vice versa. If a charge was weak, it'd be made to stick. Having a man like Troy sit before them didn't seem strange at all and the fact that he worked for Van Bruen Plc, one of the biggest professional services companies in the country, made little difference to them.

'You're a real loser,' Kearns sniped and Troy sent a menacing look her way.

She enjoyed the moment of having a person like him on his knees: a person earning three times her salary. He was too posh for her northern ideals and she tried to give the impression of keeping it professional when it was anything but.

Troy's desperation to use his *real alibi* intensified. Using it would clear this issue up but create far bigger ones. Too dangerous. Ceinwen needed to be protected at all costs and he just couldn't afford for her to be implicated in anything. Not now. Troy straightened himself up and suggested another angle.

'I think it's obvious what has happened here, I've been framed.'

'Nice try but no, I don't think it's obvious. My advice is, sign a confession to the murder and it'll all be over. DS Kearns and I can get ready for our next case while you can prepare for the punishment that awaits.'

'Punishment? OK, we'll do it the hard way. I have nothing additional to add other than I want legal representation.'

Breck turned to Kearns with a 'that's typical' expression. 'This interview is now finished.' He checked his watch. 'I have to leave for a meeting with Bashir.' Then lowered his voice. 'Are you OK to transport this idiot back to his cell?'

'He won't be a problem, I can handle him.'

Breck left the interview room and kept the door ajar so that the officer outside could enter. Kearns gathered her file but when the officer pulled out handcuffs for Troy she intervened.

'Leave it. I don't think he's stupid enough to try anything daft.'

The officer shrugged, though surprised by the order. He ushered Troy outside with Kearns following close behind and they all walked along a winding colourless corridor, each lost in their own thoughts. Troy wasn't surprised at the lack of support but he needed a sign. Maybe he could delay proceedings until he had found out more about what was going on. He needed to do something. Fast.

They stopped when they heard a fierce crescendo of noise ahead. It snapped them into life. Someone had locked the door that led to the cells. Kearns knew they would have to take a detour through reception but that's where the trouble seemed to be. It was the only way they could reach the cells.

They would never make it.

All three went through with Troy sandwiched in-between both officers. Due to the screams and chaos up ahead it sounded like a station under siege to Kearns, and when they entered the reception area she realised she wasn't far wrong. An object flew towards her head but she ducked just in time. She grabbed Troy. Then instructed the officer to help out his colleagues and watched him enter the battle against a man that wore a swastika tattoo like a new shirt. He swung his fists while spitting hate at those around him.

He was one of the Front's feared soldiers and alone he was trouble enough, but with members of his entourage trying to defend him, it became a challenge just to keep him contained. Men like these didn't care about doing time, they wanted to mark their moment in blood.

Kearns tried to think of the best way to transport Troy back to his cell and it was when she locked eyes with him for the briefest of moments, that an unexpected understanding formed. A reluctance on her part, anticipation on his. Kearns turned her attention back towards the chaos, unsure of whether to stay close to Troy or wade into the fray. While she battled her indecision, she loosened her grip from his forearm. In an instant Troy wondered if this was the *sign* he had hoped for. He hadn't been handcuffed. Kearns had seen to that.

Everything became possible. Escape and point the police toward Janet Maskell's real killer. Get this distraction dealt with. It was now or never so Troy pushed Kearns back. By the time she hit the floor he had disappeared into the heart of the melee. She jumped to her feet and scanned the room, believing she had seen him slip through a side door. One that would take him down into the basement. Someone had taken out a riot shield, and the thugs seemed to be losing the fight when a jagged path to the door open up. A flustered Kearns followed it and went through the side door, down a flight of steps, all the way to the basement that she had been in just twice before. Once by accident and the second time, to show the plumber where to go because she happened to be the nearest one standing when he came to fix the pipes.

It was not the sort of place anyone would want to visit if they had a choice and because of that, it was perfect for Troy to hide in. His desperate action that she participated in made her uncomfortable but she knew the stakes.

'Alexander, this will make a bad situation a lot worse. This isn't the way to do it.'

She didn't expect him to reply and he didn't give one which worried her even more. The dark created strange objects in front of her. Ones she couldn't decipher, and it made her apprehensive.

Bang. Kearns swung her head toward the sound and saw something scurry across the floor. A rat. That was it for her. She had enough and went back up, convincing herself that she may have got it wrong. Troy didn't venture down here. She made a mistake.

After she left the basement Troy peeled himself away from a part of the wall that a cluster of metal pipes had obscured. He edged his way upstairs and when he neared the top, he peeked through the door. Most of the trouble makers were cornered and he saw no sign of Kearns. Feeling confident, he made his way towards a clear exit, blended into the background and scooped up a discarded radio. When a WPC rushed towards him he held it close to his ear.

'We have a few officers down over there,' he said pointing, knowing that she was trying to put a name to his face. 'They need help, quick!'

She went to where he directed her, while he continued on his way out with a calculated calmness. The police radio gave him an identity and upon reaching freedom, he felt a spark of sunshine warm his face. It energised him. Troy stopped for a moment to absorb what he had done. Just a moment though, no more than that, because it had started and now there'd be no turning back.

Troy darted across the main road oblivious to the squealing car brakes wrapped around the scream of horns and saw a crowded bus. He had no change for the fare because his possessions were at the station. He knew though that sometimes problems could be solved by unexplained measures of good fortune and he found that to be the case when the bus conductor twisted his head around, distracted by a bunch of over-zealous youths on the lower deck. It allowed him to sneak on and find a seat upstairs.

After the bus pulled away, he saw Kearns step out of the station. She scanned the area trying to spot him, while he sat with the rest of the passengers, listening to their conversations overlap like pieces of paper, knowing he was now free to sort this mess out then get back to what he needed to do.

SIX

Breck found a way to differentiate between the two men both claiming to be Alexander Troy by opting for the simple prime suspect and person of interest (POI) tags. It had proven to be yet another issue solved and the day hadn't even concluded. He needed to get his meeting with Anil Bashir over with and wasn't looking forward to it.

Breck tidied himself up so that Bashir couldn't throw any derogatory comments his way as he had done in the past, then left his seat.

Beatrice hovered near Bashir's office and Breck wondered what she was up to. As he approached, she shifted to the side and called out, beckoning him to follow her. He still had two minutes to spare so he let his curiosity steer him.

'Bea, what's up?'

'I don't mean to be pushy but when can we talk?'

'I've got a lot on at the moment but I'll try to find the time. Please bear with me.'

He should have perhaps asked her what she wanted to talk about, although he had a sneaking suspicion.

Beatrice checked that no one was watching before letting her hand brush against Breck's. It turned out to be an awkward moment for him, one he never expected. However, they were colleagues and the situation needed to be handled with care.

'Bea, what are you doing? We're at work.' She pulled away feeling hurt. Breck sought to make amends.

'Sorry. I'll make it up to you but I need to speak to Bashir first.'

Beatrice forced a smile then walked away, battling with her emotions and leaving Breck feeling rotten. There was little he could do for the time being. What started off as office banter and flirtation, had now brought him to a tricky place with a colleague and it needed fixing. That would be something for later though as he readied himself then knocked on Bashir's door.

'Come in Arlo, you're one minute late.'

Breck checked his watch. Bashir was right. 'Sorry sir,' he said then walked in.

Detective Superintendent Bashir possessed two obvious points of interest – dark rings around his eyes, part inherited and part legacy of late nights and early starts, and jet black bouffant hair. The items upon his desk emitted an impressive shine and Breck spotted the framed picture of the Super's wife. She was best described as an English rose, fifteen to twenty years younger than her husband with long dark hair.

He wondered how they met and how she became his wife but wouldn't dare ask. On the shelf were Bashir's medals from a variety of sports – badminton and squash – and two non-fiction books on psychology. The stuffed toy officer pushed into the corner of the shelf at least proved he possessed a suppressed sense of humour.

Bashir threatened to suck the life from the cigarette wedged between his dry lips at the same time he invited his officer to sit. He had cleared his desk, leaving just a glass of water to his right side and a file to his left. Breck pulled out a chair and lowered himself into it but couldn't help but stare at the white strips of crispy hair that decorated the sides of Bashir's face.

'Is there something on my person that is interesting you Arlo?'

'No, sir, I'm just…nothing, sir.'

The Super removed the cigarette from his mouth then placed it on the outer edges of a silver ashtray. One that had been engraved with his initials. A reward for fifteen years' service.

'I hear we have a dead finance director of a big city company. We must manage this in the right way, which I'm sure we are doing.' Breck nodded. 'I understand you visited the crime scene. How was it?'

'Not pleasant as you can imagine. Seeing as the victim was left in a bad way. I'm thinking about running the microscope over anyone she's fallen out with in her line of business, perhaps running the rule over Van Bruen's possible competitors.'

'No need.' Bashir's words took Breck by surprise.

'I don't quite follow sir.'

'I know that as part of your investigation you have a name of an employee that works at the same company. Van Bruen are pretty rigorous with their vetting procedures so I'd imagine he's not stealing their files to sell to the Chinese, or the Russians.' Breck's stony face failed to acknowledge Bashir's attempt at dry humour. 'The other man, the one that was attacked, there might be something there so follow that line of enquiry.'

'But sir…'

'That's a direct order.'

'The suspect tried to get new business. Should I look at the company in question to see if it ties in?'

'They are legitimate. I don't want us upsetting the wrong people, so no.'

The smoke from the cigarette created a thin wall between them and Breck knew better than to challenge Bashir, so he told him what he wanted to hear.

'As always, I'll do my best to get a result sir.'

'Good because the wealthy don't like this sort of thing happening on their doorstep. It creates problems and makes us look bad.'

'I'm sure the poor would have a problem with it too, sir,' Breck retorted. 'Shouldn't everything be on an equal footing so that we investigate what we're given regardless of social status?'

'Wealthy translates as influential in my book and we're here to protect those that wield influence. It's what the SCU was set up for.'

Bashir's eyes glowed bright for a brief second before he let them return to their unnatural dimmed state. He relaxed his shoulders then took a sip from the glass of water. 'You've been here for a while now and I brought you into this cess pit of a place Arlo because I need results. It'll be difficult because the cuts have hit everyone hard, your team too.' Bashir took time to reflect, wishing he could stop the rot but knowing Breck could if given the chance. 'The whole service is haemorrhaging but we have to hit our targets. You're the senior investigative officer in the absence of a regular DCI on this case, so due to that fact, I'll be poking my nose in from time to time.' Bashir pointed to his nose just in case Breck didn't understand. 'You're also an ambitious lad, so I'm sure you'll want to be a DCI one day.' Breck wasn't even given the time to respond before Bashir continued. 'Sounds good doesn't it, DCI Arlo Breck? Imagine it lit up in lights and keep that picture in your mind. You can make it here but I want things done the correct way under my direction. I don't want us to look bad by slipping up.'

Breck had already questioned his career by dreaming of a safer environment where the chances of survival were higher than they were at present. In the last year alone five officers he knew of had to retire due to injuries sustained while in the line of duty. However, now wasn't the time to discuss that.

'With regard to the current murder investigation, sir...'

'Excuse me.' Bashir sneezed then took a silk handkerchief from out of his pocket. Breck waited until his boss was ready before continuing.

'I'd like us to keep watch on our POI.'

'Under normal circumstances that makes sense but I can't assign a budget for it. We're stretched as it is.'

'It would be very useful if we did.'

'OK, I've got no problem with you doing it off your own back, great idea. But you'll have to be resourceful with that one.'

The OK bit pleased Breck but not the conditions of the OK bit. He had enough to do already in his normal day-to-day without worrying about managing a continuous surveillance operation. He felt defeated.

'Let me mull it over, sir, no use making a rod for my own back.'

'Agreed,' Bashir said. 'Mull it over. So, what do you know about our prime suspect?'

'He's a valuation specialist with Van Bruen which means there's an obvious link between himself and Janet Maskell, with her being the finance director there. Having spoken to him in the interview room I can say that he's a bit of an arrogant sod. For us, the exact relationship between himself and Ms Maskell is still unknown. He refused to acknowledge that there was anything other than a professional one between them.'

'What's the evidence against him?'

'His credit card and a magazine with his name written on top found at the scene. No alibi for the period we believe Janet Maskell expired, and of course there's the issue of the second Alexander Troy.'

'Sounds all straightforward up until the part of the second Troy coming into this.'

'I agree. After you came into the interview room and told Kearns the news, we went to speak to the other Troy. He seemed sincere enough and if he was an actor, then I'd say give him an award now. The main thing, he has an alibi for the time Janet Maskell died.'

'Where does he work?'

'Anywhere he wants sir. He's an entrepreneur of some sort.' Breck watched Bashir rake through the data in his mind.

'Not sure I like the sound of that. As I've said earlier, focus more of your attention on the Troy that reported the attack. I don't want this to drag on and on.'

'Shouldn't the focus be on the one without the alibi?'

Bashir arched one of his eyebrows. 'I don't like repeating myself.'

'Of course, sir, I'll do what needs to be done.'

Bashir's satisfied nod opened the door for Breck to leave so he rose from the chair and walked out, careful to close the door behind him. The DI never cared much for following the strict code of authority and believed that impromptu decisions sometimes needed to be made. The rule book amended.

Despite Bashir's instruction the POI was the one with the legitimate alibi. He was at the station reporting his attack at the time of Janet Maskell's murder. Formal identification of the fingerprints found on the credit card would soon arrive and surely implicate the prime suspect. Yet something didn't add up. Why was Bashir blind to this? It didn't make sense.

When Breck returned to his desk, he was still reflecting on his conversation until the shrill of the phone made him jump. He managed to answer it after two rings. It was his girlfriend.

'I can't handle it, Arlo, I need you here.' She sounded distraught.

'Calm down, what's wrong?'

'I'm not good, I don't feel safe and my head is pounding.'

'Take some aspirin.'

'Is that the best you can offer, aspirin?'

'What else do you want me to say?'

'Why did you leave me on my own this morning?'

Breck kept his voice low. 'You told me you were feeling better, I wouldn't have come into work otherwise.'

'I was but I'm not now, not right now.'

Her distress knotted his stomach and Breck waited. Not because he didn't know what to say but because he needed to allow himself time to cool down. 'I have to go,' he said after a while of nothing. 'I'll be there as soon as I can but remember, I'm working.'

Molly's silence gave its own reply so Breck ended the call, frustrated and stressed. He stared at the floor for a few moments until he summoned enough strength to head down to the front desk, passing a few SCU colleagues along the way, and judging by the scowl on his face, they knew better than to strike up a conversation.

Desk Sergeant Clive Bird had seen enough of the world and was just happy to turn up to work and do as much as he needed to do, nothing more, then he'd get off home. His vice was fishing whenever he could and he liked to throw a few bob on the horses too.

'Have we got an address for Alexander Troy, the robbery victim?'

Clive opened his leather bound red book and scratched his head as he read through the most recent page. He then flicked through the earlier pages before returning to it.

'That's strange.'

'What is?'

'Well there are two Alexander Troy's listed in here. I don't get it.'

'Welcome to my life. I'll explain later Clive, but there's no mistake. It's the one that came here to report an assault this afternoon.'

'It looks like he scribbled it in. That's on me it is, should have checked.' Breck had a peek. Whatever POI Troy had written was illegible.

'If it helps, he just popped in again. Said he had left his car keys behind and picked them up off the table there underneath some magazines.' Breck glanced over to where Clive referenced. 'He drives one of those nice Mk4 Cortinas.'

Breck's eyes burned bright, and he was already on his way out of the station when he asked, 'What coat is he wearing again?'

'Not a coat but a green bomber jacket!' Clive replied.

Breck exited the station at a crossroads, unsure of where the POI had gone until he saw a man wearing a green bomber jacket cross the road. A Mk4 Cortina was parked in the direction in which he headed and Breck came close to calling him but held back. The POI continued past the car and then Breck followed him.

He watched him head down into the heart of Lewisham and enter the Riverdale Shopping Centre. There was a slight bustle about the area which suited Breck fine. The additional people would act as cover for his unscheduled surveillance. At one point he even crouched down and pretended to tie his shoe laces after the POI stopped to glance around to make sure he wasn't being followed.

A glut of passers-by blinded Breck's line of sight until the POI continued again with his journey. This time walking into a department store. The clothing aisles enabled customers to flitter past, browse left and right with ease, and he stopped at a rack of men's shirts to check them out. Breck stopped too but next to a line of women's lingerie. He had no choice, couldn't afford to get too close. He grabbed a bell sleeved chemise and pretended to inspect it, oblivious to the store's security guard that had taken a keen interest in him. Perhaps it was the way he caressed a garment made for the opposite sex. Or could it have been because he kept peering over? Either way, the guard who weighed in at two hundred and fifty pounds with a cloudy grey shirt tucked into his charcoal trousers, came thundering towards him prepared for a confrontation.

'You all right there?'

'Yes, thanks.'

'It's just that you're standing by the women's section.'

'Is it a crime?'

'A crime?'

'Yes, for me to be browsing through women's clothes? I might be searching for a present.' The guard considered this but while he did, he refused to leave.

'Yes you might but this department floor is my domain.'

The last thing Breck needed was for him to make a scene, so he flashed his ID and told him to, 'Piss off,' then turned his attention back to his target. Of course that just served to make matters worse because the guard blocked his path.

'I'd like to know what you're doing. Right now you're making a big mistake. Back off or you won't have a job this time next week.'

Out of pride the guard remained rooted to the spot but it was a no-win situation for him and when Breck saw the POI leave the store, he simply pushed past.

Breck maintained a safe distance while he continued to follow behind and soon switched onto Ladywell Road. He felt the ache in his feet as he trotted beyond the black steel posts on which the paint had long ago stripped away, and the other end beyond the posts opened up onto a large patch of green. The POI headed straight towards its centre.

There were a few people slotted around but he seemed comfortable enough, planted next to a mother and her screaming toddler. Minutes later a man approached, flaunting denim on denim and the two of them seemed to know each other. They began a conversation. From where Breck stood, he couldn't get a clear view and wondered why the POI had left his car outside the station to walk so far for this meeting? He'd have to get closer to them. Breck approached an ice cream van near to where they stood, hands in pockets, whistling a tune. As he closed in the other man left which was unfortunate. But not wanting to raise suspicions, he carried on towards the van and asked the woman inside for an ice lolly. He kept a discreet eye on the POI and to be honest, he had expected the tracking to be much more difficult. Tricky. As long as he wasn't spotted he wouldn't be complaining.

'That will be thirty pence,' she said.

Breck took the ice lolly. 'Thanks.' He pulled out the correct change and paid, but when he turned around his stomach flipped. The POI had disappeared. Breck's desperate stare stretched across the grassy landscape but he drew a horrifying blank. He struggled to process just how it could have happened. The POI had gone and somehow Breck suspected he knew he was being followed.

In frustration, he ran over to the mother and her child - who had now stopped wailing to nibble on a chocolate bar. The mother made the most of the few minutes peace.

'Excuse me. There was a man in a green bomber jacket sitting right next you just a moment ago. Did you see where he went?'

'Sorry, no I didn't.'

'Are you sure? This is important!' Breck failed to realise the volume of his voice had shot up by a few decibels. The woman grabbed her child out of fear but the little girl tried to struggle free and dropped her chocolate bar to the ground. She resumed her wail but Breck remained unperturbed. 'Why won't you answer the question? I need to find him!'

'If you don't leave us alone, I'll scream for help.'

Breck came to his senses and backed off. The mother's words slapped him hard and he knew he had to accept that he had been given the slip. It was a wake-up call and proof that all was not as it seemed.

Breck had screwed up. He threw the ice lolly to the ground in disgust and walked away. Lemon wasn't his favourite flavour, anyway.

SEVEN

Kearns took a bit of time out for herself in the yard, smoking as she attempted to come to terms with what had happened. And what would happen, and what might yet be. The station was already in panic mode after the fracas and although order had been restored, she needed to speak to Bashir.

Beyond the gates a young woman walked past and her svelte size and innocent face reminded Kearns of her own estranged daughter. The more she stared at her the more the woman transformed into Kim and it transported Kearns to the past. To a time where her ex-husband would be fast asleep whenever she returned home from work.

He trapped himself under the spell of booze, and she would often stop and stare at him with overwhelming sadness, disappointed that he failed to live up to the potential he had shown when they first married. The magic had long since fizzled away between them. Love replaced by hate. But the one good thing to emerge from their union was their daughter Kim - a bright and feisty young girl.

In those days, working as a WPC always tired Kearns. She'd get in, drop her handbag to the floor, slip off her shoes then open a bottle of wine. She'd eat the digestive biscuits on the sofa beside her sleeping husband and stretch out her legs to get comfortable, accepting that biscuits and wine for the third night in a row wasn't the type of diet she wanted to advertise. It had become her new bad habit and as the News at Ten flashed onto the television screen, Patricia Kearns would often fall asleep.

One morning when the door slammed shut, she jumped out of her sleep. It was bright and light surged through the window, and lit the room. She sprung up, still hazy and peered outside just in time to see Mick set off for work. It made sense now. The slamming door was a sign of his anger at having to make his own sandwiches for lunch again. She felt nothing and recalled glancing at the wall clock. No time for a bath, just a quick face wash. She had to get going, and it was after she put on her shoes and straightened up that she saw the note pinned to the door.

Mum,
I'm off to Julia's after college. See you later.
Kim x

Kearns switched back to reality. Her daughter now lived miles away and the girl that had reminded her of Kim a moment ago had gone too. It didn't take long for her steely resolve to resurface though because there would be no reunion today. Just shit to sort out.

Kearns discarded the cigarette and stepped back inside the station to see several skinheads from the fracas lined up with their hands handcuffed behind their backs. They disgusted her for their attitude but had served a purpose today. Whether or not that purpose was morally right or wrong she couldn't yet decide.

Kearns made her way to Bashir's office but stopped just outside the door when she heard him on the phone. He sounded agitated, which meant he'd soon slam it down. She counted down from ten and by the time she reached three, he ended the conversation with a bang. It sounded as if he had broken the phone in two and her pensive knock was apparent to Bashir who opened the door himself to let her in.

'You look worried.' He stepped aside to allow her to enter. 'Have a seat.'

'I'd rather stand, sir.'

'OK, what can I help you with today?'

'The suspect that we apprehended earlier has escaped. My fault.'

Bashir returned to his position behind his desk in deep thought. 'How?'

'A situation occurred in reception.'

'Yes, I've heard about it. Was just on the phone to Clive. This is not good but we can blame the fight that broke out for this.'

'The suspect saw his chance and just got away from me.'

'Yes, we'll blame the fight.'

'I didn't handcuff him.'

Bashir's eyes widened. 'No handcuffs? Are you mad?'

'Sir, after our conversation this morning I thought...'

Bashir cut in. 'Patricia, it's not for us to dictate these matters in such a direct way. Although a charge could have been pinned on him within a few hours it wouldn't have happened under my watch. He would have been bailed by tomorrow.'

Bashir put a finger to his lips to halt any more words from Kearns while he analysed the situation, and in his moments of thought he knew what to do next.

*

On his return to Cransham, Breck headed towards the exact spot he last saw the Mk4 Cortina parked. It wasn't there. This version of Troy had been smart enough to shake him, collect his car and drive away. Breck fumed. He didn't even have a registration number to check so his only hope was to get the address the POI gave upon his arrival.

Feeling deflated, he entered the station to witness a clean-up operation underway. He had no idea what was going on but saw plenty of uniforms looking dazed, juniors were tidying up, and seniors were standing around shaking their heads. Breck spotted droplets of blood on the floor where the mop hadn't yet reached and concluded that a fight had taken place. So he went over to Clive for an update, noticing a newly attached plaster on the custody sergeant's cheek.

'It looks like a hurricane has swept through here.'

'Yes, it was quite something that you missed.'

'What happened?'

'A bloke brought in for driving without a licence happened to be one of the Front's' security chiefs. He took offence at how they man-handled him and made a big noise about it. One thing led to another then he turned apoplectic.'

Breck had a look around. 'Looks like it was quite a noise.'

'It went up a notch when his mates bowled in and tried to have a go. We've currently got several men locked up but a juvenile that was with them escaped,' Clive said, making sure the plaster behaved itself by staying in place. 'Did you find the Troy fella?'

'Yes. I trailed him to Ladywell then lost him.'

'That's not like you Arlo. Rumour has it you've got supernatural police skills that are unexplained.'

'Funny. There's a comedy club around the corner if you fancy a career change. Anyway, how can I locate him when all we have is an illegible address? He's our POI and I want to speak to him now. For your reference, the other Troy is our prime suspect.'

Clive itched the scratch on his head. 'He told the interviewing officer that he had a holiday booked to Norway, planning to visit one of them remote islands.'

'What's the island named?'

'Something like Spits…Spitser…'

'Spitsbergen?'

'That's it, or it could have been Bear Island. One of the two but he said that his flight was scheduled for today.'

It wasn't the type of news that Breck wanted to hear but there was little he could do.

'Thanks Clive. I wanted to speak to him before he went on holiday but will have to figure something else out.'

Breck grabbed one of the hard-boiled sweets from the metal dish on the custody desk. The strawberry and cream flavoured sweets were reserved for visitors, but that mattered little to him as he unwrapped one then popped it into his mouth.

On his way back to his floor he stopped off at the gents, still annoyed at being given the slip by the POI, but consoled by the fact he had the other Troy at least locked up in a cell. His relief was short-lived. At the urinal he was joined by fellow SCU officer Ray Riley, a heavyset man with a small face and deep lines that tracked his forehead. His reputation at the best of times preceded him, and he did nothing to dispel them. It gave him a sick boost to be the bad boy of the SCU. He used to be on good terms with Breck until their well-documented quarrel a year ago. Since then he always tried his best to put Breck down and now was no exception.

'How is it going, still failing at your job?' Breck knew he should ignore the snipe but wanted to fire back with one of his own.

'I'm doing quite well but I haven't seen you around much. If they haven't got any work for you perhaps you should do us a favour and go home.'

Riley smiled. 'You were never in my league. Even now that you're a DI, you still ain't.'

Riley always feared that Breck would overtake him on the way up the career ladder and Breck liked to play with that.

'Did I tell you that I'm working on a big one, a dead finance director and a case of double identities? I don't think I did. You're not important enough.' Riley kept his lips sealed so Breck goaded him further. 'I'd love to know what are you working on. How to harass teenagers down at the Riverdale?'

'I'll give you that one Arlo, the older you get the sharper you're becoming but some of those coloured kids need watching. Anyway, the reason you haven't seen me around much is because I've just come back from holiday.' Riley stared straight ahead, fiddling with his trouser zipper while humming Bowie's *Starman*.

Breck feigned interest. 'Where did you go?'

'Costa Rica. Didn't want to come back to be honest.'

'So, why did you?'

'To see your pretty face and I love the power the job gives me. I've just found out that I have to help with patrolling the Front's march. Keep them out of harm's way from those anti-fascist hooligans.' The surprise at Riley's words registered on Breck's face.

'Don't look at me like that, everyone has a right to voice their opinion. Anyway, the point is Bashir has put me in charge of a specific area along the route and it made me think.' Riley acted as if time had frozen while he stared up at the ceiling. Breck had to check that his heart was still beating.

'For fuck's sake, please don't keep me in suspense.'

'It made me ask, what have you been given?' Breck ignored him but that didn't stop Riley's poison. 'You haven't been given anything with regard to the march and I thought you'd be a dead cert.'

'Why would you think that?'

Riley sharpened his next set of words. 'Well seeing as you can relate to both sides of the fence.'

Breck managed to hold himself back, left the urinal and washed his hands in the basin, wishing he knew of a way to thump Riley and get away with it. The man's ignorance was to be expected but it had no room in Breck's complicated world. A place where he would not get even as much as a second glance in most places as things stood. If it were known that a difference existed, he'd be getting three, four, or even five glances. The rest didn't know it but Riley did.

Investigations were ongoing regarding the scale of corruption in the force. Breck hoped Riley wouldn't be able to weave his way out of anything. It'd just be a matter of time before he was questioned. His conviction rate remained high, yet there were always rumours about him and the way he chose to do things. What Riley did to get those high rates, no one apart from his partner Gaz Bennett quite knew. Gaz could blow the lid off all his dealings but he'd probably implicate himself as well and it was that loyal silence which allowed Riley to play the game, and take advantage of whoever he wanted to.

The mirror above the wash basin allowed Breck to see his weary face. The odd strand of grey already tracked parts of his hair. The job had aged him and he never even realised.

Breck left the toilets and remembered he hadn't yet phoned his girlfriend. He'd be unable to pop round to see her before he finished work proper. A phone call was the least he could do. He made it a priority to ring her when he reached his desk, but he didn't get any further with that thought because he bumped into Beatrice.

The first thing to note: her upset. The second thing to note: her borderline hate. It pointed the finger at his responsibility for all of her woes and she made herself clear.

'We need to talk now!'

It wasn't the best time for him but he was fearful she'd cause a scene. Breck didn't want to feature on the station's gossip lists. Or face a difficult time while working alongside her.

'Let's go into the function room.'

He held her arm as he led her away.

The function room was where the station's officers would meet with stakeholders, council officials and prominent community leaders. Currently undergoing a refurbishment, the tables and chairs were hidden, draped in a sea of white covers. The perfect place for Breck to obtain some privacy for the conversation to come. He now regretted that drunken kiss he shared with Beatrice at the recent SCU team night out.

As soon as he closed the door she used her body to block it, sending a clear message. He wouldn't be allowed to leave until she said so. Beatrice liked him much more than a friend, and a lot of the lads fancied her which gave him a bit of a confidence boost.

However, Kearns saw her as a danger, a viper ready to sink her teeth into anything she desired. She seemed to have her eye on men that could in some way further her career but Breck didn't see her like that. Perhaps the pouting lips had something to do with it.

'Bea, why are you so upset? I haven't been ignoring you or anything like that.'

'No you haven't but you've been ignoring something else.'

'Enlighten me, just what have I been ignoring?'

'Arlo, don't pretend like you don't know what I'm talking about.'

'Do you mean when we…at the team night out?' Breck couldn't even bring himself to say it and that was when he realised things had gone far enough. 'I'm with someone, Bea. There has been too much flirting between us and it's been my fault. I accept that.'

'Too much flirting? We didn't stop at the kiss, we nearly went all the way. This is what you want otherwise you would have put a stop to it a long time ago.'

Breck hung his head and stared at the floor. She was right. Maybe their flirtatious working relationship gave him an escape route away from his problems with Molly. The truth hurt and at that moment he became confused and unsure about what to say.

'Give me time.'

'You want more time?'

'That's what I need and I'm not saying that to be difficult.'

'I thought it'd be easier than this.'

Beatrice guessed that she had little choice in the matter. Although she was far from happy with his request. There was a glimmer of hope on her part that he'd be honest about how he felt soon enough, and if giving him time would lead to the chance of something then she'd be happy to take the gamble under normal circumstances. Whatever they were.

'Say something, please,' Breck pleaded.

As he held her hands Beatrice felt the chemistry between them but a relationship needed two consenting adults to have any chance of working. The question she had to ask herself wouldn't be easy. Did she believe Breck would endanger his relationship for her? Deep down she knew the answer and refused to play the fool.

'Arlo, this is a waste of time so I've got to be professional about this. From now on we're just colleagues and nothing else. How's that?'

Breck failed to respond so she released herself from him and turned to leave. Then swung her head back and in that moment, she sent across all the hate she could muster. With nothing more to say she left and Breck felt disappointed with himself. The blame for everything that had happened lay at his door and somehow, he had to fix it.

Breck left the function room and made his way up to his floor.

Bashir blocked the entrance with a formidable scowl printed across his face and barked a stream of instructions to a faceless temp worker before she scurried away. His focus then shifted onto his DI.

'I'm going to be tied up at the anti-fascist group meeting. They want to stop the march but it's not as simple as that and it's not in my power either.'

'Does a decision like that need to come from higher up, sir?'

The strain showed on Bashir's face. 'Yes; and whether we like it or not, the march will soon be upon us. We'll have the local press there to scrutinise everything on the day and to give it to us in the neck afterwards. Bloody nuisance. Right, while I'm gone sort out the situation we had earlier.'

'Sir, I don't know much about it.'

At that moment, Kearns appeared from around the corner to confess. 'Sorry, it was my fault Alexander Troy escaped. During the mass brawl, he took his chance and made a run for it.'

Breck's jaw dropped but Bashir's intimidating stare forced him to close it back.

'We're on it,' he said turning to Kearns. 'Come on, let's go.'

Both officers made their way outside while Breck found it difficult to subdue his shock, wondering how an experienced officer like Kearns could ever have let a prime suspect in an investigation slip from her grasp.

'Pat, how did he get away from you?' Kearns was lost for words and just offered a simple shrug of the shoulders. They opened the doors to the Allegro and got in. It wasn't like her at all but he didn't want to dwell on it because he knew mistakes happened. They were a part of the job. 'Do we know where he might be?'

'We believe he's in the Deptford area. Last seen near Margaret McMillan Park.'

'Good, at least that's something. Did he hurt you?'

'No, I'm fine. I was just careless that's all. So much happened to distract us that he saw his opportunity then took it. After he made a run for it I thought he might have slipped down to the basement,' Kearns recalled.

'Ah, a great hiding place.'

'Saw no sign of him though so I got that wrong too.'

Breck realised that Kearns was still being quite vague with the exact details of Troy's disappearance but put it down to shock. It hadn't escaped him that both Troys were now on the loose, which made it a lot trickier to work out the real one.

Kearns fastened her seatbelt. The screaming siren of the Allegro allowed Breck to speed out of the yard and cut through the traffic on the main road.

'My week has already been hectic enough,' he complained. 'This morning when I woke, I had hoped for an easier day.'

'Sorry to drag you into this.'

'Hey, that's what partners are for. Don't worry about it.'

Margaret McMillan Park, half the size of a football pitch with grass cut to an inch high, had wooden benches that retained their varnish. A surreal ambiance filled the air and by the time Breck and Kearns exited the car they had a plan. Breck would scope the market area while Kearns would use the car to patrol the backstreets. They didn't want a horde of flashing blue lights to force Troy underground. They wanted him to believe that the coast was clear, so he'd reveal himself.

Breck waved off his partner and dug his hands into the pockets of his coat, wading through the ribbons of chatter which floated around. The market was busy and on any other day he might have grabbed himself a bargain. A record player or an amplifier. That would all have to wait. He took his time observing anyone that looked suspicious but regardless of how promising it seemed, it always turned out to be a red herring.

This pattern continued until he saw a man propped against a wall side-on, hesitant with his movements. Breck zeroed in to watch him glance around a few times as he walked away and the detective regained the spring in his step. Travelling into the heart of Deptford market was the prime suspect, Alexander Troy.

Breck pushed on straight ahead, past a cluster of bodies and the items for sale nestled on the ground due to overloaded tables. The barking dogs and calypso music from a radio provided an orchestrated backdrop of sounds, and every second step someone stood in his way, cursing and pin-balling him around. He became an unwanted obstacle under the din of boisterous sellers.

Troy didn't appear to have a clear idea of where to head. Once or twice he stopped and rerouted himself but Breck wasn't confident of grabbing him in such a populated area with so many people close by. He had done that once before in another case and a bystander ended up in hospital with serious head injuries. He should have been able to shake the fear of that happening again but it proved to be difficult.

Breck watched Troy perform a 360-degree loop then walk through a litter-strewn alleyway to his right, about four yards in width, and venture out towards the main road. He dipped into a nearby newsagent, but with Troy's wallet back at the station, Breck wondered where he had obtained money from. He wanted to make the arrest right there and then but there could be other people in the shop. Breck had no way of finding that fact out other than to walk in himself but it'd be too dangerous. He'd wait with his concealed baton and handcuffs, hoping it would be enough in this instance.

Breck pulled the radio from his pocket and contacted Kearns, then leaned against a bus stop. He stepped forward a bit and pretended to be interested in the timetable which prompted an old lady to smile at him. He returned the gesture and remembered that he hadn't spoken to his own grandmother for a while. That was not like him. She had brought him up after his mum passed away but life had been busy of late. Breck felt the guilt of that in an instant because he more than anyone knew that the job took people away from others all the time. His reflections ceased when he spotted Troy.

He left the newsagents but still remained cautious, though appeared to be a little more relaxed. Perhaps even believing that the coast was clear. Perfect. Kearns would arrive in any second then they'd be able to get him and put an end to this chase.

Breck expected Troy to turn right towards Brookmill Road but instead he began to head towards him, so he stared at the ground and averted his gaze. There'd be no arrest yet. Too many people around. The old lady and now a mother and her three kids. Breck stayed stationary while he passed by. Yet, when he turned to follow he stopped in his tracks. Troy had hailed a black cab and was in the process of getting in. Breck realised that he needed Kearns to arrive more than ever right now. Where was she?

A break in the traffic allowed him to step out into the main road and he could just about make out the Allegro in the distance. He waved his hands without creating a sound because the sensible option would be to see where Troy would head to. His actions brought a few curious stares his way, but when Troy's cab moved off, Breck was close to exploding after he saw the Allegro stall then stop. He dashed towards it only to stumble in the road before he could continue his jog towards Kearns.

She saw him coming and kept turning the ignition while vehicles behind didn't dare sound their horns at the police car. By the time Breck opened the door, the Allegro restarted after she tried the ignition again.

'What happened Pat?'

'Don't know, it just cut out.'

'The thing was serviced last week, it shouldn't be cutting out!'

'I don't know what to say.'

Breck thought that it was peculiar but didn't have time to dwell on it. He hopped in and pointed forwards. 'Troy's gone that way in a black cab, let's get moving.'

Kearns switched on the siren and bolted away.

'Why didn't you make the arrest?'

It was a good question and Breck could have responded by asking '*Why did you let him escape in the first place?*' After careful consideration, he thought better of it.

'Too many people around that might have got hurt if it went wrong.'

'I can't see him.'

Despite their best efforts to guess the multitude of potential directions Troy's journey might have taken, they drew a blank on his exact whereabouts. The prime suspect had escaped for a second time.

'Have we got anything else to go on?' Breck asked. 'I don't fancy going back to the station to face Bashir empty-handed.'

'Troy's boss, Lizzie Daniels, might know where we can find his girlfriend, which may lead to him. It's a longshot.'

'I'm happy to take it. Have you got her number?'

'No but it should be at the station in one of the files.'

'Pull the car over.'

Kearns reduced the speed and when the car stopped, Breck used the radio to get through to the SCU. Beatrice came on air, still seething with him and although she knew that Kearns was there too, it failed to prevent her from being unhelpful. After the update she had a quick look for the file containing Lizzie Daniel's direct number but didn't come back with any good news.

'I can't find it.'

Breck groaned. 'What do you mean you can't find it?'

'It's not where it should be.'

'OK, thanks,' he said. He ended the conversation and turned to Kearns. 'I suppose the option of ringing directory enquiries is there for us.'

'You should report her to Bashir. Her conduct is a joke.'

'We all have to work together, she's just having a bad day that's all.'

'I mean it, Arlo, get Beatrice sorted out. She's a flipping DC, nothing more than that.'

'We've all had off days Pat and I've no reason to believe she didn't make a genuine attempt to search for the file.'

'You've got a soft spot for her, haven't you?'

Breck didn't like those words but it was true, more than Kearns ever knew.

'Let's change the subject,' he suggested.

'I've got an idea, let's go and see Lizzie in person. It's not too far.'

Breck agreed and Kearns restarted the car without complaint because the journey to Van Bruen plc would make up for her absence earlier.

*

The Van Bruen building didn't look as grand to Breck as it had done earlier, perhaps it was the 'new age feeling' thing he had been reading about. He couldn't be sure. Meanwhile, the same receptionists from earlier were still on duty and recognised him, terrified he had brought more bad news.

'I'm here to see Lizzie Daniels,' he said upon reaching the desk.

'DI Breck isn't it?' The younger of the two asked.

'Yes, and this is my colleague Detective Sergeant Patricia Kearns.'

Breck chose not to sit down and Kearns followed suit. He felt that standing would shorten the wait, and he was right. After a few moments, Lizzie Daniels emerged wearing a solemn expression, looking a bit shaky. Breck made the introductions between her and Kearns then both officers followed her to Meeting Room One on the ground floor. The same room that Breck sat in during his previous visit.

Lizzie poured water from an opal glass jug into a cup. 'Do any of you want some?' she offered, but both officers declined. She placed the jug back in its place then sat down. It was a different Lizzie to the one he met earlier, and he had seen the look she wore on her face many times before on others – when the death of someone close had started to sink in.

'How are you holding up?' he asked.

'I've been comforting Janet's secretary who's been in tears, along with a few others that worked in her team. If I'm honest, it's becoming a nightmare.' Lizzie took a sip of water and stared at the cup for a while as if it might hold all the answers.

'The rumours are flying around that Alexander has got something to do with Janet's death but it didn't come from me or Wade.'

Breck cast his mind back to the two receptionists and believed if he arrested Lizzie Daniels right now, she too would be implicated in the murder on the strength of their loose talk.

'I'm going to tell you something in confidence Lizzie so don't repeat it. Alexander has escaped from our custody.'

'What?'

'As it stands, he's now a fugitive. Has he tried to contact you at all?'

'No, he hasn't. What was he thinking, running away?'

Neither officer could provide an answer so Breck broke the silence. 'Earlier, when I informed you and Wade of Janet's death, you told me about a woman he was courting named Ceinwen. Do you know where we can find her, or even a close confidant, someone he might turn to?'

Lizzie bit her lip in thought. 'I have no information on where Ceinwen could be but Troy has a friend he trusts by the name of Peter Clarke.'

'Do you know where we can find him?'

'Yes. We held a charity event here last year and he came along. Tried to chat me up too but had no idea I was Alexander's boss. He slipped me his address but it was all very embarrassing.'

'Did you throw it away?'

'Of course, but if you want it you can have it.'

Kearns couldn't understand how Lizzie could provide it while Breck knew what would come next. A perfect recall of Peter Clarke's address.

EIGHT

Peter Clarke's name rang a bell with Kearns and she wondered if he could be the same defence solicitor the CID kept an eye on a few years back. The one that wore designer suits and drove the type of flash car beyond the normal means of his salary. He also had a habit of defending the wrong types.

'So you're not sure if it's the same Clarke?'

'No, I wasn't close to the case. All I know for sure was that he had a wife and child, a little boy. The wife ended up leaving him and all of a sudden, the fancy lifestyle ended. It's almost as if she walked away with half of his cash as hush money.'

They were on their way to Greenwich and Breck sensed something hidden within Kearns that he couldn't quite identify. A distant feeling.

'Pat, you've never told me the reason why you left Sandal & Agbrigg to come down here to Cransham. That's a big step for anyone from the North.'

'You're right but you haven't told me why you moved here either so that makes us quits!'

'I fancied a change, only that. Now it's your turn.' He appreciated her bullish powers of observation.

Kearns considered her words but in the end, she delivered a terse response. 'Likewise.'

'Really? I thought it might be more to it than that,' Breck teased. He wasn't convinced.

'Sorry to disappoint.'

Breck believed that Kearns was hiding something but didn't quite know how to prove it. Then Molly and Beatrice crossed his mind, and the conversation dried up. He had a lot to think about.

They reached the border of Greenwich and stopped at a set of traffic lights. Breck opened the glove compartment and pulled out an A-Z Street Atlas, ploughed through a couple of pages, and soon found Peter Clarke's address. He directed Kearns the rest of the way and it took a further five minutes until she stopped the car.

They were a few feet away from Clarke's home, a nice place on an even nicer street and Kearns hoisted the handbrake into position then exited at the same time as Breck. She resisted the chance to take the piss as he zipped up his coat to protect himself from a breeze that wasn't even there.

'He lives at number 36,' Breck revealed, pointing a finger across the road. 'Let's go and say hello.'

*

After a multitude of knocks rattled his front door, Peter Clarke moved away from the pipes that were underneath the sink he was attempting to fix. He didn't appreciate the intrusion and lifted himself off his knees, wondering who it could be, while wiping his wet hands across his overalls. He put down his tools and went to investigate.

Kearns stood in front of Breck and Clarke eyed her up and down. She returned the favour, unsure of what to make of his bright red shoes.

'Mr Peter Clarke?'

'Yes, who wants to know?'

She pulled out her ID. 'I'm DS Kearns, and this is DI Breck. Can we come in?'

Suspicion circled Clarke's face yet the detectives knew that because of his legal background he'd respect the law. Or at least they hoped he would. They knew little about Clarke or his temperament but would soon find out.

'Can I ask what this is concerning?'

'It's best if we talk inside, I reckon,' Breck suggested.

There was an innocuous shrug from the defence solicitor before he let them in. When he did, he directed them towards the kitchen.

'We can talk in here. It's time for my cuppa anyway. Do either of you two fancy one?'

Both officers declined the offer almost in unison and Kearns sat down while Breck stood. Everyone waited with pleasant faces and fixed smiles until the kettle boiled. Then Clarke poured out the water into his white mug and joined Kearns around the table. He bought the smouldering liquid heat to his mouth and took a sip before taking great care to place the mug back down.

'So what is this about?'

'Do you know a man by the name of Alexander Troy, maybe known as Alex for short?'

The solicitor ran a hand over his thinning patch of hair and assumed that the police must already know he and Troy were friends so there was no point in lying.

'Yes, I know him. Is he OK?'

Breck failed to answer. 'When was the last time that you spoke to him?'

'We spoke two weeks ago. He said he had got hold of tickets for a football match. He asked if I wanted to go with him but I couldn't.'

'What else did he discuss?'

'Nothing much, it was a short conversation.'

'Did he seem normal?'

'Yes, he seemed normal, whatever that means.'

Kearns cut in. 'Has he got a girlfriend, someone else who knows him well?'

Peter Clarke tilted his head upwards and tapped his fingers on the table to an imaginary rhythm, giving the impression he was trying to search every loose memory in his head.

'Alexander doesn't do girlfriends, he prefers casual relationships. Likes to play the field. He flashes a smile and then lets the beast in his trousers do the talking. He's got the looks for it, unlike me.'

Kearns stifled a smile and continued. 'I understand that he's going out with a woman by the name of Ceinwen, pronounced *kine-win*.'

Clarke shrugged and Breck pulled out a seat then settled into it. Clarke brought his mug to his lips again, and this time took two mouthfuls of tea while Breck believed him to be too clever to give much away out of loyalty. For the present moment, he at least provided them with a jagged path into Alexander Troy's life.

'Mr Clarke, I suggest you help your friend by assisting us. We need him to clear up an urgent matter and he hasn't made things easy for himself so I'll ask this question just the once. When was the last time that you *really* heard from him?'

Clarke's face hardened. 'I told you, two weeks ago!'

Breck slammed a hand down on the table. 'A murder has occurred, and he has been implicated. Tell us what you know!'

Clarke rebuked the aggression by folding his arms in defiance which signalled the end of the questioning. Breck knew that and rolled his eyes. The conversation hadn't turned out the way he had planned.

'May we have a look around?'

'Not without a search warrant. You know the rules DI Breck.'

'Indeed, I do Mr Clarke. Thank you for your time and rest assured we'll be in touch.'

Breck and Kearns left, failing to spot the framed photo of a little boy and his mother. Peter Clarke peered through the kitchen window and watched them shrink into the distance then smirked. He grabbed his tools and returned to the pipes underneath the sink that he had been attempting to fix before the interruption, desperate to get it all done before Troy arrived.

NINE

West Cransham had more than a few interesting places to visit and one such place was called The Inn. The music venue brought a hazardous nightlife to the area and people from all over the UK flocked to the place frequented by a plethora of in-demand bands.

A guaranteed spectrum of noise accompanied every gig, every event, with drug-fuelled teenagers puking up

in the toilets. On a night when a band comprising of three Northern lads with sprayed hair, lean torsos and body piercings, played their last song, a majority of the crowd refused to believe that it was over.

Cheers followed, mixed with chants of, 'We want more,' but it was indeed the end of the show and the exits were opened to allow everyone to leave.

The venue had seen lots of nights like this, where many still felt the cutting edge of the electric guitar riffs, the lingering sounds of the tremolo, and the memories of the solo parts. The young began to get rowdy. The night belonged to them. Screw the establishment.

Buried in the heart of the crowd was Geraldine, a transatlantic rich girl rebelling against what she stood for, while soaking up the community tribalism at the same time. Her group were already so high they felt invincible and Geraldine felt no need to hold back her boyfriend.

'That looks like Rogers ahead,' he said. 'I never gave him permission to come to the gig. He's not allowed.' Simon couldn't catch up to Rogers as quick as he wanted. Not because Geraldine hooked herself onto his arm, but because the crowd were being drip-fed out. His best friend Tiz came along with his girlfriend Imelda, and he pitched in to back Simon's comments.

'He needs smacking up, let's do him.'

'Yeah, I like the idea of that.'

It had been a good night so far and would be even better if he ended up putting his fist through Rogers' nose.

The Inn's security made sure the crowd exited in single file and received abuse for their efforts from those who were nothing more than a colourful collective of wayward youth. By the time the group reached outside there was no sign of Rogers.

'You've lost him, maybe next time huh?' Geraldine said, unintentionally making Simon feel as if he had failed which dented his male pride.

'Let's go to the pub,' Imelda suggested but Tiz wasn't having any of it. 'We'll go there after Simon sorts out Rogers. Hang on, there he is.'

Rogers crossed the road with two mates and Simon's adrenalin reached bursting point. He squeezed through the crowd that had spilled out onto the street and Geraldine lost her grip on him. Tiz wasn't far behind so she found Imelda and both girls held onto each other for comfort. A line of cars stopped them from joining the boys as they pounced on Rogers and pinned him against a wall daubed with *Pakis Out* in large letters. Rogers' mates had legged it.

'Bet you save loads of money on dyeing your hair.' Simon pulled hard, tugging the roots out of Rogers' scalp causing him to wince.

'He's a true ginger spaz but pretends that he isn't?' Tiz said, wading in.

Rogers nodded in the hope it would make them go away but he was wrong. Simon became intent on making an example of him, just to show off, nothing else.

'I didn't give you permission to come here tonight. We didn't want to see your ugly mug.'

Simon could see fear in Rogers' eyes, so loosened his grip. He wanted a fight not a capitulation and had the intention of letting him go until Geraldine and Imelda joined them. Their disappointment in the anti-climax reinvigorated his desire to humiliate him.

'Kiss my boots, Rog.'

Rogers stared down at the Dr. Martens and didn't fancy putting his lips on the scuffed leather. Simon pushed down on Rogers' shoulders, forcing him to begin the descent to his knees but in a surprise move, Geraldine protested.

'Let him go Simon,' Rogers caught her eye, thankful for the intervention.

Geraldine knew the right thing to say to make Simon relent. 'He's a loser, don't waste your time on him. Let's go to the pub.'

Simon chewed on her words and wanted to step away but Tiz stirred it up again.

'He'll lie to his mates and say that he fought us off.'

'Is that true?' Rogers' could feel Simon's breath skate across his face and his attempts to deny Tiz's claim were fruitless.

Simon grabbed him by the neck to force him down.

'Do it, come on, do it. Lick my fuckin' boots.'

Rogers was trying to resist but when Tiz kicked his knees, his legs collapsed. Imelda cheered on the boys while Geraldine wasn't so enthusiastic. Simon and Tiz had no need to bully Rogers, but she was powerless to stop it unless she could lessen the blow herself. With nothing to lose Geraldine bowled over and slapped Rogers across the face. It stung him and interrupted the whole *shoe kissing* moment. Then she screamed at him and the wink she sent Rogers was shared between them alone. Geraldine dragged a pent-up Simon with her.

'I need a drink. Come on.'

He spat in Rogers' direction, narrowly missing him while Tiz grabbed Imelda and began to complain.

'Why didn't you do what she did?' Imelda had no answer. 'Simon, your bird doesn't mess about.' An irate Tiz pulled Imelda to one side. 'Listen babe, next time do what she does, show a bit of balls.'

Imelda elbowed him in the ribs and he told her to, 'Piss off', then he put his arms around her and together they walked off. All four of them still feeling invincible and able to fight the world.

Rogers made sure they were almost out of sight before he pulled himself up and dusted down. It was time to go home and made for a crap end to the evening. But while he walked away so did someone else. A person that had been watching everything and taking a keen interest, although not in Rogers. It was in someone else within the group that had just left. Geraldine.

TEN

The Messenger

In his mind it wasn't personal, just business for which he had been paid to complete and the evening saw him waiting by a wall, busy pretending to be nothing so that nobody needed to look at him twice.

He watched with interest when she left the pub with friends and within that group he saw her boyfriend, judging by their closeness. The arms were locked

together, the lips touched. Not the right match for her he believed and already he blamed the boyfriend for making the girl Frankenstein's monster. Dog collar around her neck, a studded leather second skin, and ripped clothes. They mirrored each other. The boy wasn't the floral shirt and sandals type, he was the Mr Angry type.

The Messenger slid off the wall and followed from far enough away for them not to notice. Not to smell him. They couldn't feel his presence, and to his own mind, he walked close enough to hear the soles of their boots tap against the cold pavement. They walked without speed, a slow tread, before splitting from the others and when she kissed the boy again, it became wild and rough. For the one who watched, bad thoughts surfaced, of her... naked... doing things... then he stopped when he reminded himself he was there for the business; nothing else.

Along a winding road, a thin mist of fog joined the two lovers and they become outlines, these punks that were unsteady on their feet. He wanted one of them to fall, to hurt themselves and call for help. Yet somehow, they struggled along just, and hopped on a bus which he caught too.

He kept his head down, heard them talk, learned things, until they abused the conductor and were forced off, thinking they could get away with anything.

They arrived at Leicester Square, the showpiece. The one they polished for the Queen's Jubilee. Tourists liked it that way, admired the sparkle and the space. But for the one who watched, it meant nothing to him

The girl stopped right outside a place to eat and the boyfriend stared through the window, pining for the food, checking his barren pockets. He clenched his fists but she calmed him, then it was over and they moved on, still thinking that they ruled the world. The Messenger watched all of this because of one simple thing. He would be visiting the girl soon and she would be next.

ELEVEN

Being a prime suspect on the run meant that Troy's flat in Cransham had been locked down. Guarded by an officer stationed outside, it was sealed off to anyone unauthorised and the officer recognised Breck and Kearns as soon as they arrived. He greeted them with a polite nod, opened the door to let them into Troy's flat, then stepped aside.

It was tidy, not a messy bachelor pad. Everything seemed to be in place and that gave them a little bit of insight into Troy. A person that liked to keep things neat and in order, organised being a key word. For Breck, he considered Troy's escape as a measured action. Not one done without thought.

The furniture was kept to a bare minimum, one chair around a small table in the dining area, a double sofa chair in the living room. A single bed for the bedroom. Breck stared at the bed and thought it must be tricky for Troy whenever he invited female company over. He moved towards the drawer in the living room and at the same time that he opened it, Kearns opened the adjoining one. They sifted through each drawer but the only thing of significance were letters from Troy's bank regarding his account. His account had been set up at Midland – the 'listening bank' and Breck found statements that covered the last four months.

Troy was spending his entire income and more or less ended each month on a minus balance. Breck paused when he saw Kearns hold up a statement confirming that Troy owed the bank money. A significant amount too.

'Pat, I have another possibility for a motive. Troy needed money and saw Janet Maskell as a way to clear his debts so must have known she had a vast amount set aside somewhere.'

'Makes sense. So it's either for that reason he murdered her, or because she caught him breaking company rules. Both sound a bit strange to me. Over the top.' Kearns then closed her drawer. 'OK, nothing in this one. I'm going to search other areas of the flat.'

Breck followed and soon unearthed a bag, the colour of which blended in with the forest green carpet. He realised it could have been missed. Inside, he found a neat pile of folded clothes and took out each item. A shirt and a pair of trousers, socks, Y-Fronts and a light brown jacket. There was also a pair of Nike Cortez running shoes. Breck pushed his hand further into the bag and found something hidden inside the lining. He had a Swiss army knife on him so he flicked it open, made an incision with the blade, then dug his hand further in to pull out a passport and a hundred pounds in cash.

'Pat have a look at this!'

Kearns returned to the room walking faster than usual and peered at the collection of items.

'It looks like a quick getaway kit if you ask me.'

'Yes it does. We'll take it with us.'

'Good find,' she said making a mental note of the items.

'Where did we get with Janet Maskell's telephone call log?'

'Forgot to tell you with so much going on. I have received it.'

'Anything to note?'

'No, nothing to help us. She made no calls on the day, or previous to it so not sure why it had been left dangling.'

Breck wasn't surprised, but they needed to leave. He repacked the clothes into the bag and carried out the statements. They would be brought back to the station and added to Troy's file.

It was when Kearns opened the door to leave that Breck remembered something and doubled back. He searched around until he found the cupboard that housed the boiler.

'What are you doing?' she asked, watching while he opened its door.

'When we interviewed Troy he said that he had taken the time off in the morning to fix his broken boiler remember?' Breck began to fiddle around with the controls.

'Yes, so it needs fixing right?'

'No, it doesn't.' Breck closed the cupboard door. 'The boiler is working fine Pat, there's nothing wrong with it which means he lied.'

*

When Kearns returned to the station she knew it wouldn't be long before she'd be discussing the morning's events further with Bashir. She expected nothing less than a very public dressing down. It was the way it had to be and she had no problem keeping secrets. Though some were bigger than others. Kearns was aware that she needed to keep the investigation on its natural path, to nudge Breck when appropriate and suggest things. It wasn't just about Alexander Troy. It never had been.

Bashir gave Kearns a disapproving stare, witnessed by a few, and summoned her into his office. Double-barrelled expletives shot from his mouth, clear and audible for everyone, and the embarrassment grew. Kearns kept her head bowed, even when Bashir's hands were knitted together over the desk while he waited for her to get comfortable in her seat.

'Now that we've got that little show over and done with do I have to remind you why you're here?'

'No sir,' Kearns said, making eye contact.'

'Good because this situation is unprecedented and must be kept from Arlo.'

He unclasped his hands and reached for a cigarette from the half-full packet on his desk. Bashir slipped one into his mouth then lit up.

'By rights, not even you should know,' he said.

'I understand so what happens next?'

'Well, you're going to sit here for five minutes while I have a smoke. After that you'll go.'

Bashir lit up and blew out a pillow of smoke, leaving Kearns to stare into space. Neither of them saw Breck arrive and stand as close to Bashir's office as he could without being accused of spying. If he were a fly on the wall he'd hear them say:

'This is difficult for me to deal with sir, let's stop the secrecy and I'll go after him myself.'

'No, you may have a stake in this but I must do what I've been instructed to.'

Breck's anonymity didn't last long. Bashir spotted him watching and instinctively raised his voice a little higher. Kearns performed an awkward shift in her seat. Bashir called him in.

Breck entered the office and Bashir's upper body remained rigid. The soles of his shoes pressed hard into the floor. He twirled a pencil in-between his fingers with the cigarette stuck between his lips. His eyes told Breck to stand and listen.

'I'm not happy with your account of things Patricia that's why

I needed a recap from you. Now you say when the fight broke out the suspect saw his opportunity to make a run for it. Yet, he was a suspect under arrest and you didn't cuff him. You're an experienced officer that failed to follow protocol so I have no choice but to give you an official verbal warning. Ensure that something like this doesn't happen again.'

Kearns glared at Bashir for a few seconds, fed up of being the scapegoat but she knew the drill. She daren't say anything. After getting bored with just standing still, Breck intervened, if just to save her from more punishment.

'We've sent the suspect's details to all ports and airports in case he tries to leave the country. We've also checked his home address to see if we can find any clue to his current whereabouts. So far we've found nothing to help us but he owed his bank money.'

'How are we with verifying who's who?'

Breck groaned. 'It's a bit of a struggle if I'm honest because I'm trying to access old files from Alexander Troy's school. We obtained the name from the CV he sent to Van Bruen plc.'

'Well you know my thoughts, let's focus on the one that reported the theft.'

Breck blew out a weakened breath while Bashir stubbed out his cigarette and rose to his feet. He walked towards his door and turned the handle, opened it by a quarter of an inch, then served a volley of warnings to Kearns.

When he had finished, she left with Breck and felt as if the eyes of the whole department were watching and they were. She didn't like it one bit and it worried her colleague.

'You OK?'

'I'll be fine. I deserved it.'

Kearns went to get a hot drink, leaving Breck to head back to his desk.

He had been sitting down for no more than a minute before he was interrupted.

'How's your investigation going then hotshot?'

He looked up to see Ray Riley using both thumbs to stretch his braces outwards. 'Am I supposed to respond to you?'

'I might be able to help, you never know.'

Breck shook his head at the insincere offer. 'Why are you wearing your dad's braces, you look daft.'

'You wouldn't understand. I'm the fashion prince around here and at the forefront of everything.'

'Bullshit if you ask me but keep telling yourself what you want if it makes you feel better.'

Riley contemplated walking away but stopped himself. 'I'm thinking about asking Beatrice to help out on my armed robbery investigation. She looks bored with you lot.'

'You'll get no success there. She busy working on my case and I've got her locked in.'

At that moment Kearns pushed past Riley and returned to her seat with a mug of warm Ovaltine. He struck up another conversation with someone while she placed it next to her copy of Woman's Own, and a stick of rock that she had won at the seaside a few weeks back.

Breck left his seat to join her. She seemed to be in a philosophical mood.

'Arlo, why do it to yourself?'

'What do you mean?'

'This place is a world away from anything that you're used to so why do it to yourself? In Cransham the racialists want to sow seeds. We have murders, robberies, and streets that are filled with piss-heads and good time girls.'

'You sound a little negative, Pat. We're supposed to be the positive ones.'

'We are but I like calling it as it is.'

'So, tell me; how is it?'

Kearns swung her chair around. 'Nothing is as it seems and I don't know who's at fault but I think I should blame someone.'

'That's how we get into trouble, trying to blame innocent parties without taking responsibility. Anyway, there's something that I don't understand regarding your incident with Alexander Troy.'

'What is it?'

'Why no handcuffs?'

Kearns' reply became stuck in her throat but Ray Riley's return gave her something else to think about. He hung around on purpose in an attempt to poke his nose in and the silence from the two officers spoke volumes. He had little choice but to leave them be and Kearns made sure he was long gone before responding.

'The handcuffs didn't seem necessary at the time.'

'It's basic protocol.'

Kearns shrugged. 'Don't start, I was careless but it won't happen again.'

'Do you know if his prints checked out?'

'Yes, we have a match on the credit card but nothing on the magazine. Just Janet's prints, no one else.'

She pawed through a few index cards on the table with names and addresses of Janet Maskell's neighbours. Breck appreciated her as a colleague and a friend but felt ill at ease. There were a few things swimming through his mind. Strange thoughts that made him uncomfortable.

'Have we set up an Investigation Board yet?'

'Not yet. It will be done soon though.'

'We shouldn't be behind with setting that up Pat. It makes us look bad.'

She disliked his sharp tone. 'As my hands are full should I get your girlfriend to do it for you?'

The underhand comment surprised him. He wanted to laugh it off he didn't quite know how to because Kearns' had hit a raw nerve.

'Why have you called her my girlfriend?'

'Everyone suspects something is going on between you and Beatrice. I know there isn't…yet, but you need to sort yourself out.'

Breck threw up his arms. 'What do you mean?'

'If you are going to cheat on your girlfriend, do it with someone that has a better personality.'

Kearns continued to look through the cards, pretending she hadn't said anything at all, while a shocked Breck tried to come to terms with being on the gossip lists. He thought that he and Beatrice were always so careful around each other. What a mess. Trying to act normal was the only thing he could do so Breck changed the subject.

'Our POI has gone on holiday to Norway so that presents us with a few problems. I think it's a good time to visit The Cambas to see if the other Troy really did have lunch there. I've also asked a contact of mine to send me a list of clients that Peter Clarke represented in the past.'

'Who's the contact then?'

'Can't say. Sorry.'

Kearns understood. 'What are you hoping to find?'

'I want to know what type of company he likes to keep.'

Breck picked out an index card from her desk. 'Do we know if Janet Maskell's nosey neighbour Wynda Brodie is in?'

'Not sure. Let me find out.' Kearns took the card from him and rang the number written on it.

'Hello, is this Mrs Brodie?' 'It is? Great. I'm Detective Sergeant Patricia Kearns and was hoping you'd be able to help us with our investigation.' Kearns winced, and seemed to be struggling to hear Mrs Brodie. 'Yes, it's about your neighbour. We tried to speak to you earlier but you weren't in.'

While she was having the conversation Breck re-read the information on the card and a few minutes later Kearns ended the call.

'Can we get something from her?'

'I believe so. I've told her we'll be on our way.'

'Good. Come on then.' Breck grabbed his coat. 'Let's hear what she has to say.'

TWELVE

Wynda Brodie's blue rinsed hair matched her hand knitted Aran cable knit cardigan. It was decorated with large circular buttons and she seemed keen to usher Breck and Kearns into her home as fast as possible, away from the prying eyes of the neighbourhood. She hobbled around aided by a walking stick and struck Breck as a woman with a keen eye for detail, nosey

some may say, but he preferred her to be the type to stick her nose in where it shouldn't be if it meant he'd get a lead. In fact, for an eighty-year-old, she very much had her wits about her.

Mrs Brodie's beady eyes found their way straight over to Kearns' standard issue black shoes and then her handbag, while Breck observed the photos of an unidentified man in an army uniform plastered across the walls.

'Is that your husband?'

Mrs Brodie paused and stared in the direction of the photos. 'Yes, it's my Cecil, God bless him.'

'Died in the war?'

The thought excavated sadness onto her face. 'Oh no he survived everything Hitler's boys threw at him. Killed by a thug in his own country. A mugging gone wrong the police said.'

Breck could sense that he had touched a raw nerve and the old woman lost a bit of her momentum.

'I'm sorry to hear that but thank you for agreeing to see us.'

'Yes of course, this way.'

She hobbled into a living room that was still stuck in the 50s, with furniture that sparkled diamond bright and a cabinet which held a history of memories on each shelf. In the centre of the room she had prepared a pyramid of teacakes and tarts, along with a large pot of tea. Both officers sat down.

'Help yourselves,' Mrs Brodie ordered.

'Er… that's a lovely spread but we can't eat it.'

Mrs Brodie wasn't used to being told no and loaded a few spoonfuls of loose tea into the pot, then poured it out into the mugs with the aid of a tea strainer. A reluctant Breck, knowing that the old lady just may have something worthwhile to share with them, relented and squeezed up next to his colleague. He picked up a cherry tart and brought it close to his line of vision before swallowing it in one go. His action caused Mrs Brodie to blossom out into a smile. It was then that he knew he had her onside once again.

She sat down on a cushioned chair and stretched out her right leg.

'Broke it years ago, it's never quite been the same since.' She stared at it with a forlorn expression.

'These are lovely cakes, Mrs Brodie,' Kearns said. 'Thank you so much.'

'You're welcome.'

Breck took a sip from his cup then placed it down in the tray. He pulled out his notepad and flicked through the pages to remind himself of what he wanted to ask.

'Right, Mrs Brodie, did you see anything suspicious in the last few days with regard to Ms Maskell?'

'Well I know most things on this street and make it my business to as I'm the longest serving resident since Mrs Snowden.'

'Mrs Snowden?'

'She moved in two weeks before I did, twenty-five years ago. Lovely woman. She died four months ago. Anyway, that lady, Ms Maskell, would go to work early come back late evening. Nothing irregular.'

'Did any friends visit her?'

'Her sister came around last year, in June. Around 2:00 p.m. in the afternoon I'd say.' Breck and Kearns swopped glances, impressed with the old girl's memory. 'Her special friend would also pop around to keep her company. He did that most days.'

'What special friend?'

'The gardener, younger than her by quite a few years he is. She loved the attention. I told her folk round here will start talking. His lot are trouble.' Kearns stopped drinking her tea and placed the cup on the table, while Breck kept his focus on Mrs Brodie.

'Do you have a name for this gardener?'

'She said his name was Benjamin or something like that but the problem is they're from two different places. Know what I mean?' Wynda Brodie ended the sentence with a wink.

'Can you describe him?'

'Difficult to say but he's one of them.'

'I'm afraid I'll need a better description than that.'

Mrs Brodie had a little think. 'He's a coloured chap about an inch or two under your height. That lady, I don't know what she was thinking employing him, let alone… well you know?'

'Can you elaborate?'

'Can I what?'

Kearns cut in. 'We need a bit more detail Mrs Brodie.'

Breck sighed. 'Is there something else about the relationship between Benjamin and Ms Maskell that we need to know?'

'Oh I see. Yes, he was her boyfriend. I saw them kissing on her doorstep once. Shocking I know.'

Breck already felt uncomfortable. 'Shocking?'

'Well a kiss can lead to all sorts and before we'd know it, they would've had half-caste kids running around the street.'

Breck noted the name of the gardener then closed his notepad. He returned it to his pocket, upon deciding he had heard enough, and wanted to leave Mrs Brodie's bigotry behind. He rose to his feet just as Kearns grabbed a cherry tart. It caused a wave of excitement to swell the old woman's heart.

'Do you need me to go to court and testify now Detective Inspector Breck?'

'Not at this moment but your information is very useful. We still have to follow the normal lines of enquiry.' Breck's response disappointed her. 'Tell me, can you remember how often the gardener visited?'

Mrs Brodie hauled herself up while refusing Breck's offer of assistance, then made her way to the mantelpiece and lifted up a diary.

'Dates and times are all in here,' she said holding it aloft. 'Keeping track of things gives me something to do. It keeps me young I reckon.'

'Thank you,' Breck said as he took it from her. 'We'll see ourselves out.'

THIRTEEN

Breck and his girlfriend were renting a two-bed home on Grinstead Road, opposite Deptford Park. The street lights had died, and the pavements weren't the cleanest he had ever encountered but it suited them both. The neighbours were pleasant and the paperboy always delivered on time.

Breck awoke to a warm ray of the sun which

crawled across his skin. Yet it did little to brighten his tempestuous mood. A lack of sleep had seen to that. He shuffled out of bed, fretful about what needed to be covered with the Maskell case and let it weigh on his mind. He needed to locate her gardener and work out where Troy was.

Breck forced himself towards the bathroom in a daze, almost tripping over his discarded slippers, and when he turned the door handle found that it wouldn't open. He was confused for a few moments until muffled sounds from inside caused him to press his ear closer to the door. He could hear Molly sobbing.

'Are you okay?'

'Sorry,' she said. 'I'm fine.'

'You don't sound fine. What's wrong?'

'I could never lie to you.' It was true but Breck said nothing, only listened. 'I'm getting flashbacks, lots of them.'

'Try occupying your mind with something, perhaps pick up one of those hobbies you used to do.'

'Hobbies? For Christ's sake, do you know what I went through?'

'Sorry, I want to help but I don't know the best thing to suggest. It's a slow process I know but I think you're getting better.'

'I don't feel that I am because I keep thinking of that night. He's going to get me, Arlo, and I'm worried he's going to step right into this house when you're not here.' Breck had hoped his girlfriend's fears were behind her but it seemed not. Molly was falling apart in front of him and a helpless Breck didn't know how to ease her torment. 'There's something you're not telling me about my ordeal, something I can't remember isn't there? I'll find out, I always do.'

'There's nothing to tell, you blacked out and the passer-by scared off that piece of scum.'

However, there was something else. Breck hadn't revealed that her attacker had struck before and she happened to be one of the lucky ones. Not all the victim's survived. Breck's silent anger continued its steady rise. He hated the person that did this, a faceless person still at large and he felt that Molly had slipped away from him.

'I can get you to speak to someone like a psychiatrist,' he suggested.

'What you went through wasn't pleasant, please don't bottle it all up anymore.' He waited for a response but nothing came. There were times when Molly appeared to be fine then something would set her off. A name, a colour, or a sound. Breck didn't know what those triggers were and wondered what would happen if he didn't get his old Molly back? 'Have a think about what I've said.'

He stood by door for a few moments before Molly's reply finally arrived.

'OK, I will.'

Breck popped downstairs, switched on the radio and turned up its volume. In the kitchen he pulled out a bottle of Bolognese sauce, tomatoes and garlic, humming along to a Donna Summer song. He opened the cupboard and grabbed the spaghetti, and was setting it to boil when Molly appeared. She stood at the entrance to the kitchen looking curious.

'Smells good, what is it?' Her eyes were still red from crying but she sounded brighter.

'This is what they call spaghetti Bolognese Breck style and it'll be ready soon. We're going to have a nice late morning breakfast I promise.'

Molly's light smile gave him hope, and that's all he needed to keep going. Hope and the belief she'd get back to how she used to be one day.

When they sat down to eat together, they talked about simple things. Not the main problems but Breck didn't mind. In fact he welcomed it and appreciated the gentle kiss she thanked him with.

Molly cleared the plates away and Breck realised the time.

'I need to get going,' he said.

'OK, get off to work. Don't make yourself late and have a good day.'

'I'll try.'

He didn't need telling twice but he felt a little deflated as it was. A failure as a boyfriend – one that should have been able to protect Molly better.

Breck returned to the bedroom to put on his best suit, pausing only to tighten his black tie in front of the full-length mirror. He combed his sideburns with gentle downward strokes and thought about his work hours. They were taking him away from home which is why he had started to believe that a change of career might be just what he and Molly needed. Police work gave him the buzz, but he was tired of being unable to carve out time for anything else. Something had to give and the interview this morning presented a way out.

Breck said goodbye to Molly then left the house with a single glance back. The location had served them well but with the property up for renewal in the next few months, he'd consider moving if a new environment would help.

He started his car but nothing happened and he continued to turn the key in the VW without any success. It failed to spark into life and he suspected that the alternator might need replacing. Determined to get to the interview on time, he left it and trotted up to the high street to find a taxi.

After a few minutes, one pulled over and Breck jumped in. He was desperate to settle into the right frame of mind but even with the troubles at home and an interview ahead, the case wasn't far from his thoughts. Solving it would be a chance to cement his worth to Bashir by locking up the right Troy. Yet, he couldn't shake the feeling that he missed an opportunity. He asked himself, *what would he do if he had gone on the run?*

He couldn't find the answer but believed he'd get it soon. In the meantime, he did some prep, not enough, and by the time the driver demanded the fare he had decided to take his chances. He paid up and scurried out.

The building where the interview would take place didn't look like much and its tidy blue sign had been nailed onto a rotting square wooden board that needed replacing. Regardless, Breck knew the job here would pay him more than his current salary. It'd be far safer too.

He straightened his tie and walked into the reception area of Hardwick Stanfield, a business security firm, convincing himself that this was what he wanted. A life away from the SCU. With his shift beginning in an hours' time, everything fitted in fine. He gave his name to the receptionist then waited, fidgeting with butterflies tingling in his stomach, until he was approached.

'Arlo Breck?'

He looked up to see an elderly skeletal man. 'Yes, that's me.'

'This way please.'

He was led through to a set of double doors by a World War One veteran. Bill gave him an overview of the First World War and swore that he knew Lawrence of Arabia.

'Small chap he was, but he weren't half bright,' he said, and Breck definitely thought Bill could be old enough to have lived in that time.

Although he walked with a limp, he had a hardened look about him and Breck sensed that his past experiences had softened him somewhat.

Bill led Breck through a maze of corridors before stopping outside a green door. He knocked twice then opened it. Breck walked through to be greeted by a man with a pockmarked face and a cushioned stomach. A poster of Cilla Black was planted on the wall behind his desk and he extended a hand. Breck shook it then Bill closed the door and left the two men alone.

'Hello, I'm Mr Garsdale.'

'Thank you for inviting me to the interview. It's nice to meet you.'

'Thank you for coming. Please have a seat.'

Garsdale waited for Breck to get comfortable before starting. 'The pay's weekly, holidays are 18 days for the year and a team of eight needs managing. They can be difficult I'll admit. Sometimes thinking that they know best but they do understand their job. I need a strong person in the Head of Security role so what makes you think you can lead the team here?'

'For the very same reason that you invited me to this interview, Mr Garsdale. I'm a copper that can cope with stressful and tricky situations by thinking on my feet.'

'I've already met many people that cope with stress and think on their feet Mr Breck. What makes you different to them?'

'I think that not all of the people you have seen would do the job the way I would. I'm pretty good at analysing situations and looking at the facts.' Breck made the mistake of telling Garsdale what he thought he wanted him to hear rather than what he really believed.

'Following the facts is fine most times but the obvious route doesn't always lead us to where it should. It's the reason why a few people get away with their crimes.'

Breck could've applied Garsdale's words to his own case which unnerved him. 'You work as a policeman, why do you want to leave?'

'I think it's time to. It feels right and it can be unpleasant work at the end of the day.'

'Unpleasant in what way?'

'Dealing with those that want to hurt others and trying to stop them.'

'I'd like to hear an example of one of your cases.'

Breck paused. 'Sorry, Mr Garsdale, but apart from what I've put on the CV, I can't say anymore. I'm in a special unit you see, and the work we do is confidential.'

An unconvinced Garsdale wrote down a few notes, then turned his attention back to Breck. 'Why is that then?'

'It's just the way it is I suppose. We deal with high profile incidents so a lot of things are classified.'

Garsdale rubbed a hand over the back of his neck and put his pen down. He was disappointed. 'My staff know that when I ask a question I expect an answer, classified or not.'

He leaned forward across his desk with an unflinching stare that must have scared many interviewees already. Breck didn't know where to start with answering the question and for the first time wondered if he'd be wasting his talents as Head of Security.

'Sorry but I have to be careful with what I talk about.'

Garsdale's mood darkened. Not a good sign and Breck was surprised by his stance. He doubted if anyone at the SCU would find out if he spilled a little bit of information to Garsdale, but he stood by his principles. He knew that if he got the job he wouldn't have to deal with any murder investigations, or put up with the likes of Ray Riley. It was a damn good chance to be free so why was he intent on ruining it?

On the whiteboard behind Garsdale's desk were child-like diagrams showing the uninitiated what the word 'security' meant. Securing business premises were the company's key focus and Breck wasn't sure how he'd fare patrolling a large building. Or asking a team of eight to do so and having to fill in when any of them were away.

'I think your managerial experience may not be enough,' Garsdale said.

'Forgive me for asking but if that is so then why call me in?'

'To see you face-to-face Mr Breck. Yes, you tick a few boxes but dealing with staff issues on a day-to-day basis requires a certain amount of skill. The management of people is key.' Garsdale shuffled through a few loose papers on his desk and somewhere along the line his face had forgotten to smile. Breck couldn't wait for it to end and he didn't have to suffer for long. Garsdale stared at him with a blank expression with his hands clasped on top of his desk, looking fed up. 'Thank you for coming, Mr Breck. I'll be in touch.'

After a brisk handshake Breck left. The whole experience felt like a chore and he wasn't pleased that he had wasted his time. He brushed off his two-piece suit and took off his tie. Then he folded it into one of his pockets and left the building.

The passing cars were all Breck had for company but he couldn't believe his luck when one turned out to be a squad car from Cransham. He flagged it down and the driver recognised him and asked how he came to be in the Tulse Hill area. Breck made an excuse that he'd forget by tomorrow and got in, pleased for the lift. Not least because he would save on the taxi fare.

Breck used the car radio to get through to Kearns at Cransham and she reminded him that he was due to attend Maskell's post-mortem. She sensed that he had the hump about something but couldn't put her finger on it. Then it became clear. Breck wanted someone else to pick up the task.

The SCU were allowed to leave the post-mortem attendance and the reporting of it to the uniforms. He made it clear they should on this occasion. He then turned to the driver and said, 'No offence,' while the perplexed officer kept his eyes on the road.

Breck also learned that Kearns had been busy arranging for Maskell's sister to conduct a formal identification of the body, which turned out to be a good thing because he remembered that he had been assigned to set it up.

A Family Liaison Officer (FLO) had been sent to the home of Maskell's sister and Breck believed her sibling might be able to give them valuable information so planned to meet her.

Kearns saw his reluctance to visit Frank Cullen's office as an opportunity to get one up on an old enemy, so she made plans to shift the task over to Beatrice. But she had a surprise for Breck, one he couldn't possibly guess. Kearns wanted him to make a detour to an address she had just acquired. Breck thanked her and admired her resourcefulness.

'Take a left here and follow the road down,' he instructed the officer. 'I'll square this with your superior so don't worry.'

The address led straight to Benjamin Genta. Janet Maskell's boyfriend was back in town.

FOURTEEN

Camberwell's hotbed of noise from its crowded streets, became wedded to the choking fumes from cars that were glued to the roads by traffic standstills. Breck had already decided to jump out whilst in the jam, instructing the officer where to park if it cleared, before walking to where Janet Maskell's boyfriend Benjamin Genta allegedly worked. From what Kearns

had been able to establish he had returned from visiting family in Wolverhampton. He grew up there but left after he finished school and moved to London. His record was relatively clean, having only been arrested once before for demonstrating. Nothing worse than that.

At the corner of Denmark Hill and Peckham Road a couple of school kids were larking about, missing valuable school time. Of course, they didn't see it that way. Pupils seldom did. Breck passed them by and reached his destination in a matter of minutes.

Benjamin Genta worked in a landscape gardening shop, narrow in width compared to other shops nearby, sandwiched between a bookmaker and a fast food outlet. As Breck neared it he saw a man fitting Benjamin's description packing up a van. Breck called out to him.

'Benjamin Genta?'

The man stopped and glanced around. 'Who's asking?'

'I'm DI Breck and I need to speak to you.' Breck showed his ID.

'What about?'

'Janet Maskell.'

'I don't know anyone by that name.' He closed the rear doors of the van.

'Don't you want to know what happened?'

The man paused and struggled to forge an answer while Breck watched, waiting to see if there were any signs of guilt.

'What's happened to Janet?'

'We should go into the shop, Benjamin.'

'Nah, I don't want my manager knowing my business. Plus, you're Old Bill, so let's do it out here where there are witnesses.'

Benjamin's distrust of the police was evident. Even so Breck just shrugged, happy to let him have it his way. 'OK then. There's no easy way to say it. She's dead.'

'Dead?'

The shock numbed Benjamin and he struggled to take it all in.

'I want to you ask you a few questions because we believe it's murder.'

Benjamin stepped back, quick to protest his innocence. 'Hold on. I didn't do it.'

He then tensed up and clenched his fists in a mixture of emotion and fear, while looking for an escape route. One he couldn't find. Breck thought it best to calm the situation right there and then because he didn't need the thrill of a chase.

'Do me a favour, don't run. I know you've been away so providing we can corroborate your alibi, there'll be nothing to worry about.'

'Why should I trust Babylon?'

The derogatory tag of Babylon didn't worry Breck because he knew that the police were often called much worse. There was still work to be done on a local level.

'You should trust me because I'm the one person that cares if an innocent man is locked up.' Breck ended the sentence with a determined stare, just enough for Benjamin to understand.

'OK, let me hand these keys over to my manager and explain what's happening.'

'You've got one minute.'

Moments later the squad car that picked up Breck from Tulse Hill, freed itself from a lane of traffic and parked behind him. Benjamin Genta emerged from the shop to find Breck waiting with the rear door open.

'Come on,' Breck said. 'Let's get this over with.'

Benjamin Genta kept his thoughts to himself as he slid into the car, then they drove away.

*

Inside one of the available rooms at the station Breck placed a cup of tea on the table for his latest interviewee. Benjamin Genta had become glassy eyed on the journey down as Janet's death became a reality. Yet he seemed desperate to conceal his true feelings in front of Breck over his lover's murder. Breck had already done his homework on Benjamin. His mum worked as a nurse for the NHS and his dad used to work for British Rail but had now retired. However, the dark cloud in his life centred around his brother's death. Wesley Genta died after being stabbed when he tried to break up a fight between two youths. Breck could feel the subtle anger brimming beneath the surface but he didn't think Benjamin was a bad person. Far from it.

He pulled his chair into position after he sat down next to Kearns and had dodged any questions about his smart appearance following the interview, by throwing his suit jacket into his locker. If anyone questioned his unfamiliar trousers or shoes, he just told them he fancied a change.

He observed Benjamin for a bit, trying to work out what he could be thinking, without much success. Then he began.

'Right, you comfortable?'

Benjamin rubbed the bridge of his nose. 'I'm never comfortable around you lot. Never know what I'm going to get.'

'I know what happened to your brother and I'm sorry but don't let that get in the way of doing the right thing here.' Breck loosened the top button on his shirt. 'Let's begin. Where were you between noon and 2:00 p.m. yesterday?'

'At church.'

Benjamin stared at the tea within the plastic cup, held it then took a sip. The confession made Kearns baulk. With an unkempt beard, uneven afro, and an opened Adidas tracksuit top which revealed a white string vest, Benjamin Genta didn't look like the type to attend church. She should have known better but she couldn't help herself and leaned in close to issue a warning.

'Let me remind you that you're looking at life in prison if you don't stop playing games. You do know that, don't you?'

Her tone became a slight worry for Breck. Benjamin was just a POI at this stage with Troy still their main suspect.

'Hold on lady, my mum asked me to drop off some flowers for the vicar ahead of the service on Sunday. I did that before I came back to London.'

Kearns shoved a notepad and pen Benjamin's way. 'I want the name of the vicar and the church.'

Obliging, he wrote in the notepad then passed it over, but when Kearns picked it up and read it, she wasn't impressed. 'You cheeky sod.'

She jabbed her index finger into the centre of Benjamin's forehead. It caused his head to jerk back. He slapped her hand away and sprung to his feet. Breck was quick to step in. He didn't want the tea to go all over Benjamin because he had witnessed Kearns splash someone before in an interview.

'Listen everyone, I'm sure that we're all on the same side here. We want to catch Janet's killer so let's just calm down.'

Breck's intervention seemed to do the trick. Both Benjamin and Kearns cooled it.

'Pat, do me a favour? Go and check out his alibi.'

'What, right now?'

Breck raised his eyebrows. 'Yes, now,' then he read the words which had been written down for Kearns and smiled. She left the room and Benjamin felt relaxed enough to sit back down so Breck resumed the questioning.

'What was your relationship with Janet Maskell?'

'My relationship with her?' Benjamin chose the moment to take a mouthful of tea. 'I am…I mean, I was her gardener.'

'And that's it?'

'What else do you want me to say?'

'Were you sleeping with her?'

Benjamin said, 'Yes,' through gritted teeth. 'We were seeing each other but she came onto me, not the other way around.'

'Hey, I'm not interested in who made the first move, or how many times she wanted it. I'm just trying to understand how close you two were. Now, did you at any time meet any of Janet's friends?'

Benjamin laughed. 'Friends? Professionally I didn't exist but she was more relaxed when I went to visit her. Even though I got disapproving looks from that nosey old neighbour of hers whenever she saw me.'

Breck assumed that by the term nosey old neighbour he meant Wynda Brodie. 'When was the last time you saw Janet?'

'It was the day before I went to Wolverhampton. A Friday night.'

'Did you notice anything unusual about her recently? Did she seem concerned about anything?'

Benjamin shook his head.' Nope, nothing. I go away, come back and now she's dead. Doesn't make any sense.'

It appeared that there would be little else to discuss but Breck wanted to be sure.

'Is there anything that you need to tell me about your relationship with Janet that you haven't mentioned yet? I don't want any nasty surprises later on.'

Benjamin shook his head so Breck shrugged and removed himself from his chair, feeling disappointed that more couldn't have been accomplished. Benjamin would be held until his alibi checked out. Until then there was nothing more to discuss.

Breck walked over to the phone on the small table at the other side of the room and dialled her extension.

'Pat. Have we got any leads on Ceinwen?'

'Nothing but I am waiting for the Vicar to ring me back.'

'OK, see you in a bit. I'm finished in here. It's been a waste of time.'

Breck ended the call but Benjamin overheard the conversation. 'Ceinwen, did you say?'

Breck turned around. 'Does the name ring a bell?'

'Janet said that one of the employees at her workplace kept recommending a woman named Ceinwen. It was to fill one of the high-profile roles that had become vacant. She planned to look at her CV and if she liked what she saw, call her in for an interview.'

Breck padded over towards Benjamin. 'Who kept recommending her?'

'Someone called, er…hmm.' Benjamin closed his eyes for a moment as he tried to recall the name. Then he reopened them. 'Sorry, can't remember.'

Breck's fixed smile hid his true frustration. He moved across the room, opened the door and allowed the officer outside to escort Benjamin to a holding cell. He had been careful not to antagonise his interviewee because he thought he'd be able to offer something significant which had so far proved wrong.

The officer arrived and applied the handcuffs while Breck remained rooted at the doorway, thinking about the best lead to pursuit next. The officer led Benjamin out but before the door closed they stopped and it grabbed Breck's attention. He wasted no time in joining them.

'I think I remember the name,' Benjamin said.

'Go on,' Breck began to burst with anticipation.

'The person that recommended her was a man. Someone called… Troy. Yes, definitely Troy.'

FIFTEEN

The Investigation Board had been set up and photos of Janet Maskell, both Troys, as well as Benjamin Genta, were attached and linked together by coloured yarn – under the case heading of Operation Nettle. The investigation room belonged to the SCU so it was used by them alone and this week appeared to be a good one. Maskell's case took up most of the board

sidelining others, including Ray Riley's armed robbery investigation.

Forensics had now confirmed that fingerprints from both Troys were found on the credit card which made sense, but the dilemma for Breck remained: one owned it and the other stole it but which one?

A list of Peter Clarke's clients had been obtained and waited for him in the post room, and as he finished off a conversation with Lizzie Daniels, Kearns entered, popping a Murray Mint into her mouth.

'Was she helpful then?'

'Yes she was. Lizzie went through a few of Janet's notes and confirmed Troy had been trying to get a job for his girlfriend at Van Bruen.'

'The position?'

'An associate director investment role. So from that we can guess Ceinwen has some financial experience that qualifies her?'

'Yes, but I want to know the real reason for Troy wanting her in there. I know Benjamin said Janet planned to look at her CV but what if he was wrong? Janet might have told Troy she wasn't interested, which would have created some animosity on Troy's part. Let's try to find her by checking the employee records of all the professional service firms in the city.'

'It will take some time. We might have to get Beatrice to manage that. I'll look into it then visit The Cambas to check out Troy's alibi.'

'Fine by me. We'll catch up later.'

Breck left to collect his envelope from the post room, while Kearns locked up and went in search of Beatrice. It wasn't a conversation she looked forward to, especially after slotting her in for the post-mortem visit, but the fact remained the department continued to be short-staffed and new faces weren't on the priority list at the moment for Bashir. Everyone had to muck in.

Kearns popped to the canteen to grab something to nibble. Just as she was about to leave she spotted Beatrice. Good timing.

'May I join you?'

Beatrice glanced up from the pages of the book she was reading. 'It's a free country. Sit if you want.'

'You not feeling too good?'

'What can I help you with, Pat?'

Kearns picked up her fork and jabbed it into the slice of cake she had picked up. 'I don't hate you. I'm not saying we'll ever be best friends but I don't hate you.'

'Nice to know. Where's your complicated partner?'

Kearns popped a bit of the cake into her mouth. The sweet taste being just what she needed to combat Beatrice's sour attitude. 'He has a girlfriend.'

'I've no idea why you're telling me that.'

'Come on, you can't fool me.' Kearns understood the magnitude of her next set of words before she even said them. 'This job brings a lot of people together. The hours we work and the stresses can make certain things happen. I've seen it and could name at least four other people within the SCU that have already become close over the past year.'

'What are you getting at Pat?'

'You're a pretty distraction for him but that's all.'

Beatrice closed her book then folded her arms, with an expressionless stare fired straight towards Kearns, knowing deep down that there was some truth to her words.

'I'm sure that you didn't come over to talk to me just about this, did you?'

'No I haven't, but if you're smart, which I know you are, you won't ignore what I've said. Now, back to SCU work. You're slotted in for Janet Maskell's post-mortem, and we need you to comb through the employee lists of professional services companies within the city of London.'

'Employee lists?'

'Yes we need to locate a female named Ceinwen. Troy's girlfriend.'

'Last name?'

'None at present.'

Beatrice sucked her teeth. 'That could take me ages.'

'I know but it's what needs to be done.' Kearns rose from her seat.

'OK, if I must.'

With a wry smile, Kearns left the canteen, unconcerned about

Beatrice's upset and was more interested in planning what she had to do next. She needed to find the quickest route to The Cambas to check out Troy's lunchtime alibi. With the Allegro being borrowed and the other police cars out of action, the journey would have to be made by public transport. Patricia Kearns didn't have any time to waste.

*

Kearns jumped off the bus and stood across from The Cambas. She crossed the road and already had a good idea of what she'd be told by the pub landlord, but understood the need go through the process and follow the normal lines of enquiry.

As soon as she stepped inside she hit a wall of smoke and the fragrant smell of beer hung in the air. She cast an eye over the customers. There were a few working-class lads, arty types, two or three couples, and wannabes that wanted to be anything. Then she spotted a man behind the bar fixing a rum and coke for a punter. She waited until he had finished. Kearns caught his attention by flashing her badge and the sight of it took the wind out of him. It made her wonder whether or not he had any dark secrets.

'Hello, officer, how can I help?'

'Are you Mr Phil Kenzie, the landlord?'

'Yes that's me, is there anything wrong?'

'I need information.' Kearns slid onto a stool, unsure of how long the conversation would take. 'Would you say that you know all your punters?'

'The regular ones, yes.'

Kearns opened her handbag and pulled out a mugshot of Alexander Troy. She rested it on the bar top then turned it around so that Phil Kenzie had a clear view.

'Does this man look familiar?' He dug his fingers into the top pocket of his short-sleeved shirt and pulled out his spectacles. While he adjusted them onto his face a few more thirsty customers appeared.

'No barmaid?'

'Susie's running late so it's just me and the cook at the moment. Bloody nightmare it is.'

He had Kearns' sympathies. Phil lifted up the photograph and kept his eyes pinned to it. 'This man in the photo doesn't look familiar. He's not one of my regulars.'

'Do you recall seeing him in here yesterday lunchtime?'

'Sorry no.'

Phil Kenzie handed back the photograph to Kearns and expected her to leave. Instead, she opened her purse and pulled out two one-pound notes.

'Let me have a glass of white wine please and a packet of crisps.' He seemed surprised. 'It's my lunch hour now. Do you think that coppers don't need to have a break?'

Before he could respond a young girl with a beehive hairdo scurried past and smiled at a few customers, then positioned herself behind the bar. Susie.

'Right, who's next?' she asked.

Her presence relieved a stressed Phil Kenzie and after he served Kearns, he watched her slide off the stool to find an unoccupied table. She waited there and checked the time on her watch. She had an off-the-record meeting and would be exaggerating the length of her visit to The Cambas because of it.

As the minutes ticked by she thought that it might not happen until a shadow appeared and Kearns raised her head to see the person she had been waiting for. Mary Tellow stood over her, late 50s, well dressed with a bit of steel in her eyes.

'Nice to see you Patricia.' She took off her coat and rested her handbag on the back of the chair.

'Hello Mrs Tellow, thanks for coming.' Both women hugged.

'You look well.'

Kearns smiled. 'Can I get you something to eat?'

'No, I already ordered something at the bar when I came in.'

Mary Tellow's daughter Louise was one of Kearns' best friends. At school they were inseparable. Known as the little schemers, they gave boys the run around playing kiss chase and got up to all sorts. But by the time their school years ended, they found that they wanted to do different things. Kearns had a yearning to be involved with law enforcement and Louise wanted to run her own hair salon.

For the next few years the girls were busy getting on with their lives but Louise's penchant for having a good time extended to gaining a collection of bad boyfriends. After a while they lost touch until they were reunited again. Although, not in the way Kearns would ever have wished.

Susie bought over a plate for Mary. 'Here you are,' she said then left, in a rush to serve the other hungry customers. Mary bit into her prawn and mayonnaise sandwich and gave it her approval.

'I hope you don't mind me inviting you here.' Kearns said. 'It's just that when I found out you had travelled up to London to visit your sister, I thought it'd be good to catch up.'

'That's sweet and it's nice to see you again. How's everything going?'

'I've split with Mick.'

'Yes, I heard about that, sorry. How's your daughter?'

'Kim's taken his side so she's not speaking to me at the moment. They're up in Glasgow together.'

'Take my advice, fight tooth and nail to get your daughter back. Once she's gone forever you'll regret it.'

'Work keeps me busy. There's lots to do but it sounds much more glamorous than it is most times.'

Mary Tellow frowned. 'In my day, we got married and looked after our husbands. We raised a family. Now, women are having careers.'

Kearns couldn't be sure if Mary had aimed that dig at her or if it happened to be just a general observation. Either way she let it slide, finished her crisps and left the empty packet on the table.

There had been enough side stepping so Kearns braced herself to ask her question. 'How are things going with you Mrs Tellow?'

Mary paused and the life appeared to drain from her while she held the sandwich above her plate. Her eyes became lost, wondering where to look.

'Birthdays are difficult to deal with, Christmas time too. I'm just glad Louise's dad wasn't alive to see what happened to her.' Kearns reached over and placed a comforting hand on Mary's arm but Mary Tellow dropped the sandwich into the plate and removed it. She couldn't hold her anger at bay anymore and it became evident as she said, 'Although it's nice to see you again Patricia, I hope that by bringing me here you're going to tell me what I want to hear. You're going to tell me that you've caught the man that murdered my daughter and made up for your terrible mistake.'

SIXTEEN

West Yorkshire
September, 1975

Some moments are etched in history. Even WPC Kearns knew that as she walked a regular route with her colleague Chris Muller, an officer with dreamy drama school looks. It sparked off without any warning when he rushed out of the newsagents with the adrenaline overpowering him.

'Did you catch that on the radio, a domestic at the end of this street?'

Kearns hadn't, her husband Mick was on her mind. She had a sneaky look and found she'd muted the radio by accident. A silly mistake that she wouldn't be admitting to.

Kearns followed Muller's rapid footsteps and in a matter of minutes they arrived at the address. It was around the corner in fact, an average-sized house with a garden full of fresh flowers and a newly painted wooden fence. It took a third knock before the lock shifted and the door creaked open.

A man with darkness in his eyes stood in front of Muller and Kearns. His chest drummed under a white V-neck. Dirt and grime lined his jeans. He seemed surprised to see them.

'Hello.'

'We've had a report of a disturbance here.'

The man added a smile. 'Really? No disturbance here, officers.'

Muller glanced at Kearns then back at the man. 'May we come in?'

His face changed into a scowl. 'Did that bitch next door call you lot?' Kearns remembered him asking. 'The bitch should keep her nose out of my business!' His excuse was ready. 'I had a slanging match with the girlfriend that's all. She's stormed off and won't be back till she cools down. I'm watching a bit of telly now pal.'

Muller cleared his throat. 'What's her name?'

Looking back, the man took too long to think but at the time Kearns thought nothing of it. She watched him rub the rugged strips of hair on either side of his jaw.

'Rhianna. Rhianna Thomas.'

'When do you expect her back then?' He shrugged. 'Mind if we take a look around? Of course you don't.'

The two police constables entered the house leaving the man bubbling with plenty of hatred but he knew it'd be better to get their intrusion over with. He watched them from a distance until Kearns returned the favour. The white V-neck overstretched on the left side. The roots of his brown hair darkened with sweat. Both images failed to correspond with a man just involved in a simple slanging match with his partner, who'd then chosen to sit down to watch television.

With Muller elsewhere, the man walked past Kearns then stopped. When she moved toward the kitchen he obstructed her path. He feigned a stumble and placed a heavy hand on her shoulder. Kearns pushed it away but he placed it back, began to squeeze, keeping a sadistic grin fixed to his face for good measure too, trying to intimidate her.

'What are you doing? I'm a police officer.'

His grin widened like he didn't give a shit. 'We're the same we are, except you wear a uniform and I don't.'

'You're obstructing an officer of the law. What's your name?'

He whispered it to her as if it were a special secret to be shared between them, while Kearns strained to peel back his strong fingers. She felt the sweat threaten to trickle down her forehead yet, she became determined that his attempt to scare her wouldn't be successful.

'We're nothing alike. Now let go or I'll make you wish that you had.'

He moved in slow motion and Kearns wanted to deck him there and then, imagining the scum spitting out teeth and spraying the place with a red mist. However, she wouldn't want to give him the satisfaction of getting any compensation.

When Muller reappeared the man stepped away, innocence personified, and Kearns bowled forward knowing it would be a waste of time reporting the scumbag for what he had done.

She proceeded into the kitchen where the bin overflowed with rubbish and dried spaghetti strands caked the outside but spotted a purse on top of the fridge. Red acrylic with a leather decoration. She sensed something was wrong without being able to say what and scanned the kitchen again but drew a blank. While the man spoke with Muller a frustrated Kearns glanced around for the next thing to search – the cupboard underneath the staircase. She moved towards it and pulled the handle but Muller appeared and stopped her.

'Let's get going. We're done here for today.'

'This needs checking.'

'Come on,' he said with a subtle wink. 'Leave it for another time.'

The two officers left the premises with Muller warning the man to keep the noise down but it left Kearns feeling uneasy, and with good reason. He waited until they were out of sight then went to retrieve 'Rhianna.'

The girl was already battered and bruised enough to offer no resistance. Just the way he liked it. He released the wire from around her wrists, took the sock out of her mouth and raised her head. One of her bruised eyes were sealed shut.

'After the noise you made, the old cow next door called the police. Why do you get me so angry? Why do you make me do this to you?'

The girl wanted to cry because she didn't make him do anything and she spoke but he couldn't hear. He leaned closer, then closer still. She spat into his face and it shocked him. He reeled back and saw it as proof that he had failed to instil enough discipline into her. Wiping away the spittle, he yanked the girl's head up by the roots of her hair, produced a knife from his pocket and drew the serrated blade's sharpest point across the soft flesh of her throat. She jerked back and forth and he struggled to contain her. The more the blood drained, the more difficult it became and he sought a quick way to end it.

He looked over his shoulder and spotted a Dorma artichoke ornament resting on the shelf. He grabbed it with one hand still gripping her hair and slammed the ornament into the bridge of her nose, breaking it instantly.

Meanwhile the two constables had now emerged onto the main road but Kearns found that she couldn't hold back.

'Why are we leaving?'

'What do you mean?'

'I don't believe she stormed out, his girlfriend I mean. What woman leaves the house without her purse?'

Muller glanced at his colleague with a look of concern. 'Where did you see it?

'I saw it on top of the fridge!'

'If she did leave in a hurry she'll return.'

'I'm not so sure. He's sick, a real piece of work.' Kearns knew her words weren't formed on a gut instinct but on a belief.

'Don't worry we'll check back tomorrow,' Muller assured her. 'He won't be expecting that.'

'Let's go back, now!'

'No, I said we'll check back tomorrow!'

Muller had been in the job longer than Kearns so it gave him the edge of seniority. Kearns continued to argue the point for a while before relenting.

*

Tomorrow arrived. Muller and Kearns returned to the house but after a few knocks on the door without reply, Muller's impatience mushroomed.

'He's taking the piss,' he said. 'I'm definitely going to nick him now.'

Muller crouched down and opened the letter box. He peered through but remained static for far too long. Not an inch of his body moved.

'Hey Muller, what's going on?' Kearns received no answer from her colleague. 'Muller?' She dragged him back.

'What's going on, what did you see?'

Muller's ghost-white gaze moved towards her and his words trickled out. 'Blood, there's a lot of blood.'

Kearns pushed him to one side and peered through the letter box herself then screamed inside. The once whitewashed walls were now daubed in red and the T-shirt the man had worn lay discarded upon the floor. Kearns raised her knee to stomach height and sent her foot crashing into the door. The blow weakened the structure but didn't do enough to break it open, so she kicked it again while Muller stood next to her still in shock. She gave it another kick, and another.

This time it burst open and she stumbled through. Muller snapped out of his shock enough to regain his senses. He stormed into the lounge while Kearns stood next to the blood marks on the wall to follow its trail. Muller came rushing out.

'Nothing in there,' he said. 'I'll check upstairs.'

Kearns stopped him and directed her fellow PC to the one place they had failed to search on their last visit. The cupboard underneath the staircase. This time Kearns pulled the cuff of her jacket over her fingers and yanked down the handle. It sprung open and a dead woman lay slumped inside, with her neck wrapped with a scarf of blood. Worse still, Kearns knew her. Rhianna Thomas didn't exist as the man had claimed but Louise Tellow did. Or used to.

The quiet girl and best friend from Kearns' school days lay dead before her and an anxious Muller paced up and down with shredded nerves. He radioed for help, leaving a shell-shocked Kearns rooted to the spot, staring at Louise and recalling the pull on the man's V-neck, the sweated roots of his hair, and Louise's purse left on top of the fridge. She remembered all the clues, hung her head and mouthed the words, 'I'm sorry, I'm so sorry.'

SEVENTEEN

London

Breck felt stressed. The whereabouts of the POI still weighed on his mind but in a way, having just one Troy to concentrate on demanded less from him. It meant that his focus could be shifted to the version he could get closest to. At the moment, a few things were not adding up but first things first. He had a contact within

the Norwegian police that had a good chance of putting a watchful eye on the POI up there.

'Hello. Can I speak to Morten Hoebeck.'

'Who is calling?'

'It's Detective Arlo Breck from Cransham Police Station in London.'

'One moment please.'

Breck hadn't spoken to Morten in a while but knew his friend would be indebted to him forever as he had once saved his life.

'Hey, Arlo is it really you?'

'I hope so. How are you Morten?'

'Oh, I have a dodgy leg and suffer from a lack of sleep.'

'Ingrid and the kids?'

'All fine.'

'Good. The reason I've called like this unexpectedly is because I need a favour. We have a POI in a murder case that has decided to go on holiday in your part of the world. I have it on good authority that he's in either Spitsbergen or on Bear Island.'

'Nice for some. What do you need from me?'

'I'd like you to keep an eye on him.'

Morten sighed. 'We are so busy here that getting someone to locate him will be tricky.'

It wasn't what Breck wanted to hear but he had faith. 'Anything you can do would be appreciated, old friend.'

'OK, leave it with me.'

'Thank you and we'll talk again soon.'

Breck ended the call then went to the post room to find it empty. A rota system existed for the junior officers but whoever was supposed to be doing it wasn't around. Breck had a choice to make. Either wait until someone turned up, or find his letter himself. He chose the latter. He walked past the franking machine, straight towards a pile of letters stacked high at the end of the room. After sifting through he found the envelope addressed to him and opened it there and then.

It had the information he requested from a friend, with the

envelope postmarked Brighton. There were still a few people around that he could trust and it pleased him.

Breck took out the two pages from inside that contained a list of names and dates of people previously represented by Peter Clarke. He had no time to investigate each one, instead he was after a quick win with a name that he recognised.

That's what he hoped for.

The first page drew a blank and it wasn't until he reached the end of the list on the second page that he found a familiar name. Jacob Simpson, a former police informer. Breck and Kearns knew him very well and he seemed the obvious choice for a solicitor who wanted to help a friend in trouble.

As soon as Breck stepped out of the post room he saw Beatrice. She spotted him too. For a moment, it seemed as if she was going to walk the other way then she changed her mind. Breck considered fleeing as well but then thought better of it. At the very least it'd be embarrassing. A charm offensive might work though.

'You look a little annoyed.'

'Pat told me that I have to search a load of professional services companies for Ceinwen's place of work and go to Janet Maskell's post-mortem. She was a bitch about it too.'

'Are you sure you're not overreacting?'

'Maybe a little but come on, Arlo, you know me. I'm learning the ropes but I want to get more involved with investigating crime here at the SCU, not do silly stuff. You'd be a good mentor.'

Breck was taken aback. Even though she was still upset with him for leading her on she saw beyond that. He felt a bit awkward and it made him wonder. Had she really accepted their now 'formal' working relationship?

'Finding Troy's girlfriend could be key to the case. We need to locate this woman. I'll also speak to Pat, tell her to ease off you.'

That seemed to be enough to placate Beatrice and she softened her stance then handed him a piece of paper with an address on it.

'What's this?'

'The address of Janet Maskell's sister, you're going to speak to her remember?'

'Oh great, thank you, Bea,' Breck said, wondering what had happened to Kearns. She should have been back from The Cambas by now.

＊

Still wiping her stinging tears from her eyes after dashing out of The Cambas, Kearns checked the time. She feared that Breck would be wondering where she had got to and become suspicious. Her eyes darted across the street where she spotted a phone box and she made her way across the busy road. As she approached a rocker jumped in. Kearns wasn't in the mood and flashed her badge. The lad, a teenager with a hairstyle that forgot the 60s had long gone, thought about ignoring her for a brief second. Then changed his mind. When he exited, a few studs from his thick leather jacket almost caught the strap of Kearns' handbag. She cursed under her breath.

Kearns picked up the receiver and dialled Breck at the station and when he asked about Troy's alibi she panicked. If she said that he had been there and Breck later found out he hadn't, it would cause a far bigger issue so she played it straight.

'The landlord Phil Kenzie didn't recognise him at all. Mind you, they get a lot of punters in there so he could've missed him. I'll make my way back to Cransham shall I?'

'No, Pat. Go to Peckham instead. We're going to visit Jacob Simpson.'

'The one that used to give us information?'

'Yes, that's the one.'

'How come?'

'He's one of Clarke's old clients. I think our solicitor is *the* dodgy Clarke you were referencing. Do you remember the address?'

'Yes, I'll make my way there now.'

Kearns worked out her quickest route to Peckham then waited, giving herself enough time to mull things over. Mary Tellow's words hurt but she just lashed out at the closest link to her dead daughter which happened to be Kearns. Those words also did something else. They destroyed any lingering doubts she had and decimated any guilt she harboured about keeping the truth from Breck. Justice for Louise was all that mattered to her and getting it would set her free.

Kearns couldn't recall much of her journey to Jacob Simpson's home, the people, the sights. Instead her thoughts were split between memories of Louise and her own daughter. Kim blamed Kearns for ending the marriage and destroying the family home. Funny, because Kearns thought the idea of a family home died long ago. Her daughter and former husband now lived north of the border, and even though Scotland wasn't that far away, when someone didn't want to see you anymore it was far enough.

EIGHTEEN

Jacob Simpson, Peter Clarke's former client and police informant, lived on the type of council estate the rest of civilisation didn't want to remember. It stood as a monument to the underprivileged. A place where the graffiti formed a sea of misspelt words and scraps of litter danced across the ground. Breck felt the pinch of an icy breeze and slowed down as soon as he recognised

the block. He waited in the car for Kearns, knowing it'd be far more comfortable inside than out and anyway, he could listen to the radio for company. A discussion on immigration dragged on, those for and those against. Some of which Breck found interesting. A caller said we should create closer ties with Europe. While another person said that if we did we'd lose our Britishness. Breck cut it short when he spotted Kearns. He switched off the radio and left the car to meet her over by the local playground.

'You OK?'

'Yes fine, why do you ask?'

'Nothing you look a bit out of sorts. So, Troy's Cambas alibi is a lie?'

'The manager said he didn't recall seeing him.'

'I'm not surprised. Right, let's go and see Jacob Simpson.'

Breck tapped Kearns' arm and pointed to a door protected by wrought iron bars. Jacob Simpson had long ago turned his back on his middle-class upbringing. He squandered the chance to apply himself to a legitimate education by laying claim to a PhD in criminality. When Breck knocked on Jacob's door he felt the whole estate were watching. Jacob wasn't the quickest to answer so Breck decided to turn up the volume.

'Jacob, long time no see. We need you to let us in!'

Jacob's croaky voice floated out from an upstairs window and he hid his face behind the once white curtains. 'Hey, keep the noise down, I'm coming man.'

A few minutes later he released the lock and greeted them with bloodshot eyes. Simpson, a self-confessed hippie that didn't want to let go of the past, styled his shoulder length hair with a parting down the middle and made sure that his shirt's yellow geometric patterns matched his crinkled shorts. The brown Jesus sandals on his feet exposed hardened toenails that had begun to curve downwards. A casual flick of his hand invited them in but he remained unimpressed and made it known.

'You want to get me killed shouting like that?'

'You took your time to open the door,' Breck replied. 'What did you expect?'

Kearns observed the cheap Beatles memorabilia propped against patchy lime coloured walls. They were life-sized cardboard cutouts of McCartney, Lennon, Harrison and Starr, placed upright. Breck glanced at the cutouts too while the sounds of Janis Joplin played low in the background.

'Where did you nick those from?'

Jacob took offence to the question. 'Didn't nick 'em. They were given to me by the manager of the cinema after their Yellow Submarine film came to the end of its run.'

'Somehow, I feel like there are more than three of us in the room,' Breck remarked in jest.

'Man, what do you SCU lot want?'

'Information.'

'I don't do that anymore man, give you lot stuff.'

Both officers ignored his statement. 'We're looking for a suspect. A close friend of Peter Clarke. Do you recall the name?'

'Not sure.'

'Clarke's a solicitor that defended you on two occasions.'

Jacob let his brain tick over for a while. 'Where's the money?'

'What are you talking about?'

'Man, I don't talk for free.'

Breck turned to Kearns. 'Is he serious?'

'Chill out brother. I just need to pay my bills.'

Kearns brought the experience of her robust policing to the fore by exerting a sharp slap to the side of Jacob's head. 'Do you think we're soft eh? You know we can't pay you for information. We'll ignore one or two things and that will enable you to continue your dealings without interruptions.'

'What dealings?'

Breck returned to the conversation. 'Well we can smell something funny in here for a start. Pat, has he been smoking pot?'

'Yes, I think he has.' Kearns sniffed the air.

'Alright, alright. Let's talk.'

Acknowledging the hopeless of the situation Jacob sat down on a tired lime green sofa and pushed a ready-made joint, the size of a large biro, between his chapped lips. Kearns exchanged a concerned glance with Breck but he put her at ease and she sat on a wooden chair with a taped right leg. Breck rested on a disconnected pine speaker box with splintered edges and they both watched Jacob light up then fire out a thick plume of smoke that mushroomed. It drowned the room in a sea of misty grey, forcing Breck to wave a clear path just to see.

'Put that out, I don't want my clothes smelling of the stuff,' Kearns moaned.

Breck placed a gentle hand on her arm because he realised how important Jacob could be for the next step in the investigation. He didn't want her to derail that.

Jacob stubbed out the joint and put it into an ashtray, sat back and sunk into the sofa. Breck wondered what would provide the impetus for him to go out and find a real job because wedged next to him was a pile of bank notes bulging from a brown paper bag. Enough to last him a few months, others a year.

It helped that everyone in the room knew the visit was off the record. There'd be no need for Jacob to worry about reprisals, or being called an informer from any of his peers.

Breck ignored the bulging bag of cash. 'Tell me something, have you had a visit from Peter Clarke recently.'

'Not seen him since the court case against the council, I swear man.'

'Ah you do recall his name. That's good. Clarke's friend is in trouble. He says he's been set up for a murder so I reckon there's no better place for him to come to than here for a bit of guidance. A bit of Jacob guidance.' Breck adjusted his position on the speaker box. 'We know you've still got your ear to the ground and might have picked up something.' Six months had passed since Jacob left Parkhurst. Breck believed he wouldn't be in any rush to return.

'Haven't seen him for ages. Sorry.'

Breck refused to believe Jacob. 'I can see to it that you end up back inside. It's the least I can do as you're not willing to help us.'

'You're going to pay me, right?'

Breck was firm in his response. 'No, we're not.'

Silence ensued where Jacob squinted a little, cracked his knuckles too before he caved in. 'OK. Clarke telephoned me, man, said he had a friend in trouble. I recommended a place outside London where he could stay low.'

'Where did you recommend?'

'A place where money is paid, no questions asked.'

The two officers sat in silence and Jacob took a while to cotton on. Then released a laboured sigh and both officers had a look of dissatisfaction which worried him. Breck stood up without saying a word and left the room which caused Jacob to twist his neck to follow his direction.

Jacob's attention reverted back to Kearns and he tried to work out what was going on. In a flash, she sprung forward and slammed an ashtray decorated with 'happy ash' into the side of his head. Jacob let out a screeching wail and held his left ear, screaming in pain.

Kearns' eyes bulged with rage and she slammed him again. This time she tore the skin leaving a distressed Jacob to wrap his arms over his head for protection. He curled up on the sofa and Kearns walked back to her seat.

When Breck re-entered the room Jacob uncurled his body. He forced himself upright and held his bloodied ear, while Breck appeared to be a little uncomfortable with what he saw but refused to comment. The result mattered. It always had.

'Nice place you have here. There are a few strange items in the bathroom that I'd usually bring down to the station but I can overlook that.' Breck received no response from Jacob so added, 'Maybe I should take another look and check them out, leave you and Kearns together for a bit longer.'

'No, man, wait.' Jacob couldn't bear the thought of being left alone with Kearns again. He lifted his hands in defeat and showed his palms. 'I have information. You'll find what you're after in a bed and breakfast (B&B) up in Yorkshire.'

'What's the name of this B&B?'

'The Clear View. Run by a shady businessman named Lance Pringle.'

Both Breck and Kearns smiled at the news but each for different reasons.

NINETEEN

Earlier

Kearns felt annoyed with herself for not wearing a scarf, and buttoning her coat all the way up was scant consolation for feeling like there was a chain of ice around her neck. She walked past a deserted playground, where the wood had begun to rot away from the seesaw, and the slide was covered in hardened bubble gum. She stared up at the block of flats,

remembering the stories she had heard about the good old days.

Back then you could leave your back door open, let the children play with freedom, where the only missing people were the ones that had become lost on their way to their destination. Lost, not snatched.

Kearns wondered if those stories were true as she lifted the knocker. The person she had come to see had already glimpsed her through the window and expected her.

Jacob Simpson offered Detective Sergeant Patricia Kearns a drink, which she accepted. He looked a bit different to how she last remembered him. Now wearing silver framed glasses, he tied his hair back into a pony tail and his maroon cardigan elevated his intelligence. Kearns pointed to his frames.

'How long have you been wearing those?'

'About a month or so. They're for reading.'

Simpson offered her a seat while he popped into the kitchen. Kearns chose the cleanest one to sit on and noticed the cardboard cut outs of the Fab Four on the floor. Poor Ringo was stuck at the bottom, squashed by the other three.

Simpson came out with a mug of tea in one hand and a beer in the other. He gave the mug to Kearns. She offered him a polite smile and took it. Just as she was about to put it to her lips she spotted a loose strand of his hair floating at the top so placed the mug on the floor without highlighting her disappointment. Simpson sat down and opened the conversation.

'Your call sounded urgent, detective, and desperate.'

'Urgent yes, desperate no.'

'Have it your way, what can I help you with?'

'You are going to be visited in a few hours by myself and another detective and when that happens, I'll need you to follow a script.'

The request took Simpson by surprise. He swigged his beer.

'That's a lot of pressure on me, I might mess up. Hey, don't you trust your colleague?'

'More than I trust you.'

Simpson laughed. 'Then why ask me, I was never your favourite.'

'And you still ain't but I need you to buy time for me. In the end it will lead to lives being saved.'

Simpson drained his drink. 'That sounds like some far-out shit. I need another beer.'

He left his seat to head back to the kitchen and Kearns became impatient while she waited. She felt rotten doing this but Breck followed his nose so she needed to do her job.

Simpson returned to the room but this time he decided to stand.

'What if I don't want to do what you're asking?'

'No choice, I've got too much on you.'

Simpson held up an unsteady hand. 'You're one tough chick. I need an incentive detective you know that.'

Kearns did indeed know that and rose to her feet, then stepped away from the chair she was sitting on. Simpson saw the envelope that she left behind. Neither needed to discuss it.

'Didn't like the tea?' Simpson eyed the untouched cup.

'No, too much milk and a strand of your hair was in it.' Kearns took her time to circle the room. 'I know you've enrolled yourself on a college course and I can see that you've tidied yourself up a bit but I need the Jacob Simpson of a few years ago in a few minutes' time.' Simpson stood still, absorbing her words. 'Make sure those cut outs are standing up. Lose that academic cardigan, the glasses, and for goodness sake, loosen your bloody hair.'

Simpson took offence. 'What's wrong with the hair?'

'It makes you look too slick at the moment, and I don't trust anyone that looks too slick. If I don't, neither will my partner and if that happens we'll have a real problem.

'Cool.'

'I might need to be a bit rough with you too so don't take it personally. Now pay attention, this is what I want you to do.'

TWENTY

Breck slammed a fist onto the desk and a box of paperclips fell off but he didn't give a damn and left them where they were. He regained his concentration enough to analyse a printout of Janet Maskell's bank statements. She paid a fixed sum every month to B. Genta and he didn't need three guesses to work out

who that could be. He'd have to get Benjamin in again and find out why he kept those payments a secret.

A check of Troy's dental records became a new item on his checklist and Breck wondered why the SCU were always a few steps behind. According to Jacob Simpson, Troy had left London to travel to Kearns' old stomping ground in Yorkshire. A good place to lay low for a city worker he thought.

Breck stared at the clock hanging in the distance. He picked up the phone and dialled his home number. After seven rings Molly answered.

'Hello?'

'Hi, it's me. How are you doing?'

'Not bad, better than of late I think.' Although it pleased Breck to hear the admission it still surprised him. He grew suspicious but didn't want to upset the moment. 'Things have been a bit clearer,' she said. 'I can't explain it. What time are you home?'

'Not sure. I'm investigating a murder don't forget and these things can take unexpected twists and turns.'

'You make it sound like a drama.'

'It might as well be but I can't control the ending.'

A long pause followed but he waited until Molly broke it. 'Let me know when you're on your way then and I'll cook us something nice to eat.'

'I will. Look, I better go, speak to you later.'

He heard a soothing calmness in her voice which he hadn't heard in a long time. Their relationship had been affected by her failure to cope. Not her fault but it had made him feel alone for a while.

No sooner had the call ended than Beatrice appeared by his side. She stared at him in an awkward way. He knew why but chose to ignore it and instead fixed a blank expression in place, forcing her to release a forlorn sigh. The chemistry between them remained and he felt her anger towards him diminishing.

Beatrice handed him a note which he read with a great deal of interest.

Another way to identify the real Troy and been scuppered. There had been a fire at the POI's dental surgery. All records destroyed. Maybe the fire wasn't an accident, maybe it had been done with the intention of covering something up. Either way it left him in the same spot. Bringing the POI in for another Q&A now became the obvious thing to do. If he could locate him.

Beatrice tapped his shoulder.

'Have you forgotten?'

'What are you on about?' She pointed at her watch as a reminder of the meeting in the Briefing Room. 'The meeting.'

Breck thanked her, then she left. He took his time to leave his seat and grabbed Janet Maskell's financial statements, along with his jacket. He met Kearns at the lifts and filled her in on the new information while praising Beatrice.

'She did well getting that info.' Breck pressed the button.

'You think so? Isn't she just doing her job?'

'Do me a favour, go easy on her. We're all one big team.' Kearns rolled her eyes and gave him a false smile, so he took that as a sign she'd meet him halfway. 'What do you think about the fire?'

'Let us make it easy for ourselves,' she advised. 'We've got our eye on the wrong Troy. Why would a city high flier murder his own finance director? It's too crazy.'

'How do you explain the escape and the non-alibi?'

'He panicked, became scared. Anyway, while we're wasting time with him. The most probable murderer is relaxing somewhere in Norway.' Breck felt uneasy at the suggestion.

'I've spoken to my contact in Oslo. He'll keep a lookout for him.'

'It's cut and dried so let's focus on the POI. Wrap it up and take the plaudits. It'll keep Bashir happy at any rate.'

'I'll think about it. In the meantime, we'll go to Yorkshire and follow up on what Jacob said. Although, something doesn't smell right.'

'Like?'

'Like why did the prime suspect live his life everyday as Alexander Troy for so long? Why did he work at Van Bruen for a number of years?'

'He's the real Alexander Troy and the other one has made him look like the murderer. Simple.'

'Maybe you're right,' Breck said.

His fading resistance increased because he wanted closure too. Kearns released a satisfied smile, believing her colleague had already started to wilt under the pressure but she couldn't tell him what she knew. *She wouldn't dare.*

The lift doors opened and it was already 90% full but both officers were still able to squeeze in. Within a few moments, they reached their floor and forced their way out.

They entered the Briefing Room where a cluster of conversations simmered inside. Beatrice had taken the stairs up and had already found a spot, while Breck and Kearns found theirs too as Bashir took centre stage. He puffed out his chest like a peacock and his eyes scanned the room, stopping at Beatrice. Bashir often took an unorthodox approach in these sessions.

'The victim in Arlo's and Patricia's Operation Nettle case has got a sister hasn't she?'

Kearns nodded.

'Yes sir. We're due to speak with her.'

'Good. Use the resources at our disposal.'

Bashir then covered other issues while everyone tried to look attentive even if they weren't. He had an elephant's memory and no one wanted to get on the wrong side of him. He also liked the SCU to look good at all times.

When he drew his session to a close, he notified Breck that due to external pressures, he'd have to run a press conference on the murder investigation. Breck's reluctant nod followed but he accepted that certain matters couldn't be delayed any longer. The case had gained press attention and now everyone was out in the open to be shot down.

*

Kearns pressed her back against a brick wall in the yard while having a smoke when Breck approached. He gave her a wink then she livened up, stubbed out the cigarette and opened the door to the Allegro. They were on their way to visit Janet Maskell's sister so he handed her a note that contained the address. Kearns memorised it then pulled out onto the main road while Breck went through the questions that he wanted to ask.

When they passed Lewisham Library, Kearns heard Breck's frustrated tut from behind.

'Traffic's moving slowly isn't it?'

'No point in having a flashing blue light if it can't be used. Are we on an emergency call?'

'I guess we are.'

Kearns let the sirens scream which allowed them to carve a path straight ahead and in a relatively short space of time they reached the home of Janet Maskell's sister.

Outside Gabriella Maskell's home in Brockley, ribbons of paint peeled away from the window panes and wilting flowers were the most impressive things to decorate the front of the garden. The curtains were drawn tight and after the fourth knock, the door opened. Gabriella stood before them wearing a loose-fitting pullover that hung over a pair of baggy shorts, and her gaunt face accentuated the pink puffiness around her eyes. Breck couldn't fail to notice her skeletal frame. A Family Liasion Officer (FLO) stood in the hallway.

'Hello Ms Maskell, I'm DI Arlo Breck and this is my colleague DS Patricia Kearns.'

Gabriella's nervous smile flittered between the two officers before she left the door ajar and walked back inside. Breck shrugged then followed her in, while Kearns entered afterwards and closed the door.

Old newspapers were scattered across the floor in the hallway next to bits of broken glass and in the lounge the lights were burning on full power. Used tissues occupied a section of the floor next to the sofa chair upon which Gabriella sat. Sorrowful and depressed were words which sprung to mind to describe her sorry state. Her lifestyle seemed the opposite to that of her dead sister and she gave a longing stare at the mantelpiece which displayed a framed photo of Janet.

'Thank you for seeing us,' Breck said.

Gabriella's response was curt. 'No choice have I?'

She lurched forward and clutched her chest which scared Kearns for a brief second. Then she watched her stare into space, lost in her own world, while letting her arms dangle over the side of the sofa chair as if the last breath had been taken from her.

'Can you tell us about your relationship with your sister?'

'We weren't close growing up. I was always jealous of her but we got on better in later years. I know what she could be like sometimes with me, quite sharp. She made a success of herself but me...well look around.' Gabriella turned her head from left to right. 'I should have done better but I didn't.' Breck and Kearns just listened, feeling that it wasn't their place to cast judgement. 'So have you caught the killer?'

'Not quite but we're working on it. We're hoping that you'll be able to tell us something which may be of help.' Breck sat down opposite Gabriella. Kearns sat beside him.

'Want a drink? I've got this.' She turned to open a new bottle of the hard stuff which she lifted from the floor. 'Or there's lemonade in the fridge.'

Breck declined. 'No thank you we're fine.'

He gazed at the many photos of Janet planted across the walls and beside the TV. It almost turned the living room into a shrine.

'I should've been a better sister I admit but I made up for it later though. Do a bit for charity now too.'

She tipped a mouthful of vodka into a glass and stared at Breck and Kearns with empty eyes. Breck waited until she swallowed her medicine before speaking again.

'What can you tell us about her?'

Gabriella blew out a tired breath. 'Not much, I mean she telephoned most times and asked how I was. Asked if I needed anything. She had plenty of money too, loved it more than life itself.'

'Do you know of her relationship with a Mr Benjamin Genta?'

'You mean the gardener, ten years her junior?' Breck nodded. 'She invited me around to meet him.'

'Did you approve of the relationship?'

'At first I was worried for her because….' Gabriella paused and Breck wondered what she'd say next. 'You know what folk are like.' Kearns understood and nodded. For Breck, Wynda Brodie sprung to mind. 'Mind you, he's quite handsome and such a strapping bloke.'

In that moment Gabriella lit up and it made Breck smile before his next question.

'Did you know that she sent generous amounts of money to her boyfriend?' Gabriella shook her head. 'Do you think he could have had something to do with her death?'

'No, he loved her. She said to me once, he doesn't carry knives, he's not in a gang and doesn't go around trying to mug anyone. He just wants to run his own gardening business one day. That's it. He wouldn't harm her, take my word for it.'

Kearns cleared her throat and leaned forwards. 'Did she have any enemies that you knew of?'

Gabriella yawned then stretched down to pick up a discarded elastic band off the floor, pulled back her hair then used it to hold it in place.

'Sorry, say that again.'

Breck repeated the question on Kearns' behalf.

'Enemies, did she have any?'

'No,' she said then her face froze as she tried to hold onto scattered memories of the past. 'Jan could be a real party girl when she wanted, handled her drink better than me.'

'How much of a party girl?'

'She had calmed down of late but there was a time when she'd become very flirty with anyone, men or women.' Breck's gaze caught the floor as Gabriella added, 'Don't be shocked, we came from a liberal family but it's just us…' Gabriella realised what she said so readjusted her words. 'It's just me now.'

Breck nudged Kearns. She rose to her feet and headed off towards the bathroom while a sorrowful Gabriella poured out more alcohol. She raised the glass to her paper-thin lips, and threw her head back before swallowing another mouthful. Her eyes fizzled. Then her tears fell like rain and Breck grabbed a tissue from the box on the floor then handed it to her. She struggled to wipe her eyes and a little while after Kearns returned.

'We'll need you to formally identify your sister,' Breck informed her.

Gabriella stiffened. 'I can't face seeing her dead body. Is there any other way?'

Kearns pulled a Polaroid photograph of Janet from out of her handbag to be used as a reference point. Gabriella's eyes locked onto it. 'That's her, that's my sister Janet.'

Kearns gave Gabriella a sympathetic look. 'Try and get some rest love.'

'The drink will let me rest, never lets me down.'

Kearns crouched and touched Gabriella's arm. 'Hey, go easy. I know it's a difficult time but I'm sure your sister wouldn't want you to throw your life away.

'You think so?'

'Yes, I do.'

As Gabriella let the words seep through, Kearns reminded herself that this was a part of the job she'd be happy to avoid.

Breck said, 'I know it's short notice but maybe you can attend the press conference? It would be a great help.' He rose to his feet.

'Yes, I'll try.'

'Thank you. Right, we'd better be going.'

The officers let themselves out but the FLO remained behind and when they reached the car, Breck asked for a favour.

'Speaking to Gabriella made me realise once again that family is important. Pat, I need to make a visit before we head back. Nothing to do with the case.'

'Where to?'

'You'll see.'

The vision of Gabriella Maskell made Breck felt a little bit emotional and it scared him. Maybe he was tired of encountering sadness and neither he or Kearns spoke much on the journey. Time to think had become a precious commodity.

Kearns pulled up outside the care home in Southwark and lifted the handbrake into place. Breck cast his eyes towards its orange-brown brickwork and dusty glass windows that were supposed to be cleaned every other day. In the wettest months, the rain would transform the brick into candy apple red and wash away the algae, as well as the dust from the glass. The manager, Emma McNamara, had been running the home since 1972.

Kearns' subtle shake of the head went unnoticed as both officers left the vehicle and walked up the steps, then through the main doors. Breck gave his name to the male receptionist while Kearns grabbed a seat in the waiting area. The place carried a fresh smell which made for a great advertisement to any visitor.

Kearns looked at the health posters on the wall, along with selected magazines on the table. It was a stream of shouting which broke her concentration, Breck's too when he joined her.

'Come on Reggie, calm down.'

'No, no, no, I want to speak to the manager. He hit me. He hit me so hard he did.'

Three people came into view from around the corner. Reggie a pensioner and two care workers, a man and a woman. They held him tight and he appeared to be confused while resisting them, still dressed in his pyjamas. They man-handled in a way that suggested he could be a threat and when Emma McNamara trail-blazed along, she pit-stopped. They had a few quiet words and then his anger dissolved away in a matter of seconds. Breck believed through a mixture of bribery and fear. They led Reggie back around the corner out of sight and Emma approached Breck.

'Hello, Arlo, how are you doing?'

'Not too bad, Emma. You look busy as always.'

'Yes, Reggie can be like that sometimes but we care for our residents here as you know. I'll try to catch up with you later.'

She dashed away, then the male receptionist called Breck's name and he turned to Kearns. 'I won't be long.'

She watched him walk through a set of double doors to the main activity room of the care home. It had been pushed to its limits to include a huge television that flickered and a seating area with a spot reserved for board games.

A row of cushioned chairs were outside in the garden, picturesque for when the sun shone through and not quite so when it didn't. Just a few of the old folk seemed with it. Most didn't and amongst them was the person Breck had come to see. Wrapped in a dark shawl, an old woman with a sandy beige complexion, stared straight ahead with her old skin stretched to breaking point over the brittle bones underneath. She looked frail but her mind remained sharp and it was on her insistence that she wore a faded hazel wig as a replacement for hair.

'Have you been behaving yourself?'

'Sometimes, where's my fruit?'

Arlo gave the woman a hug. 'I never had time to pick any up for you. This is an unofficial stop off.'

She frowned. 'What's wrong?'

'Nothing, I just wanted to see you.'

'They'll sack you if you don't be careful.'

Breck laughed. 'They'll need a better reason that this.'

Kearns decided to stretch her legs. The curiosity gripped her and she peered through the glass panel of the double doors to watch Breck, wondering what on earth he was up to. She saw him pull something from his pocket and hand it over to the old lady. Then he gave her a goodbye hug.

Breck came out and Emma happened to be standing nearby, talking to a member of her staff. When she spotted Breck she killed the conversation and almost pounced on him.

'It's so good to see you, Arlo. You look well.'

'So do you Emma, how are things?'

'Well, I've split up with my boyfriend.'

'Who's the latest one?'

'A painter and decorator who's crap at his job and a few other things too.' Breck felt embarrassed, he didn't want the details. 'So I'll have to move on.' While he smiled, Emma felt Kearns' *back-off* stare and decided to close the conversation. 'Well if you ever want to check up on her but are too busy to visit, just give me a ring.'

Emma handed over her personal telephone number and Breck did something with his eyes. A deep stare thing that made her blush. An uncomfortable Kearns coughed in an effort to grab his attention but Breck couldn't understand why she wanted to be so protective. He struggled to fathom Kearns' dislike of Emma's flirty nature, ignoring the loosened buttons on her blouse, or the flickering light simulation of her eyelids. A typical man.

Breck thanked Emma then left the building with Kearns by his side, fully expecting her next question as they walked down the steps.

'Who's that old lady at the care home? You said this visit has nothing to do with the case.'

'In a loose sense of the word it has.'

'How do you mean?'

'Her grandson is the senior investigating officer.'

'What are you talking about? Oh.' Kearns' words became lodged in her throat midway much to Breck's amusement.'

'Yes she's my grandmother.'

'That old lady is your grandmother?'

Breck opened his wallet and dug a finger into one of the small pockets. He pinched a finger-sized photo and pulled it out.

'Who's that?'

'My mother. She died in '65 and my grandmother took me in after that. Kearns saw the resemblance between Breck and the woman in the photo. The eyes and the shape of the face were the same but her skin was just a shade darker.

'Don't be afraid, there's plenty more like me around. People with a mixed heritage and paler skin that allows them to be whatever they want.'

Kearns offered an understanding smile. 'You kept that quiet.'

'I used to a lot more as a kid, easier to get along with everyone that way I thought. Not now though. I just don't shout it from the rooftops.'

'I'm glad you told me.'

'Apart from you, only one other person knows.'

'Who's that?'

'Ray Riley.'

Kearns' face clouded over. 'That idiot?'

'He found out by accident but it's a long story for another day, Pat.'

'Well, I'll be waiting for that day you can be sure of that.'

'Let's head back to the station and get the Maskell press conference out of the way. Then we'll prepare for our trip to the Yorkshire B&B to locate Troy.'

They neared the car and Breck stopped for a moment and watched a mix of people going about their business from across the street. He realised he could choose his identity just like people choose their friends. Yet, in these troubled times of division and difference, he couldn't determine whether that choice was a gift, or a heavy curse.

TWENTY ONE

New Jersey

The thing that attracted Ceinwen Phelps to Alexander Troy was his kilowatt smile. She witnessed it first hand after he had sent over a bottle of champagne while she lunched with a friend in Mayfair. He wasted no time in waltzing over to their table; full of himself, but what could have been a short-lived meeting turned out to be something much more. She accepted his business

card, laughed about it too. When she arrived home she summoned enough courage to dial his number and speak to him. They had a lot in common and she knew that they'd end up together.

Dressed in a smart flared trouser suit, Ceinwen's chocolate brown hair hung loose over her shoulders and the gold stiletto heels tapped against the floor. She pulled her wheeled suitcase through the airport, although many people still carried luggage the traditional way. The wheeled suitcase had been bought from Macy's in New York and the store was amongst the first to stock it. For Ceinwen, it amounted to a kudos thing. It served as a great conversation piece.

She made her way towards the airport's exit and dreamt of a better life with an air of optimism that refused to be diminished, swearing to never give her love to the wrong man. She'd made the mistake more than once before and she still found herself paying the price for the biggest one of all.

Ceinwen raised a hand to hail a cab. A stranger appeared out of nowhere. Her eyes had to look up to see his face and the striking line of smoke coloured hair on his chin would make him stand out in crowd.

'Ms Phelps, I'm Eddie and transport's been arranged for you.'

'By who?'

'Your company laid it on.'

His arrival took her by surprise but after the long flight she was in no mood to turn him down. Eddie took the suitcase from her and she followed him to a black Cadillac, one that would have trouble squeezing onto a majority of English roads. She strapped herself in and listened as the engine grunted into life, while Eddie moved the vehicle away and upped its speed, switched on the radio then turned it down low.

Ceinwen Phelps, Senior Mergers and Acquisition Manager, at Xenon, saw New Jersey as a world away from her discreet corner of South East London. However, the trip would be another string to her bow. A step up the career ladder beckoned and although there'd be obstacles, she wasn't afraid to dream.

The journey didn't take long and when Eddie slowed the vehicle to a stop, Ceinwen peered through the window. The champagne coloured canopies of the hotel were eloquent, just as she'd heard, and she couldn't wait to go inside. Ceinwen opened her purse and offered Eddie a tip but he refused. He retrieved her suitcase and she left the Cadillac to see him walk towards a payphone. He beckoned her over but she didn't understand why. She pulled her suitcase along and joined him.

Eddie handed her the phone. 'It's for you.'

'For me?'

'Take the phone damn it.'

She took the phone and pressed her ear against the receiver. She didn't expect the voice on the other end and the shock crippled her.

Eddie waited for a few seconds then unpeeled the phone from Ceinwen's tight grasp. He watched her while she remained stock-still. When he had amused himself enough, he jumped back into the Cadillac and parked it across the road. Ceinwen's head began to spin and she had to accept the truth. Even with being thousands of miles away in New Jersey, she wasn't safe.

*

She walked into the hotel and checked-in, glancing back while she spoke with the receptionist to see if she could spot Eddie from across the street. She could. He sat in the Cadillac, chewing on a piece of gum, looking like he had all the time in the world.

The concierge appeared and showed Ceinwen to her room. She gave him a tip and after he left, locked the door, pressed her back against it and slid down. It felt safe there and she sat staring across at the light which filled the frame of the window, wondering how everything could turn sour so fast. The past had come back to haunt her and she needed to prepare for the worst.

The voice.

This was just the beginning.

Eddie had been sent by the man in her nightmares. A man she had a relationship with before Troy. A man named Marcin Dvorak. Her biggest mistake. He had provided an escape route for her at the right time in her life once upon a time. A bit of light-hearted fun that a causal relationship brings. She never meant it to be serious but Marcin wouldn't let go. His obsession suffocated her.

Ceinwen left her room, exited the hotel, and welcomed the soft breeze that greeted her outside. She still found it difficult to come to terms with the situation and hopped on a bus, unsure of its destination. It didn't matter much, she just wanted to get away.

A mix of people were inside and she slumped down onto a window seat for a cut-price sightseeing tour. A few stops later she jumped off and stepped out onto the street, wrapping her arms around her body and followed the path of the wind. She ended up in an unfamiliar place in front of a Two Guys department store sign, amongst parked cars, where a girl in a dazzling rainbow coloured shirt swigged beer from a bottle. The girl sat on the back of her boyfriend's Harley Davidson. Her mini-skirt rode high on her thighs.

'Excuse me, Ms. See, you don't look like you from round here,' the girl said. Neither was she judging by her mid-western accent.

'I've flown over from England.'

'England? Cool. Have you … ah … come over to party?'

'No, I'm here on business.'

The girl swung her head back towards her boyfriend and smiled. Not a nice smile, more crooked and twisted. She took another mouthful from the bottle and brought her voice to a whisper. 'You like him?' Ceinwen looked at the man in the blue T-shirt and ripped jeans, with a moon-shaped scar on his left cheek. The sun had tanned his skin and he looked like he worked on bikes or even cars, because grease stains were still trapped underneath his fingernails. The girl became impatient. 'Don't leave me hanging.'

The question seemed to be an odd one and with all she had to worry about, it confused Ceinwen.

'I don't know what you mean by do I like him. I need to get going.'

'But see, I was thinking, um, that maybe we could all go to the bar across the street and ah, well you know, do some drinking. Get to know each other see, and go to a motel for some fun.' Ceinwen stepped back, baulking at the salacious invitation but her reaction caused immediate offence. 'C'mon, loosen up bitch!'

Ceinwen jogged away, unaware that Eddie had been observing on the other side of the road from inside the Cadillac. After a few moments of walking when she attempted to cross the road, she saw him too. She stepped back onto the pavement and scurried away, almost in a blind panic.

The biker and his angry girl rode after Ceinwen. She still swigged from the bottle while his eyes were dead and they both focused on their prey. The roaring engine made Ceinwen turn around to see them mount the pavement and she spotted a diner up ahead. They'd catch her before she'd reach it.

Ceinwen moved as fast as she could but missed Eddie sprinting over. She missed the kick that he flung at the Harley which made it zig-zag then crash.

She watched him walk over to the rider while the girl laid on the ground clutching her bloodied knee. He pulled the rider away from the bike and used his head as a punch bag. Ceinwen thought he was dead, so did his girl.

She hobbled up on one knee and seeing her boyfriend's face in pieces made her want to kill Eddie. She turned her bottle into a weapon and Eddie shook his head, then clawed away one side of his opened leather jacket to reveal his Smith & Wesson Model 27. With its six-inch barrel, a .357 bullet would punch a tennis ball-sized hole into her and the thought of Eddie's six-round cylinder opening her up scared her enough to force her back.

Ceinwen turned around and ran into the diner. It was a half-full with a shallow stream of chatter and one of the employees kept her in his sights after she entered, wondering if she was a problem waiting happen. She asked for a table and he handed her a menu.

'You okay, ma'am?'

'Yes fine, thank you.'

'You sure?'

'I said I'm fine!'

Ceinwen tried her best to appear normal and even ordered a drink to calm herself. It took its time in coming but when it arrived, any chance for a moment's peace evaporated. There was Eddie again. This time inside the diner. He seated himself just three tables away and pulled out a newspaper. Ceinwen, couldn't take the mental torture anymore so she balled her fist, sprung from her seat, then stormed over to his table.

'I want to speak to him,' she demanded.

'You want to talk to him?'

'Yes, right now!'

Eddie fumbled around in his pockets for loose change and folded away the newspaper. Then left the diner with Ceinwen to walk to a payphone nearby.

He dialled a number and followed it up with a mumbled conversation then passed the handset to her. She stared at it, recalling the time fate intervened and freed her from Marcin's grasp. The police forced him to disappear and it allowed her to return to a normal life. Now he had come back and the option of going to them for help didn't exist.

Ceinwen valued her life. Marcin, nephew of one of Europe's most feared criminals, never failed to get what he wanted. With his shadow looming, the danger now extended to Troy as well as herself. But Marcin didn't know about Troy, yet. If he did, he'd go after him so Ceinwen needed to think fast and figure a way out of this mess. As soon as the event she had flown over for ended, she'd be heading back to England.

No choice.

Ceinwen took the handset, readied herself then spoke.

'Marcin just tell me what you want me to do and I'll do it,' she heard herself say. 'I want you to leave me alone, that's all I want, and I'll do whatever it takes to make it happen.'

TWENTY TWO

London

Breck did his one hundred press-ups, which he tried to do most mornings then went to check on Molly. Still fast asleep, she hadn't given him an answer yet on whether or not she wanted to speak to someone professional about her ordeal. Although he wanted to give her time, he feared that she might be running away from it all. His own guilt at handling this very personal

matter had become a problem for him but he kept that from her. As an officer of the law safety should have been his middle name. Yet when Molly needed him where was he? Pissing it up in their local boozer and ending up falling asleep, while Molly had her life torn apart, bit by bit.

He always reassured her that the search was ongoing but energy and hope and been depleted from him long ago, snatched away and replaced with a reluctant acceptance that he had tried everything. He called in all of his favours and used police resources without success. He couldn't tell her anything else other than he still believed he would catch the man whose face she didn't see on the night she walked home alone.

Breck had a shower. The warm water felt good on his skin and freshened him up. When he finished, he popped down to the kitchen with a small towel wrapped around his waist and made a slice of toast. He adorned it with a thick spread of honey.

After he finished he grabbed the phone and rang the main number for the care home, ignoring Emma's personal number.

'Please put me through to Imelda Breck please, it's her grandson.'

He waited a while for them to get her to a phone but when she came onto the line it made it all worthwhile. 'Happy birthday, gran!'

'Arlo! Thank you. Yes, I'm another year older now.'

'Maybe so but you don't look it,' he said, hugging the phone between his shoulder and ear while pulling out a box of cereal and a bowl.

A raspy chuckle came back through the line. 'Thank you for the present. I opened it first thing this morning.'

'Do you like it?'

'The gold bracelet is lovely, thank you. Emma's going to put me in my nice dress later for when they sing happy birthday to me. There'll be a cake with a million candles on.'

'That's sounds great.' His gran then went quiet for a bit, enough for Breck to become concerned. 'You all right?'

'I received a birthday card from your dad.'

Breck should've been happy that his dad hadn't forgotten his former mother-in-law but he wasn't. His father had schmoozed his way back into her life a few months ago, cap in hand, spinning a sad story. She gave him money then he left without word. No change there then.

'I'd rather not know, please.'

'He's given me an address if you want to contact him.'

Breck didn't. 'I've got to go.'

'Arlo.'

Breck wanted to be there to help her celebrate but the demands of the job prevented him from doing so. He couldn't get time off. And even if he could, he wouldn't want any discussions about his father to dominate her day.

'Take care, gran. I hope you have a great time.'

'OK then. Be careful.'

He ended the call, pleased that he'd managed to keep his anger at bay. His gran had always been his rock but his father was another matter.

Breck heard the clink of bottles from the milkman's delivery and went to the door to collect the milk. He opened the door and picked up the two bottles from the doorstep, brought them inside, peeled back the silver foil from one and poured out the milk. A dollop of cream fell out onto his cornflakes as it always did the first time with new milk.

Breck stood by the fridge to place the bottles inside when Molly entered the kitchen, holding one of his shirts.

'I didn't expect to see you there,' he said.

'I just thought I'd pop down for breakfast while you were still here.' She held the shirt aloft, aligning it with her face.

'When did you get this?'

'The other day why?'

'It's not something you'd go for that's all.'

'I fancied something different.'

The shirt was a present from Beatrice, one that he never told Molly about so he agreed with her. It was lime coloured, had frilly cuffs, collars the length of eagle wings and large white buttons. Definitely not a shirt he'd go for.

Molly placed it on a stool then joined him at the table, neglecting to tell him that she had acted on impulse and searched his pockets to look for any signs of cheating. She went through his drawer to see if she'd come across a love letter but the only thing she found was the shirt. She knew for certain he didn't buy it.

Breck gave Molly a soft kiss on the cheek. He handed her a bowl, the milk and the box of cornflakes.

'You look brighter today.'

She ignored his compliment. 'Where did you get it?'

'What?'

'The shirt. Where did you get it?'

Breck's heart drum-rolled. 'You're obsessed by it. Should I look for a female version?' Molly ignored the joke to stare into her bowl, stirring the cereal and milk together over and over again. 'Off a market stall down Portobello Road why?'

'Nothing, just curious.'

Breck didn't know whether to believe her or not and became anxious, fearful of her next question so he came with one of his own.

'Have you thought about going to speak to someone, to get you back on track?'

'Off the rails, am I?'

'Come on, you know what I mean.'

'I might. I don't know. I suppose seeing someone could help. I'll think about it. Best to make sure it's with someone I'd be comfortable with but I need to find something to do. I miss Woolworths and going into work to talk with the girls.'

'I know but you didn't want to go back.'

'Couldn't face the questions or the sympathy after what happened.'

Breck felt Molly's sadness. 'I heard MFI were recruiting. One of our old sergeants works there now. I could have a word. It'd be useful if you were there anyway, we'd get discounted furniture.' Molly didn't seem enthused by the idea. Taking things one step at a time might be best, Breck now began to believe. 'I tell you what, let's see how you feel in a few weeks before you go rushing back to work.'

The phone shrilled. Molly's aunt Kathy had decided to check up on her niece. For once he had good news when she asked, 'How is she doing?'

Breck turned in Molly's direction with a deep sense of pride. 'Molly is...' He stopped because he couldn't find the right words so he said, 'I'll let her tell you herself.'

He signalled for Molly to come over then stepped aside when she began her conversation.

Breck popped upstairs to change into his clothes for work. He threw on a black sweatshirt and jeans, alongside, his sandy brown leather jacket. Perks of being in the SCU that would allow him to retain a bit of cool or so he hoped.

By the time he returned downstairs Molly was still on the phone so he gave her a wave as he left. He breathed in some of that Deptford air and the VW started up first time, but he knew better than to question divine intervention.

The main road played host to thick walls of traffic so Breck turned the car up onto Deptford High Street, with the intention of driving towards Pagnell Street. Once there, he'd join the A20 towards Cransham and all went well until his stomach churned. He still felt hungry but there was a solution and that solution also presented him with a longshot for something else. Breck pulled over next to the Paradise Lane Caribbean takeaway. A place where he'd stand out a mile.

Paradise Lane's pastel coloured decor and picturesque images of palm trees, and sandy white beaches didn't quite fit in with the downcast morning. Breck made his way past a group of youths that eyeballed him and received a surprise.

Benjamin Genta blocked the doorway.

'I ain't done anything,' he said in protest.

'I wouldn't agree. We need to talk about the money Janet put into your account every month. First though, I want to fill my stomach. Don't go anywhere.'

Benjamin stepped out of the way and watched Breck order at the counter. He even swore he heard him switch to mild patois as he spoke to the owner Marla. A true out of body experience. At the same time a local face that Benjamin knew as a gun man, with links to notorious groups in Brixton and Ladbroke Grove, made his way out with food in hand. He swung a look towards Breck inside the shop and after being satisfied he offered no threat, he moved on.

Benjamin had already been seen speaking to Breck so if it became known that he was a police officer then he'd have a problem. A big one.

He turned around to see Breck collect his food and when the detective walked past, he urged him to follow. Benjamin waited until he reached his car first then pounced. Breck wound down the window leaving him to stand outside.

'How did you know that I'd be at Paradise Lane?'

'I didn't know for certain. Call it a wild guess. I'm also hungry.'

Breck showed off his food bag that contained curried goat, plantain, and fried dumplings.

'Are you saying that you've bought food from there before?'

Breck pulled a dumpling out and began to eat. 'What do you think?'

'Bullshit.'

'Ask Marla. She'll tell you that I visit almost every week.'

Benjamin grinned. 'I'll be back.'

Breck watched him head into Paradise Lane and wished he was in there to see his face when Marla spoke to him. Moments later Benjamin resurfaced. Breck revved the engine.

'I can't believe it.'

'Good, now get in and tell me what I need to know otherwise I'm taking you in.'

'What for?'

'Perverting the course of justice.'

Benjamin made sure that no one was watching as he opened the door to the car and slid in. Breck moved onto his second dumpling and waited until his guest became comfortable.

'Tell me about the cash gifts.'

'The money was for the anti-fascist group that I'm a part of. We needed extra funding for leaflets and stuff like that. Janet agreed with what we were doing. Said she wanted to help.'

'You need to be careful. Activists are being monitored.'

'Someone's got to keep up the fight. It's us and them. We all heard about the punch-up at the station involving one of the Front's men. At one of their rallies he said we were all muggers. Then he started talking about the Third Reich and said he'd shake us out of the trees. We've got to keep up the fight.' Breck couldn't really dissuade him. He felt the burn in his own chest too. 'I get stopped on average about three times a week. They never find anything. Your boy Riley loves me I swear, always got something to say when he sees me.'

Breck folded the top of the paper food bag and rested it on the back seat. The current social climate affected both of them in its own way.

'It's not easy that's why I need you to be straight with me when I'm trying to do the right thing in finding out who killed Janet and why.'

'There is something else that I didn't tell you.'

'What?'

'Janet said that she saw someone following her.'

'She told you that?'

'Yeah, the last time we saw each other before I went to Wolverhampton. She said she spotted a man outside her workplace. He stood out because he wasn't the suit type.'

'What type was he then?'

'A baseball cap and dark clothing type.'

'What did he look like?''

'White, powerfully built and wore a baseball cap. She told me that she couldn't see him in great detail. It was getting dark.' Benjamin rubbed his hands together as if the cold from outside had found its way into the car. 'She spotted him again lurking around near her home for a bit then he disappeared.'

'Why didn't you reveal this at the station?'

Benjamin shrugged. 'I didn't like what you represented.'

'Fair enough but your girlfriend is now dead and that could be a credible lead.'

Benjamin accepted that he had made a mistake. 'Sorry, I know you've got your job to do. Look, come down to the Jupiter Club.' Breck tried to place it. 'It's the community centre in New Cross.'

'Oh yes, I know the place.'

'Your colleagues damaged the sound system there and made arrests for no reason. We're having a meeting there next week to talk about it.' Breck recalled the incident. It occurred a few years back and remained unresolved. His silence gave Benjamin the answer. 'Marla told me you're a regular in Paradise Lane. Even said your grandma's from Ocho Rios. Shit, I never reckoned that.'

Breck smiled. 'I want you to keep out of trouble. Do you hear me?'

'I hear you but The Front are going to march near here soon and fight to "reclaim the streets" as they say. We're not going to let them past so keeping out of trouble might not be possible.' In his head, Benjamin was already somewhere else.

Breck understood the failings of his own words and he let his eyes follow the alcoholic hovering outside the bookmakers, holding a part-concealed can of beer in a paper bag, talking to anyone foolish enough to listen. Ahead of him, a drug-addicted prostitute with tawdry dark hair and black heels, walked up and down in a skirt which refused to hide her milky white thighs. She had been brought into the station a few times. A sex-seller that knew how to play the game and often offered cut price deals. Ahead of her time many said. Four BJs for the price of two was a summer special other girls now copied. Breck's observations became of great interest to Benjamin.

'What are you seeing?'

'A lot of problems,' Breck admitted, 'problems that need fixing.'

'That's right but not just here, everywhere. We're in the dead lands, a place where you're judged solely by the word of others. No one ever gets out. They stay trapped in it forever.'

Breck didn't want to hear that. To keep him going, he needing to know hope lay ahead somewhere along the line. He leaned across to Benjamin, opened the door and let him out.

'Thanks. Remember what I said, keep out of trouble.'

Breck watched him walk away like a street solider. One that had readied himself for an urban war.

Dead lands, a place where you're judged solely by the word of others.

Breck sniffed the air and inhaled a sweet spicy smell. The food. He noticed that a vast amount of heat had already escaped from the bag which he could do little about so he tried to look for the positives. Lukewarm food had to be better than nothing.

*

At the station Breck padded past Clive and saw Beatrice up ahead carrying a bunch of files that threatened to topple over. He side-stepped a few people in his way and morphed his walk into a light jog so that he could catch up with her.

'Need any help?'

'Thanks.' Breck lightened her load by taking some of the files.

'Any developments with the Nettle case?'

'We may have a breakthrough.'

'In what way?'

'I just bumped into Maskell's boyfriend, Benjamin Genta. He revealed that a man had been watching her.'

'That sounds positive.'

'We're being given the run around at the moment so I'll take what I can get. What are you doing with these?' he asked referring to the files.

'Bringing them to Bashir so that he can better organise our ring of steel for the march.'

Breck saw Kearns in the background and wanted to speak to her. 'I'll bring these up in a sec.' Beatrice didn't feel like sticking around so went on her way.

'What were you two talking about?' Kearns asked.

'Police work so no cheeky comments. New information from Benjamin Genta. Maskell saw a man outside her place of work and near her home on the same night.'

'When?'

'A week before her murder.'

'What have we got to go on?'

'A white male, powerfully built, wearing dark clothing and a baseball cap. Run a check on all known local possible suspects. See if we can get a match. Might lead to something. It could've been our fugitive Troy.'

'OK, let's hope we get something from it.'

'I need to give these to the boss, see you in a bit.'

Breck made his way to Bashir's office to deliver the rest of the files. Kearns went in the other direction to her desk and stared at the paperwork.

It had to be done but something else tugged at her. Against her better judgement, she reached for the phone and dialled her daughter's number. She hoped she'd pick up. After a few rings it went through to the answering machine. It wasn't the result she wanted but she chose not to waste the chance to show she cared.

'Hello Kim, it's me love. I'm just calling to see how you are. I'm OK but I do miss you and we should talk. I'm not sure what you've been told but you should hear my side. Look, it'd be great if you could…um…give me a call back and let me know what you've been up to. Take care, love you.'

Kearns ended the call and became tearful. Would Kim pick up the message? If Mick found it first he'd delete it without saying a word to their daughter. Despite the anxiety, Kearns didn't mind taking that chance. Kim was her weak point and always would be.

TWENTY THREE

The Messenger

He sat inside her flat after letting himself in without her knowledge. Sprinkles of cigarette ash littered the floor, discarded crisp packets overflowed from a coffee table. Damp and mould were embedded into the ridges of the skirting boards and he knew her name as he always had done. Geraldine. They said she was rebellious and

could have anything she wanted with a wealthy daddy happy enough to indulge her.

She partied like any other student, alcohol and drugs, and applied eyeliner in a way that created a look of anger. To scare the non-believers but he believed.

He watched her from behind while she used the mirror as a guide. She massaged a thick layer of cream into her pink hair with black roots before sharpening the ends into spikes, then paused. She could feel his presence so he shifted out of view until she resumed. His eyes followed her over to the sofa upon which she stretched out, causing her T-shirt to rise up enough to expose her stomach. The stereo continued to blast out punk, deafening anyone at close range and the noise threatened to break the speakers. A relaxed Geraldine made an attempt to sing along until a number of ultra-loud knocks at the door disturbed the moment.

She didn't want to move, that much he could tell, but she did and expelled a lazy groan while her hidden guest watched her pad over to the door.

'Who is it?'

'Delivery,' a baritone voice fired back. 'Can't fit it through the letterbox.'

'Hang on,' she said, mumbling afterwards.

She unclasped the chain and when she opened the door the delivery man's eyes scooped up the image on her T-shirt. A cut out of breasts printed across her chest, and he watched her finger the silver hooped ring that crossed over from her left nostril to the right.

Geraldine signed what she needed to, then took the box without giving any thanks. After the door closed, her uninvited guest smiled. She belonged to him now.

He waited, gave it enough time until the delivery man had long gone then the Messenger's smile tightened into something hideous.

He moved with speed.

He wrapped a hand around her mouth and expected a struggle like many had given him before but fear gripped her. He spun Geraldine around so that she could see the whites of his eyes from beyond the mask. And witness the burning flames that began to rise from within them. When she convinced him she understood, he removed his hand.

'Bedroom,' he whispered.

She begged him. 'Don't hurt me, don't rape me.'

'This is just business.'

'Please.'

'Shhh.'

He pulled a heavy-duty pipe wrench from his pocket and began to flip it up like a toy, wondering how best to finish her off, and happy that the location of the bedroom deescalated the volume of the music the closer they got to it.

Once inside, he could barely hear vocals, the drums or the guitar, but the heat distracted him. It began to welt his skin so he removed the mask. Geraldine scrambled around on all fours and when she found her purse she pulled out forty pounds in cash and handed it to him.

He never asked for it.

Did she believe that she could buy her freedom?

He popped the 'tip' into his pocket and decided to play on it. 'I want more. Write a cheque now.'

Somewhere inside Geraldine had hope after he said that and with cheque book and pen ready, she battled to stop her hands from shaking.

'Who should I make it out to?'

'Mr Alexander Troy and sign it.'

She tried to recall the name but couldn't. 'How much do you want?'

'Leave it blank and bring it here.'

Geraldine tore the cheque out of the stub and brought it over. She handed it to him and expected her escape route. It never happened. He knocked the cheque away.

Geraldine tried to run.

He grabbed her hair, spun her around then squeezed her throat. She wanted to fight and scratched his face but it had little effect. He raised her up onto the tips of her toes and imitated her voice.

'*Please let me go.*' Then changed it back to his own. 'You've seen my face.' And back again. '*I'm good at forgetting faces, please don't hurt me.*'

He increased the pressure around her throat and kept increasing it until the struggling stopped. Until her body became limp.

He threw her away and ignored the thud of the floor because at that point he thought about her boyfriend, and wished he was there. He'd provide more fun. And while he thought this, Geraldine crawled across the floor, scared and shaken. She could only find the wall.

He couldn't bear to see the suffering, so out of frustration he threw the wrench at her to end it. Geraldine raised her hands to protect herself but the tool bullied them out of the way. The wrench struck her head. To watch her roll over and clutch the dent in her skull fascinated him. The Messenger drew closer and kneeled over her, showing no emotion as he returned his hands to her throat. Geraldine couldn't even muster a scream as the colour drained from her. And he examined the process while being a part of the process. Squeezing and squeezing until her eyes threatened to pop out of their sockets.

Then it was over.

He repositioned her head on the floor in the way a father would place the head of a newborn child onto a pillow. Then he stepped away and collected the wrench, leaving the written cheque on the floor. She would never have a family or get married, never enjoy the right to experience old age or see her loved ones again.

'I'm just the one that has to bring the message,' he whispered to her, knowing that if it wasn't him, it'd be someone else.

There wasn't any cellophane to use like before. Took too long to wrap the body last time so he kept things simple.

Geraldine scratched him. She had the skin from his face but he knew how to fix the problem. The Messenger pulled a paper bag from his pocket and lifted up her hands to inspect her fingers. He could see beyond the chipped multi-coloured nail polish that they were perfectly shaped, but that did little to deter him as he said to himself, 'Right then, where were we?', and pulled out his knife.

TWENTY FOUR

Since Breck had asked her to go easy on Beatrice, Kearns decided to conduct the mortuary visit herself, to show that she had a heart. It wasn't her favourite thing but she liked the idea of Beatrice being unable to bad mouth her due to her kind gesture.

Kearns zeroed in on the red brick exterior in the knowledge that it housed one hundred and twenty

refrigerated storage spaces with one perhaps waiting for her.

She left the car to be surrounded by a blustery wind and accepted that she should be more awake for a pathological examination seeing as the rest of the country had woken up a long time ago.

Kearns waited at the entrance for around a minute or so before being met by Home Office Forensic Pathologist Bart Redmaine. He liked the look of Kearns but she always rebuffed his approaches. He was a handsome man with inviting eyes, shored up by thick eyebrows, and he offered her a warm smile.

'How are you, Patricia?'

'Not too bad, and you?'

'Busy, so many bodies to look at nowadays.'

'Keeps you in a job.'

Bart offered a thoughtful nod. 'Yes, there is that.'

Kearns followed him into the briefing room, while his assistant entered the storage area where the bodies of the dead were cocooned. She stood before a seven-foot door marked with the numbers, twenty-six to thirty-one, and extracted number twenty-eight. The corpse of Janet Maskell. With help from another assistant, she brought the body through to the examination room.

They had covered the corpse from head to toe in a white sheet and when Bart removed it flashbacks of the crime scene met Kearns head on. The collar of Bart's baby blue overall, covered in part by a green protective plastic pinny, flapped up around his shoulders and Kearns looked a little queasy. He noticed that Kearns' eyes darted back and forth as she fought to control her anxiety.

'Don't worry we've all been there,' Bart said in an effort to calm her.

'I'll be all right. I will,' she tried to convince herself.

The assistants fetched a few instruments from the other side of the room while Bart lifted the white sheet and moved a hand towards Janet's face. The assistant returned and placed the instruments in a tray. Bart began.

'There's bruising to the temple and also here.' He moved around the victim's face and ran a gloved finger just above the brow, tracing the crown of her head. 'The blow caused severe internal bleeding around this region.'

'Damage assessment? In layman's terms I mean.'

'Her skull was cracked like a walnut, Mrs Kearns.

'It's Ms Kearns, I reverted back to my maiden name.'

The mistake embarrassed Bart. 'I see, apologies. Her skull was cracked in several places and the sacrum destroyed. My guess is from a blunt instrument, judging by the circumference of the marks.'

Kearns knew they already had an approximate time of death from Frank Cullen's early estimate. It had allowed them to proceed with their investigations but they still required confirmation.

'What's the official time of death?'

'Judging by the body temperature when I recorded it at the scene after you left, I estimated it as being between 1:00 p.m. and 2:00 p.m. on the day found. Pretty precise I know but I like precise.'

Kearns knew that Frank wasn't in the habit of getting things wrong so she welcomed Bart's confirmation.

After it ended, Frank was on hand to deliver his findings as a fast-track measure and recorded asphyxiation as the cause of Janet Maskell's death. Upon leaving, Kearns pondered over the timescale it happened within, aware it coincided with the exact period the fugitive Troy failed to provide an adequate alibi for. She realised that in different circumstances it would be perfect. Instead, it still left him chained to the crime and wouldn't deter Breck from chasing him. Not one little bit.

*

Breck's decision to stay away from the post-mortem somehow led him into the station's yard, kicking around an empty coke can, pretending he was playing in the FA Cup Final. When he heard a light giggle from behind he turned to see Beatrice. He had no idea how long she had been there watching.

'Having a schoolboy moment are we?'

'Don't be cheeky.'

'That's right, she shouldn't be cheeky.' Riley appeared from around the corner like a contagious bug, stopping in between both Beatrice and Breck, an unwanted obstacle in the way, puffing on a cigarette. 'You need to learn the ropes, darling, so you'll have what it takes to be a good detective.' Beatrice held her tongue because of Riley's seniority. 'Fancy a bit of extra tuition over at my place? I'm always willing.'

'You're allowed to tell him to piss off,' Breck told her.

Beatrice fired the words towards Riley. 'Piss off.'

'I'll let you have that one but normally you wouldn't be able to talk to me like that DC Beatrice whatever-your-name-is. With Prince Charming here looking after you, I guess you'll have an easier time, perks, promotion....' he said, letting his words linger.

An incensed Breck bowled forwards and balled his fist. Riley tensed up. Breck snatched the cigarette from his mouth and stubbed it out. Now wasn't the right time for Riley to get his comeuppance. Yet his nemesis felt humiliated in front of the DC and stormed off.

'Bea, if he gives you any hassle, let me know.'

'Will do...I didn't know you cared anymore.'

Breck pretended that he didn't hear the last part of her sentence and made sure they stayed in work mode. 'How's the professional services search for Ceinwen progressing?'

'It's still ongoing. I'm still wading through a list and waiting for some people to get back to me but there's something I need to discuss. It's about my job.'

'I'm listening.'

'As I mentioned when we spoke in the post room, you'd be a good mentor. I want a bigger role in things.'

'In this investigation?'

'I suppose, yes.'

Breck slipped both his hands into his pockets. 'That's not possible, you know that. I'm leading and Patricia is my deputy.'

'Patricia's got her eyes on the Flying Squad but I want to build a career with the SCU.'

'Your time will come Bea, just be patient. We can look at the set up on the next case.'

'It feels like I've been waiting for long enough,' she moaned. 'Can you trust Kearns like you can trust me? I'd be a better partner for you and you know it!'

'I can't believe you just said that.' Breck released his hands from his pockets and aimed another kick at the can. It flew up into the air and bounced off the wall.

'It's true. Remember, I did some good surveillance work on the European criminal operation.' Breck struggled to recall the fine details of that so Beatrice helped him out. 'We wired up a Rolls Royce Silver Shadow which belonged to a big figure in the Eastern European underworld named Aychm. We found out that several of his businesses were scattered around Europe and had been set up an age ago as safety nets.' Breck began to remember it now. 'Riley decided that it was nothing that we could arrest him for. He led the investigation.'

'Do you think he knew he was being listened to?' A suspicious look spread across Breck's face.

'I doubt it.' Although she said it, Beatrice began to wonder too. 'He used coded language. We believed he was making reference to someone that betrayed him. Body parts were wrapped and buried somewhere we believe.'

'Come on let's go back inside. This Aychm fella sounds like a nasty piece of work.'

'You wouldn't be wrong there. He's a Slovakian Roma of Polish descent with criminal contacts all over Europe. The Polish cops have an unsolved murder of two Ukrainians in Wroclaw which he had a hand in. He also ran a prostitution racket in the city of Lviv. But he has never even been charged with anything.'

Breck ruffled his hair as they walked back inside, impressed with the sharpness of mind which Beatrice displayed.

'Please don't worry about your career,' he told her while being as sincere as he could. 'I think you're an asset. Just keep doing what you're doing and your chance will come eventually. I'll catch you later.'

Beatrice watched him walk away, still hearing the words… 'your chance will come eventually,' but she didn't want to wait. She wanted it now and had a few things up her sleeve. The chance to stick two fingers up at Kearns and show Breck that she'd be better placed as his partner. Beatrice hadn't told the full truth. While they had struggled to locate Ceinwen Phelps she had found her, in a loose sense of the word, along with an astonishing discovery. One she couldn't wait to reveal.

TWENTY FIVE

Anil Bashir brushed down his uniform before he went in to see his boss Patrick Rose. Rose was visiting the borough on his way to a meeting in Birmingham. He started his career in the same year as Clive Bird, yet while Bird reached the level of custody sergeant, Rose catapulted himself to the role of detective chief

superintendent. That gave a little insight into his character. Rose wasn't one to sit down and let life pass him by.

Bashir and Rose often never agreed completely but Bashir mastered the art of knowing when to put up and shut up. It was something he had become an expert in as soon as he suspected that Rose wanted to reform the SCU, meaning redundancy for him.

'Anil, fancy a drink? Tea or Coffee?'

'Drink? No thank you.'

'You sure?'

'Yes, absolutely sure.'

Over time Bashir had learned how to respond in a way Rose would understand. He still had his eye on his pension and wasn't going to give Rose an excuse to destroy all his hard work.

'So what have we got this month?'

'Quite a lot has been going on and we've made inroads on a majority of things.'

'Give me the detail Anil, that's what I want.' Bashir opened his file and angled it so that Rose could see what he'd be referring to. Rose took it from him and read the first page. Bashir expected to get it back because he wanted to run through it line-by-line. It wasn't going to happen.

'Give me the stats. As Detective Superintendent I expect you to know these off the top of your head. You're on a good wage as we all are, so we have to earn it, don't we?'

Bashir found Rose's attitude infuriating but kept a lid on his emotions. Being tested like this could only mean one thing. Rose planned to discredit him as part of his latest set of mind games.

'Where do you want me to begin?'

'Give me Cransham's crime statistics for the current year.'

'So far we've had fifty-four robberies to date and…'

Rose cut in. 'Is that on business or persons and do we have suspects for those robberies?'

'The split is twenty-five per cent on businesses and seventy-five per cent on persons. Muggings are a problem but my investigating officers have identified suspects in forty per cent of those cases overall.'

'Go on.'

There have been four armed robberies but the stand out one involving a councillor is being looked at as a priority. The investigating officer is close to making an arrest.'

'Who is that officer?'

'Detective Inspector Raymond Riley.'

'So he's still serving with us. Hasn't he got an attitude problem?'

'His conviction rates are amongst the best in the department.' Bashir waited for a reaction from Rose. None came. 'There are so far just eight reported incidents of gun crime for the area, twenty reported incidents of motor vehicle crime, and a spike in racist and religious hate crimes.'

'You haven't mentioned murder yet Anil.'

'I'm getting to that, sir.'

'There's one in particular I'm thinking of.'

Bashir stopped to think about it but Rose liked to throw a red herring in every now and again to win those bloody mind games. So far, so good. Bashir had recalled the correct data from the file.

'Can you be more specific?'

'I'm talking about the death of Janet Maskell.'

'Everything has been complicated by the instruction to…'

Rose stopped him. 'We don't need to discuss any complications. I'm the one that first gave you that instruction so informing me of it would be a waste of time would it not?'

Bashir gripped the side of the chair. The blood drained from his fingers but he kept his smile intact. 'Yes. I have two of my best officers on it in Arlo Breck and Patricia Kearns.'

'The suspect escaped from the custody of Patricia Kearns so how can she be one of your best officers? For many different reasons it makes us look inept.' Bashir tired of the hard ball game. It was put up and shut up time. Rose pressed his long fingers together to create a triangular shape which he then balanced in line with his chin. 'I want an answer.'

'There were mitigating circumstances. A fight had broken out in reception and the suspect took his opportunity to escape.'

'And Breck, is he being a good boy with what we need done?' Rose released the file onto the table, not interested in reading any more. Bashir thought of the amount of time he had taken to compile it and wanted to cry. Rose only read the first page.

'No problems with Breck. He's being steered in the right direction.'

'What about Kearns?'

'She's fine, sir.'

Not for the first-time Bashir felt uncomfortable. Rose hadn't permitted him to discuss the situation with anyone else. He expected him to manage everything from afar but he didn't believe he could. Not without having Kearns onside. Bashir's mind wandered off somewhere.

'Are you not with it today, Anil?'

'Sorry, I've just got a lot on my mind, sir. It's all under control.'

'Good, glad to hear it.'

A light knock on the door followed and Gloria, Rose's secretary, entered the room with his prep paper. She was in her mid-forties, straight-laced and pragmatic. Rose continued the conversation after she had left.

'Be careful with this Troy case,' Rose warned. 'Van Bruen has a lot of influential friends and the problem he has now, is the very type the SCU was designed to solve. We should be in control of this, all the way. Instead, we have suspects and POI's running around all over the place. Get this to a satisfying conclusion.' Rose raised his eyebrows as a warning. 'Let's not get the wrong man eh?'

'No we won't sir. The press conference for the investigation will be underway soon. I'll be there after this meeting.'

Rose delivered a sharp and decisive nod, and Bashir wondered if his officers ever felt about him the way he felt about Rose. He wanted to escape but knew it was far from over.

'Next on the agenda is the march. Tell me how the preparations for it are going,' Rose demanded. 'If the mayor rings me again I'm putting him straight through to you! I'm fed up with discussing it.'

Bashir exhaled a measured breath. It was going to be a long day.

TWENTY SIX

Scoop-hungry journalists occupied the press room and three rows of four chairs were separated by a TV camera positioned in the middle. It pointed straight towards the main table at the front. A solemn-looking Breck entered alongside Gabriella Maskell, with Kearns and Beatrice behind them. Gabriella paused when she saw the enlarged photo of Janet on the wall and

Kearns could see the effect. She urged her to move on. A couple of uniforms stood just outside of the camera's scope and Bashir, happy to survive his meeting with Rose, observed from afar, at the entrance to the room. Breck waited until the simmering whispers died down and a blanket of silence fell. He cleared his throat then began.

'We are still appealing for help regarding the murder of Janet Maskell, a fifty-three-year-old finance director from the Cransham area.' Everyone zoomed in on him which was strange. It made him tense. After having second thoughts Breck decided to scrap his planned script. He sometimes worked better that way. 'We want to keep our streets as safe as possible and need the public to be our eyes and ears.'

A journalist raised a hand.

'Vic Gera of the *Cransham Gazette* here. What can you divulge about the exact type of injuries the victim sustained?'

'She suffered appalling injuries but I won't specify the exact type. We're requesting for witnesses to contact us. We don't want members of the public to be looking over their shoulders all the time, so we need to stop whoever's out there from doing this again. I urge anyone with information to contact us.'

'Was the victim married? Did she have any family?' Gera liked the sound of his own voice and his Latin features enabled him to live long in the memory - along with the overdose of hair that perched on top of his head.

'I'm sure you know the answer to that already but for those of you that don't, the answer is no. She wasn't married, nor was she a mother but she had a boyfriend.'

'Is the boyfriend a suspect?'

'At this stage no.'

Breck scoped around for anyone else with a question then took a moment and glanced at Gabriella. He feared she wouldn't be able to hold it together for much longer due to the trembling which started in her hands. It now reverberated throughout her whole body. She'd break soon and Breck needed to bring her into the conversation without delay.

'To help with our appeal I'd like to now introduce Ms Gabriella Maskell, sister of Janet.'

Gabriella forced her head upwards, allowing her puffy eyes to catch the full glare of the lights. They made her squint and she hated being in the room.

'Ms Maskell, how has this tragedy affected you?' a voice called out.

'I just want justice.' Gabriella squeezed the ball of crumpled tissue in her hand. Her voice wavered. 'I want it... for my sister so... if anyone knows anything please get in touch.'

That was it. She couldn't manage anymore. Gabriella broke down and Breck turned to Beatrice, giving her the signal to switch on the large OHP monitor.

A blurred photo took everyone's attention away from Gabriella and caused most people more than five yards from it to strain their eyes. Beatrice sharpened the focus to fix the issue.

'This is the man we want to question and he's using the alias of Alexander Troy. He's a blond Caucasian male, 6'1 tall and dangerous. Members of the public are advised not to approach. If you see him contact us. I repeat, do not approach.'

Bashir turned purple with rage. He had no idea Breck planned to show Troy's face to the press, let alone the whole country, and when an officer led Gabriella away, the ticking wall clock became the most prominent sound.

Vic Gera raised his hand again.

'Is it true that the secretive SCU tend to operate outside the law, and are you doing so now with regards to this case?'

The question stunned Breck. It was clear that Gera wanted to make a name for himself and Breck promised to make a mental note of the mischief maker.

'It's not how we operate here. Next question.'

Breck shot a glance over to Bashir and the volcanic look on his face suggested something was wrong but what? He'd find out soon.

Breck went through the paces and answered other questions until the press conference came to a close, and while a few journalists milled about and others left, Breck went in search of his boss outside.

'Is there a problem, sir?'

'Yes, there is. Who told you to push out the photo of Alexander Troy? I didn't authorise it.'

'I didn't know I had to get authorisation as the SIO, sir?'

'You are supposed to run anything that might compromise the case past me.'

'Not sure how showing the face of our prime suspect compromises the case.'

Bashir glared at him but Breck hadn't yet overstepped the mark. Bashir had to 'sell' his argument. 'It sends out the wrong message to the other Troy that went to Norway. I want him to know he hasn't gotten away with anything.'

'Sir, with all due respect he's a POI in this. The evidence points to the man whose face I've just put up on the screen.'

'I know that Patricia feels the same way I do about who you should be spending time on apprehending so don't get smart with me.'

Breck hadn't seen Bashir on edge like this before. He didn't like it one bit. It reminded him why he had sought a way out of the SCU by way of a new job, and while Bashir stood in front of him, there were a million things Breck could have replied with but saw no point.

'Is there anything else, sir?'

Bashir's eyes illuminated like a beacon but Breck's decision not to meet fire with fire worked in his favour.

'One last thing. The Front's march is still going ahead and the whole country will be watching us. Leave is cancelled for most officers except your lot.' Bashir lowered his voice to a whisper. 'The reason I've not called you into helping with it is because you've still got what is fast becoming a high-profile murder investigation to solve. I want results.'

'Yes, sir.'

'Good. You can go.'

Breck broke away shaking his head and cursing. Meanwhile, the Detective Superintendent stormed to his office and reached for his cigarettes. He opened the packet like his life depended on it. Deep down Bashir wished that he could do things his way and conduct proper policing. As it stood, losing his pension remained at the forefront of his mind and he found it hard to stomach. Let alone allow one of his brightest detectives to swim up a false stream. He lit up then locked the door and continued to puff the life out of the cigarette but couldn't remain still. He grabbed the phone and dialled a number which answered after two rings.

'Hello it's me. It's about that thing we discussed before, hold on, yes I know we're not supposed to talk about it again but I'm uneasy with it.' Bashir stopped a bit so he wouldn't muddle his words. 'All I'm saying is let my guy in on this. He might be able to...' Bashir stopped again, angered this time. 'Of course I'm not stupid. As I said when I spoke to Rose, I can assure you that no one else knows.'

Another lie. Kearns knew. He believed she had a right to. Bashir detested being spoken to like a little child and it appeared that the conversation would end an old friendship when a revelation was made. Bashir took a few moments to absorb it.

'What do you mean it'll be shut down? They're willing to take that risk. No support? Does Rose know?'

A stark warning to Bashir filtered through the receiver before the line died and he knew then that he had done all he could.

The Detective Superintendent had a heavy heart and knew that he couldn't look at himself in the mirror. He wasn't just ashamed at what he had become a part of, he was afraid too.

TWENTY
SEVEN

Breck walked past a junior SCU officer guarding the communal door that led to the new crime scene and after he stepped into the Cransham flat, it wasn't long before Kearns stopped him in his tracks.

'You're late this morning.'

'Sorry, got held up.'

A look of concern engulfed her face, followed by a

stark warning. 'It's not pretty so prepare yourself.'

'I always try to.'

Kearns moved aside while Breck went in to observe the marked areas. The speckles of blood. A cheque book and a clump of the victim's hair. He then took a closer look at the body of the teenage girl propped against the wall. She had been left in a similar way to Janet Maskell. Her pink matted hair glued itself to her face by dried blood and the most poignant thing were her eyes. Left wide open as if trying to say something and point Breck in the right direction.

Kearns stood close by and opened her notepad to relay the information she already had.

'Just waiting for confirmation on her identity. Her bag's missing. In the meantime, this is what I've found.' She unveiled a clear plastic wallet from underneath the notepad.

'What's that?'

'A blank cheque.'

'Why are you showing me a blank cheque?'

'I'm showing it to you because it's written out to a Mr Alexander Troy. There's also a missing cheque page from the cheque book on the floor. The numbers on both correspond. This cheque page was torn from it.'

Breck restrained his surprise. 'So it confirms that our prime suspect is implicated in yet another crime. Why did he leave it behind?'

'He could've been in a rush but that's not all. Look at the name of the account holder.'

'Breck squinted so Kearns held the blank cheque closer. He couldn't believe it.

'This is going to be a real problem.'

Kearns witnessed the concern on Breck's face. 'I know what you're thinking but just consider this. Our POI might have slipped back into the country from his jaunt in Norway – if he ever went.'

'What are you getting at?'

'It's a set up by our POI to send you in the wrong direction.'

Breck noticed that Kearns said 'you' and not 'us' but kept his thought to himself.

'When we get official confirmation of the victim's identity, send an officer over to notify her next of kin.'

'And we know who that is don't we?' Kearns said it with dread while Breck sucked in both cheeks and ran through a few scenarios, trying to figure out Troy's plan.

Kearns' eyes were busy scanning the area near his feet.

'What's on your mind?'

'I couldn't find a murder weapon but traces of cocaine were found on the floor,' she commented.

'I don't believe the drugs belonged to anyone other than the victim. There's no cellophane this time, so is it a different killer?' Breck questioned. He crouched in front of the victim and felt his own heart sink at the sad sight in front of him. A minute afterwards, Frank Cullen padded in. He greeted Kearns first.

'Pat.'

'Frank.'

'Arlo.'

'Hello Frank.'

Frank lifted each side of his trouser outseams then crouched alongside Breck. It didn't take him long to assess the damage.

'No cellophane this time eh?'

'I just said that before you walked in.'

'Do you think it could be a different killer then?'

'I just asked that question too more or less.'

'Have you two finished?' Kearns wanted Frank to get on with it.

'What do you think?'

'At the area of the head we have a severe wound that appears to have cracked the skull. That's my guess. There's ligature marks around the throat too. Most disturbing though, one of the fingers on the right hand is missing.'

'Why is that most disturbing?' Kearns asked.

'I believe it was done for no other reason than to punish her. Maybe the killer had been scratched. Anyway, we'll see what Bart says. I hear he's a few minutes away.'

'How long do you think she's been left like this?'

'Not long but I'd say several hours at least.'

Frank rose to his feet. Breck followed then turned to Kearns.

'Make sure she's checked for traces of semen please.'

'You think she was raped?'

His eyes ran to one corner of the room. 'Well her cut down studded shorts are over there.' Then he brought them back to where he stood. 'And her T-shirt is over here. Let's just make sure we're thorough with this because whoever did it is nothing more than an animal in need of putting down. Fast track everything.'

'I'll do the paperwork again, shall I?'

Breck didn't care who did the paperwork. He just wanted to catch the bastard that did this. He left the flat and inhaled the air outside, glad to be away from such a macabre environment. He sought sanctuary inside the Allegro.

There were now two dead bodies, connected by the name of Alexander Troy and Breck remained on course to unwittingly deliver Kearns' long awaited personal retribution. The knock on the window by his partner grabbed his attention. Kearns had something to say so Breck wound it down by a quarter.

'We can now officially confirm her identity and it's as we feared. She's Geraldine Van Bruen, daughter of Wade Van Bruen.'

Breck held his head in his hands and mumbled words along the lines of, 'Oh shit.'

TWENTY EIGHT

Ray Riley couldn't peel his eyes away from the voluptuous stripper dancing in front of him. He became hypnotised and aroused at the same time while she tossed a mane of hair from side-to-side. His visit to the club was made under the guise of 'a lead to follow' for his armed robbery investigation. No one questioned him because he led it. Riley had a habit he

needed to feed and he knew how to navigate the club enough to stay out of the view of its security camera.

In the backroom, Simon the assistant manager, placed his feet upon the desk and began to draw pictures. His mind was on the next concert that he wanted to go to with Geraldine and he loved showing her the punk life. He reached halfway through drawing a space-aged Fender Stratocaster when he saw a figure beyond the glass door. He crapped himself, dropped the pencil and removed his feet from the desk.

The door burst open and Ray Riley entered with the girl that danced for him.

'Get out. Me and Delilah need some private time.'

'What, now?'

'Yes now Simon, or you can watch if you want. You might learn something.'

Delilah giggled and it wound Simon up knowing she'd be untouchable as long as she remained Riley's plaything. It wouldn't be long before she started throwing her weight around either. Even demand preferential treatment.

A vexed Simon took himself out of the room and glanced back to find they hadn't even bothered to wait for him to leave. Riley had unbuckled his belt and pulled down his zipper by the time Delilah dropped to her knees, pushed a hand inside then pulled him out.

*

The brakes screamed when Breck took a sharp corner. It forced Kearns to hang on to the car's interior but she didn't say a word.

'I do understand what you said, Pat, about Geraldine's murder being a set up and the other Troy sneaking back. Me being sent in the wrong direction and all that. I get it, but I've got to follow my instinct on this.'

Kearns had tried. Breck would be difficult to control now but what would she do if he got in her way? Would she stop him herself –

do what she needed to? Breck shifted the car down into second gear.

'One of the officers found out from her neighbour that Geraldine's boyfriend works in a strip club around here somewhere.'

'There it is.'

Breck brought the car to a halt outside the Starlight Club. He had heard about it from Riley but never paid any attention. Never had any desire to visit. He pulled out a pair of knuckle dusters from the glove compartment and slipped it inside his coat.

'Come on, let's see if the boyfriend is one we should be taking a closer look at. You never know.'

Breck and Kearns went over to the club's entrance and were met by a bouncer. Breck showed his ID. 'I'm looking for Simon Wensthorp, the assistant manager.'

The bouncer twitched and Breck guessed that he must have had a brush with the law in the past somewhere.

'I don't want no trouble. He's inside.'

'Behave yourself and you won't get none.'

The bouncer let them through and the SCU officers walked into the seedy club. A few middle-aged men were scattered about, a drugged-up DJ, and a young lad who sat at the bar. His black trousers, shirt, and waistcoat, didn't match his punk hairstyle so Breck closed in on him.

'Do you work here?'

The lad turned around. 'Yeah, I'm the assistant manager.'

'How old are you, twelve?'

'I'm nineteen and as I said, I'm the assistant manager.'

'Simon Wensthrop, we'd like to ask you a few questions.'

'How do you know my name?'

'I'm DI Breck and I'd like to know where have you been for the last several hours?'

'I've been here working the night shift. Started from eleven yesterday. I agreed to do 'extra hours' that's why I'm still here.'

'Do you have anyone that can corroborate this?'

'I can.' It was the man operating the bar. 'Simon has been here. We've worked the same shift officers.'

A girl walked past and caught the barman's words.

'Are these lot police?' She didn't wait for the answer. 'They must be, I can smell the filth on 'em. Simon's been here for ages, we can't get rid of him.' Then she left satisfied, having played a small part in her boss's exoneration. Breck refocused his attention back on Simon.

'Is there somewhere we can talk?'

'Can't we talk here?'

'Let's go to the managers' office,' Kearns suggested. 'That's the best place.'

Simon panicked. Riley would go mental if he was disturbed and ended up being embarrassed. With little choice Simon slowed his walk when they left the main area of the club and this continued all the way through the corridor to the manager's office. As he neared he began to raise his voice, hoping Riley and Delilah would hear him.

'I wish you'd tell me what this is about, officers, I'm so tired and my shift ends soon!'

Kearns clocked on. 'Why have you raised your voice, you suffering from something?' She quickened her steps and brought Simon with her by dragging him along.

'Hey, what are you doing?' he protested.

Breck knew better than to intervene and at the door, Simon pulled out a set of keys then dropped them – on purpose. Kearns picked them up, now guessing he had something inside he preferred them not to see. She forced him to select the right key and he took an age to open the door that he never locked in the first place. An impatient Kearns barged past him and Simon feared the worse but didn't hear anything. Eventually he walked in with Breck following close behind.

Riley and Delilah had left. Simon sat down with a smirk on his face while Breck stood and fired off the questions.

'Do you know Geraldine Van Bruen?'

'Yes, she's my girlfriend.'

'Well I'm afraid that we have a bit of bad news.'

The smirk slipped off of Simon's face. 'What's happened?'

'Geraldine has died. She was found in her flat earlier today.' Simon stared at them as if the words didn't make any sense. 'The death is being treated as suspicious at present so I can't tell you any more.'

'What does that mean? I don't understand.'

'It means that the cause is inconclusive and we're trying to determine it.'

Simon became more confused by the minute. Breck positioned himself on the side of the desk and had a quick look at the security camera monitors. There were two of them. One picked up the bar area and the other spied on the punters entering the club. Breck rewound the tape and soon confirmed Simon's presence inside. When he spoke to him next, he wore a look of sympathy.

'We believe that Geraldine was murdered, Simon.' Kearns shot Breck a disbelieving stare at his unforgiving bluntness. 'Do you know anyone that would want to harm her in any way?'

Simon shook his head while the tears began to stream down his face. He refused to wipe them away.

'Is there anything you can tell us that would be helpful?'

'Dunno.'

'Were you two close?'

'Real close.'

'So it was a serious relationship?'

'We are…were serious. We had things in common and both hated law and order. Liked to do whatever we wanted.'

'The punk movement, right?'

'Yeah and I got her a friendship ring. Here's my one.' Simon held a hand up and showed Breck his ring. A silver band with a Greek key pattern.

'I need to know. Did you two have an argument recently or anything like that?'

Simon slammed his fists down and sprung to his feet as the anger poured out. 'I didn't kill her!'

It shocked Breck so he jumped off the table, slipped a hand inside his coat and thrust his fingers into the knuckle duster he had brought along. 'Relax. Getting wound up like this is not going to bring her back.'

Simon zoned out and whacked the telephone off the desk. He

looked like a bull about to charge. Kearns attempted to calm the situation.

'We know you're upset, love. It's OK to be upset but we're trying to help and want to catch whoever did this.'

'Fuck off.'

'Simon, please. My DI will put you down if you become a danger to us. Geraldine wouldn't want you to be like this.'

Those words seemed to seal it. Simon inhaled and exhaled at a furious pace then groaned before his legs gave way. He slumped back down in the seat and cradled his head in his hands. Breck slid his fingers out of the knuckle duster and put a hand on his shoulder.

'I know it's hard and a bit of a shock for you but if there's anything that springs to mind in the next couple of days please let us know.' Breck turned to Kearns. 'Wait here with him for an officer to arrive, then bring him home.'

'I'll make sure he's all right then look into the man that followed Janet Maskell lead you acquired through Benjamin Genta.'

'Great. I'll go to see Wade Van Bruen. See you in a bit.'

Kearns pulled out her radio and called for the nearest squad car to pick her up at the Starlight Club then cast an eye on Simon, a young lad in a big man's world. One that would swallow him up if he wasn't careful.

Geraldine's father, Wade Van Bruen, had already been notified. The next conversation with him wasn't one Breck looked forward to but one he had to have.

On the bustling streets outside the club Ray Riley kept his head down as he left via its rear exit. To meet Breck and Kearns in the compromising position wasn't part of the plan. Simon would keep his mouth shut about his visits. That's all that mattered.

Riley opened the door to his car, grateful for the security camera in the manager's office that allowed him to spot his colleagues when they entered. Ray Riley, one step ahead as usual, just the way he liked it.

TWENTY NINE

The embossed Van Bruen logo looked impressive but a sombre mood had already engulfed the entire company after news of Geraldine's death. It spread quicker than wildfire. Business was business and it remained open although Geraldine's father's grief increased after having just returned from identifying her body. Staying in the building helped him and being in a familiar

environment made him feel safe. Funeral arrangements were pushed to the back of his mind. He couldn't deal with those yet.

The receptionist with high cheekbones and a perfect fringe, directed Breck to the CEO's office so that when he walked out of the lift, he'd know where to go. He reached the correct floor and saw two security men guarding Van Bruen's office. Their threatening stance surprised him, even after he flashed his identification and the not-so-slim one stared at it in a way that suggested he had failed to complete his school education.

'No one's allowed in.'

'Mr Van Bruen's expecting me.'

'No one!'

A flicker of tension grew. 'You're making this harder than it needs to be.'

'I've got a job to do.'

The not-so-slim one went to push Breck away but before he could touch him, Breck took a step back, grabbed his fingers then twisted them. He cried out in pain.

'Let go!' he begged.

Breck released him and prepared for whatever would happen next but the slimmer of the two guards had a quiet word with his colleague. Then both men stepped aside. Breck entered Van Bruen's office and saw the man himself, standing by a window while staring down onto the streets below with his hands locked behind his back.

'Mr Van Bruen.'

Wade Van Bruen didn't face him, not yet anyhow. 'I know who you are,' he said. 'The first thing I did was find out who you were after we first met. How long you've been serving, who you served under and what you're like.'

Breck walked to the centre of the room then Van Bruen turned around.

'May I ask why?'

'Because you were investigating a murder involving one of my employees. Now you will be investigating my daughter's murder too. Have a seat, please.'

Breck sat down at the pine desk and his own reflection shimmied off the surface. Van Bruen moved away from the window to step across the thick carpet to the safety of his seat. The office didn't contain much clutter and the sheer size appeared to be just a statement of power and wealth. Close up, Breck could see that Van Bruen's eyes were red from crying. He watched him as he pulled out a drawer.

'Do you have children, Mr Breck?'

'No.'

'Well let me tell you that even when they grow up you still remember when they were young. When they depended on you. As a parent you never forget that so let me show you what I want to do to the bastard that killed my little girl.'

Breck raised a hand. He couldn't let Van Bruen's grief dictate the proceedings.

'I know you're going through a difficult time, Mr Van Bruen, but I need to ask you a few routine questions.' Van Bruen gestured his agreement by the use of a hand and pulled out a box of tablets from his drawer. When he saw that the box was empty he tossed it to the side and slammed the drawer shut.

'Was she in any trouble?'

Van Bruen shook his head. 'We both know my employee Alexander Troy is behind this, as a sort of twisted revenge. He's sick and I want the son of a bitch caught.'

'At this stage sir, we don't know for certain.'

The phone rang and Van Bruen switched his attention towards it without any desire to pick it up. The phone shrilled until it died and Van Bruen's mood worried Breck. He considered if it was worthwhile continuing.

'Do you need a moment?'

'No, Mr Breck. Did you know that Geraldine's mom died when she was two-years old? I had to make sure she'd be safe always and thought that would be the case if she studied over here in England.' Van Bruen's eyes began to wander, as if trying to remember the thing they were supposed to find.

'When did you last speak with your daughter?'

'Day before last. We had planned to meet up tonight for dinner. In some ways, she was becoming a ghost figure to me and I wanted us to reconnect.'

A knock at the door interrupted the conversation. Lizzie Daniels entered. She paused as soon as she saw Breck but Van Bruen beckoned her in.

'Do you need anything, Wade?'

'More aspirin,' Van Bruen said. 'My head hurts.'

Lizzie picked the phone and buzzed through to Van Bruen's secretary. 'Bring in two aspirin and a glass of water please.' Then she turned to Breck. 'Sorry to interrupt.'

'That's fine. It's good that you're around to support Mr Van Bruen.'

'I don't know what's going on, first Janet and now this.'

She threw a worried glance over and Breck left his seat to walk over to the window where the CEO had stood just moments earlier, intrigued to see what he had seen. People, taxis, red buses. A vibrant London. Breck turned around and aimed a question at Lizzie.

'Did Geraldine ever meet Troy?'

'I don't think so,' she said.

Van Bruen jumped in. 'Are you saying that my daughter and Troy we're together?'

'No I'm not. Troy is in a relationship and your daughter had a boyfriend who we've spoken to. I just want to know if they have ever met.'

'Is my daughter's boyfriend a suspect?'

'No. Simon's devastated and happened to be working late at the time of her death so he's in the clear.'

'Saw him once and told her to end it. Of course, she didn't listen to me and became involved with the punk scene. I hoped it would just be a phase,' Van Bruen reflected.

Breck opened his notepad. 'From what we know Geraldine was last seen arriving home alone so I have officers speaking to a host of her student friends to see if we can gain any significant information.'

'Tell me, Detective Breck, do you believe Troy is responsible?'

'I don't know but we found a cheque written out in his name.'

'Is this about money?'

'Not sure but I shouldn't have even told you that, I'm sorry.' Breck figured that there was nothing much more to gain by questioning the mourning father any further. 'If Troy makes any contact Mr Van Bruen please let me know.'

'I'll kill him myself first if he does.'

Breck understood how he felt, how any father would feel in his situation and left the office, ignoring the glare from the two security guards until a recollection of the past forced him to stop.

'Wesley Thomas. I remember you now, I locked up your dad.' The grimace from the not-so-slim Wesley became fierce. 'How's he doing? No, don't answer that I can only guess. He's got a fifteen-year stretch because he fell asleep at the wheel. Not a good advert for a getaway driver is it?'

By this point, Wesley's colleague held him back, much to Breck's amusement. After getting the reaction he sought, he walked away and left the Van Bruen building.

*

Breck neared his desk at the station to hear the buzzing tap of Kearns' fingertips on the Olivetti Letterra, typing up the latest report.

'How's Simon doing?'

'He's in pieces but his dad was at home. He looked like a waste of space to me but at least the boy's not alone. He has a lot of anger buried inside him so this won't help but what can we do?'

'Not much I suppose. Any news on the man that spied on Janet Maskell?'

'No, nothing. It's a total dead end. I checked the most obvious candidates on our list but I couldn't prove any of them followed her that day.' Breck was disappointed,

Kearns paused the typing. 'How did it go with Wade Van Bruen?'

'Painful to say the least and rather sad watching this powerful man that can get anything he wants, be in so much pain.'

Kearns slid over a message for Breck. He angled his head sideways to read it.

'Duty calls,' she teased. 'You were the one that wanted everything fast tracked.'

'Thanks for the reminder.' Just the thought of the mortuary – this time for Geraldine' post-mortem – made him queasy. 'Well seeing as you filled in for her with Janet Maskell's one, get Beatrice on it.'

'I knew you'd say that. It's already sorted and she's on her way. Once it's done Frank will prioritise getting his report finished to help us.'

THIRTY

Breck waited for Beatrice by hovering around her desk, eager to hear Bart's findings from Geraldine Van Bruen's post-mortem, and Frank's official cause of death. To pass the time, he considered giving Molly a ring to see how she was doing when Beatrice appeared.

'Who are you waiting for?' she asked.

'You.'

She offered a tired response. 'Me?'

'What's wrong?' She didn't want to say so Breck pushed her. 'Come on, spill it.'

'I thought it'd be easier working alongside you by drawing the line after our chat in the function room, but it's proving difficult sometimes.'

'I don't get it. Since then you said you wanted to partner me and that I'd be a good mentor.'

'All those things are true but sometimes when I get a quiet moment and think about us...'

Breck stamped out this pattern of thought before it went any further. 'It'll be fine, we're working together well. As far as I see it, we shared a drunken kiss that's all. We didn't sleep with each other so don't worry about it,' Breck, said, gaining the confidence to admit what had happened between them.

Beatrice considered his words unsure of whether or not to accept them as the truth while she dug out the report and her notes from her handbag. The notes were separated so she put them into order before she began.

'Ignore me, I'm being silly.'

'Right, what have you got for me?'

'As you instructed Kearns when you inspected the body, Geraldine was checked for traces of semen but there was no evidence of rape. Bart said that the temperature of the body indicated she'd been deceased for several hours before the officers found her.'

'Several hours. OK, just as Frank said,' Breck recalled.

'Her body displayed traces of cocaine and cannabis use, and the jagged teeth pattern against the bone of the severed finger tells us it was caused by a serrated blade. Bart found haemorrhaged tissue at the injury point.'

'Cause of death?'

Beatrice flipped over to the next page. 'As recorded by Frank at the Coroner's Office, asphyxiation. From what Bart said, her windpipe had been broken and he found haemorrhaging around the eyes. Bart identified two ligature marks around the neck which meant that her oxygen supply became limited at some point. He also found evidence of cyanosis around her lips.'

'I'm no expert but the asphyxiation suggests the mutilation occurred after death. Anything else?'

'Bart mentioned that the severance of her finger was not done with any surgical skill, and that a blunt instrument caused the head wound that cracked her skull.'

'Thank you, Bea, that's very helpful.'

Janet Maskell and Geraldine Van Bruen had both been strangled in their flats. Both victims were female, and both were linked together through the Van Bruen name. Breck made his mind up. It had to be the same killer. Regardless of what Kearns had said or would continue to say, his eyes remained on the prime suspect as the one to bring in. First, Breck needed to anticipate Troy's next move and he knew how to play dirty if he had to. The B&B lead that Jacob Simpson provided now grew more important by the second.

THIRTY ONE

It happened by accident. Breck found Kearns sitting in Bashir's office again and they were talking at length, but Bashir spotted Troy watching and raised his voice. It prompted Kearns to perform an awkward shift in her seat. It wasn't long before Bashir called Breck in and Kearns switched the conversation when he entered.

'I take full responsibility at the time of the incident, sir.'

Bashir's upper body remained rigid while the soles of his shoes pressed hard against the floor.

'Detective Chief Superintendent Rose is not happy with your account of things that's why I need this recap from you. Now you say a fight broke out and the suspect saw his opportunity to make a run for it. That bit I understand but Troy was under arrest and you failed to cuff him. Come on, Patricia, you're an experienced officer.' Kearns feigned embarrassment. 'I have no choice but to give you an informal verbal warning. You will get it confirmed in writing and it will remain active for a period of six months.'

She glared at Bashir for a few seconds. It was all a big show but she knew the drill and daren't say anything, which left Breck to intervene just to save her from more punishment.

'Sir, we've sent the suspect's details to all ports and airports in case he tries to leave the country. We've also checked his home address to see if we can find any clue to his whereabouts. So far we've found nothing apart from bank statements.'

'How are we with verifying who's who?'

'It's a bit of a struggle if I'm honest. I'm now trying to get access to old files from Alexander Troy's school. Both men highlighted the same one from what we can see on various documentation we have obtained.'

Bashir waved them away and Kearns went to get herself a glass of water while Breck headed straight to his desk and rang Morten Hoebeck in Norway. He wanted an update on the POI.

'Ah Allo. Help you, can I?'

'Hello. I need to speak to Morten Hoebeck. It's Arlo Breck from the SCU in London.'

That seemed to excite the young man on the other end of the line. 'Wait, wait. I get him. Yes, wait.'

After a few moments, Morten arrived.

'Hello, my friend. You good?'

'Yes, well as best as I can be. How are things your end?'

'Ah busting drug dealers seems to be the thing at the moment. You ringing about your POI?'

'Yes, any news?'

'Well my boss has been off ill for a few days so I was able to deploy someone to check with passport control. I'm afraid his details haven't appeared anywhere. You sure he came this way?'

'That's the information we have. Can you keep this open for me?'

'Yes, I'll continue to keep an eye on things here and will let you know if anything arises.'

'Thank you, friend. Take care.'

When Kearns returned to her seat she placed her water on the desk. Breck joined her.

'What's next on the agenda?' he asked.

She was mindful of keeping the options open for him. 'Maybe we should be looking into the payments Janet made to Benjamin. Do we believe him?'

'I don't see why not. He's got no need to lie about that and he has an alibi.'

'It's possible he may have had an accomplice.'

'I don't understand why you'd think that.' Kearns had no answer for the suggestion either and to herself, blamed it on her desperation to keep him away from the prime suspect.

'Come on, let's go. I want to get out.'

They left the building and sat in the car, debating where to go to next. The visit to the B&B would be later. Train tickets had been booked. So what to do now, visit Benjamin Genta again or Peter Clarke? This debate continued until the rear door opened then the conversation ceased. Beatrice hopped in with her coat on and handbag over her shoulder. Breck went first.

'What are you doing?'

'Joining the both of you.'

Kearns stepped in. 'Why?'

'Because I know where Troy's girlfriend Ceinwen works.'

'Where is she then?'

'I'll show you where. She holds a senior managerial position within investments.'

'Give us the address and then you can leave our car.'

'Sorry, no can do.'

Kearns became agitated. 'Listen, Bea, we'll need to speak to her bosses and find out what they know.'

'I've already done that. She's been at her place of work for four years, achieved their star award for best yearly performance, and is currently away on business in America. I've seen a photo of her on their marketing material so I know what she looks like too.' Breck half-turned his body to get a better view of Beatrice.

'What's going on here, Bea?' he asked.

'Ceinwen returns to the UK today and I know where she is going to be.' Kearns swore under her breath. 'We can stay here all day if you want but we're running out of time,' Beatrice reminded them, 'and if Bashir finds out that you've let a genuine lead slip then someone will be for the high jump.'

Breck could see the thunder clouds circle above Kearns but ambition wasn't frowned upon at the SCU. If someone showed the aptitude for getting things done they'd be encouraged. It's how Breck got to the rank of detective inspector.

'She's done well getting this information, Pat. She can ride with us.'

Kearns couldn't disagree even if she wanted to, for good reason. Breck turned around.

'That's settled then,' he said. 'Let's get going. 'Where to Bea?'

'Heathrow.'

Kearns spied on Beatrice through the rear-view mirror, secretly proud of the way the detective constable had the audacity to force their hand. It reminded her of when she started out with the ambition and determination to get ahead. Of course, she'd never tell Beatrice that and no other words were spoken on the journey, but they all knew that finding Ceinwen would be one of the most significant steps in the investigation.

THIRTY TWO

Hunger had already begun to sting the inside of Troy's stomach so he bought a sandwich from a kiosk near Waterloo Station. The seller didn't even look at him. He just wanted the money and Troy paid then devoured the sandwich in seconds. He pulled a hat borrowed from Clarke, down over his head and went in search

of a phone box. The last thing he wanted was to be seen, so his heart almost stopped when a police officer walked by. Much to his relief nothing happened, so Troy went on his way, jumped on the Vespa that Clarke had rented for him, and went looking for a phone box. He found one at the other end of Waterloo Bridge.

He jangled the loose change that Peter Clarke had given to him and recalled their discussion. They had looked at the various ways of clearing his name and being a defence lawyer for a few individuals the law would describe as wrongdoers, Clarke also submitted other options. Last chance options. Troy knew Breck and Kearns' had visited his friend, knew they were on his tail and wouldn't let up. And if they caught him then what? He hoped it wouldn't come to that because if it did, he'd make sure he'd be the last one standing.

Troy pushed money into the coin slot and dialled a number from memory.

'Hello?' The velvet voice was female and one he didn't recognise.

'I'd like to speak to Proctor please.' He could ring the number another five times in the next few minutes and it'd be a different voice every time. That's how it worked.

'Primary extension?'

'It's 445883221.'

'Secondary extension?'

'It's 900100134.'

'May I ask who's calling?'

'Alexander Troy.'

'One moment please.'

Troy hated these periods of silence where he had to wait, hanging on for the unexpected and always fearing the worst. He needn't have worried.

'Hello, Alex, you well?'

He recognised the voice this time. It was Proctor. An old Etonian with impeccable manners and a penchant for loyalty.

'I'd love to say yes but I'm in a bit of a tight spot.'

'I'm listening.'

'The police pulled me in and now I'm implicated in the murder of a finance director at my firm. It's bullshit but I guess you may already know this?'

'Conversations have already taken place.'

'Did those conversations discuss how to get me out of this mess?'

There was a long unexpected pause from Proctor which worried Troy. 'It's all ongoing but there's also a lot of other things happening here that is slowing the process.'

'What things?'

'Nothing for you to worry about.'

Troy's grip tightened around the receiver. 'Are you sure about that?'

'Yes I am. Now, we don't know who is behind this yet but we're working on it. There is the chance that you are being followed too so be aware of that.'

'Anything else that I should know about?'

'Ceinwen will be back in the country today on flight 4407 and when she is, take her under your wing. There's a safe house for you in Cardiff so I'll get the address sent to you.'

'But you don't know where I'll be, I don't even know where I'll be.'

'Don't worry about that part.'

'Let's get this sorted out because what's happening at the moment is becoming very dangerous to everything we're trying to do.'

'Agree,' Proctor said then the line went dead. He and Troy never said goodbyes. Didn't believe in them.

Troy left the phone box. He jumped on the Vespa and surprised himself by enjoying the ride until he spotted a Ford Capri through the wing mirror. He remembered Proctor's warning. It followed him at every turn and his first thought was to shake it, but then he had another idea. Troy travelled to Blackfriars and once there, parked the Vespa outside a pub and hooked the open face helmet on the handle bars.

Inside, photographs of professional and amateur boxers adorned the walls with many of them having trained in the working gym upstairs. Troy had visited once and always felt that it was a good place to 'hang out' for a while. He found a spot by the window and waited.

The silver Capri swept in and stopped outside. Then a man with shoulder length dark hair and blond highlights jumped out and walked across the road, perhaps believing Troy had headed in that direction. Troy left his seat by the window to investigate but by the time he reached outside he had lost him.

Troy peered into the Capri via its side windows but saw nothing of significance inside. He knelt down in front of the car and toggled the registration number and within moments the fake number plate loosened. He was about to snap it off, then he saw the man return, so he dashed back into the pub.

Troy skipped up a few flights of stairs to the entrance of the gym. A woman sat behind a desk, flicking through a magazine, with a mesh of hair obscuring one of her eyes. Her lips were full and under a different set of circumstances and in another lifetime, Troy might have asked her for a date.

'I'd like to use the gym. Do you offer a try-out session first?'

She smiled then reached down into a box beside her chair and pulled out a form.

'Fill this out and you'll be entitled to one free session.' She handed it over to him. 'Just write down your details.'

Troy filled out the form then slipped it back to the girl. She checked it with a glance and placed it into a tray. When she handed him a temporary gym pass Troy said, 'Thank you,' then waltzed through a set of double doors.

Men sparred with each other in the main single ring, while shouts of encouragement from their trainers floated in between the boisterous clank of creaking iron. The weight machines were located at one side of the gym, occupied by a few males obsessed with rivalry. One or two raised their heads, flexing sculptured bodies, while completing two to three reps with free weights.

Troy ventured into the changing room which was nothing to sing home about. The lockers were two feet in length and about a foot and a half in width. He needed to have his own padlock to use it which he didn't, so he placed Clarke's borrowed coat on a peg then went back into the gym. Troy grabbed two dumbbells and stood near a window.

It allowed him to peer straight down onto the Capri to see that its headlights were on. Troy didn't know what to make of it until the lights went off and the man exited then made his way into the pub.

Troy prepared for him to come up to the gym and swapped the dumbbells for a curling bar. Then positioned himself next to a group of guys that were shadow boxing.

A minute passed, then two, then three. No matter how long he waited the man never emerged, so he handed the curling bar to a young hopeful and went back to the window. He was just in time to see the man return to the Capri and start it up. Troy planned to tail him so he bolted into the changing rooms, grabbed the coat, and rushed out to see the Capri fade into the distance once he reached the Vespa. Too late.

Troy threw a fist into the handle bars, frustrated at his obvious failure without wanting to dwell on it. These things happened so his mind moved onto flight 4407. Go to the airport and collect Ceinwen. However, his frustration continued. After starting the Vespa Troy realised he never had enough petrol to get him there. Troy secured the helmet to the scooter and went in search of a taxi. As luck would have it, he found one but knew he didn't have enough money for the fare. He played along as if he did and once he arrived at Heathrow, he waited until the driver slowed down.

Troy bundled himself out.

'Hey, stop. Where's my money?' the driver yelled in the distance. 'You crook.' But Troy ignored him and merged with the crowd.

When Troy bowled into the airport, he refused to make eye contact with anyone. Ceinwen's flight had arrived and he soon found her. A chic pair of sunglasses hid her eyes but it there was no mistaking the swing of her hips. But his smile turned into a look of concern when he spotted a security guard tug the arm of his colleague and point in her direction. He feared the worse before a man emerged from just behind her, well-built in a tatty brown suit. He made a run for it and airport security gave chase. Troy quickened his steps, followed Ceinwen outside, then hooked an arm around her waist.

'Hey, it's me,' he said, 'don't scream.'

Ceinwen stopped walking out of fear then she realised it was Troy. 'Why are you trying to frighten me to death? What are you doing here?'

'I missed you too.'

Ceinwen flung her arms around Troy. 'I've taken a much earlier flight so how did you know when I'd be returning?'

'I phoned your hotel and took a wild guess,' he lied.

He didn't feel it was right yet to tell her about his new status as a wanted man. Instead, he'd turn his appearance to his advantage. 'Let's go to your place and relax,' he suggested. 'I've missed you.'

*

The main décor colours inside Ceinwen's home were black, white, and grey. Anything with more than two month's collection of dust she binned. She had the tag of being high maintenance but that didn't matter to a man like Troy.

'We need to talk,' he said. 'A few things have happened to me while you've been away.'

'Fill me in.'

Troy inhaled a deep breath. 'There's no easy way to say this but the police think I killed someone.'

Ceinwen began to laugh. 'What are you talking about?'

'They think I killed Janet Maskell.'

She stopped. 'Your finance director? Are you sure?. Ceinwen ran her fingers through her hair. 'I don't believe this.'

He waited for her to speak again but the words failed to arrive, and when the passing cars from outside splintered the silence, they both became lost in their own thoughts. Troy still needed her to trust him.

'Say something, please.'

'This is real isn't it?'

'Yes, but I'm going to fix it.'

Ceinwen had missed him and if it were ever to be them against the rest of the world, then she'd live with that. She pressed her lips against

Troy's mouth which surprised him at first. Then he understood, and ran his hands underneath her blouse. He struggled to unclip her bra but it soon fell away and then he hoisted up her skirt. He ran his hands over her thighs and their warm bodies pressed together, wedded by the anticipation. Ceinwen felt the urgency of his excitement and drew him in closer still. Maybe it was because she missed him, or because she wished to escape a past that repulsed her. Whatever the reason may have been, when they had sex, it was the best she had ever had.

THIRTY THREE

Breck stopped the car outside the airport and lifted the handbrake. Kearns and Beatrice bolted away and he raced out too, determined to keep up.

The airport was busy as to be expected, and they believed Troy had been beaten to the punch by their arrival. Ceinwen would be able to fill in the blanks on the prime suspect, and give a bit of insight. Apprehending

her shouldn't be a problem. All they had to do was to locate her on arrival and then take it from there.

Breck caught up with Beatrice and Kearns who had now reverted their run to a trot. All three headed towards the terminal Ceinwen was due to walk through and Breck busied himself observing everyone they passed. Half-a-minute into their journey a large family had converged ahead to block their path. Several of the little children bounced around on space hoppers which made it impossible for the detectives to burst clean through.

'We need to pass, we're police,' Breck stated and that line would've worked on many families except this one's grasp on English wasn't so good and the chatter continued. 'Come on, we need to get through!'

'Vogliamo mangiare ora o poi?' one of the family members said which prompted Kearns to comment. 'I don't think that gentleman understands you, Arlo.'

'Great, this is all we need.'

It was then Breck heard someone in the group say, 'Papa, have you got all of your things?'

He homed in on the voice and approached the young woman.

'Hello there, we need to get through without delay. We're police.'

'Oh, so sorry.'

The woman began to instruct her family to move aside and let the detectives pass, while Breck worried that the delay could harm them.

With everything back on track, they continued to the arrivals lounge to find it almost deserted.

They saw a member of the airport staff standing around, so Beatrice and Kearns spoke to her. She confirmed the passengers from Ceinwen's flight had already passed through arrivals and checked out their luggage.

They were too late.

Breck noticed a bit of activity behind them between a group of security guards. He trotted over, hoping it might lead to something. He showed his badge.

'Couldn't help noticing your discussion I'm DI Breck from Cransham Police Station, is everything all right lads?'

'We're holding a man that's been acting suspiciously. We think he came to meet someone here but they either didn't turn up or he missed them,' one of the guards said.

Breck wondered if it could be Troy.

'What does he look like?'

'Around 6'1, well-built, light brown hair.'

'Can you take me to him? There's a small chance he may be the man that I'm looking for in connection with my ongoing investigation.'

'Sure, come this way.'

Breck followed the guard to the holding room believing the chase for Troy had gone on for long enough and had started to dent his reputation. It wasn't his fault Troy escaped from Kearns but he became implicated by association and wanted it rectified.

They turned into a restricted area then through a short corridor until they reached a white door.

'He's in there being interviewed,' the guard said. An excited Breck peered through the glass panel on the door but his face said it all when he saw the man in a tatty brown suit. 'Not him?'

'No, that's not him.'

The guard offered to walk him back but Breck refused. He knew the way and when he found Beatrice and Kearns, they were sitting down in the lounge.

'Where did you go?' Kearns asked him.

'Round the back, I thought we had a lead. False alarm, so it looks like we've missed her.' Breck turned to Beatrice. 'Do you think her workplace got her flight time wrong?'

'They seemed certain about it when I spoke to them.'

'Do we know her home address?'

'I can ask Xenon to give it to us. They're a bit difficult to deal with but shouldn't stand in our way if we mention she's part of our murder investigation.'

'There's something else I found out too.'

'What is it?'

'Troy's girlfriend shares the same employer as her husband.'

'Her husband?' Breck repeated while Kearns cursed.

'Yes, she's married to a Richard Phelps.' Breck and Kearns never expected to hear that and it explained why Troy had been so vague about her. 'Ceinwen's husband was overseas as well on the same trip.'

'OK, get what you can from Xenon.'

All three of them then left the airport. For Beatrice, there was no reward for her tenacity. For Kearns, it happened to be another mishap in her favour. For Breck, knowing Troy had reached Ceinwen first pissed him off and made him more determined than ever to get him.

THIRTY FOUR

A susurrus of wind rattled the window to break the silence and Troy turned to see Ceinwen fast asleep. He admired the perfect shape of her lips and the smoothness of her skin. He planted a gentle kiss upon her cheek then nudged her awake. She smiled but recent events worried her.

'We should go to the police and tell them what you

told me. You could say that you went for a walk during the unaccounted time and you just wanted to be by yourself. That's your alibi.'

'There's no one to verify it.'

'We have to do something now. I mean it.'

'I agree, perhaps soon.'

'I'll even cover for you if I have to.'

It was a sweet gesture but one that Troy knew his lover couldn't fulfil. 'Ceinwen you can't because you were on a plane. Also, being associated with me would be bad for you in every way.'

'I'm saying use the alibi, no matter the repercussions. For me, please.'

'What about your career and my career?'

She threw her hands up. 'We'll start again, get new jobs. Change our names and make a fresh start.'

Troy rolled his fist and bit into his knuckles. Ceinwen needed to stay put and run her life as normal, for everyone's sake.

'Just hang in there for me a little longer, please,' he begged.

Ceinwen she said nothing more and stormed out of bed. Troy followed her to the kitchen and the lapse in time did not alter her mood. He noticed that the sense of adventure she used to have had been replaced by dread and uncertainty, so he wrapped his arms around his frightened girlfriend. They spent a few moments listening to each other's heartbeat, feeling the warmth of each other's bodies, and Troy knew he shouldn't be in so deep. He had grown too close to her and broken his own rule. One day soon he'd have to pay the price. Ceinwen unburied her face from his chest. She had made her decision.

'OK, I'll hang on in there for you.'

'It's for the best.'

'When this is settled and you're free, have you ever thought about what would be next for the two of us. I'll be divorced from Richard soon I'm sure.'

Troy pretended the world wasn't that bad and held Ceinwen just that little bit tighter. He hadn't given much thought to the future – they were having illicit fun. The thought of something permanent was an idea he never considered. Although he knew other men like him who had taken that route he just couldn't envisage it. His conscience wouldn't allow him to.

Troy released Ceinwen from his grasp and switched on the television but while they were both watching, he witnessed her tenebrous expression. He hoped it would pass but it remained for a long enough to bug him.

'What's weighing you down?'

She couldn't hold it in anymore. 'There's something I have to tell you,' she said. 'It's about my ex-boyfriend. I know this may sound far-fetched but I fear he's going to hurt us. He really will.'

'What's his name?'

'Marcin.'

'Isn't he just a loudmouth. An idiot?'

'Maybe I overplayed that bit. Over in New Jersey he sent one of his thugs to follow me around.'

'What did he look like?'

'A tall man, said his name was Eddie and he had a distinctive goatee.' She drew the outline.

'Did he hurt you?'

'No, just scared me a bit. I'm fine.'

Troy didn't want to make a big deal of it. He needed her to carry on doing what she did without any distractions and unbeknown to her, he had anticipated the emergence of her ex-boyfriend.

*

Late into the night when Troy had fallen asleep, Ceinwen changed her clothes and left the house. She walked down the darkened street with her gaze pinned to the ground, battling to keep her courage up. She had told them where to collect her from in a bid to retain control. They didn't know she lived nearby and after she turned the corner a waiting Granada swung its door open.

Ceinwen paused and recalled the first time she met the man that would become her nightmare. She remembered travelling into work thinking about her latest argument with Richard that morning. It poured with rain too. She felt ruffled when she emerged from Goodge Street Underground Station, realising that she had left her umbrella on the train. If that wasn't bad enough, the heel broke on her shoe. Exhausted and fed up, she stood in the rain, looking at all around her and wanted to cry. The tears refused to fall. Then the raindrops stopped hitting her, but she could still see other people around getting wet. Ceinwen struggled to figure it out. Until she saw a man next to her holding an umbrella aloft. He held it over her head and she was lost for words. She thanked him and he introduced himself as Marcin, and he gave her his umbrella, insisting that she keep it. He made his request in such a way she couldn't refuse, and when he left, she watched him melt into the crowd.

Ceinwen arrived at work on a high. Being drenched didn't matter, neither did her earlier argument with Richard. Or the broken heel. It was as if someone had opened her eyes and she couldn't shake the feeling. She decided that the umbrella should be returned to its rightful owner so the next day, she completed the same journey. Left her home at the same time, exited the same underground station, walked towards the same bus stop. She didn't spot him but she continued the pattern the next day, and the next. On the fifth day she saw him again. Marcin said he had been hoping to see her too and a happy Ceinwen handed back the umbrella. They spoke for longer this time and he bought her a coffee. Afterwards, she accepted the invitation to dinner.

Marcin wanted to know so much about her that it became overwhelming. He showed interest in her work and thought her business skills could be better used. She asked how, he remained vague with the answer. He showered her with gifts and attention. A week later their affair began.

The change occured when he knew she had fallen for him. He began to take her for granted. His threats were veiled at first but very real and it scared her. Business became the one thing he did not wish to discuss in any detail. He told her he imported and exported goods but the drugs made him careless. One morning she saw more money than she had ever seen before and confronted him. By then, he had become a servant to the temptations around him, and it made him snappy and short tempered. He began to terrify her and almost broke her fingers once too. Then he was arrested and they locked him up.

She would've visited him in prison but he didn't want her to. Had he grown tired of her? Ceinwen felt confused so tried again with her husband Richard, and learned to hold back the words of protest when he'd say something she disagreed with. She put up with his petty behaviour and so it went on until she met Alexander. In an instant, Richard became a noose around her neck once again.

Ceinwen's recollections forced an impatient Eddie to push his head through the opened window and beckon her into the car. She jumped in, convinced that she was doing the right thing, all the way to Pimlico.

When Eddie pulled up outside Marcin's home he left the engine running, leaving Ceinwen to let herself out. She caught her reflection in the rear-view mirror. Her hair, lipstick, and mascara, made her feel cheap but she pushed those thoughts to the back of her mind as Eddie drove away. She walked to main door alone and remembered the house in better times, but these set of circumstances made it a much more difficult journey. Ceinwen took the deepest breath she could, readied herself, then pressed the doorbell.

A butler with the physique of a body builder, forced to squeeze into a uniform made for someone half his size, let Ceinwen inside. Overpriced paintings still hung on the walls – Marcin's attempt to appear cultured to his guests, and mini statures of naked Greek athletes were positioned in a line along the hallway floor. The butler led Ceinwen towards the dining room where she saw a table adorned with lit candles in beautiful bronze holders. They provided a romantic setting and an opened bottle of champagne had been placed on the table in full view. The butler pulled out a seat for her and by setting up the room, it was as if Marcin had stepped back into the past before the drugs, mood swings, the lies. Before the hunger for power took over.

Ceinwen never had a plan or an escape route. She used to be

able to manipulate Marcin and hoped she still could. Regardless, she wanted to feel positive so reached over and poured out some of the champagne into a glass. She swallowed it in one quick burst to steady her nerves. It worked.

She didn't hear the door open but felt a presence from behind and turned to see Marcin, standing in the doorway. His appearance hadn't changed much since the last time she saw him, and he stared at her with thoughts of yesteryear. Wondering what could have been. His dark sunken eyes were a testament to his lack of sleep and the smell of paprika, and garlic clung to him tighter than a vest.

Marcin placed his hands into the pockets of his beige trousers and rounded off his look with a lilac shirt. He stepped into the room and signalled to the butler to leave then grabbed a seat and placed it beside Ceinwen.

'You look great,' he said. 'We have food coming soon.'

After a lop-sided smile cracked his face he held her hand in a way that amplified his desperation. She shrank away.

'You said you just wanted us to talk,' she reminded him.

Marcin straightened up. 'Yes and we are doing. It's just that I haven't seen you in a while.'

Ceinwen had no idea how long the 'meeting' would last but she hoped it wouldn't be for an eternity. She felt uncomfortable sitting next to him, and although the dining room was filled with fragrant sweet smells, it made her wary. She drank some more champagne but decided against eating anything. Marcin would poison her given half the chance.

'Marcin, I haven't come here to dine with you. We were good once but that's all over with and I just wanted to tell you that face-to-face.' Marcin hung his head in a rare moment of vulnerability. 'Please just let me go, so that I can get on with the rest of my life.'

'You said you'd do anything to make me leave you alone, remember?'

'Yes I remember.'

'Sleep with me.'

'I can't do that.'

'Why?'

'I know what I said but you've twisted it. You'd force me to do degrading things just to prove a point.'

'You sound like you don't trust me.' Ceinwen silence spoke volumes. 'I guess you don't. I hear you have a new man and I'm not referring to your husband because he was never new. Does this new man treat you well?'

He knew about Troy.

'Yes and he's completely different to you.'

'Maybe I should tell your husband about your affairs.'

'We'll be divorced soon enough so you'd be wasting your time.'

Marcin could tell she had toughened up since they were last together and lost some of her fear for him. He needed to rectify that.

'You can't trade me in so easy. You go when I let you, not before.'

'I don't love you Marcin, don't you get it? Why send someone to follow me around in New Jersey and how did you even know I was going to be there on business?'

Marcin refused to answer and kept his gaze fixed to the floor like a sulking schoolboy. Whenever he did that something bad often followed. It would be no different this time.

'You're wrong.' He lifted his head. 'Maybe if I get rid of your new lover there'll be room for me again in your life.'

The musclebound butler returned to the room with food and Marcin rose from the chair to sit at the other end of the table. The butler filled the plates then left the room.

'It's time to eat,' Marcin instructed and Ceinwen's face crumpled. 'Anything wrong?' The change in him had begun.

'I'm not hungry. I've already eaten.' Ceinwen twisted her napkin in frustration, tired of his churlish manner. 'Leave me alone otherwise I'll go straight to the police.'

She gambled with that response but had nothing to lose. It didn't work. Marcin became incandescent with rage while she became determined to destroy the sick world which he had invited her into.

'If you go to the police you know what will happen don't you?' I'll wipe out your father then come for you.'

Ceinwen pushed back the seat and attempted to stand. When she did, she experienced a see-saw effect. Her head felt woozy and she couldn't work out why. Then she found the answer. The champagne had been drugged. Marcin's sucker punch.

Ceinwen tried to walk away, but had to hold onto the side of the table for support until her legs lost their strength and buckled beneath her.

She collapsed onto the floor after losing control of her body. She couldn't move and the drowsiness proved hard to shake. In a matter of moments Marcin stood over her, seething and clenching his fists.

'Understand something Ceinwen. I can do whatever I want, whenever I want and until I say otherwise, you belong to me.

THIRTY FIVE

Troy awoke on the sofa with blurred eyes, cursing his poor night's sleep. Too many things continued to occupy his mind so he thought it best to go for an early morning jog and clear his head. He toppled out of bed then hauled himself to his feet, completed a few stretches, then slipped on a red Slazenger tracksuit he had left behind the last time he visited Ceinwen.

He put her hideaway home at around two miles from the Surrey Commercial Docks area, and Troy left the house, and found himself running in that direction. The roads were quiet enough for him to be comfortable and it gave him time to think. He loved the freedom that a run offered him and everything rolled along just fine until he jogged past a familiar face. Troy held back and watched the man with the dark hair and blond highlights leave the Capri that had followed him. The man popped into a newsagents and Troy couldn't believe it. He didn't return to the car when he left so Troy tracked him, being careful to keep out of sight and at a safe distance. Or so he thought.

For a few moments after he crossed the road, Troy lost him and remained in limbo until a hand gripped his forearm, forcing him to stop. He had found him. Or was it the other way around?

'We like to bury the dead quick in my country so I'll afford you the same privilege,' the man said.

He hooked his arm under Troy's and shoved something sharp into the base of his spine, quelling any attempts to pull away. His eyes were devoid of life, nothing but a lingering quagmire of anger and hatred as he forced Troy to walk towards the Surrey Commercial Docks area nearby. Now closed and landfilled, some would say the perfect place to make a person disappear forever.

'I've been looking for you but you're a hard person to find.'

'Who sent you?'

'I can't tell you that but you've done bad things and there's a price to pay for doing bad things.'

'Who are you?'

'Call me Blondy.'

That didn't make too much sense considering the highlights took up just twenty-five per cent of his hair with the other seventy-five per cent being a natural brown, but Troy rolled with it.

The two men walked across the earthy cold landfilled ground and Troy began to drag his feet as a way of postponing the inevitable. He knew that everything would be over soon, a permanent over, so he needed to think fast.

'I'm going to be sick.'

Blondy's grip tightened. 'That's the least of your problems.'

'Come on, please! Give me a break.'

Blondy paused, considered it, then relented to allow Troy a moment. A silly mistake and he glanced up at the sky in a show of arrogance, which gave enough of a window. Troy pushed him and sent an uppercut crashing into Blondy's jaw. He watched him tumble then Troy straightened up and fled.

He ran back along the way they came, worried that more men might soon be on his tail, so his next steps were simple. This was beginning to look like something he'd need more help with so he found a phone box and dialled the number he never ever wrote down. After five rings a man answered.

'Hello?'

'I'd like to speak to Proctor please.'

'Primary extension?'

'It's 445883221.'

'Secondary extension please?'

'Yes, it's 900100134.'

'Name?'

'Alexander Troy.'

'One moment please.'

Proctor came on the line.

'Alexander. Why have you called?'

The greeting took Troy by surprise. He may not have expected a welcome party but he at least believed he warranted a warmer welcome.

'My problem still exists.'

'I'm aware but you need to give me time to fix it. '

'No progress?'

'We think the other Troy has ventured to a northern European country. They can't track him.'

'That's not so good for me.'

'Anything else?'

'After I spoke to you last time someone followed me. I lost him then but he found me again, just now. It almost ended for me in a bad way but I escaped, so it's a good time to get to that safe house in Cardiff.'

'The address is on its way, just keep Ceinwen safe and don't ring back until it's is all over.'

The line died.

'Proctor! Hey, Proctor!'

A furious Troy slammed the receiver multiple times against the inside of the phone booth littered with call girl business cards until he cracked it.

Don't ring back until it's all over.

What was Proctor thinking? Troy realised there was little he could do but something significant had changed. He needed to adjust too. Troy dialled the police switchboard and kept his message brief.

'This is for Arlo Breck of Cransham Police Station. I'm Alexander Troy, wanted for Janet Maskell's murder.' He paused for a second as the word murder reverberated around in his head. 'I'm innocent, didn't do it, but I've gone and done your job for you. A man followed me to a pub in Blackfriars. I was able to evade him by hiding out in its upstairs gym but I think he could be the one setting me up.'

The operator attempted to cut in. 'Sir if you could just...'

'Listen to me!'

At that point the Capri crawled past with Blondy inside, and the words became wedged in Troy's throat. The receiver fell from his hand and he eased himself out of the phone box after the car stopped on the other side of the road. The voice of the operator faded when Troy began to walk away with one thought continuing to warm his heart. He spotted the Capri before Blondy spotted him, otherwise he'd be dead.

THIRTY SIX

Troy tried to deal with his disappointment upon realising his message for Breck was vague with not much to go on. He blamed the stress of the situation and the fatigue for the loss of focus and noticed that Ceinwen had been downcast. When he pushed her on it she said she had visited a friend but he didn't know

who, if that friend was ill, or had if they fallen out about something.

He travelled upstairs to find her camped in her bedroom and no matter how many times he asked, she refused to open the door. He wanted to know if she was OK but received no answer.

'Ceinwen, say something. This is not right. I'm getting worried.'

'I'm fine,' he heard her say.

'Listen, you don't sound fine. What has happened and which friend did you go to meet?'

After a few moments Troy gave up and moved away from the door, certain that she would reveal the crux of the problem in her own time.

He used her telephone to notify Clarke about the Vespa and ended the call apologising, then considered leaving another message for Breck. He wanted to but convinced himself that trying to get the detective onside wouldn't work. Breck would not act on the strength of the message alone.

Troy walked away from the phone and swigged a bottle of beer he had taken from the fridge. He slumped down in a chair moments before Ceinwen entered the room. She moved away from him when he tried to touch her.

'Are you OK?'

'Everything is great. Stop asking.'

'You were crying upstairs.'

She ignored him and stared straight ahead. Troy shrugged and left the room to dispose of the beer bottle. By the time he returned Ceinwen had begun to wipe away fresh tears. She struggled to speak with any real clarity and Troy watched her begin to walk back out. Then she stopped, knowing that to leave him feeling guilty would be wrong.

'What's going on, why are you so upset? You can't just leave without saying anything. What have I done?'

'It's not what you've done it's what I've done.'

'I don't get it.'

'I went to visit Marcin, not a friend.'

'Why did you do that?'

'I went to see him because he promised he'd leave me alone if

I did. Since it happened though, he's threatened me again if I don't return.'

She began to cry so Troy sprung across and gave her a hug. She clung onto him for dear life, glad to have him near.

'What happened when you met with him?'

'He drugged me and the next thing I remember I woke up on a bed in one of his spare rooms.'

'Did he touch you?'

'No, I still had all my clothes on. He just wanted to show me would he could do.'

The colour drained from Troy's face. He knew of Marcin more than he cared to let on and his emergence at such a delicate time was not good news. In fact, he had become a serious threat to everything Troy planned.

THIRTY
SEVEN

The paperwork piled sky high on Kearns' desk but it didn't matter. She had other things on her mind and would be off to Yorkshire soon.

By her own deduction, they were a few steps behind with everything. She tapped Breck on his shoulder and gave him an update. 'Beatrice has liaised with Ceinwen's

workplace Xenon, she's registered as living with her husband so we sent an officer to their home address.'

'What did they find?'

'Ceinwen wasn't at the home she shared with Richard Phelps.'

'That means she and Troy are hiding together somewhere.'

'That seems to be the case. Her return to work date at Xenon isn't for a while yet so there's no point in keeping her office under surveillance.'

Breck's phone shrilled so he picked it up. Molly sounded distraught so he signalled to Kearns to move away, and made sure there were no other officers within earshot before he felt comfortable enough to speak.

'Molly what's wrong?'

'Arlo, it's like the world is swallowing me up. Can't take it anymore.'

'You seemed brighter of late, baby.'

Her voice escalated. 'I don't know what's happening!' I saw his face again as he pinned me to the ground.'

'Calm down, try and get it out of your mind. Everything takes time.'

'I can't! Come home, please. I need you here now.'

'Molly, I think we should see someone about this?'

'No, I don't want anyone to think that I'm crazy. I won't be strapped down and evaluated like a guinea pig.

Her tone worried Breck. 'That won't be the case. You'll have a conversation with someone that will listen.'

'You better get here now, Arlo. It feels like my head will explode, I'm telling you it does.'

'OK, I'm on my way, stay put.'

Breck ended the call and asked Kearns to cover for him so that he could sort out his personal issue. He kept an eye out for Bashir while he made his way to his car. He started it up then sped home.

Molly had no real family apart from an aunt so she depended on Breck quite a lot and when he arrived, he found her in the living room with the curtains drawn in broad daylight. She sat on the sofa and it took her a while to acknowledge him which didn't help his confidence.

He walked over to her and sat down.

'Molly I'm here now, baby.'

'It is you?' she almost whispered.

'Why are you asking me that? You know who it is.'

'What happened to me in the hospital? I want to know.'

'Why are you going back to that when we're trying to move on from it?'

'I want to know, please.'

Breck felt the time had come to be honest with her. 'You were in a coma Molly for a week and I thought you'd never wake up but you did. I visited every day, didn't leave your side at all.'

'You told me I was unconscious for a few hours.'

'A few hours, a few days, what's the difference?'

'Plenty, why hide that from me?'

'To spare you the trauma of it.'

Molly shook her head. 'I don't believe any of this is real right now. It can't be.'

Breck outstretched a hand. 'That man is not here, but I am and I promise you that I'm searching for him. I'm always searching for him.'

'Make me believe you.'

'I'm closing in, Molly. He won't be able to evade me for too long.'

Breck felt no guilt at his blatant lie. He had little idea where to find her attacker but his lies were what his girlfriend needed to hear. Hot warm tears trickled down Molly's face.

'What did he do to me?'

'Nothing, you were saved in time. Let's stop this now and go upstairs. You can get some rest.'

Molly nodded. Breck guided her to the bedroom and coerced her into sitting down.

'I don't feel tired enough to sleep.'

'Is there anything that I can get you?' he asked.

'Yes, a new head. Christ, I need a new head.'

'Stop it. What are you saying?'

'I'm saying, maybe you should send me away and let them lock me up. You know something's wrong with me.'

Breck refused to entertain the extreme idea of sectioning Molly. She'd get better, he just didn't know when. Right now, he didn't have a choice but to leave her alone for the journey to Yorkshire. There was little he could do but it seemed as if Molly's ordeal had taken a firm hold of her all over again. Before Molly's attack, their conversations were carefree and light. She'd talk about her job but he wouldn't mention his because he needed a place to hide away from the violence and the trauma of murder cases. Home provided it. Breck never believed that he'd hanker after those days again but he did now.

Breck went downstairs and made a phone call. It didn't take him long.

Upon his return he had a surprise. 'We're going to take a ride.'

'A ride to where?'

'You'll see. I'm dropping everything to do this now. I've just had a thought and I'm going to act upon it so help by trusting me.'

*

The car journey had been pleasant and Molly still didn't know where they were heading to. Although she wasn't quite herself Breck felt that a short trip would do them the world of good.

'Why won't you tell me where we're going, Arlo? I know it's not to a picnic.'

'You'll see when we get there. It might turn out to be the most important thing we do.'

'I want it to be something romantic like a picnic.'

'I can't promise that but I'll make a note of it for next time.'

They drove for another mile before Breck spotted a service station and pulled over. He felt peckish. Molly felt hungry too and was glad for the stop off. They left the car and made their way to the service station which was quite clean inside but carried a strong smell of petrol if one stood at the wrong end. A trucker with hands covered in grease, eating an egg sandwich, seemed to be the culprit so Breck chose to sit away from him at a table further down.

'Arlo, it's strange spending this time with you and unexpected, because I'm not used to you staying put for more than five minutes.'

'Hey, I'm not that bad am I? Anyway, what do you fancy?'

'A cup of tea and…'

'A full English? You can leave what you can't manage. Better to have the choice.'

That seemed to swing it. 'OK.'

Breck went to the counter to order but the woman behind it directed him to the waitress. He pointed across to her serving a couple of indecisive guys.

'I have no plans to wait here for the next couple of years. She's busy.'

The woman relented and took his order but her annoyance with his attitude didn't worry Breck in the slightest.

He returned to Molly.

'What's bothering you, Arlo?'

'Not sure what you mean.'

'Do you think I'm not going to notice you getting ready for an interview when you put on a suit that you haven't looked at in months, or a tie I last saw you wear to a funeral?' Breck was surprised by the fact he had been so obvious. 'So how did it go?'

'Not great. It was for a head of security position. The boss man, Garsdale, wanted me to go into detail about the work I currently do, to measure my suitability for the role. He didn't get it.'

'Did you tell him you couldn't talk about some of that stuff?'

'Yes but he didn't appreciate that fact.'

Their order arrived, a full English for Molly and a fried egg sandwich with a black coffee for Breck. He stuffed the sandwich into his mouth and drained his coffee, and while referring to Garsdale said, 'I didn't want to scupper my chances but I couldn't tell him anything much, you know that.'

'Yes, I know that you're some secret super cop.'

Breck smiled. 'The interview finished a bit quicker than I thought so now I'm just waiting to hear from him.'

'Do you even care if you don't get it?'

'Not sure. The SCU frustrates me at times but I wonder what else is there for me to do. Anyway, I need to tell you that I'll be off to Yorkshire soon, although I don't want to leave you alone.'

'Stop it. Make sure you go. You've got a job to do.'

'I guess you're right.'

'When are you off?'

'Next few hours.'

Molly rolled her eyes. 'Thanks for the notice.'

'I considered not going because I didn't want to leave you alone.'

'Alright, I'll let you off.'

Molly held Breck's hand and began to reminisce. 'Remember when we used to visit the lions down at the zoo?'

'When we were younger and carefree you mean?'

Breck glanced at the wall clock in the service station. 'We need to get going.'

'Where to?'

He almost told her then but held back. 'Get your coat on.'

They returned to the car and Breck sensed her growing frustration at being kept in the dark. He moved off and drove for a bit, before taking a turn up a dirt road. They were moments away from his surprise.

'You have to close your eyes,' Breck told her but Molly didn't cooperate and they were at the last hurdle. He pictured himself on his knees begging, so asked her once more. 'Please.' This time she played along.

'This better be worth it,' she warned.

Breck parked the car and led her out over the rocky ground, to where a swell of noise could be heard. Her pace quickened from the excitement. Then he allowed her to open her eyes and when she did, Molly saw the circus. Music and cheering emitted from the huge ivory tent.

'I can't believe you've taken me here.' She wrapped her arms around him. 'What are we going to see?

'The lions of course!'

'I just mentioned it in the café, this is mad.'

Breck felt that he had done something good at last by springing the surprise as they queued behind others waiting to get in.

'What about work? How did you sort this time off?'

'Don't worry, I'm taking care of it all. This is important.'

Breck didn't want Molly to feel any guilt at him being with her. He made the decision but hoped his half-truth wouldn't come back to haunt him. He had taken legitimate time for the extra hours he had worked. Hours that were never logged as overtime. He believed that he had a right to claw some of that back and Molly deserved a moment out of the house to free her mind. He realised something else too. He needed time away from the case. Whether it be a few minutes, an hour. Whatever time he could grab.

THIRTY EIGHT

Yorkshire

The murky Yorkshire air became blurred by thin sheets of silver mist and Kearns sat in a cafe staring out of the window, while the sound of sizzling bacon crackled. Breck went to the toilet, which left her to battle her own demons. Of which amplified, because she had returned home. This would be a fleeting visit without seeing any of her family. Dad died a few years ago but

her 'mam' was still around. A jealous woman and a master of put downs with a sharp tongue to boot. No wonder she didn't want to call home. Her sister could fuck off too.

Kearns took a sip of tea with a strained face because she had forgot to ask for sugar then Breck swaggered back in. He pulled out the money to pay for the tea and sandwiches, by which time, Kearns was already waiting outside.

She hailed a taxi and both of them carried their small bags inside for a potential overnight stay at a hotel, in case they needed to stop over. While Kearns spoke with the driver Breck pulled out his notepad which contained the address of the B&B that Jacob Simpson gave them. Breck hoped for his sake that it wouldn't be a waste of their time.

He stared out of the window taking in the sights like a tourist, and along the journey the driver began to talk about his life. He came from Uganda, one of the many booted out by Idi Amin, and complained about how hard it was to make a living in Callaghan's Britain. Discussing it seemed to be his therapy, not anyone else's, and about ten minutes into the journey Kearns signalled for him to stop the taxi.

Breck became curious. 'Why have we stopped here, Pat?'

'I used to live there,' she said so Breck stretched his neck out. Kearns pointed. 'The house with the green door.' Breck could sense that the place held a lot of memories for her, good and bad. 'Let's take a detour on our way to the B&B.'

She instructed the driver. 'Two roads down on the left, then straight down and turn right at the end of that road. Then left again.'

The taxi moved away and followed the route. It reached its destination then slowed down waiting for Kearns to confirm.

'Stop here.'

She popped a stick of gum into her mouth, stepped out of the taxi and stared at the house. Breck felt obliged to leave the taxi and join her.

'Are you all right?' She nodded but Breck sensed her vulnerability which surprised him a little. 'You don't have to talk about it if you don't want to.'

'Maybe I do. There was a domestic situation inside that house many years ago and a colleague and I went to investigate.'

'What happened?' Kearns wondered how best to answer the question and zoned out. She separated it into what did happen and what should've happened. The time had come to face the past because that day tied into what they were facing now.

'You said you and a colleague went to investigate.'

Yes, and met a man that scared me that day though I didn't admit it at the time. One of the worst.'

'Who?'

'His name was Larry Sands.'

'What did he do?'

'He committed a murder by slicing an innocent woman's throat. Then I believe he fled to Europe because his trail went cold.' Kearns spat out her chewing gum. It had lost its taste. 'He's still out there though, I know he is.'

The door of the house opened, neither expected that, and a wasted teen staggered out. Breck tugged her arm and as sympathetic as he was to Kearns' past, he realised that they needed to get going.

'Let's be on our way, Pat. Memories can sometimes weigh us down.'

They returned to the taxi and went straight to see Lance Pringle, the owner of the B&B. Breck instructed the taxi driver to stay out of sight around the corner, in case they needed to make a quick getaway.

Pringle's Bed & Breakfast had a lick of fresh orange paint splashed along the window sills, with little else to point to any evidence of a refurbishment. Breck pressed the doorbell with Kearns beside him and a woman greeted them with a face like death.

'We're here to see the owner.' She stared at Breck so he added another line for clarity, 'Mr Lance Pringle?'

'Me speak no English,' she said. 'No English.'

'Let us in or it'll be a long day for you,' Kearns warned and after the woman stepped aside to let them in, she remarked, 'It's a good thing she can understand it.'

A sheet of dust lined the surface of the reception desk along with a few unopened letters and several moths rested on the curtains.

The woman who let them in slipped away into an adjacent room so Breck pushed his ear up to the door and kept it there for a while.

'What can you hear?' Kearns asked him.

'It's not clear. I think she's speaking to someone.'

He heard her return so stepped back. The woman said nothing when she emerged and just carried on with her cleaning duties, so he pressed the desk bell, hoping that Pringle himself would greet them. By chance he saw figure flash by the window and alerted Kearns. Breck then bolted out of the B&B to see Pringle already in his white BMW attempting to start it.

He yanked open the door and Lance Pringle pulled a screwdriver from his pocket. He jabbed it forward and Breck tried to swing out of the way. Too late. It pierced his skin. Breck cursed then tightened his fist and threw a punch that smashed the bridge of Pringle's nose. Pringle groaned and held his face long enough for Kearns to reach the other side of his car and drag him out. She pinned him up against it.

'Cuff his hands behind his bloody back,' Breck barked.

'Who are you lot?'

'SCU,' Kearns informed him while applying the cuffs.

'Where are your uniforms then?'

'It's dress down day, mister.'

'I want my solicitor.'

Breck stayed on the other side of the BMW, easier that way. 'OK, let's do this out in the open shall we? Where is Alexander Troy?' Pringle turned his head away. Kearns gave him a clip around the ear. 'He's the man Jacob Simpson sent your way. That's the only information we've come for.'

Pringle's brain clicked into gear. He didn't need this hassle, especially today. He had an important meeting to attend later and couldn't afford to be delayed by anyone. His life depended on it. Screw Simpson.

'Troy never came.'

That reply confused Breck. 'What are you on about?'

'He never came because he was never going to. I owed Simpson a favour and he warned me you lot would be on your way down. He wanted me to make something up regarding Troy's whereabouts but I can't afford to be locked up right now. This has got nothing to do with me, honest.'

'You're lying.' Breck scowled, failing to pick up on Kearns' silence. 'I'll be back in a minute, Pat, just going to check inside.'

Kearns kept Pringle pinned against the car while Breck returned to the B&B. He checked every room, opened drawers and moved furniture around, but found nothing. Maybe Pringle had told them the truth. If so, why had Simpson sent them here and what he was protecting?

Breck returned to Kearns and Pringle with an option. He could bring the B&B owner to the nearest station and interrogate him but in doing so, would waste even more time.

'Where were you going when I caught you trying to make a run for it?'

The sun caught Pringle's eyes making him squint. 'I have a bit of business outside of town. I'm a business man, that's what I am.'

'You'll need to do better than that.'

'It's nothing illegal, honest. I've just got to meet a few associates, pay off a debt. Being late would be bad for my health if you know what I mean?'

Breck had enough. Pringle and his activities were a job for the local constabulary not them. He lashed out by kicking an overflowing wheelie bin, the nearest thing to him, and the rubbish spewed everywhere. Breck gave it a couple more kicks, imagining it to be Jacob Simpson's head as Kearns looked on.

'Come on,' he said to her. 'Release this idiot, we need to catch the train back to London.'

Kearns let Pringle go and the B&B owner wasted little time in getting as far away from them as possible.

'Instead of rushing back to London let's go to the hotel instead,' she suggested. 'It's already booked. We'll clear our heads and be fresh for when we head back.'

Kearns' suggestion made perfect sense and sounded better than anything Breck's muddled mind could manage, but he didn't want to. For him, there was still much more to do and not enough time to do it in. Breck declined the offer and went to find their waiting taxi.

THIRTY NINE

London

After arriving back in London with Kearns, Breck excused himself and made an unofficial visit. Ralph Jenkins, a fit man in his early sixties, raked up the leaves in his front garden with a purpose. He wore sturdy wellington boots and a body warmer while whistling Tom Jones' Green, Green, Grass of Home. By the time

Breck reached him, he happened to be midway through the chorus.

'Who are ya and what ya doin' sneakin' up on me?'

'Sorry Mr Jenkins, it's not intentional. I wonder if I can have a few minutes of your time.'

'If ya sellin' then I'm not buyin' from ya.'

'No, I'm not selling. I'm here to ask you about the night of November 1976 when you scared off an attacker.'

Ralph stood still for a while and gripped the rake even tighter.

'Wot about it? Ya not him are ya?'

'No, I'm not.'

'Come on, who are ya?'

'It was my girlfriend that was attacked.'

Breck felt a tightness in his chest when the words crept out. Ralph lightened his grip on the rake and expressed sympathy.

'I'm sorry, thought ya were a weirdo. Can't be too careful round 'ere.'

'I know that you gave a statement to the police at the time but if there's anything that you can remember which wasn't mentioned, it would be a great help.'

Ralph propped the rake against the wall of his home and walked around to the back. Breck couldn't be sure if his action was a rebuke or an invitation but followed all the same.

Ralph sat on a deckchair right outside of his garden shed. From the pocket of his body warmer, he took out tobacco and began to chew. Breck watched Ralph battle with himself. What did he want to get off his chest? He started to tap his knee about eight chews in then began to speak.

'I woz on me way home from work, retired now though I am. Anyways, mindin' me own business when I saw a man and woman in the distance, tusslin'. Never knew wot to make of it. Thought it woz just a couple arguin'. Put me head down and waited for me bus. Then he dragged the woman by her wrists, well I sed to meself summink's not right 'ere.' Breck's fists clenched instinctively. 'He woz pullin' her towards the bushes but the woman's screams shook me. I just knew summink woz wrong. I ran over. A jog to some but it woz a run to me.

Anyways, I ran over and started shoutin' all sorts. He came out, lookin' all bothered and I didn't know whether he…' Ralph appeared to be vexed. 'I know it woz ya girlfriend so I don't wanna cause offence.'

'I've come to hear what you have to say so please continue, Mr Jenkins.'

'When he came out of the bushes I didn't know wot he had done to her, so I clenched me fists, went up to him. Ralph imitated the moment. 'He woz panickin', I could see that. Then he ran away. Ya girlfriend had her clothes on but woz out cold. I sed in me statement, the man I saw had shoulder length hair.' The recollection affected Ralph a little and he took a few moments for himself. 'As he ran past me I swear I saw summink.'

'What was it?'

'Didn't wanna say at the time in case I got it wrong but I fink he had a tattoo on his neck. A triangle.'

'Anything else?'

'No, it's like I sed back then. I called the police and waited with her until they arrived.'

'Mr Jenkins, thank you so much.'

Ralph rose up and shook Breck's hand. 'How's she doin', ya girlfriend?'

'Struggling a bit with it all still.'

Ralph rubbed the base of his chin. 'I take it ya haven't caught the bastard then otherwise ya wouldn't be 'ere.' Breck neither confirmed nor denied it. 'No one bothers me 'ere and I'd like to keep it that way. This is not official police business so how about this, if ya forget ya came then I'll forget ya visited.'

That sounded like a deal that Breck was happy to agree to.

FORTY

Breck's focus now shifted towards Jacob Simpson. The squad car sped from the yard with a back-up vehicle following close behind. Despite Kearns trying to delay him, Breck needed answers from Simpson now. He didn't like being duped.

They arrived at their destination and waited at the

east entrance of the Riverdale Shopping Centre, where market traders sold bed linen, batteries and cleaning products, fruit and vegetables. Along with imported toys which would do well to last a quarter into their warranty. A consistent stream of people passed by and Breck held his radio close, ordering the other car to cover the back entrance. The voice on the other end snapped the line into life but interference disrupted the signal. An irate Breck slammed the radio against the car's interior.

'Come on, Beatrice,' he breathed, 'bloody answer.'

Kearns cracked her knuckles to ease her nerves hoping that Simpson wouldn't divulge their little secret. Beatrice's voice soon became audible.

'He's walking your way now, heading towards the exit!'

Breck and Kearns jumped out. Not wanting to arouse any suspicion they browsed at the closest thing while Simpson walked with a swagger towards them. He never saw Breck, who he headed towards as Kearns switched her position behind him. He had no chance when Breck sprang into life and blocked his path. Simpson tried to double back but Breck grabbed him and buried a fist into his left ribcage then stomach in quick succession. It knocked the wind out of him.

'You lied to me. I'd like to ask you a few questions so if I were you I wouldn't cause a fuss.'

There was little danger of that as Simpson remained doubled up in pain and on his knees. Kearns handcuffed him then led him away to the van in front of a crowd of people that had stopped to gawp. They acted as if they had witnessed the Second Coming. The arrest had been straight forward and with everyone back in their vehicles Beatrice offered Breck a 'well done' smile.

The journey to the station took just a few minutes. With no sympathy on display they handled Simpson with strong hands and his brittle body gave the impression it may break.

Beatrice led him to the interview room and then exchanged places with Kearns who paced up and down outside. It was all good and well arresting Simpson but Breck hadn't let her in on what had been going on in his head. Had he begun to mistrust her? He joined Kearns outside and peered into the interview room.

'Apart from leading us up a garden path, what else have we got on him?'

'Nothing much! He had a large amount of money on him which he'll claim he won at bingo or on the pools.

'Clarke and Troy must have plotted with him to send us down to Yorkshire so that should be good enough. Let's get this started.'

Kearns swung open the door to find Simpson slouched in the chair. She went through the legalities as he tried his best to appear disinterested and in a petulant act, threw the hood of his jogging top over his head. It infuriated Breck because he didn't like being messed about and he pulled it straight back off.

'You can be out of here in tick if you cooperate,' he advised but Jacob Simpson stared straight at him in defiance. 'What's wrong? You're not one to be lost for words.' Still he refused to speak. Breck sat down. 'Jacob, your reason for being here is quite simple so let's get straight to the point. You lied to us.'

'To us?' Simpson laughed. 'No, I might have lied to you, man.'

Kearns fumed. What was Simpson playing at? If she had a gun nearby she'd shoot him.

'What do you mean by that?'

'Nothing, just having a bit of fun. You should remember that everything has a price brother.'

Breck now understood the reason behind his misinformation. Money. Simpson not being paid created the problem, but unbeknown to him it was yet another lie. Simpson wouldn't tell him the part Kearns played in the whole saga. Breck turned to his partner and lowered his voice to a whisper.

'Do you believe he did this because of money?'

'Pay him and he'll do whatever you need him to do. If you don't pay him then he'll throw his toys out of the pram. But something else is going on here. I think he told us the truth about Troy travelling down to Pringle's B&B but let me have a few minutes with him. He owes me a few favours.'

Breck agreed. He needed to go to the gents anyway, and Kearns waited for the door to close before she spoke to Simpson in private.

'You'll tell Detective Inspector Breck that Pringle lied us. Troy did go and see him but he moved to an unknown destination.'

'What if I don't?'

'Do you really want me to answer that, love?'

Simpson shook his head. 'Hey, why hit me with the ashtray when you came over to my place. I've still got the mark. That weren't cool.'

'It had to look convincing, so get over it. Now back to business. You'll say afterwards that you think Troy won't return to London for the time being.'

'I don't get it.'

'You don't need to get it, just do as I've said.'

Breck re-entered the room and gave Kearns a quizzical stare, so she shook her head knowing he would assume Simpson had refused to cooperate. Breck returned to his seat.

'I want to know where Alexander Troy is.' Jacob Simpson stuck two fingers up which made Breck chuckle for a while before he erased his grin. 'Let me make it clear. If you make this difficult for me I'll push out word on the street that you've been helping us to catch all of your lovely non-law-abiding friends.'

'You wouldn't dare, you stinking lot still need me, man.'

Simpson had a point but Breck wasn't planning to let him know that and the detective sat motionless with a haggard frown, letting the seconds tick by. 'By the time I've finished bad mouthing you, they'll be scraping your body off Peckham High Street.'

That did it. Simpson began to scream obscenities but his throat soon dried and his tongue became a heavy weight. Breck's words preyed on his mind and destabilised him, so much so, that he hardly noticed Kearns.

'You lot make me sick. You're nothing.'

'No, I'd say we're something because we have you here and you can't leave. Now, we've had a few murders which appear to involve one key suspect. Troy. We know you've got a seat at the table with all your contacts, so we want to know what the guests are eating.'

Kearns wanted to move this along and prompt Simpson to follow the script.

'Let us cut you a deal,' she said. 'Someone's got to be held accountable. You know how it is, Jacob. We know that you're on probation for previous fraud offences so it will be easy for your associates to believe you've stitched them up in order to get away with a few things.'

Simpson wasn't pleased. Whatever he had given the police in the past, it was not something they were later supposed to threaten him with. That pissed him off.

'Right, looks as if you'll be spending a longer period of time here because we've made no progress,' Breck concluded. 'I'll arrange for officers to go to your flat and search the premises. Who knows what they'll find.'

'They won't find anything, man.'

'I urge you to tell us what you know about Troy,' he warned. 'We can't protect you if you don't.' Simpson threw up his hands.

'Pringle lied. Troy did go to see him but has now moved on to an unknown location.'

'How do you know?'

'Pringle told me after you let him go. He phoned me. I'm telling you, Troy is on a tightrope.'

'How do you mean?'

'You know? Tightrope, lose his balance and he'll fall off.'

Breck turned to Kearns and pointed towards Simpson. 'This guy's got a future in show business. Say hello to our resident Tommy Cooper here.' He returned his attention back to the hippy with a stark warning. 'Tell me what Troy is up to?'

Simpson winced. 'OK, you didn't hear it from me but Troy placed a passport order with a forger. He'll come back to London to collect it.'

Kearns' look of surprise wasn't picked up by Breck. From not initially following her instructions, Simpson had now gone over the top with information that even she didn't know about.

'How did he get in contact with the forger?'

'Through Clarke of course.'

'That bit will be hard for us to prove. OK, who's the forger and where is Troy planning to go to?'

'Man, you can find the guy at Bill's Snooker Hall most days. Everyone knows who he is.'

'Well I don't so have you got a description for us?'

'He's a bit of a fruit, in his mid-fifties, and goes by the name of Maurice Mace. Most people call him Mo.'

Breck knew him. 'Mo Mace?'

'Yep, I don't know where Troy is planning to go to but Mo's turnaround is several days if that helps.'

'Several days?'

'He's old school and won't rush. Got this thing about quality.'

'When did Troy first meet with him?'

'Not sure brother.'

An almost satisfied Breck aimed a wink towards Kearns at a job well done.

She remained in shock at the new revelations, while Breck hoped that the information which Simpson provided would jump start the investigation. He needed it to before it became too late.

FORTY ONE

Several cold black coffees were on either side of Breck's cluttered desk. He stared at it all, imagining that a letter from the Hardwick Stanfield security firm was just visible underneath a pile of papers. It caused him to panic. He had yet to hear from Mr Garsdale and didn't believe he possessed a realistic chance of landing the

job – a job which he was unsure if he wanted anyway. With weary and stretched faces, he and Kearns continued to mull over Simpson's information.

Kearns stretched her fingers out on the table and tilted her head towards the ceiling, pretending to be in deep thought.

'Jacob Simpson is a fantasist, making things up. As for inventing this scenario, I don't know, I don't think I buy it.' Kearns sniffed a couple of times although her sinuses were clear.

'OK, so we let him go?'

'He'll want a deal.'

'What for?'

'Future cooperation.'

'Confiscate the large sum of money he had and tell him we won't raid his flat. That's the deal!'

'If we do that then he might not help us in the future.'

'We've got other people to turn to if that were ever the case. He just happens to be the man of the moment. The best of the bunch for this situation.'

Breck reached for one of the coffees until he remembered it had lost its heat, and followed his realisation with a deep sigh. 'His future cooperation is not our problem, Pat. I don't want Jacob Simpson thinking I'm soft. In Troy, we've got a killer roaming around London, getting ready to leave. I aim to stop him.'

Kearns stepped in to steer Breck's thinking back in the direction she wanted.

'I understand but I do think we should focus more attention towards Norway. It's too much of a coincidence that our POI had a flight booked on the day he reported the attack. We may not know how he is linked to the victims at this moment but we know their connection is Wade Van Bruen. Our POI could have an unknown issue with the CEO.'

'I'm not going there Pat and I've been getting the impression that you think I'm wasting my time following our prime suspect.'

'To an extent, but I know we have to look at all avenues. Contact your man in Oslo and see if he's heard anything. It might even be an idea for you to pop over there.'

'Let me give you an update on something. I have our POI's car registration number which the yard's security cameras picked up when he arrived at the station to report his attack. From that, we now have an address so I plan to send a few officers up to his Camden home for a surprise visit. Even though he is missing somewhere in Norway his home just might reveal a few important clues.'

Breck had kept that from her and for the first time, Kearns noticed a real look of suspicion on his face. It made it harder for her to keep up pretences while Breck felt that they needed to put their heads together and figure out the whole stolen identity issue. Not waste time on Norway. They were decades away from pressing a button on a computer and getting an immediate answer. A little bit of indecision followed until Beatrice popped up with a message for Breck. Before she could deliver it though, he asked her a question.

'Bea, got any ideas on how we can pinpoint the real Troy?'

'What have we come up with so far?'

'Well...'

Kearns jumped in. 'Excuse me. This requires real detective work, Arlo. Not for a DC to give us three guesses.'

'Give her a chance. She's entitled to have her say. At the moment, if Bashir wanted me to give him a result I wouldn't be able to, and I don't want him to force additional assistance on me in the form of someone like Ray Riley.'

Kearns' partial sulk did little to dim Beatrice's enthusiasm, but after much head scratching she drew a blank too. They all took turns to stare at each other until Breck called an end to the informal gathering. It saw Kearns disperse back to her desk while Beatrice saw Riley head over, looking like he wanted trouble so stayed put.

'I heard things are not going so well for you,' Riley said when he reached Breck.

'Where did you hear that?'

'Everywhere I turned, people told me things. You can always join my team if this case becomes too much. I'll give you easy tasks that you can manage. Like, getting my tea and cleaning my shoes.'

Breck shot up from his seat and went nose-to-nose with Riley. He had enough and Beatrice intervened when Breck looked like he'd thump him.

'I've got a message for you and it's from a male,' she said. Breck backed down. 'He claimed to be Alexander Troy, the one we've been chasing.'

For Breck, no one in their right mind would pretend to be Troy right now so it must be genuine. He wondered why the message had just reached him but carpeting the lazy sod that handled it seemed fruitless. It would take an age to sort out and with things as they stood, it wasn't worth the hassle.

'What did he say?'

'The transcript is on my desk, come on.' Beatrice pulled Breck away from Riley, as she had intended, to diffuse the situation. 'You shouldn't let him wind you up. He's not worth it.'

'He'll get what's coming to him one day, you can be sure of that.'

She handed over the transcript and Breck let the delicate touch of her hand brush his for longer than he should have.

'I thought you said it was on your desk.'

'I didn't want to see you get into trouble over Riley. It was best to get you out of the way.'

Breck appreciated the thought but it became an awkward moment for them both until he focused on the transcript and began to read it.

ALEX TROY: This is for Arlo Breck of Cransham Police Station. I'm Alexander Troy, wanted for Janet Maskell's murder. [Pause]. I'm innocent, didn't do it, but I've gone and done your job for you. A man followed me to a pub in Blackfriars. I was able to evade him by hiding out in its upstairs gym but I think he could be the one setting me up.

OPERATOR: Sir if you could just...

ALEX TROY: Listen to me!

The call ended abruptly.

'Why did he just stop?' Breck asked the question but Beatrice couldn't give him the answer. 'Where did he make the call from?'

'He made it from a public telephone box in the Rotherhithe area.'

'I'm handing this to you. Check all the pubs in London Blackfriars and find the one with a working gym on its top floor, clear?'

'All clear,' Beatrice said.

Breck wasted no time popping over to Kearns. 'Pat, I need you to get Peter Clarke here pronto. I want to question him about his meeting with Jacob Simpson.'

'It's a bit short notice isn't it?'

'Tell him it's important.'

Breck readied himself for the meeting he had arranged until the phone rattled and he prayed it would be good news from somewhere, anywhere. After a brief conversation with Home Office Pathologist Bart Redmaine, Breck felt a whole lot better.

He now had the name of a man that could help him determine which Alexander Troy had been telling the truth, and which one had been lying. He couldn't wait to find out. Breck still wanted to believe in his own competence and looked forward to his impending chat with Peter Clarke, to see what he could extract from him.

FORTY TWO

Peter Clarke appeared to be relaxed. He reaffirmed the identity and occupation of his friend Alexander Troy, while still demanding the arrest of the man that he believed had been impersonating him. Breck closed the door to the interview room, knowing the time was right to question him again. His one regret: not having

the resources to plant an officer on him 24-hours a day. Peter Clarke possessed the eyes of someone that knew far more than they cared to reveal. Today though, it was Breck who carried the surprise

He ran through the usual legal spiel and proceedings which Clarke knew inside out anyway, and watched the defence solicitor sniff the stuffy air in the room.

'Does it bother you being here?'

'A little but I understand your need to do these things in order to prove the innocence of my friend. What circumstance makes a person steal the identity of another? What sort of rat would do that?'

The question ended with a curious stare and Breck planted his forearms on top of the table, palms flat on the surface.

'Have you any idea why anyone would want to impersonate Alexander?'

'For money Mr Breck; people kill for it, don't they? The man that is impersonating him is delusional so get him the psychiatric help that he needs.'

'We'll offer it after we catch him I can assure you.'

'I have something you may be interested in.' Clarke dug into the pocket of his trousers and produced a document. He handed over Troy's birth certificate. 'I helped with a bit of financial advice before this whole thing blew up and it was left behind.'

Breck never recalled seeing Troy's name anywhere on Clarke's client list but kept that to himself.

'Thank you for this, I'll need to take a copy.' The satisfied look upon Clarke's face blossomed even though Breck wasn't finished. 'Let me be honest here and say that we're at a crossroads. I want to know just who is pretending to be who, and bring justice to the dead.'

'I applaud your work ethic Mr Breck but in this country a man is innocent until proven guilty. Alexander escaped from custody but it's not a crime for a man to be scared.'

'No but it is a crime for a man to protect another that has killed, isn't it?'

'Quite.' Clarke shuffled nervously on his seat.

'Did you visit a Mr Jacob Simpson, with the prime suspect?'

Clarke had a blank expression ironed into his face. 'You represented him once on a case,' Breck stated.

'Ah yes, a housing issue. Why on earth would I want to see him?'

'You tell me.'

'Well I haven't. Not since we were at court and certainly not with Alexander.'

'Does Troy know Wade Van Bruen's daughter?'

'Sorry, who's Wade Van Bruen?'

'The CEO of his firm.'

'Not that I know of. Should he?'

The two men locked eyes in a mental game of chess that neither would win.

'Mr Simpson told us you visited him with Troy, and that he recommended a B&B outside of London, owned by a Mr Lance Pringle.'

'Why would he say that he recommended a B&B?'

'For Troy to hide out at.'

Clarke's face tightened. 'He's lying and that's a dangerous accusation. I'm willing to break him down in court to prove it.'

'There'll be no need for that, Mr Clarke. I appreciate you coming in at such short notice. Thank you for your time.'

Breck rose to his feet and showed Peter Clarke the way out.

FORTY THREE

Ceinwen's visit to Marcin still left Troy shell shocked. He underestimated the strength of his feelings towards her, which meant he failed to detach himself from the hurt and humiliation. However, with the situation calmed, she told him she'd take a nap. Troy tried to forget about it.

He switched on the television to take his mind off things but received a shock. Troy increased the volume because against a backdrop of blue partitioning, he saw his photo and that of Janet Maskell's on display. Flanked by Janet's distraught sister, a pre-recorded press conference saw Detective Inspector Arlo Breck address a room with a dozen microphones pointing towards him. The broadcast appeared to be a replay from a previous day and nearing its end. Breck seemed to be staring straight at him through the television as he described Troy as dangerous and advised members of the public not to approach him.

Troy switched off the television in disgust and paced up and down, trying to prevent his temper from exploding. Breck now believed he was an imposter and not the other Troy. Of that there was no doubt. His movements which were once cloaked, had been made much more difficult because everyone now knew his face. He'd lost a crucial advantage and he needed to react.

It took Troy a few seconds to reach the bathroom and locate a pair of scissors. He hacked off his flowing locks without a second thought and watched the long strands of hair fall like autumn leaves. Troy opened the cabinet to see if he could find anything useful to colour his shorn hair, and spotted the hair dye that he bought last month. Back then he toyed with the idea of changing the colour and left it in Ceinwen's bathroom. Now he needed to. After reading the instructions he applied it to his hair and it wasn't long before a new black no nonsense military cut, made Troy look older and more distinguished. Added to the stubble of growth hedged around his jaw, he could see the dramatic change in his appearance which pleased him. But the knock on the door didn't. Troy froze, dropped the scissors into his pocket, while Ceinwen slept.

He inched downstairs to see that someone had popped a note through the letterbox and peeked through the window. He didn't spot anyone. He returned to the folded note and opened it up to see Tyler, Cardiff, and an address, written inside.

He needed to speak to Proctor.

Proctor always seemed to know where to find him, a job which he did rather well. Yet, it made Troy wonder who had tracked him and when? Did Proctor always have his back or was that an illusion? It was hard to say but he'd rather have someone like Proctor with him than against him.

Troy dialled his number but the phone continued to ring. He hoped that someone would answer but they never did. He recalled Proctor once telling him that the number would never ring without answer. He lied. After ending the call Troy tried again but received the same outcome. It worried him and he wondered what had happened to Proctor.

Troy called Clarke then re-read the note that pointed him towards the safe house in Cardiff. After that he waited around for a while, spinning a lot of scenarios though his mind, then took a few five and one pound notes from Ceinwen's emergency money tin. She still slept and he didn't know if she'd be safer staying, rather than going with him. In the end, Troy grabbed a rucksack and decided to bring her along. He called out to her but received no reply.

Troy trotted up to her bedroom to find it empty. She had slipped out of the house without telling him. He had little option but to leave, he couldn't hang around, and when he heard Clarke arrive he opened the door and rushed out to meet him. Through the open window of the Range Rover, Troy handed the Vespa keys to Clarke.

'It's outside the pub in Blackfriars that I told you about, but I've got to leave now. I need to get to Paddington to catch a train to Cardiff.'

Clarke's face curled. 'Are you trying to do a runner?'

'No, just getting help. It's complicated.'

'I've a bit of bad news.'

'What?'

'The police contacted me again. Breck interviewed me not too long ago.'

'Why?'

'He found out that we went to see my contact Jacob Simpson.'

'Does he know about my passport request?'

'He never mentioned anything but it looks like Simpson told them you travelled down to Yorkshire. He might have done it to buy you some time.' Clarke paused, what he had to say next wouldn't be easy. 'He threw a strange one at me though. Breck asked if you knew Wade Van Bruen's daughter.' Troy was as puzzled by that as Clarke expected him to be. 'From my time as a solicitor I know they only ask questions linked to a case so I did a bit of snooping outside your workplace before I came here. I had a conversation with one of the employees who had popped outside.'

'And?'

'Van Bruen's daughter is dead and there are whispers that it's murder.'

'Are you saying Breck believes I did it?'

Clarke gave his friend an unconvincing shrug. 'When is your train due?'

'In about fifty minutes.'

'Come on, let's get going.'

Troy was about to hop in until he spotted a man hanging about at the end of the street. The tall man dressed in black, had a distinctive goatee and looked suspicious. Troy jumped into the Range Rover but kept an eye on him and after they moved off, he checked to see if they were being trailed. They weren't.

Troy relaxed but during the journey something inside his head clicked and the identity of the man became clear. Based on the description that Ceinwen gave him, it appeared to be Eddie hanging about at the end of her street. Marcin's Eddie.

Troy opened Clarke's glove compartment and forced his hand inside to grab a pen. He wrote down a number on the back of a torn envelope, while Clarke wondered what he was doing. Troy waited until the train station came into view before he tucked the envelope into Clarke's pocket.

'Ring Ceinwen,' he heard himself say. 'Her number is on the envelope. Tell her to go to her father's home and stay there until I contact her.'

Clarke gave him a bemused look. 'But I've never spoken to her before.'

'No time to explain. Just tell her that I think Marcin knows where she is.'

'Who's he and what does he know?'

'He's an ex-boyfriend, a violent one by all means, and now he knows about the home she's renting to be as far away as possible from her husband.'

Clarke shook his head in disbelief. 'I never knew you were with a married woman, and now there's a violent ex-boyfriend lurking about. You don't make things easy for yourself.'

'No, I'm not known to.'

Clarke refocused enough on the driving to swing off the main road and park. He switched off the engine while looking a little perplexed. Troy hooked the rucksack by his feet, over his back.

'Take care of yourself.'

'I'll try.'

'When will you collect the passport from Mo?'

'Not sure, but soon. I'll know when.'

Troy opened the door and slapped the roof of the Range Rover. Clarke gave him a thumbs up, hit the gas and sped away.

Troy crossed the road, pleased he hadn't been followed, and just happened to glance back without knowing why. Good thing too because a Granada came into view, and he saw the stranger that he spotted at the end of Ceinwen's road behind the wheel. Troy kept calm and ducked down, darted across the road then ran into the station to catch his train.

FORTY FOUR

Breck left Kearns inside the car and jogged across the road to enter Bill's Snooker Hall, where a few regular customers sat inside passing the day with idle chat. The Italian manager stood behind the beech-wood bar wearing a fugazi smile while touting for business. A parade of snooker tables covered the main area and

Breck soon located the person he had come to see. Maurice Mace. Better known as Mo.

Breck slammed a hand down upon the smooth baize and the tepid man closest to the impact froze. The outline of the nipple rings were visible from under his vest, and for Breck, his leather trousers were a tad too tight for anyone in their early sixties.

Mo stood maybe a few feet or so to his left, in ripped jeans and plain shirt, and showed a bit of savvy by urging his friend to go. The man fizzled away while Breck used his discarded cue to fire the black ball into the middle pocket. It signalled the end of the game and time for business. Mo placed his hands into his pockets and sucked in his stomach.

'I thought you were playing it straight nowadays, Mo.'

'Are you jealous?'

'Of course I am.'

'I pushed out the straight rumour to drum up business. Being treated like a leper is bad in these parts. We all got needs.'

'Let's talk.'

Mo realised Breck wasn't going anywhere anytime soon so released his stomach and saw it droop. He beckoned Breck over to a quiet part of the room where they'd be able to talk in private, and both men faced each other around a small circular table.

'To what do I owe the pleasure, DI Breck?'

'I want to know the whereabouts of a suspect in a murder investigation by the name of Alexander Troy.'

'You come here asking me that. I thought you were the law.'

A perplexed Breck replied, 'I am.'

'I'd love to help but I can't.'

'Well the department I work for operate a little different to the rest. Let me show you.' Breck reached across to Mo's left hand then squeezed the life out of it. Mo yelped and slapped his free right hand on the table. 'All right enough, let go.' If you screw my fingers up I won't be able to work.'

'Now you're catching on. The way I see it, your fingers allow you to illegally forge, for which you can earn good money. I'd be doing everyone a favour if I broke them.'

That infuriated Mo. 'If I talk to you my business is dead.'

'I want to know when, Mo.'

'When what?'

'I want to know exactly when is it that Troy's planning to collect the passport from you so that I can nick him.'

After rubbing the top of his left hand, Mo dug into a bag hooked onto the back of his chair and pulled out a gift.

Breck examined the passport which gave Troy a new name and nationality. A new start. His pathway to a new beginning.

'It's all done. He said he'd call me when he'd be ready to collect it. That's not the way I work so he paid me extra for the inconvenience.'

Breck returned the passport to Mo with a warning. 'Don't tell him I've been sniffing around and when he calls you, tell me. Not a week after, not a day after, but straight away.' Mo held his head in his hands but Breck was in no mood to administer sympathy. 'Are you listening to me, Maurice?'

'Yes, got it.'

Breck rose to his feet and extended his hand in friendship but Mo was hesitant, recalling the sharp pain that cut through his fingers just a few moments ago.

'Suit yourself but I'm expecting to hear something from you very soon.'

Breck left the table and padded out of the snooker hall, updated Kearns in the car, then they sped away.

FORTY FIVE

Cardiff

Troy's tired eyes sprung open. He peered out of the window just as Cardiff Central Station came into view and a cluster of butterflies crowded the pit of his stomach. Although he was still in a tight spot with his options limited, he knew a solution existed, albeit a dangerous one. He needed to push for it if he was ever to get his old life back.

Troy hopped off the train and left the station. The taxi driver's flat cap covered his eyes so it was a miracle he could ever see the road, and after Troy told him where to go, he said he knew the place. Along their journey they drove past a boarded-up shop, its name now forgotten by most, and a youth club with bandaged windows. They stopped at a street in Cathays that pretended to be asleep when its eyes were wide awake and Troy paid up and jumped out.

Dai Kyler, a friend that mixed with the wrong types, possessed similar brooding eyes but had been lost for a long time. Bin bags blocked the entrance to his garden, which Troy bypassed and when he reached the door, he slammed down the knocker.

Kyler soon appeared wearing a smile and a white vest while holding a can of Carlsberg. Scars marked his arms like tattoos.

The size of the house was deceptive from the outside. Its rooms were larger than expected with embossed water blue wallpaper that had been in existence since the early 60s. Kyler rumbled through a few loose papers on the sofa, bills, telephone, and electric, while Troy observed the overflowing ashtray.

'Have you started smoking again?'

Kyler shook his head. 'Nah, the bird I'm poking does. She stays over sometimes, lives across the road. You know how it is, I need the release but relationships are hard.'

'Your accent's thicker.'

'I've been working on it. I love nothing more than blending in but I'll take that as a compliment.'

Kyler grabbed a shirt that hung on a nearby chair and buttoned up. 'Who else knows you're here in Cardiff?' He checked his wallet

'Just the friend that drove me to the station. He won't say anything.'

'If you're here it means there's a lot of shit flying. What about the help at your disposal? You know people.'

'There's no help. Proctor didn't pick up when I last called so it's just me it seems.'

'What else?' Kyler noticed Troy's hesitation.

'There's a stranger claiming to be me and I guess I didn't expect that either.'

'What rock has he crawled out from?'

'No idea. I can't even track him.'

'This is madness. You're in a crazy situation, a dangerous one.'

Kyler moved across to the half-opened window and peered out, leaving Troy feeling unsure about whether or not he wanted to help.

'I was told it'd be safe here for me.'

Kyler took a few moments to think before explaining his own situation.

'Things are tricky right now. You can't stay for more than a day or two at most.'

'Then why have I been sent here?'

'I can't answer that but it's not been great for me either.'

'Maybe I can blend in with what you're doing here for a while. It'll take me out of the limelight because they've put my face on the local news.'

'Hey, hold on. I haven't heard from you in ages and now you want to just break all the rules.' Kyler's face tightened at the thought. 'There's a line and we don't cross it. You know that. Stay away from my space and I stay away from yours.'

'I understand but Proctor sent me here. Don't forget, before this crap swallowed us up we were good friends, and after it we still will be. Look, forget about me blending in. Get me what I want and I'll leave.'

'What is it that you want?'

'A gun, one that's untraceable. Everything is moving the wrong way and I don't like it one little bit. Total silence from Proctor, accusations of murder, and now trouble for the woman who I have to protect. I don't trust anything much so I'll finish it then get away.'

'Wait a couple days and I'll see.'

'I can't. I'm getting ready to skip the country for a while and it's better to do it sooner rather than later judging by how things are panning out. I've got a guy setting me up with a passport but I'm running out of time to wrap everything up. They've pinned me down for the murder of my finance director and now the daughter of my CEO.'

'Okay but haven't you got an alibi?'

'For the first one yes, but I can't use it, not yet anyway.'

'I don't get it, why not?'

Troy took a deep breath. 'There's a line and we don't cross it. You stay away from my space and I stay away from yours, remember?'

*

The evening arrived and both men tried to find the resolution they were unable to earlier. Troy watched Kyler stare into nothingness and contort his face like a maths professor attempting to solve the most difficult of equations.

'My view is that if an ex-boyfriend is causing your lover problems then so what? He'll tire of it and judging by what you've said, there are bigger issues to deal with.'

'You don't understand.' Troy frowned. 'Marcin deciding to drop his interest in Ceinwen, would be like an Atheist wanting to hold hands with a Christian. It's never going to happen.'

Kyler slung a protective arm around him. 'It'll be fine but when this is all done and dusted, for the sake of our health, maybe we should both consider new careers. You've had a long day and I've got a great bottle of Scotch. Let's relax this evening and then I'll get you what you want tomorrow.'

Troy smiled. It sounded like a good idea.

FORTY
SIX

The faint sound of jingling of car keys hovered over Troy's head and stirred him awake. Kyler playfully pulled him upwards by his collars and then stuffed a bread roll into his mouth which Troy spat out. He made a weak attempt to tidy himself up seeing as the bottom half of his shirt hung loosely over his unbuckled trousers. His head felt like someone had stuck it in a vice and left it there.

'What time is it, Dai?'

'It's before dawn, the early hours of the morning. Time to get going.'

'What's the strength of that Scotch that I drank yesterday?'

'No idea. Stuff like that doesn't bother me, I'm too busy lapping it up.'

Troy staggered out to the car, amazed that Kyler appeared to be unaffected by their late-night bonding session.

On their journey, they spoke about sport and politics in an attempt to keep things as normal as possible. It served as a silent denial of who they were and what they had become. Kyler drove along Richmond Road then onto Fitzalan Place, trying to get to Butetown as quick as possible by taking the route to Bute Street. The car continued for a little while longer until Kyler slowed down across the road from Old Joe's, a local cafe sandwiched between a dry cleaner and a newsagent.

Troy walked in with Kyler and noticed the menu on the wall that tempted customers with plenty of options. The owner, Joe, drank out of a mug from behind the counter. His tired eyes were glued to the black and white television, and he wore his chequered shirt rolled up at the sleeves. Kyler greeted him with a warm handshake then Joe lifted the counter to allow both men to walk through.

They padded to the back of the café, then opened the door at the end only to be met by a sheet of darkness. Kyler hit the light switch which revealed a narrow staircase. It led to the basement. He stepped down first and Troy followed behind.

They passed a box-sized room with its door left ajar, inviting them to glance inside. Hiding their discomfort proved to be difficult when they saw a man attached to a meat hook that hung from the ceiling. He had a bloodied face they couldn't put a name to. Lance Pringle, proprietor of Pringle's Bed & Breakfast, had been beaten, and with the life draining from him, he realised that he should've stayed in Sandal & Agbrigg. It'd be doubtful he'd live to see the end of the day.

Kyler and Troy continued onwards until they entered the basement to see a young man sitting on the corner of a worktop peeling an apple. An older man sat around a glass table counting vast bundles of money. His head was covered with a flat cap, semi-hiding his rich brown hair that flowed down either side of his face. Grey whiskers around his jaw sprung outward and the buttons on his shirt were opened to half-way down to show off the array of gold chains around his neck.

The man in the flat cap continued to count crisp twenty and ten-pound notes until he reached two-thousand pounds and stopped. During this interval, Dai Kyler stepped forward and introduced Troy. The man stared at Troy with a blank expression at first, then clicked his fingers. An employee the size of a steam locomotive train approached, making the ground shudder under his weight, and Troy almost shit himself. He never saw him standing in a darkened corner of the basement. Nevertheless, he threatened to push his intelligence to its limits as he tried to work out how best to tie the counted money inside a black bin liner before hiding it.

The man Troy now knew as Dexter Wright, took off his flat cap and with it came the most strangest of moments. The carpet of brown hair that Troy thought belonged to him, was actually attached to the cap, and the light shimmered off his bald head. He ran a hand over it but no one seemed surprised and Troy found it hard to take his eyes away from self-made flat cap hair piece mash-up.

'Silas, fix us a couple of drinks,' Dexter instructed the apple peeler. Yet another youth wasting his life after making the wrong career choice. He then outstretched a hand towards Troy. 'Please sit.'

Troy sat down at about the same time Silas moved off the worktop and found his way to the fridge. Troy watched him grab an unbranded bottle along with a can of R Whites lemonade, and mix them together into two separate glasses. Meanwhile, Dexter reached into his pocket and grabbed a Cuban cigar. He lit it up seconds before Silas delivered the drinks.

'Who do you think set you up then?' Dexter swallowed his drink in one go and waited for the answer.

'Not sure, I'm working on finding out who it is.'

Dexter's fingers curled around his empty glass and he took a few hard puffs on his cigar. 'I thought you might be able to do better than that.' Dexter held out a manicured hand and Silas stretched an arm underneath the worktop. He pulled out an object wrapped within a towel and handed it over, so that Dexter could unravel it on the table to the beat of the imagined drum roll.

'This is a SIG-Sauer P220 semi-automatic, a darling of the Swiss Army. Have you used one before?' Troy shook his head causing Dexter to puff out his cheeks in surprise. 'What have you used then?'

'This and that.'

Dexter glanced at Kyler then back at Troy. 'This and that sounds like the name of the gun I wanted once for Christmas to shoot my older brother with. I was ten years old at the time.' Dexter turned to Kyler. 'Imagine that, ten years old and I wanted to do my own brother in.'

Kyler remained nonplussed so Dexter returned his attention to Troy once again.

'Back to the point. Do you know about me?' Troy shook his head, he hadn't been filled in about Dexter's background. 'People say I've done things, questioned how I've got to where I am but they don't understand what a struggle it's been. A boy from a Welsh mining town has made his mark up here.' Troy watched Dexter puff the life out of his cigar. 'I also don't let just anybody into my circle but Dai told me you're a wanted man, and a wanted man is my type of man.' Dexter laughed after that which allowed Troy to relax a little.

He lay the SIG on the table, nothing more than a trophy, a precious black market prize for all to see.

'Drop the SIG into the Thames when you've finished. I don't want it back down here.'

Troy wondered how many times it had been used to kill as he picked it up and tucked it away.

'Thank you.' He shook Dexter's hand.

'You're welcome. Any friend of Dai's is a friend of mine.'

Kyler and Troy left the basement to walk back the way they came. Neither saw Dexter beckon Silas. Neither of them heard him say, 'Gather a couple of trusted men and head up to London to deal with the Dvoraks, before they come and deal with us.'

By the time the bright light of the cafe greeted them, Joe had switched off the television and was standing by the door with his coat on, fidgeting and looking anxious. Kyler handed Troy the keys to the car and told him he'd be along soon, then engaged in a hushed conversation with Joe.

Once inside the car, Troy adjusted the passenger seat and let it recline back, almost disappearing from the view but not quite. He saw Joe leave the café in a rush but Kyler hadn't emerged. Seconds later a red Rover P6 pulled up and four men got out. He couldn't see the faces but assumed they came to conduct business. They went inside just as a wave of tiredness swept him up, and not for one moment did he believe he'd fall asleep, but he did.

*

Troy's eyes flapped open. Kyler was back in the car but different. Dazed and zombie-like. Red marks were smeared on the collar of his shirt, and across the cheeks of his face. He turned the key in the ignition and floored the accelerator.

'What's going on Kyler?'

'Four men came and attacked us. Kept hacking away!' Kyler swerved to avoid a cyclist.

'Who's hurt?'

'Dexter's been shredded.'

'What are you talking about?'

'He wasn't moving.'

'Are you hurt!'

'No I don't think so.' Kyler was still in shock and stared at his shirt while pelting along at high speed. 'This is not my blood, it's someone else's.'

'Keep your eyes on the road damn it!'

Kyler broke every speed record known before screeching to a halt outside his home. The burning rubber marked the asphalt and the smell of petrol wafted in through the open window. Troy noticed the blood encased around Kyler's fingernails.

'Did you touch anyone there?' he asked.

'Huh?'

'Can it be proved that you were there?'

'I can't remember.'

Troy lost patience and jogged round to the driver's side to help Kyler clamber out, then got him inside.

'You need to get cleaned up straight away.'

'Yeah, you're right.'

Kyler struggled up to the bathroom and looked a sad sight. Troy bit his nails like they were food. Why the hell would Proctor send him here? The safety had long ago disappeared. And what if he had been at Old Joe's Café at the same time as those men? It didn't bear thinking about and for the first-time Troy began to wonder just whose side Proctor was on.

Retching sounds filtered down from upstairs so Troy rushed up to see Kyler coughing up blood. On his knees and bent over the toilet, mumbling incoherently. Troy spotted patches of red from around his left side and feared the worse. A knife wound. Kyler would have to return with him to London but none of this made any sense.

'You're going to have to come with me. We're leaving Cardiff.'

'No, I can't.'

'You're in a bad way. No choice.'

'I'm not going.'

A fed-up Troy left him but when Kyler drifted out of the bathroom he stumbled down the stairs. He regained his footing then made a move for the door. Troy blocked his path.

'Do you want me to take you to a hospital?'

'You know I can't go there. Those guys might be looking for me.'

Troy recalled Kyler's hushed conversation with Joe, and Joe looking anxious as he left. A few things weren't adding up. 'Who were the men that did this?'

'They travelled down from London.' Kyler paused to catch his breath. 'Don't worry, I'm almost finished here. There's a lot of money involved.'

'Who's behind the Dexter hit?'

'I can't say.'

Kyler's reluctance to open up annoyed Troy. 'I need to know the part you played in this!'

Kyler refused to talk about it anymore so Troy moved aside to let him leave the house. He retrieved his rucksack and cursed, but when he made his way to the door, he found Kyler on the floor. The colour had drained from his face.

Troy took a closer look at his finger-deep wound and wiped away the claret. Someone had twisted the knife after inserting it, and Troy couldn't stem the flow of blood that pumped out. He could see Kyler fading away and the deafening wail of sirens forced him to make a decision. They were getting closer. The police were moments away. Troy checked Kyler's pulse. He was gone. The shock froze him but he had to move. He knew that.

Troy escaped through the rear of the house and burst through the patio doors, straight into a weed infested garden. Amongst the broken bits of wood scattered like debris, a Vienna Flared stone vase was the prettiest thing to admire.

Troy scaled a high fence and landed on top of a pillow of prickly thorns. When he fought free of them, they scratched his skin but the adrenaline kicked in hard and numbed the pain. He found a spot to hide, next to a wild stretch of bush and rested there. He allowed the memories to flood in, feeling devastated and emotional, because he had no way of bringing back his friend from the dead.

Troy soon found enough courage to peer out from beyond the bushes. The way ahead seemed clear so he moved out and followed a path to a main road. Nothing mattered except his escape and in order to stay off the grid, he slipped down a side road and soon found himself standing in front of an abandoned house.

Troy forced open the door to the boarded-up property and the smell of damp, which carried a pungent kick, hit him. He traipsed into a ground floor room lit by a beam of light that shone through a crack, and a broken stool had been propped in a corner. Troy sat down with the SIG in his hand and took off the safety, just in case he needed to use it.

*

One minute turned into two, then multiplied into many more, before Troy felt safe enough to leave. He walked away from the house without a nearby destination and passed a street where he spotted a man working on a car. The engine purred and the vehicle had its door open so Troy hung around. When the man popped into his home he grabbed his chance.

He walked towards the car, closed the bonnet then jumped inside. Troy released the handbrake and made the car crawl away until he reached a main road. From there, he upped the speed without knowing how far the car would take him. It didn't matter because one thing ran through his mind. Kyler. A good friend for many years.

The time had come to return to London and he planned to collect his new passport and find out who framed him. But most of all, with an untraceable gun in his possession, he promised himself he wouldn't end up dead like his friend.

FORTY
SEVEN

London

Arlo Breck stood at bottom of the stairs staring at Molly's suitcase. They enjoyed their impromptu visit to the circus but the 'psychiatrist' conversation cropped again afterwards. This time Molly decided to meet him halfway and agreed to stay with her aunt who once worked as an assistant clinical psychologist. On paper, she possessed enough useful knowledge to be

of help to her niece. Molly still struggled to move on so it seemed for the best, and it'd be a good idea for her to spend a bit of time in Tunbridge. She had coped well enough when Breck travelled to West Yorkshire but different surroundings might swifter aid her recovery. Breck wanted to move on from the past too. He just didn't know if it would ever happen.

Molly edged her way downstairs by holding onto the banister and Breck rose to his feet to help her down. She refused his offer in an attempt to display her own strength which he understood.

'The taxi is outside. Sorry I can't come with you to the station. Are you sure you have everything?' Molly nodded but her eyes were distant. 'It will be nice to get out of London for a while don't you think?'

She gave Breck a gentle kiss before he picked up her luggage and walked her to the taxi. The driver popped her belongings into the boot while Molly climbed onto the backseat.

'Ring me when you get to Tunbridge.'

'Yes, OK,' she said. 'Arlo, one thing.'

'Yes of course, what?'

'You wouldn't be unfaithful to me, would you?'

Breck felt a lump in his throat, taken aback by the question. He wondered why she had asked that unexpectedly, then when he considered it, found the answer. The shirt. The one he wouldn't buy in a million years. He needed to reassure her. 'Don't be silly, what made you ask such a thing?'

'Oh nothing.'

Breck didn't believe her. 'Give me a ring when you get there.'

'I will.'

When the taxi pulled away, a morose looking Arlo Breck stayed in place until it disappeared from view. He hoped Molly would return to him as she once was and remain so, and he saw her trip as a step in the right direction. Breck opened the door to his VW and made his way to the station.

*

When Breck reached his desk, he received good news straight away. Beatrice had located Troy's Blackfriars pub and showed him two signatures.

'This is something that I collected from my pub crawl.' Breck didn't smile. 'I'm joking,' she said. 'One of the signatures on this list confirms that Troy did in fact sign into a working gym in Blackfriars. It validates the story to some extent I suppose, of a man following him. The one he thinks could be setting him up. What do you want to do?'

'I want to find Troy and his married lover then wrap this bloody thing up. That's what I'd like to do but it's not going to happen yet. Since the press conference and subsequent media coverage, we've received many calls but most have turned out to be false leads. Good work anyhow.'

Breck dialled Morten Hoebeck in Norway, fearing he was beginning to look out of his depth. There'd be someone within the SCU waiting to jump into his shoes should he fail. Not just Riley. After a few rings he got through to Morten.

'Hello, Morten, how are you?'

'I was minutes away from ringing you, and in answer to your question I'm good and bad.'

'How come?'

'Good because I had the breakfast I wanted this morning and bad because of the news I have to tell you.'

'What news?'

'We've found your POI.'

'That's great news.'

'You don't understand. The POI is dead. We believe murdered.'

'No, no.' Breck couldn't believe it.

'We found the body in a small fishing boat floating out to sea, wrapped up in a net.

'How did he die?'

'The harpoon through the eye that came out the other side of his skull, is a big clue, but our pathologist will confirm the exact cause.' Breck felt defeated. 'Here's a break for you though. It looks like the killer was a bit careless.'

Breck gained some hope. 'In what way?'.

'The victim's wallet had been stripped of cash and most other things but we found a folded scrap of paper inside that his killer missed. On it is a UK 01 phone number. A lead perhaps?'

'I don't know how to thank you.'

'Bavarian sausage and sauerkraut normally works with a flask of beer to wash it down with.'

'I owe you one, friend.'

Morten gave Breck the number. 'We'll run through the normal processes here but is there anything else you want me to do while that is ongoing?'

'Get an odonatologist at your end to carry out a test on the POI.'

Forensic odonatologists were used to either identify human remains when fingerprints were unobtainable. Or to examine bite marks in a criminal investigation. They could also be called upon to determine age by examining a subject's teeth. Breck suspected a slight difference in age between the two men at the centre of the investigation. Although the procedure carried a chance of being less accurate on anyone over the age of fifteen.

'OK, I'll fix it.'

Breck hung up with Beatrice standing beside him looking a little bit anxious.

'Do you know where Pat is?'

'No idea but can I help?'

'They found the body of our POI in Norway, but this number was found in his possession. Here it is.' Breck handed the number over. 'Find out who it belongs to, Bea, and make that your top priority.'

FORTY EIGHT

The Messenger

No one would have blamed Jacob Simpson for feeling relieved after escaping from Breck's clutches. The sour smell of the interrogation at Cransham station still clung to him, and made him feel more uncomfortable than seeing scattered cat faeces at the entrance to his block. He side-stepped a few broken syringes on his

way up the stairs and even a used condom didn't register.

Simpson pulled out his key and opened the door. Then it happened.

Someone pushed him inside. Simpson's feet disappeared from underneath him and he fell flat on his face. A boot slammed down on top of his head, pinning him to the floor.

'Hey, this must be a mistake, man.'

No reply.

A subtle rustle of a plastic could be heard before the foot was released then a bag slipped over his head. Simpson felt his body elevate upwards and he was pushed onto the sofa. A small hole had been cut out at the front of the bag to allow him to breathe, but there were no eye slots. He had little time to think before a boot crashed into his chest, jerking his body backwards, and although the sofa cushioned him, the sting still forced him to let out a faint whimper.

Simpson must have guessed something terrible would befall him. He sprung up and made a desperate run for the door but was pulled back. A barrage of blows rained down on him. Each punch zapped Simpson's resistance. He felt himself being dragged along by his ankles, and being taken to, what he believed to be his bedroom, where he was forced to his knees.

Simpson's hands were pulled back and tied together.

This was a pro at work. He had upset the wrong people and Simpson understood what this was about – the very public arrest by Kearns and Breck outside the Riverdale. Simpson knew a lot of secrets that plenty would want him to keep quiet about, but the way he had been subdued carried its own signature. He knew who was in the room with him and what to say.

'The pick-up was routine, nothing else.' Footsteps moved away from Simpson but when they returned, the atmosphere worsened. Another blow connected with Simpson's head and sweat crawled down the side of his face after he felt something grip his pinkie. He let out a horrifying scream. 'They wanted to know about guys I met!' He became breathless from the pain and felt what he believed to be a nut cracker, grip the next finger on his hand. Simpson flopped to the ground. The lever was released from his finger. 'Peter Clarke and his mate Alexander Troy. They wanted to know who set up Troy, man. Simpson used to be my solicitor that's why they visited me. Troy is looking for way out of his mess but they're amateurs. I ripped them off for couple of quid and spun a story.'

Those desperate words flicked on the light switch within the mind of the man that intended to kill him. He had the option to allow Simpson to plead for his life until the fear paralysed him. Until it polluted the core of his mind. Then grab a pillow from the bed and press it against his head before pulling the trigger on his Beretta. Not once but twice. The silencer would dampen any noise and he'd scoop up Simpson's body, throw it over his shoulder, and walk out of the flat like he owned it. For the grand finale, he'd use the sole of his boots to crack a few fingers or a forearm, Simpson's neck even, and grind the bones into dust, then dump Simpson down the rubbish chute. The other option was to show leniency. Let Simpson live to serve him another day. Him not his bosses. He weighed it all up with the Beretta pressed against Simpson's head and Simpson feared the end unless he gave up something valuable.

'Wait, there's something you don't know. It's about one of the coppers investigating Troy. It might be useful.'

The movement behind him ceased. 'Her name is Patricia Kearns and she's a DS.' The Beretta eased away from Simpson. 'Let me live and I'll tell you what she asked me to do.'

For the one they call The Messenger, the deal interested him because after this visit, he had an important meeting, and the keys to a greater kingdom lay just ahead.

*

A flurry of people, joggers and dog walkers, had begun to pass through Greenwich Park to make the most of the day's sunshine, while The Messenger walked like someone in a rush and headed towards Aychm Dvorak – a man of advanced years dressed in an immaculate dark suit. Aychm sat on a park bench with polished Cuban heels on his feet while two men stood at equal distances watching over him.

The Messenger joined him on the bench.

'Thank you for coming,' Aychm removed his hands from his pockets. 'You know, we should make the most of every day is what I say to whoever will listen. No one wants to listen. Not even my nephew. People want to complain and get greedy. Even those closest to you. I've seen many friends fade away and when you get to my age, it can wear you down.' Aychm patted the knee of his guest and inhaled. 'No one knows your true name and it's difficult to contact you but I've considered your request and it sounds reasonable.' He paused. 'I understand that you just want to know where to find the man that attacked her is that correct?'

His guest nodded.

Aychm sat like a king surveying land he'd be happy to plunder. Men like him didn't get to where they were by being foolish or rash. They considered their options. Every single last one, and the man sitting next to him could be invaluable.

Aychm leaned over and whispered a name and The Messenger reeled back. 'Don't be surprised that I know who you are. I'm very good at finding out what I need to. It changes nothing between us.' Aychm rose to his feet and The Messenger followed suit. Although the revelation had shaken him, the two of them then strolled through the park, towards Aychm's Rolls Royce, and the bodyguards followed. The Messenger had heard about Aychm's unpredictability. His temper and ruthlessness were well known. 'If I'm in the US then it's the feds, over here it's the Yard trying to snare me, so I am careful, always careful,' he admitted. 'Don't put me at risk, or I'll attach your tongue to my wall.' One of the men opened the door to the Rolls but Aychm paused before getting inside. 'Loyalty is what I value and weak links are what I detest. It makes me not a heartless man but one that is pragmatic so this is my wish.' Aychm whispered into The Messenger's ear with an emotional request, then he entered his car and said, 'Do that for me and I'll put you where you deserve to be.'

*

In West Cransham, the houses were beautiful monuments with one lane of the road equal to the width of two out on the main. A maroon Jaguar XJ12 parked half-way up the hill, so The Messenger wandered up to it and opened the passenger door. The smell of paprika and garlic hit him straight away, which he refused to comment on as he shook hands with the driver. Ever cautious, he spotted another man sitting in the back with blond highlights that illuminated the ends of his flowing dark hair. He shifted in his seat. Marcin Dvorak, the driver, noticed.

'Blondy's a trusted confidante. Don't worry,' he said, seeking to reassure his guest.

'Glad to hear it,' he replied.

Marcin focused on the man's reflection in the rear-view mirror. 'His hair looks pretty? It takes him a long time to get his hair like that; it's a technical process.' The Messenger relaxed due to the reassurance, and the strange hair care insight. 'Large chunks of his hair are pulled through the holes in a plastic cap that he wears and then a hooked needle is used to isa, icy, iso…'

'Isolate?' Blondy chipped in.

'A hooked needle is used to isolate the strands for bleaching. Very technical.'

Marcin held a silver key which he rotated between his fingers before he dropped it into The Messenger's hand. 'That is the key to a different property. Not the one we agreed. I need to make one final trip to the old place, but I believe it will be compromised very soon. This new property is up for sale so no one will be there. Go in and act normal then the neighbours won't be concerned. They're used to seeing different people come and go, but if you stand around like you're looking for trouble, they will be. I know you won't do that. Get the job done.' Marcin pulled out a bottle, unscrewed the top and inhaled whatever was inside. 'Let me tell you something. My uncle and I don't like liabilities. As my uncle always says to me, they're bad for business.'

'Smart man, your uncle.'

'Yes, his decisions are always the right ones.'

Marcin's need for recognition, mixed with delusions of invincibility, saw him boast about various things. The sort of things a man in his position shouldn't talk about. Many times his uncle had warned him to keep his mouth shut, and many times he had failed to.

The end of the meeting saw The Messenger pull out a gift, a white paper bag which he handed over, knowing that Marcin had a penchant for mementoes. Then he left the Jaguar. Marcin's eagerness saw him untie the knot and peer into the bag, and he smiled because it confirmed one thing. He had the right man for the job.

Yet, Marcin had no idea his guest had conversed with his uncle prior to their meeting. If he did, he'd reconsider his opinion and discard his plan. In fact, he'd change everything.

FORTY NINE

Breck was in the Major Incident Room (MIR), transferring his case updates onto the board. A board now clustered with other cases. It would soon make for difficult reading, yet another reason to get things resolved sooner rather than later.

When he finished, he received a visit from Kearns and saw her wipe away a tear. Mary Tellow had called

her. She wanted an update on the whereabouts of her daughter's killer and used emotional blackmail to try and get it. Kearns couldn't tell her anything and Breck wrongly assumed her upset was in some way linked to her estranged daughter. Kearns thought it best to play on that.

'My Kim still believes the poison that my ex-husband is spewing. I've made a right mess of things.'

'You can fix it. I know you can.'

'Not this time, Arlo. Do you know why she won't speak to me?'

Breck often wondered but Kearns always seemed reluctant to go into detail.

'Only if you want to.'

'His name was Dean. She loved him. And when it suited, he acted as if butter wouldn't melt in his mouth. Kim met him while they were both first year college students. Dean was a bit of a lad, full of himself and had the physicality of John Wayne with Donny Osmond looks. His dad happened to be one of Mick's work colleagues. As time went on, I noticed Kim become more withdrawn. Some of her spark had disappeared but it didn't make sense why, so I followed her one evening, blame the detective in me. I followed her and found out Dean was pushing her around. That son of a bitch bullied my daughter and I witnessed it all.'

'So what did you do?'

'I lost it, Arlo, and ended up hurting him. It caused an almighty row but not in the way I expected. Kim sided with Mick and refused to speak to me. They both felt I went over the top and it also gave Mick the excuse to walk out and leave me. Just another example of my unreasonable behaviour he said.'

'You did the right the thing.'

'Kim's love for Dean blinded her. They split up in the end but she still blamed me then left with Mick when he decided to go. So now you know, I'm a bad mother. One that drove her own daughter away.'

'Nonsense. I'm sure she'll return Pat, you've just got to give her time. To me, it sounds like you were doing her a favour and she'll realise that one day.'

Kearns' emotions had begun to get the better of her, so Breck opened his arms and gave his partner a hug. It was the least he could do.

They stayed in the MIR for a bit until she felt ready enough to resume work. Then they left together.

*

Late into the evening, Kearns' mood still appeared to be sullen which was no good for her, the team or the case. Breck lifted his head away from his paperwork with a suggestion.

'Fancy a drink, Pat?'

'Are you asking me out on a date?'

He laughed. 'Molly's staying with her aunt for a bit so I'm lonely.'

'Come on then,' she said as she grabbed his arm. 'I know a place.'

They were on their way out when they passed Beatrice, packing her things away, so Breck invited her too. She agreed to come along despite the presence of Kearns and all three stepped out of the of the station, and headed towards Breck's car.

The bar in Crystal Palace, best described as a place full of tired faces desperate to put the day behind them, played soft jazz with the potential to induce sleep. Kearns ordered a Gin & Tonic while Beatrice settled for a glass of white wine. Breck killed his thirst with a pint of lager. After Kearns got the second round in, the conversation between the three relaxed, but it was inevitable that the case would crop up.

'I want to lay the cards on the table,' Breck began.

'I don't see any cards,' Kearns joked.

'No, I'm serious. Our department is always under scrutiny from those at the top, and the media profile of the double murder case is snowballing. We've had a press conference and it's been discussed on local radio, appeared in local newspapers. As well as one of the nationals. Yet, we are still no closer to solving it. One version of Troy has escaped and now the other one is dead. Found overseas in a fishing boat.' He broke off to take a mouthful of lager.

'Some cases just don't get solved,' Kearns remarked.

'Well the ones I'm working on do.'

Beatrice cut in. 'How do you sum up this case at the moment, Arlo?'

'It's tricky. I don't know what Alexander Troy is hiding, or why he is trying to convince us he is not the killer by leaving me a message, and a trail for us to follow.'

'A trail?' Kearns questioned.'

'The Blackfriars pub,' Breck reminded her.

'You know my view, Arlo, I definitely believe our dead POI was involved with both Janet and Geraldine's deaths. Someone silenced him.'

Breck needed another opinion. 'Beatrice, what do you think?'

'I don't know. I'm just wondering, why would someone kill our POI and equally, why is our prime suspect still on the run?'

'Maybe it isn't just us he's running from,' Breck suggested. 'Looking at where we are with this I think that if we find Troy again, we'll get the answers we need. Mo is going to call me when Troy arranges to meet him. Then we'll nab him when he collects his passport and squeeze the truth out of him.'

Breck had a wild-eyed and determined look about him that Kearns had seen before. She knew she had to swing with it for now and reflected on her partner before Breck. An absent minded chauvinist prick, that liked his own company. He barked orders when it suited and he'd let her take the flak when he didn't have the balls to. When a back problem forced him to retire, she told him how sorry she was to see him go. She lied. Kearns celebrated that night like she had never celebrated before.

Breck in contrast, acted completely different, and showed her respect which made the situation more difficult. She could just about justify her betrayal, but the guilt of hiding the secret from him, long ago began to eat away at her soul.

*

The light had left the sky when the phone woke Breck. He bolted upright with a see-saw feeling inside his head, his hands clambered around in the dark, attempting to reach the phone. He toppled over an empty glass and a half-full bottle of white, but his eyes were quick to refocus and soon became accustomed to the darkened setting. He used a few tissues to mop up the spillage and hoped that he didn't drive home drunk. He threw a hand against the wall to balance upright. The phone kept ringing so he staggered over to it.

'Huh? Hello.'

'It's Pat, sorry to bother you. I know it's late.'

'Hi, what's wrong?' Breck heard a noise from upstairs. 'Hold on, just a second.'

He moved the phone away from his ear. The floorboards were definitely creaking overhead. It served as a sharp slap in the face and forced him to come to his senses. Someone else was in the house.

Breck threw the phone to one side and left the room. He grabbed the golf umbrella propped against the wall and went to investigate, feeling embarrassed that his intoxicated state made him rely on an umbrella for protection.

The tentative steps he took allowed him to inch his way upstairs until he saw the outline of someone. A woman. She stood by the entrance to the bedroom. The woman stepped forward wearing one of his shirts, unbuttoned all the way down the middle.

'I see you've woken up then.' Beatrice couldn't stop smiling.

Breck discarded the umbrella, displaying no emotion but the guilt of knowing what he might have done, began to cut him open.

'What's going on here?'

'I guess you'll be wanting this back.' She grabbed his attention by playfully slipping out of his shirt – the one she bought for him. Breck felt uncomfortable while she stood before him semi-naked. He needed a way out. Then he remembered Kearns.

'I'll speak to you in a bit, I'm on a call.'

Breck drifted back downstairs in a daze to pick up the phone.

'Hello, Pat sorry about that. What's wrong?'

'I'm just checking that you got home all right. Beatrice said she'd drive you home in your car because you had a few.'

'Er yes, she did. I woke up with a pounding head though.'

'Anyway, I just wanted to make sure that you reached home safely. How did Beatrice get home?'

And there was the real reason Kearns had called – to see if Beatrice had stayed the night.

'Don't know. When I woke up she was gone.'

'Ah she must have caught a cab. OK, I'll let you rest – see you tomorrow.'

'Bye.'

Breck ended the call then heard Beatrice call his name. He found her sitting on the lower stairs, this time with the shirt back on.

'Was that Pat checking up on you?'

'Yes.'

'She needs to get a life she does. Anyway, you don't look happy to see me.'

'Bea, thank you for driving me home. Please tell me what happened afterwards?'

'You just saw me almost naked standing by your bedroom and you ask me what happened afterwards. Are you serious? You want to know what we did?'

The venom in Beatrice's words shocked him. Breck shook his head. He didn't want to know but Beatrice wouldn't let up. She grabbed him, so that she could whisper it in his ear, and she watched his exasperation as her words slipped out, resenting him for the fact he'd never leave his girlfriend.

If true, Breck was aware that what Beatrice claimed, could damage both their careers, alongside his marriage.

Breck walked away, determined to let things run their course. Beatrice would stay the night and they'd leave for work in the morning together. Once they reached the station, they'd walk in separately, minutes apart, and try not to talk about this night ever again.

FIFTY

After arriving at the station, Breck travelled to the MIR. A letter with the Hardwick Stanfield postmark dropped through the letterbox, before he had set off for work this morning. He didn't feel relaxed enough to open it with Beatrice around so popped it inside the glove compartment to read when he was ready.

In the MIR, Beatrice remained distant after what

had happened which Breck expected. The other SCU members in the room were junior but with the march approaching, it was all Breck could get. Once he had everyone's attention he began to give an update of key movers and major events of the case so far. Yet, when he took a step back and thought about it, they had a lot of information already. It just needed piecing together.

'The last thing I'd like to mention is that we've now got a warrant to raid the Camden address of our deceased POI. We obtained the address through his car registration number and planned to wait until he returned. That will now not be happening so a few of you are going in. Beatrice will lead.'

The revelation bolted Beatrice upright and caught her unaware. Was this her prize for being with him last night? Breck on the other hand preferred her to be out of the way.

Kearns had a question. 'Has Morten given you any more information?'

'Not yet but I'd love to know how our POI ended up with a harpoon embedded in his eye socket.' The room fell silent. 'Right everyone, we're done.'

The group began to disperse but Kearns had a quiet word with Breck.

'We can win this by pinning it all on our dead POI. It'll cover up for the fact we can't piece together the information we have.'

'Pat, this can't be closed until I catch our prime suspect and question him. You know that.'

'Fair enough, you're the SIO. It was just an idea.'

'Yes I am the SIO.'

'Take it easy. I didn't mean anything by it.' Beatrice passed by and Kearns noticed her lack of communication with Breck. 'Why has she been given the lead on the Camden address raid?'

'It'll be good for her. I think she feels that things are moving slowly in her career.'

'She lacks patience that one. Anyway, I've got to sort something out so I'll see you in a bit.'

Breck gathered his file then returned to his desk to find a letter which had been couriered. It originated from overseas. He used a letter opener to lift the seal of the odonatologist's report sent from Morten Hoebeck. The report had been written in Norwegian, but the key parts were translated and highlighted. A lot of it made for unexciting reading but the parts that mattered were clear for anyone to see. The odonatologist had reported that the dead man known as Alexander Troy, was in the age region of 40-45 years old. Not the 32 years of age his 'official' documents stated.

It astounded Breck and he couldn't peel his eyes way from the report but he required one more favour from Morten. If the POI wasn't Troy then he needed to know the dead man's real identity.

FIFTY ONE

Breck had his conversation with Morten and now sat in Bashir's office to give him an update of the case so far.

'Beatrice has led the raid on the empty property in Camden and checks revealed that the owner had been paid three month's rent in advance, via a recognised estate agent. Plus a deposit too. Both parties are innocent of any wrong doing.' Bashir's searching

gaze gave the impression he expected to hear more than he had. 'I asked my contact in Norway to get an odonatologist to carry out oral tests on our dead POI, which he did. There was a non-match to the specified age.'

'A non-match?'

'Yes sir, Morten my contact, also ran a check on our man with other international agencies like Interpol and the FBI. They matched his photo so I can now confirm his real identity. He's Jean-Marc Alper, an accomplished conman of French origin. Never been caught and speaks English better than most.'

Breck expected Bashir to ask why he had never thought of contacting one of the international agencies before but he never did. Perhaps because Breck's main focus had been on the other Troy.

'Is there anything else?'

'Beatrice is running a trace on a UK phone number found on Alper's body. We're hoping to get an address.'

'Is this a solid lead?'

'I believe it to be so.'

'I've cancelled our one-to-one today to enable you to concentrate on this. At least we can refer to the prime suspect as *the* Alexander Troy. Make sure you update the team on the identity issue now.'

Breck nodded then left the office, while Bashir watched him gather a small number of SCU officers in a circle to inform them. He realised he couldn't pull Breck back from this, even though it was all snowballing to the wrong conclusion.

Bashir made a mental note to organise a separate briefing for those involved in the impending right-wing march. He planned to discuss strategic positions around Lewisham, Cransham, and New Cross. And how best to keep the two factions – The Front and the anti-fascists at the heart of it, apart. That filled his mind as he stepped outside his office, but as soon as he did, Kearns grabbed him, unable to contain her bewilderment at the news she had just heard.

'What's going on, sir? Did you know about Alper?'

'Keep your voice down. I didn't know anything beforehand. Just stick close to Breck and intervene if you have to.'

Bashir waited for Kearns to give him the impression that she understood.

'Yes, I will.'

'He also got his contact Morten, to speak to international agencies without your knowledge so he may be starting to suspect something. We can't afford that at this stage.'

Kearns agreed but said nothing else, aware that Breck had been watching them both.

FIFTY TWO

Troy dumped the car he stole from Cardiff on the back streets of Greenwich and unpeeled his eyes from the pull of the skyline. London's air carried its own unique taste; the type which could either hardened the soul or break the spirit and he knew that he had returned a different animal to the one which left. Nothing offered any surprises.

He found his way to Clarke's home and Clarke ushered him inside. Troy filled him in with an edited version of his trip to Cardiff, leaving out Kyler's death, along with a few other things, such as the SIG he received from Dexter.

'Sounds eventful.' Clarke had a smile on his face. 'I've got Breck and Kearns waiting for you in the other room.'

Before Clarke even took another breath, Troy pulled the SIG and Clarke felt his legs weaken. He held up his hands.

'Hey Alexander slow down. I'm joking. It's a joke! They're not here.'

'You don't know me or what I'm capable of!'

'What do you mean by that?'

Troy got a hold of himself. He was losing it and putting everything at risk by doing so too. He lowered the SIG and reached for the bottle of gin left out on the table. He poured out a decent amount into a glass and swallowed it whole. Clarke had never seen him like this before. It concerned him. Troy felt no embarrassment, just the burn of the alcohol travelling down his throat. No buzz, or relaxation of the muscles.

During this time, Clarke couldn't take his eyes off Troy's SIG. He became tense and Troy realised.

'Sorry, it's the stress,' he said with a little remorse. 'It's making me do crazy things.'

'I shouldn't ask you where you got the gun from then?'

'No don't.' Troy hid the SIG inside his jacket. 'I want to stay here until tomorrow at least. I'm tired and need a rest.'

'Fine. I could do with the company but no more John Wayne moments.'

'You've been a good friend Pete. I won't forget it.' Something sprung to Troy's mind. 'Did you speak to Ceinwen?'

'Yes, all done. She's gone to her father's home.'

'Good. One less thing for me to worry about.'

Clarke wished he could do more for his friend. Troy looked close to breaking point. They first met when Troy stepped in to save Clarke from a beating and he had been there ever since, watching his back and taking an interest in what he did as a solicitor.

Troy threw his head up towards the ceiling and stretched out his legs, knowing that their friendship hadn't occurred by accident. He hoped that Clarke wouldn't hate him if the truth ever surfaced. And as for Ceinwen, what would she say? He didn't have an answer for that but at least in his current crisis, he knew she was safe.

*

Ceinwen Phelps stared blankly at the half-completed page in her typewriter. She didn't want to stay at home with her father anymore, regardless of Troy's warning. Instead, she chose to go to work to take her mind off things, and hoped the message he gave to Peter Clarke was just an exaggeration. She didn't know where to find Troy, and Richard still pressured her for a reconciliation.

Ceinwen opened the blinds to let the sun glide through and seconds later she heard a tap at the door. Richard barged straight in.

'Hello,' he said then tried to kiss her full on the lips but she turned away. He pulled himself away.

'You're back already?'

'Yes, flew in this morning and I thought I'd go over the preparations for the November event with you. Have you picked any suitable venues?'

'Yes, I have the information in my file.'

Richard sat down and folded his coat over the side of the chair. He glanced over towards the windows.

'It's not a bad day today, what are you having for lunch?'

'No idea.'

He placed his briefcase on the floor while Ceinwen popped behind the desk to grab the file. She handed it to him and he examined the information. He seemed pleased.

'Don't look so worried. I promise not to talk about us and give you the space you've asked for, but I'll be honest. I want you back.' Ceinwen felt uneasy which Richard noticed. 'Anyway, this is great.

We've got a board meeting tomorrow so I'll discuss it with them. How did you find the New Jersey experience?'

'It was OK.'

'It surprised me that you chose to fly back straight after it finished. Because of that, I didn't stick around too long either but it doesn't matter. I have great news,' Richard sensed her unease. 'You've been selected as the best person for the Head of Acquisition role. It comes with a global remit, so you'll be managing a team of specialists to identify the best businesses for us to acquire.' Richard returned the file and picked up his coat.

'This is a bit sudden isn't it?'

'You're not complaining are you?'

'No but it's quite sudden that's all.'

'We'll discuss the fine details of your good news another time. I'll see you around I'm sure.'

After Richard left, Ceinwen became desperate to leave the office. She wanted to clear her head so grabbed her bag and took the stairs down to the ground level.

Outside the building, a car pulled up with a familiar face behind the wheel. A face that she didn't see. She had taken a short cut through a side street, and when a hand covered her mouth to stifle her scream, Ceinwen fought and kicked with everything she had. To no avail.

After she passed out she was bundled into a car and her abductor would've liked nothing more than to snap her pretty little neck. He would have too, if he didn't have orders to deliver her in one piece.

FIFTY THREE

Tension bubbled ahead of the Front's controversial march, with the local community preparing for lockdown. Most observers feared it would set race relations back years and Breck agreed. Currently, he had the phone glued to his ear on other business. Molly's train had pulled into London and she had called to let him know. When their conversation switched to

her well-being, the past cropped up and it now seemed to be part of her therapy. Breck wanted to reassure her.

'Molly, I'll never give up searching for him. I want you to know that.'

'If you ever do find him, what then?'

'I'll bring him to justice.'

'Thank you for not giving up. I'm going get a bite to eat before I come home. How's your case going?'

'Things are progressing so I won't complain. Look, I'll speak to you later.'

Breck ended the call and pushed the full list of witness statements for both Janet and Geraldine to one side. They contained nothing of significance which just served to annoy him and he mulled things over, but no matter how he tried, he couldn't shake the picture of Kearns and Bashir colluding together. They had a shared secret and he wanted to find out what it was.

Breck shifted his focus back to the case. Troy surfaced in August 1974 when he got the job at Van Bruen. His CV – which Breck obtained from their HR department – listed the companies they received his references from, but those companies had now gone into administration. Coincidence or something else?

Breck didn't have the answers and needed to be elsewhere anyhow. He collected his jacket and left the station without telling Kearns, and along the way he bumped into Beatrice. She had news for him.

'I've got an address for that number retrieved from the dead POI in Norway. It's in Rotherhithe.'

'Rotherhithe?' Beatrice nodded. 'Find out who lives there because I want as much information as possible before we make a move.' She didn't say anything, although she wanted to. 'Bea?'

'OK, I'm on it,' she said then she fizzled away.

Breck went in another direction. He left the building, started up the Allegro and drove out of the yard, enthused because he had something important to collect. Information that could blow the case wide open.

When Breck neared Shooter's Hill he recognised the police squad car parked half on and half off the pavement. He also recognised the person slammed down across its bonnet. The Allegro screeched to a halt and he jogged over.

'Riley what's going on?'

Ray Riley swung his head around with a vicious scowl. His partner Gaz Bennett kept himself hidden in the background when he realised Breck had arrived. The two of them already had an infamous run in, resulting in hospital treatment for Gaz, but the SCU had a straightforward approach go that sort of thing. Three strikes and you were out. Breck had two more strikes left.

'Keep out of it, Arlo, this is routine police business.' Breck observed Riley as he kept a hand pressed down on the windpipe of a handcuffed Benjamin Genta. Breck ignored Riley's warning.

'What has he done?'

'Mind your own business.'

'You can't handcuff him if he hasn't done anything.'

'It's my right to stop him under the sus law.' The sus law allowed officers, on suspicion alone, to stop and search individuals they believed were intent on wrongdoing. But Riley wasn't the type of person to use it fairly.

'I aint…done…anything!' Benjamin just managed to squeeze the words out.

'Shut it boy. No one's talking to you.' Riley pressed down harder. Benjamin became increasingly agitated and breathing became a struggle.

'Let him go, Riley. I'm not asking, I'm telling.'

'Arlo, please fuck off. There has been a spate of robberies in the area and this coon fits the profile of the man that we want to question.'

Breck went toe-to-toe with Riley who saw the intent within his eyes, which confused him. 'Come on tell me. Why is this one so special? Do you and him have a love-in eh?'

Breck exploded and gripped Riley. He forced him to release the hand which he held Benjamin down with, but Riley then used it to fend off Breck. Meanwhile Benjamin staggered over to the side of the kerb and collapsed to the ground, gasping for air.

'Gaz, give me a hand,' Riley shouted across.

'Stay put,' Breck warned.

Gaz weighed up his options and decided to remain in the car. Safer that way.

'You'll be out of a job soon if you don't keep your anger in check, Arlo.'

Breck and Riley began to roll across the bonnet as they wrestled each other, while Gaz lifted the police radio. He didn't know whether or not to use it, even when Breck bent back one of Riley's fingers then rifled a punch into his stomach. Then another one, and another. Riley dropped to the floor.

'I'll have you for that. You're finished,' Riley threatened as he winced.

'It's my word against yours Ray.'

'Gaz is a witness, two against one. Isn't that right, Gaz?'

'No, it's two against two.' Benjamin had now risen to his feet, a little unsteady, but on his feet all the same. 'I didn't see anything. Detective Inspector Breck didn't touch you at all.'

Breck signalled for Gaz to throw over the keys to the handcuffs which he did, and while Breck freed Benjamin, Gaz crept out of the car. He helped Riley to his feet and the two men watched in silence as Breck ushered Benjamin into the Allegro.

FIFTY FOUR

Benjamin's temperament bordered on volcanic after the treatment dished out by Riley, and he was still fuming although they had been driving for a while.

'Do you want to go to hospital to get checked out?'

'For them to ask me a bunch of questions. No thanks.'

'You looked in pretty bad shape back there.'

'I said no.'

Breck gave in. 'OK. Have it your way.'

'What happened back there is the reason why there's big problems. I was minding my own business when Riley pulled the car up in front of me and pinned me down. All the brothers know him. He likes to harass us. I bet he's even looking forward to the march.'

Breck spotted a side road up ahead. The perfect drop point. 'Why do you say that, about him looking forward to the march?'

'Saw him speaking to the Front's security chief the other day.'

Although Breck understood what Benjamin implied, he had no grounds to pursue it. Breck pulled up the car at the side road recognising that he was in danger of being late for his meeting.

'If you jump out here and walk to the end of the road, it'll take you to a bus stop. From there you can catch a bus to Cransham.'

'I know.' Benjamin opened the door and put one foot on the pavement then paused. 'Thanks for what you did back there. It took guts.'

'Just doing my job.'

'We need more people like you doing their job and less people like Riley.'

Benjamin stepped out and zipped up his tracksuit top. He fixed both hands inside its pockets and strolled away, while Breck waited until he was out of sight and hoped for a better tomorrow.

Breck refocused and picked up his route again. He had ten minutes left.

*

Somewhere west of Plumstead, Breck waited in a car park. To bide his time, he opened the glove compartment and planned to read the unopened letter from the security firm. Yet, while he held it in his hands he found it difficult to. The thought of rejection overwhelmed him, he couldn't deal with just yet. Breck returned the letter. He'd open it another time.

A brown Talbot entered the car park and a floppy beige fedora hid the driver's face. When the door swung open, a small package flew out. Then the car then flashed its lights twice as if to say deal done and pulled away. Breck exited the Allegro and collected the package, hoping his gamble had paid off.

He unwrapped the brown paper and butterflies lined his stomach. When he opened the file inside, the shock of what he read made him gasp. It gutted him and made his head spin too. The new information turned everything on its head and a stunned Breck mapped a plan of action. Things would never be the same again.

*

Kearns, took a call from Mo Mace.

'What have you got for me?'

'Troy's coming to meet me.'

'When?'

'You can't let him know I told you anything - it'll ruin me and could put me in danger. Maybe rough me up a bit, not the face though.'

'Relax, he won't have a clue, love. Now when is he coming to collect?'

Kearns saw Breck return to his desk and wondered where he had been.

'Are you still there?' Mo asked.

'Yes, got distracted.'

Mo told her the time and she thanked him because she would make sure that they turned up late. Too late.

Kearns rolled over to Breck. 'You look like you've got something to say.'

He came close to accusing her of all sorts but then held back.

'Who were you speaking to? It looks like something is going on.'

'No nothing is going on. It was just a sales call.'

If Kearns told him her daughter had called Breck might have believed her, but to palm it off as a sales call was a lie as far as he was concerned. The last time Kearns took a sales call, she sent a barrage of expletives straight to the salesman not a hushed voice.

'Anything else happening?'

'No, nothing.'

Breck wanted to see how far Kearns would keep up the pretence. When she least expected it, he'd reveal what he knew and it would bring the whole lie crashing down.

FIFTY FIVE

Troy waltzed into a pub in Marylebone determined to finish what he had started. He headed straight to the men's toilets and slipped on a pair of gloves. Once inside, he tipped over the dustbin which left rubbish strewn across the floor and began to dismantle the bottom of the bin. Then someone walked in. Troy

placed the bin back and grabbed a broom that had been left in the corner and began to sweep. The intoxicated man used the urinal without uttering a word then left, neglecting to wash his hands in the process, and as soon as he was out, Troy used the broom to wedge the door tight. He didn't want any more unwanted interruptions. He returned to the bin and cast his mind back to the most recent message he left for Proctor. He made it when he last stayed at Clarke's home, he had risen early while Clarke slept and begged for help. Now he'd find out if he had been disowned.

Troy removed the bottom of the bin, unwrapped the bundle inside and read the typed note that accompanied it.

Get What You Can. Then Out. END.

Troy would have to wait for the explanations later but it became clear that Proctor kept the lines of communication open just for him.

Troy unblocked the door and exited the men's toilets. He knew there'd be just one chance to get this right, and he reminded himself of that small fact all the way to his meeting with Mo Mace.

*

Troy travelled past a couple of kids. They were performing bicycle tricks over a makeshift ramp made of broken shards of wood, and had slanted the wood on top of crumbling bricks. One of them decided to sit it out, choosing to suck on a lollipop with a comb stuck into the roots of his tired afro. Up ahead a few people were drifting into the snooker hall but Troy's focus centred on just on one thing. Mo Mace and his passport. Mace wanted to meet at the snooker hall and not anywhere else.

Troy asked the Italian behind the bar if he had seen Mo but the question drew a blank expression. A tap on his shoulder forced him to turn around to be met by a stranger wearing a grin and blond highlights at the ends of his hair.

'You after Mo?'

'Yes, do you know where he is?'

'Sure do. He's waiting for you over there.'

The man directed Troy to the back room and everything was at least going according to the adjusted plan. Or so it seemed. Troy turned the handle of the door and stepped into the room.

Then came face-to-face with Marcin. Troy stood close enough to see the bristling pinpricks of grey upon Marcin's chin and the trouble in his unmistakable sunken eyes. He panicked and pulled out the SIG, quick to jab the tip of it into his stomach.

'Step back,' he warned. 'Where's Mo?' His finger tightened around the trigger and he prepared himself to use it.

'You should move that away. It makes me feel uncomfortable.'

Troy mocked him. 'I'm so sorry about that. Now answer my question!'

'You're playing a dangerous game by threatening me.'

The conversation never progressed any further because Troy never heard Blondy creep up behind him. The blow to the back of his head knocked him out cold. Meanwhile, Mo Mace sat in the corner hidden by the shadows, epitomising the very reason why he had been able to survive in his industry for so long.

*

Troy's eyes flickered open. The taste of blood soured his mouth. His hands were tied but he had space to manoeuvre. The room reeked of a lemon scent. Troy saw the frames of a set of windows ahead, but the windows were covered with wooden boards that had been nailed down tight. Whisky coloured linoleum stretched across the floor and the oddest thing lay in the centre of the room. A knee high square oak table with rope tied around its legs.

Troy used all his strength to roll over onto his stomach. When he did, he wormed his way forwards but breathed in the dust from the floor, which floated up and scratched at the back of his throat. Unintelligible sounds soon separated into individual voices, and Troy pushed his face as close as possible towards the gap between the door, and the surface of the floor.

FIFTY
SIX

Kearns decided the time was right to inform Breck that Mo Mace had tried to contact him with the exact time that Troy planned to meet. She waited until he finished his conversation with a junior officer then pounced.

'Mo Mace called for you.'

'When?'

'Not long ago. I couldn't find you.'

'What did he say?'

Kearns smiled. 'Troy's on his way to meet him.'

'About time too. We'll keep our arrival low key, no sirens or cavalry. I'll meet you outside in ten minutes. I'm going to stop off at the armoury.'

Only a small number of SCU of officers were allowed to be armed and Arlo Breck happened to be one of them.

*

The double doors of the snooker hall creaked when Breck and Kearns walked through, and Breck seemed to be still adjusting to the weight of his firearm in its holster when he approached the man behind the bar.

'What can I get you to drink?'

'Nothing, it's information that I'm after.' Breck showed his ID. 'I want to speak to your manager.'

'He's not around at the moment but maybe I can help?'

'A man by the name of Mo Mace frequents this snooker hall. I'm looking for him.'

'Maurice left about twenty minutes ago.'

'On his own?'

'No, with a group of men.'

'What men?'

'Sorry, I don't know. Never seen them before.'

Breck glanced towards Kearns but she couldn't offer any suggestions.

'Did he look uncomfortable like he might have been in danger?'

'No, I wouldn't say that. He seemed relaxed.'

Kearns stepped forward. 'He's lied to me about all of this. I'll throttle him.'

'This is not what I need right now.'

A disappointed Breck left the premises while a secretly satisfied Kearns followed behind. Inside the car she tried to offer a solution.

'You may not want to hear it but we still have a way out of this.'

'No, Pat, I'm not going to pin all of this onto our dead POI Alper. Not when Troy is hiding something. We both know that.'

'OK, I tried.'

By the time they arrived back at the station, Breck's foul mood had diminished enough for Beatrice to feel comfortable enough to approach him.

'I won't ask what's annoyed you,' she said. 'I've got a result that might cheer you up though.' The word *result* pricked Breck's interest enough for him to take notice. 'I've finally got a name of the owner of the house linked to phone number, found on our dead POI in Norway.'

'Who does it belong to?'

'A person named Marcin Dvorak.'

'The name doesn't ring a bell for me. Do we know who he is?' Beatrice shrugged and felt a bit embarrassed because she hadn't researched that bit. 'Please find out who he is and get me some time with Judge Palmer – I'll need a search warrant.'

Beatrice left and more than ever before, Breck felt the strain of the job. He suspected that Kearns fed him false information regarding Troy's meeting with Mo Mace and he wanted to confront her. Somehow, he held himself back and a move away from the SCU seemed a real option once again. Breck needed to believe that he could trust his colleagues.

While he agonised, Bashir caught sight of him and walked over, noticing his mood.

'What's getting you down, Arlo?'

'Nothing sir, just a little tired with this case that's all.'

'I know our resources are stretched because of the march today but have you got all the help you need?'

'I think for where we are now, it's sufficient.'

'Don't worry, I've got a feeling it will end soon. I don't know why but I do.' Bashir began to reminisce. 'I worked on a case back in '68 similar to this. Went for a bit without any real feeling of progress, followed the wrong leads and all sorts we did. Then we got a result unexpectedly.'

'Well, I'm always hopeful sir.'

'Good. Glad to hear it.'

'How are we set up for the march?'

'I'm drafting in as many officers as I can. In fact, I'm looking at a few thousand and I hear the council are moving the elderly and disabled away from potential areas of trouble. Last ditch meetings with the Front and the opposing groups, failed to find a compromise in my eyes.'

'That doesn't sound good.'

'No and our intel tell us there might be an anti-fascist gathering around Clifton Rise. So Arlo, in the words of many who have faced a battlefield before the advent of war, God help us all.'

Bashir strolled away and in a case of perfect timing, Beatrice came rushing over.

'I have news on Marcin Dvorak.'

'Go on,' Breck urged. 'I'm listening.'

'He's the nephew of Aychm Dvorak.' The name sounded familiar to Breck. 'His uncle is wanted by the Yard, Interpol, everyone.' Beatrice couldn't contain her excitement at the discovery. 'He's the one I told you about. I bugged his car on Riley's old operation.'

'Why is our dead POI linked to him?' Beatrice was at a loss to explain. 'It's all right, I don't expect you to answer that but we need to move fast on this. We'll need an instant response car (IRC) behind us so I'll sort that out now.'

Breck knew he had been given another chance and he was intent on grabbing it with both hands.

*

Breck acquired a search warrant for the property in Rotherhithe in record time. While he, Kearns, Beatrice and officers in the IRC, rocketed to the address, Breck felt it could lead to something. His mind tried to balance many different bits of information, anomalies, and things that were strange enough to drive him crazy if he let them. Deep down though, he knew he was edging closer to the truth.

They arrived at the house in a squad car rather than the Allegro. Breck approached the door of the four-bed detached house first. The IRC boys, led by Francis, stood beside Breck. Ten years' experience, lean and focused.

'We're not sure what we'll be dealing with so everyone be on your guard,' Breck warned. Then he counted down. 'Three, two, one.'

The door burst open with the first kick he executed and they all rushed inside. Kearns searched the ground floor with Francis, while Breck led Beatrice up the stairs for a quick sweep of the place. Everyone remained on their guard. Breck soon ventured into a bathroom big enough for one. He opened the cabinet and found half used tubes of shaving foam and razors. Behind the bath taps lay a small comb with hairs trapped between its teeth. Judging by the length of the comb's teeth whoever used it preferred to keep their hair low. Breck bagged it so that samples could be extracted and he had expected to find more. When Beatrice called him, the sharp urgency that infected her voice forced him to rush out and witness a sight that took him by surprise.

FIFTY SEVEN

The march

Inside the home registered to Marcin, one of the bedroom walls were covered from top to bottom with photographs of a woman. Beatrice recognised her straight away. Kearns bolted upstairs and entered the room after hearing her call Breck. Beatrice had their full attention.

'That's Ceinwen Phelps, Troy's married girlfriend.'

I remembered her from the marketing material that I saw at Xenon.'

'What's her connection to Marcin Dvorak?'

'I've no idea,' Beatrice confessed.

Breck ran it through. 'The POI is connected to Marcin, and Marcin is connected to Ceinwen. What are we missing here?'

None of them had the answer.

Breck stepped in closer and inspected the photographs. 'In a majority of them, Ceinwen appears to be relaxed but unaware they have been taken. While the others, the Polaroid snaps, have been shot from a shorter distance and she's looking straight at the photographer.'

'What are you getting at?' Kearns asked.

'She either knew our dead POI, or she knows Marcin somehow,' Breck deduced.

Beatrice stepped away from the wall and opened the wardrobe nearby. It seemed a pointless action until a white paper bag fell out and rolled to a stop by her feet. Breck gave her the nod to untie it and she reeled back when she did.

Breck peered inside. 'That looks like a human finger.'

'Definitely a finger,' Kearns added after she had a look too. 'There's a friendship ring on it.'

'Pat, the silver ring with a Greek key pattern is the same one Simon showed us at the strip club. We know which of our deceased had a finger missing don't we?'

'Geraldine.'

Breck stepped away to view the photos on the wall again. 'If that is Ceinwen in the photos then that at least gives us a motive for Troy being set up wouldn't you say? She's at the heart of this.'

Kearns had seen enough of the severed limb and joined Breck near the wall. 'Set up by who though, our dead POI or Marcin?'

'Seeing as Jean-Marc Alper is dead, I'd say Marcin pulled the strings on this one.'

The shocking discovery allowed Breck to shift the killer tag away from Troy at least, and shift it over to Marcin Dvorak.

Breck stared at the paper bag. 'We now have evidence to connect

Marcin to at least one of the murders.' He turned around searching for Kearns. 'Where's Pat gone?' He didn't notice she had left.

'Maybe she went outside,' Beatrice suggested.

Breck moved aside the curtains and glimpsed Kearns talking to a group of kids on bicycles. He didn't understand how she could be with them one minute then gone the next, so he made his way down to investigate, only to bump into her upon her return.

'What were you doing out there, offering to buy them sweets?'

Kearns ignored the biting remark. 'We now have a registration number for a maroon Jaguar XJ12. Those kids out there saw it speed away from here not too long ago.'

'Sorry, I shouldn't have barked. OK feed that back to the station then finish off searching down here.' Breck turned around and caught Beatrice on her way down, holding the bag. 'Bea, please get someone at the station to ask Clarke if he knows where Troy is. Let him know that we now believe his friend to be innocent of Geraldine's murder, if not yet Janet Maskell's. Tell him he may be in grave danger. It might make him cooperate with us.'

As expected a small crowd had gathered, and while Breck moved beyond them, his radio snapped into life. They received a positive ID on the Jaguar after it became involved in an incident with a motorbike as it turned into a residential road in West Cransham. Breck gathered the team and informed them. After that, he buckled up and he leaned across to Kearns in the car.

'I need you to get us there fast, Pat. Every second counts now.'

'Every second always counted, Arlo,' she said the under her breath afterwards. 'You just didn't realise.'

Kearns shifted the gears and nailed the accelerator to the floor. In seconds, the streets became a blur. Breck took out his standard issue firearm to make sure the safety was off, while Beatrice felt nervous. Although situations like these were what she wanted to be involved in.

No one had mentioned it but the shadow of the march tainted the air and it stoked Breck's curiosity.

'How many Front demonstrators have turned up?'

Kearns tried to think. 'Not sure, someone guessed it to be around five hundred or so. Could be more, even up to a thousand.'

'Less than we anticipated. What about the other side?'

Kearns made a sharp turn which shifted everyone to their left. Breck banged his head on the window. 'Ouch.'

'Sorry. From what we know, there are several anti-Front groups.'

'How reliable is that intel?'

'Shall I give you that piece of string metaphor?'

In a rare light moment Breck shook his head. 'No, don't bother.'

'Anyway, we've got everything there, horses, riot shields. The lot, Bashir made sure of it.'

Kearns attempted to loop onto the A20 before being forced to slow down due to the large crowds, but Breck's frustration ballooned.

'Why have we come this way? We're touching the edges of the march.'

'You told me to get us there fast. This is the quickest way!' Kearns snapped.

Beatrice chipped in. 'Everything is blocked. We were working on this case so we're probably a bit behind with any last-minute arrangements.'

Though Breck didn't want to admit it, Beatrice's explanation made sense as they witnessed New Cross Road become bottled-necked with a slew of bodies, placards and angry faces. The Front demonstrators, protected by the heavy police presence, shouted obscenities at the anti-fascist opposition, who weren't shy in giving it back. Bits of wood, empty cans and bottles cut through the air, while the radio airwaves were congested with all things concerning the march. Something had already kicked off nearby. It concerned Breck

'Do you think that's Clifton Rise their talking about?' Kearns asked.

'Could be. The march started from somewhere near, perhaps Pagnell Street. We need to get out of here. Francis' team in the IRC are following as close as they can.'

Streams of people were now running after a few of the Front's footmen. The police protection ring had been broken and Breck saw Benjamin Genta, squaring up to a Front demonstrator twice his size. His 'Stop The Muggers' banner had been unfurled on the ground and he gripped Benjamin's shirt collars, then administered a tight bear hug. His python grip squeezed the life out of Benjamin and Breck feared the worse. He couldn't get to him with what was happening all around. He needn't have worried. Benjamin fired-forward a head butt which split the man's nose. Blood pooled out of his nostrils and down into his mouth, forcing him to let Benjamin go.

Breck glanced up. Eggs sailed through the air and failed to reach their targets, but ended up hitting the car. A brick sent in retaliation the other way failed to find its target too. It cracked the windscreen.

'Pat, turn us around and get us the hell out of here. We'll go the other way,' Breck said.

'Alright, I'm doing it now.'

Kearns winced and performed a U-turn, hitting one or two bodies in the process, but not seriously injuring anyone. With the horn blasting, they burst through and left behind the devastation.

Kearns used her intimate knowledge of the back streets to loop them onto the main road again, in order to reach West Cransham where the Jaguar was last seen. Breck urged Kearns to up the speed even more, and the IRC came into view behind them.

While they sped along, the crack in the windscreen became a problem. It continued to impair Kearns' vision. She tried to angle her head away to an undamaged part but in doing so she swerved. Breck panicked. He grabbed the wheel so Kearns hit the brake. The car spun out of control. Beatrice didn't have her seat belt on and the momentum tossed her around in the back seat like a rag doll.

No one saw the lorry.

It had stopped just ahead, with scaffold spiking out from its rear, and the car's momentum brought it racing towards them.

The impact took out the windscreen.

When the glass exploded inside, it missed Kearns' face but a shard sliced Breck's hand. He released an agonising scream. The IRC approached from behind at breakneck speed and their lead officer

Francis, saw the danger but not in time. It collided with the left side of Breck's squad car then bounced off, and spun several times, hitting a sea of loose scaffold. The debris strewn road caused its tyres to lift off the ground and the IRC flipped over onto its side.

A deafening silence followed.

FIFTY EIGHT

Breck opened his eyes without recalling when they had closed, and turned back to see Beatrice out cold on the back seat. He leaned over and checked her pulse then felt a jabbing pain in his leg. She was breathing so he checked on Kearns who mumbled a few incoherent words. Red marks were pencilled across her forehead

and Breck grimaced as he unbuckled his seatbelt. He tried to move the top half of his body before tapping Kearns.

'How are you doing?'

'A bit …shook up…I think I'll live.'

'Something hit us at speed. Not sure what though.'

Breck unlocked the door of the car to step out, but the sharp pain stabbed him again. He could pinpoint it now. The length of scaffold that smashed the windscreen, had wedged itself against his left thigh.

'Pat, can you get out?'

'Think so,' she said, still dazed.

'If you can, get this sodding thing away from me so that I can move.'

Kearns gathered her strength, all she had, and stumbled out of the car. The gashes on her forehead were more evident now, and she hobbled over to the front of the vehicle. She opened the door and just managed to push the scaffold back far enough for Breck to reposition his leg, and clamber out.

He felt the trickles of blood run down his leg. 'My hand feels red hot,' he told her.

The nosey parkers were out in force but Kearns ignored them enough to find her bearings. Breck watched the whispery smoke escape from the engine of the IRC but saw movement. Breck beckoned Kearns over.

'Phone the emergency services, and help them over there.'

He took several steps forwards but found his natural movement a bit hampered from the injury.

'What are you trying to do?'

'I'm doing what I have to. You've been hiding something from me, Pat. Something concerning Troy.' Kearns opened her mouth to speak but Breck cut in. 'Save it. I need to locate Marcin Dvorak because Troy will be there or thereabouts I'm sure. If I don't then he's going to die, if he hasn't done so already.'

Breck didn't mention the package he collected at the car park in Plumstead. The records stated that Alexander Troy had died in 1941, aged five, along with his family during one of the World War Two air raids on Birmingham. If that were to be true, then just who was Breck on his way to save?

*

Troy's arms were heavy weights. He couldn't move them, even when Marcin Dvorak entered the room, laughing to himself. Marcin used his strong hands to hoist his love rival up and in a bizarre act, pressed his nose against Troy's cheek to smell him in the way a wild animal would. The Alpha male laid down the gauntlet then threw Troy away. It amused Marcin to see his head slam against the wall. A defenceless Troy couldn't see his loaded SIG anywhere and Marcin made no mention of it.

Visually things were still a bit blurred for Troy, and double vision ensured two versions of Marcin were in front of him. He ran a hand across his chest and realised he could still do what he had to. For that he was grateful.

'Marcin, what have you done to me?' he asked.

'I fed you Ketamine so you might be feeling groggy. The horse tranquilliser may also cause you to see things that are not there. Hallucinate.'

The sardonic expression across Marcin's face accentuated his dead sunken eyes. 'Is this about Ceinwen?'

'I heard about you a long while ago. How you were courting my woman while I was locked up inside. Some city high flier with big dreams. To kill you straight away became my first wish, but then I thought about it. First, destroy your reputation then have my fun.' Marcin's face twisted, he wanted the recognition. Needed it. 'I found out where you worked idiot, dangled the carrot for the deal you broke the rules for. I made it easy for Janet Maskell to find out. Then had her killed so the finger could be pointed at you.'

Troy struggled for breath brought on by his anxiety. 'Why murder the girl. Young Geraldine?'

'Another connection to your place of work. That's all.'

Troy's eyes burned. Marcin's failure to keep his mouth shut would come back to haunt him for sure.

'And what about the other Troy?'

'I threw him into it to add to the confusion but in the end, he knew too much so had to go too. I don't like loose ends.'

Marcin glimpsed the time on his Rolex then left the room without saying anymore.

Troy pushed himself into the corner with every last ounce of strength, hoping to use it to leverage himself up but failed. Then Marcin returned, this time with someone else. Ceinwen.

She refused to look Troy straight in the eye and Marcin noticed this. He left her side and gripped Troy's jaw, letting his fingers dig deep, and they threatened to rip the flesh from Troy's face.

'Look at him! You left me for this?'

She gave no answer and that infuriated him, so he let go of Troy then leapt towards her. Marcin grabbed the roots of her hair and Ceinwen screamed as he began to twist them. It amused him for just a short while however, because he soon stopped. But when he spotted her mouth the words, 'I love you,' to Troy, he exploded. Marcin pushed her away, causing her to lose her footing and Ceinwen hit her head on the floor. Marcin watched as she lay unconscious.

It incensed Troy but he had to play it smart. 'You'll get locked up again after this. For a longer time too.'

'I'm untouchable you idiot. My uncle Aychm has many people on his payroll.' To Troy's surprise Marcin rolled off a few names of those people but ended with a deadly warning. 'There will be no charges even if I kill her and you.'

Marcin's smugness became too much to bear, but the fear which once inhabited Troy had all but diminished. He caught a glimpse of the time on Marcin's Rolex and knew the end had come. He had done the best he could, with what he had been given.

'I don't need anymore,' he told him. Then Troy began to laugh.

'What do you mean? Why are you laughing like a crazy man?'

The answer to his question never came so Marcin replayed the words in his head.

I don't need anymore.

I don't need anymore.

I don't need anymore.

Marcin's gut twisted and the most horrific look spread across his face. Raging, he sprung forward and ripped open Troy's shirt to see a book-sized tape recorder strapped fast with adhesive around Troy's waist. The wires to the microphone and the mic itself, were taped to his chest.

'You've been recording me?'

'Yes, with every single fucking word captured.'

It sounded crazy, but after having concealed the recorder for so long, Troy now felt exposed. He closed up the torn shirt with a satisfied smile, while the confession pushed Marcin over the edge. He'd been tricked. He had set himself up to be convicted by his own loose tongue. His revelations threatened the dealings of his own uncle too. Only one thing rushed to the forefront of his mind.

Kill Troy.

Marcin released a heart wrenching wail then unleashed a machete from his waistband. His fury forced Troy to cower, while he held the blade aloft, but before Marcin could thrust it down, an interruption occurred. The door opened and the man known as The Messenger walked in.

He assessed the situation in the room – Troy in the corner, Ceinwen on the floor, Marcin about to kill. He grabbed Marcin's arm, which left the blade hanging in the air.

His action confused Marcin. 'What are you doing?'

'Maybe you forgot, but that woman on the floor over there was important to everything your uncle wanted to do, pal. The murders you're behind have created a problem. A big one. So here's a message from him to you.' Marcin's eyes were still so wild with anger that he struggled to latch onto the true meaning of those words. Regardless, The Messenger concluded. 'Liabilities are always bad for business.'

Then it happened in a blink.

The machete was twisted away out of Marcin's grasp and Troy saw the foot-long blade skid across the floorboards. The Messenger knocked him to the ground, pressed his right foot down into his chest, and pulled out the Berretta. He fired three shots in quick succession and two of those, blew a clean hole through Marcin's chest, separating his oesophagus from his stomach. The last shot ripped a hole just above the centre of his eyes. Right through his glabella.

A sea of red began to nestle around his body, while the smell of gun smoke floated through the room. Troy thought his end had come but he never figured in the equation. Aychm viewed a civilian like Troy as no threat. He just got caught up in bad shit.

'It's your lucky day, pal. You'll live to see another one, but if you talk about what you've seen I'll come looking for you,' The Messenger warned him before calmly walking out.

FIFTY NINE

Breck heard the gunshots from outside and it startled him. He took off his jacket and used it to wipe the sticky claret away from his hand, as well as from the top of his shoes. Then he threw the jacket onto the kerb, knowing that entering the house alone would be crazy. Breck radioed Kearns and although the sting of

his wound continued to hurt, he pushed on. He had no plans to wait.

Breck approached the opened door where he believed the shots came from, and reached for his standard issue gun. Problem. It wasn't in its holster. He couldn't figure it out until he realised he must have lost it during the crash. The most probable explanation being, he didn't secure it properly after taking off the safety. Breck still had his baton and knew what he had to do, so proceeded inside.

On the ground floor of the house, amongst the silence, he felt a deep sense of trepidation and wondered where to go first. Then he heard a shuffle of feet and a pressing down of the floorboards overhead. He used the sounds to direct him and edged his way upstairs.

With clenched fists and an extended baton, in case he needed to use either at short notice, Breck struggled to settle his nervous tension. He had been in the job for years but knew a bad situation when he saw one. He had it confirmed when he came face-to-face with a man standing at the top of the staircase. A man dressed in stonewashed jeans and a black leather jacket with epaulettes, wearing Ray Bans that hid his eyes. A rock star killer that carried an air of confidence and both men waited and watched each other like two dogs about to battle for territory. Until Breck initiated the conversation.

'I'm a police officer, Detective Arlo Breck. I've got back up on its way here so let's be sensible.' Breck held his baton up in the hope that it would serve as a deterrent.

'I've been looking forward to meeting you, pal. It's been a long time coming.'

'What do you mean by that?' Breck remained on his guard, aware that the man was armed after hearing the gunshots.

'Choices. We all have them and this is yours. You can pretend like you haven't seen me and run upstairs. Be the hero.'

'And if I do that what will I find up there?'

'Three people. One dazed. The second unconscious. The third, almost dead.'

'Almost?'

'Almost, but not quite.'

Breck felt the stinging pain in his leg again but pushed it to one side. Could the third person be Troy?

'You know I won't just ignore you, whoever you are. I can't do that.'

'If you knew what I can give you then yes, you would.'

Breck leaned against the banister in obvious discomfort. 'We'll discuss it at the station. How does that sound?'

'It sounds like bullshit to me.'

The man pulled away the lower part of his jacket to reveal his Beretta as a warning.

'You don't scare me,' Breck lied.

'Don't you want to know what I can give you?'

'A confession?'

He stepped down the stairs towards Breck, who then raised his baton up to head height, ready to strike. The man stopped just short of the baton and lowered his voice with a surreal amount of confidence.

'I give messages to people. Some are good, most are bad, but for you, I can give something far greater than a confession. I can give you the man that attacked your girlfriend.'

Breck zoned out then his mind boomeranged back in. What did this man know about Molly and the attack? Did he know the person that did it? Breck battled to calm down otherwise he'd drive himself mad.

'I don't know what you're talking about.'

'Yes you do pal, and the more time you waste, the closer to death someone up in the room above gets.'

'So if I let you go you'll tell his name and then what?'

'You'll be the hero as I said, and you'll owe me. That's how it works.'

The conversation had brought the 'man who sends messages' close enough for Breck to have a chance of hitting him. A bullet would beat a baton, but a baton would beat a fist.

'Give me his name,' Breck demanded.

'Have we got a deal?'

'Give me his name and where I can find him, then I'll tell you if we have a deal.'

'At 6:00 p.m. he'll leave the Pear Tree Pub in Cransham and go to the number twenty-three bus stop. That's your man, one hundred per cent pal. Now, have we got a deal?'

Breck gave the man his answer. He smashed the baton over his head. The man groaned and fell back, and Breck surged forwards, but his blind enthusiasm made him careless. He was caught with a boot to the groin and a sharp punch followed to his temple. Breck toppled down the stairs.

As soon as he hit the ground he tried to climb to his feet, but his leg pulsed and slowed him down. The blow had scrambled his brain. Meanwhile, The Messenger's Raybans were in bits from the strike, and the cut to his head pushed him over the edge. Before Breck drew his next breath, the daylight which lit up the floor, illuminated the figure of The Messenger, who now stood over him. The Berretta was drawn with the wild fire of death evident in his eyes. The same fire that had been witnessed by Janet Maskell, Geraldine Van Bruen and Marcin Dvorak, now had its fourth witness.

In those moments Breck thought about Molly. He thought about his life and those he loved, and wished he could have had more time. The Beretta was raised so that its barrel levelled with Breck's line of vision. Then a burst of gunfire cracked the air.

Confusion followed. Breck could hear his own heartbeat. The Messenger remained standing.

Then his arm lowered and Breck watched the Berretta fall from his grasp. He toppled onto Breck, and while the detective wrestled the body off, he saw the bullet had entered his back and burst through his heart.

Kearns stood by the open door, pointing what appeared to be Breck's missing standard issue firearm. She gazed at body she just felled and stepped forwards, devoid of any emotion. Almost in a trance.

'That's him.'

'Breck's eyes darted over towards the lifeless corpse he had just pushed away. 'Who is that man?' He pulled himself up.

'Larry Sands,' Kearns replied as she placed the gun on the floor. 'The man that played a big part in ruining my life.'

*

Troy realised that Ceinwen Phelps and Peter Clarke would now be consigned to the past. Getting a job with Van Bruen, befriending Clarke and winning over Ceinwen, were all part of the plan. Except for one thing. Falling in love.

Breck and Kearns walked in as Ceinwen started to stir and Troy made sure his recorder remained hidden. It wouldn't be long now.

Breck glimpsed Ceinwen. 'How is she doing?'

'She'll need a visit to the hospital for treatment but she should be all right.'

'And you?'

'I'm doing better than him,' Troy said, while he stared at the lifeless Marcin.

Breck cut across the room towards the body and Kearns followed. They both wondered the same thing. Why did Sands leave Troy alive?

The arrival of two vans interrupted their thoughts as they screeched to a halt outside. Kearns went out onto the landing to investigate, and after hearing the cattle of feet and feeling relieved the cavalry had arrived, Breck soon despaired when they appeared.

'Lads, pleased to see you. I'm Detective Inspector Arlo Breck from the SCU.'

'Out of the way!'

Kearns returned to the room. 'Arlo, what's going on?'

'I don't know.'

Their highest-ranking officer, with twenty years unblemished service, stood in front of them with a stark warning. 'You two stay out of this.'

Breck challenged him. 'On whose authorisation?'

'From the person that tells your boss's boss what to do. How to do it and when.'

The officers grabbed Troy without handcuffing him and used a blanket to cover his head. Breck protested but one of them shoved him out of the way, and they bundled Troy out of the house. They pushed him into one of the waiting vans, came back for Ceinwen, and pulled her out too. While Kearns remonstrated with the lead officer, Breck watched as they directed Troy's married lover into the other van and he wondered what an earth was going on.

SIXTY

Kearns sat in Bashir's office and felt drained after going through a catalogue of emotions. Bashir wanted them to keep up the pretence one last time.

'They kept Beatrice in hospital overnight as a precaution but she'll be fine. As for Arlo, it's for the best that he believes what we discussed. It at least

covers us.'

'You think it's best that he believes a lie rather than the truth?'

'Yes, I think so, Patricia.'

Kearns disagreed. 'We should let him know sir.'

Bashir rested a hand on his desk and stooped his back to lean towards Kearns. 'I was sworn to secrecy. I told you because I felt you should know. Had a right to.'

Kearns felt disgusted with herself and at the bullshit Bashir spewed. He didn't tell her out of any moral duty as he claimed. He did so because he needed help in controlling the investigation. Breck presented too much of a risk to toe the line, but Kearns' personal interest in Larry Sands guaranteed her compliance.

'He has a right to know as the SIO in this case,' she said.

'I can't tell Arlo an unnamed officer assumed the moniker of Alexander Troy and had been working undercover to flush out his target, and that we hid it from him. Patricia, I'm sorry if it displeases you but I'm not going to entertain that idea.'

Kearns tried to better understand the motives for her own sanity. 'So they found out Aychm Dvorak wanted Ceinwen to acquire new business, due to her specialist background, in his bid for legitimacy, and sent Troy in to influence her.'

'By overseeing her induction into Aychm's close circle.'

'And siphoning information from her?'

'Yes correct. The whole operation had been running on a need-to-know basis since 1974. Until the order came in just days ago to pull the plug. They also felt the operation might be compromised after another one of theirs, Dai Kyler, lost his life. From what I gather he operated a Plan B in their attempt to snare Aychm.'

Bashir shook his head at the tragedy of it all but there was something Kearns wanted to know. 'Why couldn't Troy use his alibi when we arrested him? It would have saved him a lot of hassle.'

'Troy met with his handler Proctor, at the time of Janet Maskell's death. He couldn't disclose that for fear of blowing his cover. We'd have to record that.'

Bashir leaned away from the desk and slid back into his chair. 'The decision to end the assignment infuriated Proctor so he delayed Troy's termination process.'

'To ensure Troy received help or assistance if he needed it?'

'Correct, and we believe they executed Marcin as a damage limitation exercise. His infatuation with his former lover Ceinwen, screwed things up for him. Anyway, are you feeling all right?' Bashir frowned. 'You look pale.'

'Don't know. I put everything on the line to get Larry Sands. I spoke to Louise Tellow's mother and told her what happened. She thanked me and I thought I'd feel better for it but I don't. It doesn't bring Louise back, or change the fact he slit her throat.'

Kearns' trembling fingers pulled out a cigarette and she waited for Bashir to OK it before she lit up. 'What will happen to Troy or whoever he is?'

'After his debriefing they'll release him, while we pick up the pieces. That's how it is, Patricia. It's a small win and a sorry state of affairs. It's the people like Peter Clarke and Ceinwen Phelps that I feel sorry for.'

'Having the trust broken you mean?' Kearns said it like she had first-hand experience.

'They'll be spun the witness protection line just like Arlo will be, but it's best they forget about him and move on.'

As if by fate, a knock at the door interrupted the conversation and Breck limped in with frustration painted all over his face.

'They've ferried Troy away into witness protection because he's an informant eh? I didn't see that one coming.'

Bashir cleared his throat. 'He'll be safer there but this case will be boxed up and closed now.'

'Why did you keep me in the dark about what he was?' Kearns and Bashir waited to see who would respond before Kearns looked away, leaving Bashir to explain.

'It was difficult for me, a top-level decision. Patricia had inside information on Sands that allowed her the special insight. We heard he had been offering his services and had become close with the Dvoraks.'

'You didn't trust me, sir?'

'Don't talk nonsense Arlo, I just explained.'

Breck remained far from convinced. The armed officers that arrived at that house were not even from Cransham station, so just how high profile was Troy? An uneasy silence swamped the room and from his own investigation, Breck knew that whoever they were protecting, it wasn't the real Alexander Troy.

'I need to move on from this, as other major issues are pending.'

'You mean the march, sir?'

'Yes, we lined up a field of horses with men and riot shields, still more than a dozen officers were seriously hurt. With far more injured. It's not good.' Bashir visibly shook while he spoke and Kearns in particular, began to feel sorry for him. 'We've got more anti-fascists locked up than Front marchers, the Bishop holding prayers, and community leaders are protesting. The national press are having a go and Rose screamed at me down the phone.'

'Maybe it will die down soon, sir.' Kearns blew smoke up to the ceiling.

'I wish it would but the Home Secretary is now involved so I doubt it. I expect it to be a tough couple of days for me. You two go and take the rest the day off. You've both earned it.'

They were surprised by Bashir's rare gesture of appreciation for their work but knew well enough to grab it. Breck escorted Kearns out of the office and it seemed like a good moment to speak in private with her. They ended up at a spot close to the canteen and he could sense her nervousness.

Breck wanted everything out in the open.

'Pat, the lies end now. I know that the man we've recently referred to as Alexander Troy, is not the real Alexander Troy any more than the POI was.'

Kearns held her chest and tried to steady herself. 'I'm not feeling well.'

'You'll be fine, just answer me.' Kearns couldn't see a way out. No where to run to, so she threw her arms up, almost in despair. 'What do you want me to say, Arlo. There were things happening that you didn't need to know about.'

'Yes, I know, according to what Bashir said.'

Breck punched the wall near to Kearns' head. It startled her.

'It's not his fault. He broke protocol and told me because I had a personal connection in Larry Sands.'

Breck recalled the trip through Sandal and Agbrigg. The story of Kearns' time as a WPC, and finding the dead girl.

'Yes, I know he killed one of your childhood friends. This was all about Sands?'

Kearns leaned against the wall. 'Yes, for me it was, but for other people it was other things. I don't know.'

'Why was I kept out of it, Pat? I want the real reason.'

Kearns sighed. 'You reported Riley a year ago for using excessive force on a suspect. Too clean for some, so Bashir couldn't trust you'd go along with it. Troy needed to complete the job he was sent in to do.'

'Sent in to do?'

'Keep this quiet or I'll be sacked.'

'What are you on about?'

'He's not an informant in the way we've tried to lead you to believe. This was a 'level one' assignment. He's an officer, part of the Yard's undercover unit.'

'The son of a bitch is an undercover operative?' Breck was staggered by the news and dizzied by the betrayal.

'Don't just look at me like that. Say something.'

Breck turned around with the turmoil building inside his head. He walked away thinking about the case, leaving a distressed Kearns leaning against the wall to watch him shrink into the distance. On a day of surprises, he would play his part in one more.

*

Breck stood outside the Pear Tree Pub in East Cransham. The clammy palms and palpitations were evidence of his anxiety, knowing that 6:00 p.m. would arrive in a few minutes. He felt guilty for having to follow the tip-off given to him by Larry Sands. But no other option existed. His own police work had resulted in nothing. So what if Sands had used his criminal network to obtain the information as his bartering tool? With Sands now dead, Breck would benefit from the ground work he put in.

Breck livened up when an unidentified man made a swift exit from the Pear Tree Pub at 6:00 p.m. sharp. Just as Sands had said. Breck couldn't see his face from where he stood, the heavy coat and flat cap put paid to that. Even when the man checked both sides of the road before crossing, he couldn't get a clear view.

Breck watched him pad along to the bus stop then zero in on the timetable.

'Come on,' Breck said under his breath, 'turn around.'

Sometimes we should be careful what we wish for.

When the man peeled his eyes away from the timetable, to stretch them down the road in the hope of seeing a bus, Breck shuddered then took a step back. Then another. He recognised the face straight away and it sickened him.

A shaky Breck lifted his radio and gave the order, and out of nowhere a squad car pulled up in front of Ralph Jenkins. The man that pretended to come to the rescue of Brecks' girlfriend on the night of the attack, was her assailant. He squared up to the officers but they took him away in spite of his protests and denials, and Breck took a moment for himself.

He could have administered his own justice and got away with it too. If he had known when he went to see him. He felt foolish because he even thanked Jenkins for saving her.

As things stood, Ralph's old witness statement would be re-examined and his whereabouts on that night too. No matter what it took, Breck would do his utmost to make sure he'd find enough rope to hang him with.

Then he lost track of time.

When Breck eventually opened the door to his VW and sat inside, he retrieved the unopened letter from the security firm regarding the interview. He ripped up the letter into little pieces and threw those pieces out of the window. They floated out like paper butterflies and he watched the breeze carry them along. Whether he got the job or not didn't matter, because he still had work to do at the SCU. There were people he wanted to trust once again, things to iron out, and for now that was quite enough for Arlo Breck to be getting on with.

Acknowledgements

It's only right that I thank those who have helped me along this epic journey, without rambling on too much or being clichéd in the process, so I'll try.

First and foremost Matthew Smith, the publisher that has made this possible. Foresight goes a long way in any industry, and Matthew has shown his own, by believing in this story and giving me the platform to share it with everyone.

My heartfelt appreciation to Row, for being a constant support and putting up with me endlessly typing away for hours on end. And Mum for always listening.

My gratitude to Keshini Naidoo, who used her sharp 'crime reading' eyes to give me valuable pointers on a few chapters of the story's earlier drafts. Also to Livvy, for her editorial reading on later editions. My thanks go out to retired officer Brian Robbins, who gave me valuable insights into 70s policing with a trip back in time, and a mention must go out to Maggie Smith, a great former tutor and friend. A person that truly loves and understands the essence of writing. I can't forget Leigh Russell for her professional advice and dedication in selling over a million copies of her books. Inspirational.

My thanks also, to those writers that provided me with plenty of good conversations, insights and truly funny times along the way – you know who you are. It's a writing community that has made me feel welcome.

Fiction allows for many enjoyable freedoms. The area of Cransham is totally fictional. However, with regard to a brief moment in history, I have tried to stay as true as possible to the 'Battle of Lewisham' referenced throughout as 'the march'. Any mistakes are my own.

Finally, a big thank you to family and friends who have been genuinely pleased that Dead Lands has arrived, and to the ever-supportive network of amazing bloggers and reviewers who love reading just as much as I do. Keep on doing what you do best.

About the author

Lloyd was born in London and attained a BA (Hons) in Media and Communication. After gaining several years of valuable experience within the finance and digital sectors, he completed a course in journalism. Under the pen name of Paige, he has interviewed a host of bestselling authors, such as Mark Billingham,

Hugh Howey, Kerry Hudson, and Lawrence Block. Two of his short stories were selected for publication in the 'Out of My Window' anthology, and he currently works as an Editor.

@lloydotiswriter

http://www.lloydotis.com/

facebook.com/LloydOtisWriter

Urbane Publications is dedicated to developing new author voices, and publishing fiction and non-fiction that challenges, thrills and fascinates. From page-turning novels to innovative reference books, our goal is to publish what YOU want to read.

Find out more at

urbanepublications.com